Stamets rolled his eyes. "For the nine hundred and twenty third time, no." As much as he intellectually wanted to deny Tilly's notion, however, there was a part of him that did feel something special about those dreams. They were becoming a passion unto themselves. He would dread their return but also feel empty without them if one didn't occur. The voice in the dream, both familiar and yet unknown, did more than call to him on a literal level—it had an emotional pull.

"I don't mean it like you think I mean it, sir. I mean something totally different." Between bites of her de-breaded sandwich, she explained. "I had a dream about your dreams, but mine was a *normal* dream where we were discussing the possibility that your spore dreams were really communications. Like, someone warning you about something or reaching out for first contact."

He offered her a blank look in the hopes she would retreat and rethink the discussion.

"Are you, uh, following me so far?" she pressed on.

"Unfortunately." He grumbled and surrendered to the inevitable. "Go on."

"Mycelial communication. Why not? If a ship can travel the mycelial network, why can't a signal?"

Stamets had been down this road before. "Straal and I tried that. Subspace communications won't work in the network."

"Who said subspace?" Tilly said. "Did you ever try actual, old-fashioned radio?"

Stamets was intrigued, if a bit stunned he'd never considered it. "Uh . . . no. No, we did not."

She grinned. "Maybe you should."

He waggled his finger between them. "By 'you,' you mean 'we.'"

"Oh, yah, I totally mean 'we.'"

"And you think the captain is going to let us just"—he shrugged—"play around with this?"

A twinkle in her eye, Tilly said, "We're a science vessel. This is very science-y."

**Don't miss these other
exciting books in the world of**

DESPERATE HOURS

David Mack

DRASTIC MEASURES

Dayton Ward

FEAR ITSELF

James Swallow

THE WAY TO THE STARS

Una McCormack

THE ENTERPRISE WAR

John Jackson Miller

STAR TREK®
DISCOVERY

DEAD ENDLESS

DAVE GALANTER

Based on *Star Trek*®
created by Gene Roddenberry
and
Star Trek: Discovery
created by Bryan Fuller & Alex Kurtzman

G

GALLERY BOOKS

New York   London   Toronto   Sydney   New Delhi

G

Gallery Books
An Imprint of Simon & Schuster, Inc.
1230 Avenue of the Americas
New York, NY 10020

First Gallery Books trade paperback edition December 2019

GALLERY BOOKS and colophon are registered trademarks of Simon & Schuster, Inc.

For information about special discounts for bulk purchases, please contact Simon & Schuster Special Sales at 1-866-506-1949 or business@simonandschuster.com.

The Simon & Schuster Speakers Bureau can bring authors to your live event. For more information or to book an event, contact the Simon & Schuster Speakers Bureau at 1-866-248-3049 or visit our website at www.simonspeakers.com.

Manufactured in the United States of America

10 9 8 7 6 5 4 3 2 1

Library of Congress Cataloging-in-Publication Data

Names: Galanter, Dave, author. | Roddenberry, Gene, other. | Fuller, Bryan, other. | Kurtzman, Alex, other.
Title: Star Trek, Discovery : dead endless / a novel by Dave Galanter; based on Star Trek created by Gene Roddenberry and Star Trek: Discovery created by Bryan Fuller & Alex Kurtzman.
Other titles: Dead endless
Description: First Gallery Books trade paperback edition. | New York : Gallery Books, 2019. | Series: Star Trek: Discovery; book 6
Identifiers: LCCN 2019030890 (print) | LCCN 2019030891 (ebook) | ISBN 9781982123840 (trade paperback) | ISBN 9781982123857 (ebook)
Subjects: LCSH: Star trek: Discovery (Television program)—Fiction. | GSAFD: Science fiction.
Classification: LCC PS3557.A378 S73 2019 (print) | LCC PS3557.A378 (ebook) | DDC 813/.54—dc23
LC record available at https://lccn.loc.gov/2019030890
LC ebook record available at https://lccn.loc.gov/2019030891

ISBN 978-1-9821-2384-0
ISBN 978-1-9821-2385-7 (ebook)

For Delilah, Alden, and Imogen

Time is too slow for those who wait, too swift for those who fear, too long for those who grieve, too short for those who rejoice, but for those who love, time is eternity.

—HENRY VAN DYKE

1

Captain's log, supplemental. Discovery *is en route to Mantilles Colony upon report of their possible Symbalene blood-burn outbreak. This is the sixteenth such call we've answered in a handful of days, as we attempt to outrun the spread of the virulent disease. Mister Stamets has performed admirably, as use of the spore drive is the only way to quickly traverse between infected colonies, but I do have concerns about the demands this mission has placed solely on him.*

"*Paul?*"

Had someone really said his name, or was it merely a chug from the cooling unit of his EV suit switching on? If it was a voice, it hadn't come over the communicator. Besides, protocol would have suggested he be addressed as Lieutenant or Mister Stamets. Unless there was an emergency.

It didn't *feel* like an emergency.

The forest stretched out around him, unending. This, he knew, was the mycelial plane, where spores sparkled in a dance of eddies created by his every move. Hyphae as thick as tree trunks; small, red florescent sprigs of fungi; broad splayed blue translucent biota; and countless interwoven masses of mycelium stalks like those he grew on the ship. But this was so much more varied and wide ranging than *Discovery*'s cultivation bay, which he thought of as his forest. *But this is a real forest*, he thought as his gloved hand touched the dark trunk of a fungal tree. *What I have is a flower box.*

"Paul?" The same whisper.

He glanced around, and saw no one.

Alone.

The forest floor was uneven and he nearly lost his balance, but seemed to steady himself without consciously trying, as if the wind had pushed him out of his stumble.

Astonished by an entirely new ecosystem, Paul Stamets marveled at the diversity. He saw representations from the entire fungal kingdom. And three others that defied categorization in astromycology as he understood it. How many more might he find?

I want to live here, he thought. *I never want to leave.*

"Ahhhh." More than a whisper. A wail?

Stamets twisted around. "That sounded like a sob," he told himself. As he turned, he thought he saw a form in the distance, but in that instant it disappeared.

The brilliant forest collapsed in a whirlwind of sparkle.

A flash of white followed . . . and it was over.

———

"Sequence complete." The computer defined the end of a mycelial jump. To Stamets it felt less a leap than a dance, and he often lost himself to it. Sometimes, like this time, there was the dream.

"You okay?" Ensign Sylvia Tilly glanced up from her console as the crewperson next to her slid the spore canister out of the injection console and back into the storage rack.

He saw her, peripherally, but his mind's eye was still focused more on the vibrant images from his vision than on her.

"Lieutenant?" Clearly Tilly could tell something was amiss.

"Yeah." He forced himself to focus on her. "All good." That probably didn't persuade her. He wasn't convinced himself.

The biomechanical shunts that linked him with the spore drive's navigation computer retracted, releasing him from its connection. There was always a little tug, and the skin under the implants itched in a place impossible to reach, so he scratched around them. No matter—the feeling was gone as quickly as it came.

He gathered himself, rolled down his uniform sleeves, and waited for the reaction cube door to open.

"You seem wrong, sir," Tilly said as she offered him a bottle of water.

"Wrong?" He waved away the bottle and stared at her, which he hoped would be unnerving.

"I don't mean you're wrong about anything—except maybe that you're good, but . . . you seem a little off?"

He continued his hard stare.

"Annoyed," she said, quickly, offering the water again. "I'm definitely getting 'annoyed' more than 'off' now. I don't mean *I'm* annoyed—"

"I'm fine, Ensign. I promise." He shook his head to the bottle a second time. "I'm not thirsty." He actually was, but didn't want to give in to Tilly's hovering. He moved past her, studying the readout of the jump, and checking for anomalies he knew wouldn't be there because he would have felt them . . . but one couldn't put feelings into a report.

"It just seems that these last few jumps are making you, well, jumpy. I'm calling it jumpy. Ha!"

"Rest mode, Tilly. At ease." He pursed his lips and put up a hand.

"Oh, okay. Yeah."

Stamets liked Tilly. Almost no one appreciated his work

more than she. Maybe Justin Straal, who had begun it with him, but they were older now. Tilly was young and full of verve and boundless energy. He still had some of that, but it was less boundless than it used to be.

"I'll take it down a level," she promised.

He took in a breath and tried to soften his tone. "Look, there's just a lot of jumps recently with little downtime. I'm . . . I don't know, I guess I'm daydreaming in there and sometimes it's hard to snap out of it."

"I understand. Or I sympathize. Just . . . you know, I'm worried about you."

He turned on his most friendly I'm-fine grin. "Permission to worry: denied."

"It's kind of my thing, though." She smiled nervously.

"*Denied*, Ensign," he grumbled more harshly than he'd intended.

"Yes, sir." Tilly's eyes sparkled. Her too-happy acquiescence didn't help his mood as it should have.

As Stamets turned toward the door, Crewwoman Enav approached with a report for him but he motioned her toward Tilly.

"Something wrong?" Enav asked as Tilly reached out for the data card.

"Nothing, Orna," the ensign assured her. "Not a thing."

Tilly, Stamets thought, *you're a horrible liar.*

———

Commander Saru approached Stamets just before he was able to escape through his cabin door. "Mister Stamets, are you unwell?"

He'd seen the towering Kelpien first officer across the corridor when he'd exited the turbolift, but avoided making eye contact and hoped Saru would show pity and let him get some much needed rest. "No, sir. Just tired. All these jumps . . ." The astromycologist tried to make his expression as bright and positive as possible. "Why do you ask?"

Saru hesitated, smoothed his uniform jacket, and angled his head down at the human. "Despite your protestations, Lieutenant, I sense something awry." Kelpiens relied on their intuition more than other species, and Saru was inclined to let his ganglia be his guide.

"I'm fine, sir," Stamets promised, glancing just a bit to see if, in fact, Saru's threat ganglia were showing. They were not. "Just lost in thought." He realized he might more accurately describe it as lost in a feeling, like he'd left a part of himself behind in his mycelial dream. *It was a dream, wasn't it?*

"Very well. The captain *will* want to know if these numerous short jumps are affecting you. It's the first time we've clustered so many together."

"Yes, sir, being the jump-*er*, I'm aware," he replied.

"Yes, well . . ." Saru's apprehension was reasonable, but his hesitation suggested he wasn't willing to act on it. Yet.

Stamets *should've* been concerned as well. And yet, he wasn't. "I promise I'll monitor the situation and keep checking in with Doctor Pollard." Hoping the first officer would let it be, Stamets edged close enough to his quarters for the door to slide open.

Nodding cautiously, Saru wasn't convinced. "The captain may want to order an examination anyway. Our current mission—"

"Is more important than my being a little preoccupied, isn't it?" Stamets knew that if the doctor grounded him, the *Discovery* wouldn't make it quickly enough between the Symbalene blood-burn outbreaks they were trying to suppress. There was no way a normal starship could arrive as quickly, given that even with a spore drive they needed to jump the instant an infection was reported.

Saru spread his long fingers as if fanning playing cards between them. Stamets always felt it was the Kelpien's version of a shrug. "I do not disagree, Mister Stamets, but I'm already on record that we may have stopped monitoring your physiology too soon after your DNA splicing. At the very least, we should be keeping a closer eye on your well-being, not just for your own safety but *because* so many lives are currently at stake."

"With all due respect, sir, I think . . ." He let his sentence trail off because he wasn't sure what he thought. "You know what? I *will* check in with the doctor and let you know."

"Excellent. Thank you."

"No, sir. Thank *you*." He stepped into his cabin, hoping Saru hadn't picked up on the lilt of sarcasm.

As the door closed behind him, Stamets could hear Saru say, "Uh, dismissed, then, Lieutenant."

———

When *Discovery* used the mycelial network, it was as unnatural as warp speed or transporters or any piece of tech to which Stamets was accustomed. But when jumping, he'd never gotten used to the gulp in his throat and the bowling ball in his stomach as time and space seemed to melt and re-form around him. They shouldn't be called jumps, but trips, he told Tilly once, and as soon as that word passed his lips, he'd wished it hadn't.

"Shroom trips," Tilly suggested when they—mostly she— were discussing it at the next jump.

"No."

"Displacement Activated Spore-Hubbings. DASHings?"

Stamets groaned.

With one eye closed, he made a fine point with his right hand, as if holding a stylus. "Can we work on you having *unexpressed* thoughts?" He honestly felt that was a legitimate request.

"Oh, uh-huh, I promise to try," she cheerfully replied.

Glancing at the engineering console's display, Stamets double-checked the next jump's coordinates. He easily read the screen backward; that and reading upside down were two of his hidden talents. Sliding through the door to the reaction cube, he nodded at Tilly. "Ready."

"DASH lab to the bridge. Spore drive is online."

"Acknowledged," Airiam replied over the comm. In the background, Tilly could hear Detmer say, *"Course confirmed,"* then the captain ordered, *"Let's go."*

"Black alert," intoned the computer a moment later. *"Black alert."*

The kinematic articulators of the computer bioconnection slid into Stamets's forearm ports. As he closed his eyes . . . he opened his mind.

———

"Paul? It's you again!"

That voice—the same voice—but . . . from where and from whom?

Everything around him was filled with spore sparkle. Usually translucent, the harmonic energy in *Discovery*'s reaction cube excited the spores, making them glow.

But he wasn't in engineering. He didn't think he was aboard *Discovery*. And yet, he also wasn't in an EV suit like the last dream; he was breathing normally and could move about easily. But where was he?

Stamets looked at his hand. Was it really his hand, or some astral projection? There *were* aliens who could broadcast their thoughts across great distances. How did they picture themselves if not with a body? Perhaps that's what astral projection was and he should believe in it. At least for aliens. Not so much for crazy Aunt Sarah, who also kept data cards filled with journals about how many strokes she brushed each of her dozen cats.

I'm all over the place, Stamets thought. *I don't know where I am, and I'm thinking about Aunt Sarah? Well,* she did *make a great chicken curry.*

"It's me, Paul! It's you!"

The voice again. The ever-familiar, unknown, barely audible voice that somehow was both warm and accusatory.

"It is?" Stamets heard himself say . . . or *think?*

"Yes, it's you," the formless voice replied, sounding simultaneously relieved and irritated. *"Help me find my way!"*

"Where?" Stamets called out. "Where are you?"

Before an answer could come, a bright flash enveloped everything and a discordant cacophony of either close whispers or too-distant bellows called out to him. *"No! Paul, come back!"*

Stamets felt himself try to scream in response, but he had no voice.

Reality returned and he was in the spore reaction cube, aboard *Discovery,* as if he'd been nowhere else. Of course, he hadn't. Other than the brief moment he, and the ship, had traversed the mycelial network.

———

"Sequence complete," the computer reported. Stamets had silenced that function months ago, but it had been reset during a starbase diagnostic and he'd not taken the time to mute it again.

"Bridge acknowledges." Tilly let Enav work up her reports as another engineer took the empty spore canister to refill it.

"Lunch?" the young ensign asked Stamets as he exited the cube and rolled down his sleeves for the nineteenth time that week. "We have a few hours before the next one."

He was ready to decline, but knew he shouldn't just return to his cabin without social interaction. If Saru had voiced his concerns to the captain, interacting with other members of the crew could be evidence Stamets was fine. Even if he wasn't sure that was true. "Sure. Why not?"

The look of happy surprise on Tilly's face at his acceptance was amusing enough to boost his spirits—just a little.

Once they'd ordered, and he'd gotten over the disappointment of the processors being out of what was supposed to pass for avocado, they moved, trays in hand, toward the tables.

Tilly led him away from her usual cohorts of various bridge crew and toward a less crowded area. "Over there."

Stamets was a bit surprised, but assumed Tilly wanted to discuss work. His interactions with the bridge crew were fairly limited, and that was generally fine by him. Perhaps she didn't want any awkward silences. Tilly always seemed to prefer awkward conversation instead.

As they lowered themselves into their seats, Stamets nodded toward the table they'd avoided. "Are you compartmentalizing?"

She looked up innocently, but kept her mouth on her straw, still drinking. "Hmm?"

"Is there a bridge-crew table and a spore-drive table and you have to pick one?"

Tilly laughed, and he wasn't sure if she found it funny or it was yet one more nervous tic. Though with her it was usually both. "Oh, no. That would be silly. I just wanted to talk to you alone."

"Why?" he asked matter-of-factly.

"Well, uh . . ." She checked inside her sandwich as if she'd forgotten to order an ingredient, then back at the food synthesizers. She removed the bread and began to eat the contents with her fork.

"Forget something?" He decided to encourage her to change the subject.

"Rigellian mayo."

He pointed to her meal with the business end of his fork. "For the baked potato or the no-longer-a-sandwich?" He had mayonnaise on the side, and pushed it toward her. "This isn't Rigellian, but you can have it."

"Oh, no, I don't want it. I mean, I *do* want it, but I don't. So, you know, I didn't forget it. I just wish I had forgotten to not forget it. Does that make sense?"

Kinda sorta? "On a scale of zero to Vulcan, it's a Tilly, so . . . draw your own conclusions." He pointed to the small sauce cup. "I don't think mayonnaise is bad for you. Unless you plan to eat it by the bucket."

"It's not," she agreed around bites of salmon, "but it was brought to my attention by a certain maternal figure that I don't taste my food because I use too much mayonnaise and so . . . I am trying to taste my food."

He took a bite of his turkey wrap and lamented the lack of avocado. "When did mayonnaise lose its standing as food?" Around another bite he added, "Was there a vote?"

"One vote," Tilly said. "Taken after my mother realized I like mayonnaise?"

"Ah." Stamets never quite connected with *his* parents either; perhaps that's why he didn't have the urge to be one. Then again, *they* never understood him, so at least the miscommunications were equitable. He decided he wasn't going to share that with Tilly, and said, "Please tell me we're not sequestered away because you want to talk to me about your mother."

"Oh, no." She laughed after a long pull from the straw in her orange juice. "Not at all. In fact, probably never."

"Then if this is a date, I want you to know we're impossible, because you report directly to me. And you're several years my junior—in so many ways—and I like men."

"N-no, I . . . I know that," she sputtered, making only a sideways glance at the untouched mayo between them. "On all counts. Why would you think—"

Midbite of his wrap he put up a hand to stop her, and after he swallowed said, "Tilly, I was kidding. What do you want to talk about that you can't seem to?"

"I think your spore dreams have meaning," she blurted out.

Stamets rolled his eyes. "For the nine hundred and twenty-third time, no." As much as he intellectually wanted to deny Tilly's notion, however, there was a part of him that did feel something special about those dreams. They were becoming a passion unto themselves. He would dread their return, but also feel empty without them if one didn't occur. The voice in the dream, both familiar and yet unknown, did more than call to him on a literal level—it had an emotional pull.

"I don't mean it like you think I mean it, sir. I mean something totally different." Between bites of her de-breaded sandwich, she explained. "I had a dream about your dreams, but mine was a *normal* dream where we were discussing the possibility that your spore dreams were really communications. Like, someone warning you about something or reaching out for first contact."

He offered her a blank look in the hopes she would retreat and rethink the discussion.

"Are you, uh, following me so far?" she pressed on.

"Unfortunately." He grumbled and surrendered to the inevitable. "Go on."

"Mycelial communication. Why not? If a ship can travel the mycelial network, why can't a signal?"

Stamets had been down this road before. "Straal and I tried that. Subspace communications won't work in the network."

"Who said subspace?" Tilly said. "Did you ever try actual, old-fashioned radio?"

Stamets was intrigued, if a bit stunned he'd never considered it. "Uh . . . no. No, we did not."

She grinned. "Maybe you should."

He waggled his finger between them. "By 'you,' you mean 'we.'"

"Oh, yah, I totally mean 'we.'"

"And you think the captain is going to let us just"—he shrugged—"play around with this?"

A twinkle in her eye, Tilly said, "We're a science vessel. This is very science-y."

"We're in the middle of a medical emergency requiring an unprecedented number of jumps. As soon as we deliver the antivirals to one planet, another colony or outpost finds an outbreak. I'm not sure we want to risk mycelial experiments right now."

"Nothing we do will keep us from jumping when we need to." Tilly's expression saddened without becoming a full-on pout.

"Have you ever seen someone with Symbalene blood burn?"

She shook her head.

"Me neither. Because if we had, we'd probably be dead. That's how fast this thing moves. *We* need to move faster, and the spore drive is the only way."

"We can at least run simulations. That won't interrupt any jumps."

He inhaled a breath and let it out slowly. He liked the idea in concept. In fact, he very nearly loved it. But part of him didn't want to know if there *was* mycelial communication. Something about his "spore dreams" was personal, and he didn't want to share them. If a presence was trying to communicate with him—an alien presence . . .

If this is real, he thought, *then something knows me*. The voice did more than call out to him—he got the impression that it *needed* him. And in return, something within Stamets felt that need as well. Then again, what if there were life-forms trying to communicate and they could only access him this way?

The tardigrade creature from which they took the DNA now spliced into him had established a precedent for intelligent life-forms who traveled mycelial space. Perhaps there was another sentient species calling out to him.

Stamets decided right then that it might be best to know if he was either dreaming this presence or simply receiving it. "Okay. So long as we can fit it in between jumps, we can run some simulations. But no practical tests. We have to be ready to jump anytime we get word of an outbreak."

"Agreed!" Tilly's grin was nova bright. "Yay!"

Stamets frowned and mock-chided her. "Did you actually just say 'yay'?"

"I did! I'm excited!" She finally grabbed his mayonnaise and began spreading it on her half-finished sandwich.

"I thought you—"

"The mayo?" she asked. "Yeah, well, I think I've earned this."

———

"Paul? Can you hear me?" Always the same tone, neither close nor far, and yet infiltrating his very being. *"Paul?"*

Yes, I hear you! Stamets thought. He didn't know how else to cry out in a mycelial dream. Still assuming it *was* a dream and not, as Tilly implied, an alien attempt to communicate.

"Why can't he hear me?" the voice demanded. It was an irritated, hushed, ethereal question. *"You said to call to him and he should hear me! You have to help me get through to him!"*

"I said he might. Sometimes he just can't," came the answer. A different voice. And still, oddly familiar as well. *"You say he is your beacon, so you must also be his."*

I'm a beacon? How? Instinctively, Stamets could feel the jump coming to completion. He knew it took mere fractions of a second, but in the network, time was not beholden to natural laws. That's the way it was in dreams, too, wasn't it? They could linger . . . but this one did not.

"Paul? Hear me! This is you!"

Me? Stamets wondered.

"It's you! Please hear me, Paul! It's you!"

Growing in familiarity as well as urgency, the voice demanded to be recognized at the same time it faded. Stamets struggled to find who was speaking, but saw only the dark sparkle of shut eyes he could not open. The determination in the voice—its purpose and desperation—flowed into him and he began to feel it as well. The presence he experienced was more than calling to him—once again, it was as if it *needed* him.

Before he could resolve that feeling, it was all ripped away as the alabaster flash of the jump's end came abruptly—as if he'd managed to finally open his eyes and look into the sun.

2

"*Why can't he hear me?*" the man demanded. "*He can never hear me!*"

"*Or,*" his companion said, "*he eternally hears you, but cannot always respond.*"

"*Is that it? Is that why? I tried to connect! I told him who I was and I didn't connect!*"

"*I'd like to think that's so,*" the figure grumbled in what the man knew was really a sigh, "*though I suppose it depends on the interaction.*"

"*Dammit, why can't you ever answer directly?*"

"*Ever? So you remember me now? I was pleased you remembered your name this time.*"

"*I—this time? Y-yes.*" The man hesitated, uncertain. "*I think so. No, I'm not sure.*" He slumped to his knees. "*I don't know I don't know I DON'T KNOW!*"

"*Then I suppose you have trouble with opaque answers yourself.*"

Recovering his wits, the man took a moment before replying. "*Yes, I . . . It's like déjà vu. I think I know you. I do, don't I? Don't I?*"

"*You do,*" his companion said. "*And have, and will again, and also won't.*"

"*That makes no sense,*" he barked. "*I need you to make sense. I need something—anything—to make sense!*"

"*It makes complete sense. Or will . . . and did . . . and, sadly, also won't.*"

"No. You won't derail me. I have a thought. Let me finish my thought!"

"Of course."

"I reach out to him, but instead I find you. Why?" The man turned to the entity accusingly, but kept close enough to the yeel tree to feel safe.

"I think it's less that you find me, and more that I find you."

He shook his head and quietly sobbed. *"I—I'm not looking to be found anymore."*

"Oh, that is far from true. I find you because you reach out. Your very thoughts, your essence, are constantly probing and searching this place."

"Liar!"

"I have no reason or desire to be dishonest."

Shaking his head, the man slumped against the tree, closely hugging the trunk. *"I hate this place. I hate you!"*

"I don't understand your feelings," his companion said, crestfallen. *"I am trying to help calm your mind."*

"You're in charge here, aren't you? Let me go. Let me leave this place—and I'll . . . I'll do whatever you want. Please! I am begging you!"

The entity bristled and shifted uncomfortably. *"I am sorry. It is not within my abilities to excise you from this place. From your perspective, that moment has yet to arrive."*

"B-but this will end?" the man asked as he slowly pushed himself upright. *"The burning will stop and I will be free?"* He took the dust from the yeel bark that had settled on him and rather than brushing it off, rubbed it in, covering what was left of his clothing as well as the exposed skin behind the tatters.

"Everything ends. And everything begins again. That is in-nate not just here, but to existence itself."

"Riddles!" the man snarled. *"Why always riddles?"*

His confidant shuddered sympathetically. *"I do try to make you understand."*

"Don't talk down to me. Don't patronize me!"

"I promise you, friend, I am not."

The man looked slowly up to his companion. *"Y-you're my friend?"*

"As I've come to understand the term, I think so. I admit 'friend' is an easier concept for me than 'enemy.'"

"I always thought enemy was the easier concept," the man bitterly scoffed. *"Enemies don't disappoint. Friends do."*

"How so?"

"Arrrgh!" He slammed his eyes shut and pressed forward into the tree again, beating the trunk with balled-up fists. *"You're always asking 'how so?' How so this and how so that! Why? What am I? A lab experiment gone wrong? An alien creature you've captured to study and test? Why are you torturing me?"*

"I would not," his companion assured him. *"Is it common to capture aliens and show them brutality?"*

The question landed hard and jarred the man, pushing him toward a troubling recognition. *"W-we tortured you . . . didn't we?"* he asked, his anger crystallizing into self-loathing.

The figure was noncommittal. *"'We'?"*

"Humans. People from my ship." The man straightened again, studying the entity with more empathy now than anger. *"Well, a human from— No, I don't know. Others were complicit, too, so that's no excuse, is it?"*

Without guile, without resentment, his friend replied nonchalantly: *"One universe is much like another."* He cocked his head left and then right. *"And, I suppose, also completely different. I admit they blend together, even for me. But I notice you remember a ship now? And that you're human? And that there is more than one universe, as your kind conceives?"*

The man's brow furrowed. *"I—I think so. I remember an-other. Or both. Two? Different universes?"*

"And no others beyond that?"

"Beyond th—? No, I . . . What universe are we in right now?"

His friend spread his arms wide. *"We inhabit . . ."* He struggled for a way to put it so as to not confuse the man further. *"I suppose you'd call it a conduit between universes. One that connects them all. Well, most of them. And yet, it is a universe unto itself."*

As if struggling with a conclusion he'd long ago made but never came to terms with, the human began pacing, kicking up black soot as he walked. *"So I'm not dead? For certain not?"*

"Do you feel dead?"

The man shrugged. *"What would dead feel like?"*

"I don't know." His companion tried to make the same movement, which on his form appeared awkward, if not painful. *"I've never known death."*

"But if I'm not dead, why am I stuck here for eternity?"

"Is that what dead is? Being 'stuck' somewhere, forever?" The question was sincere.

The human caustically chuckled. *"Some people think so. I never did."*

"Then what is death to you? And why do some people think it is a forever place? Is 'dead' endless?"

"I don't know why people believe what they believe," the man admitted with a grumble. *"I'm not sure what I believe anymore. But, yes, death is supposed to be endless. But I don't think it should feel endless."*

Truly curious, his companion moved closer. *"I'd like to know what you believe happens when the death of beings like you transpires."*

Struggling to remember philosophical views rather than

the emotions that roiled within, the human slowly plied out a cogent thought. *"I think . . . that I believed there was nothing after life ended. That when our brains stop functioning . . . we are just gone . . ."*

"But?" his friend gently prodded.

A memory surfaced, though the man couldn't place the where or when, so instead latched on to the notion itself. *"I remember wondering what happens in that moment just before death."* Calmer now, he slowed his stride and their march became an almost leisurely walk through the forest. *"As the brain's function diminishes, perception changes, distorts . . . and—and perhaps in the final seconds before it stops, you feel love . . . you think you see family . . . and for you, time slows . . . to an eternity."*

"Do you believe this?"

"I believed in science . . . before I died." He stopped, lowered his face into his hands, and wept. *"But now I'm locked in this place."*

"You're not here forever."

"You say that but I need you to prove it!" He continued to cry. *"And you say I'm not dead, but I feel dead."*

"You said you'd feel nothing if you were dead."

"Then I was wrong. I'm buried, in space, or at sea . . . not afloat but not sinking."

"That's very poetic for someone who thinks they're dead," his companion pointed out. *"But since I'm with you, I thought we decided we're both alive."*

For a long time, the human was silent, and the entity just watched as the man softly, slowly bounced his forehead on his own fist. *"If I'm here . . . and not there . . . I have to be dead."*

"We also decided 'dead' wasn't a place, didn't we?"

"I told you," he snapped, *"I don't know!"*

Giving the man some physical space, his companion

backed away a bit, but pointedly asked, *"Tell me what you* do *know."*

"I know that . . . Paul is my anchor. My beacon, like you said. But he can't hear me now. It has been forever and I think he's forgotten." As the air cut into his cheeks where the tears washed away the bark dust, he smeared his dirty palms across them to soothe his skin. But then his hands didn't have enough of a coating, and the harassing sparkles in the air bit into him again.

"The air burns me!"

"The JahSepp. They ride the wind and recondition this plane."

"They try to erase me. Is that it? Is that why Paul can't hear me? Because I've been erased?"

"Erased?"

"From reality." The man looked up mournfully at his companion. *"Are the JahSepp erasing me, and when I recover, I'm not me anymore? Have I been wiped out of time and no one remembers?"*

His companion didn't hesitate to answer. *"Paul remembers you."*

"He does? Are you sure?"

"He does, and he doesn't, and he will, and he won't."

"Yes, I . . . I remember a Paul who didn't remember me right. He wasn't my Paul. He tried to trick my Paul. He wasn't good—wasn't right."

"Figuring out who is and is not 'good' can be as difficult as learning what good means."

The human snuffled a sob and searched the mycelial sky. *"I don't know where I am! I don't know where he is and—"* Suddenly he twisted, as if hearing a faraway call. *"Is that him again? I feel him. I think. But . . ."* He searched left and right. *"From where?"* After a long moment, he dropped his gaze down again, disappointed and dejected. *"Gone."*

"*Was that him or another him?*"

"*What does that even mean?!*" the man shouted.

"*It means my efforts to explain are not helping. But I will continue to try. We must find you a clearing. It is the only way to reorder your mind.*"

"*A what?*" The human skewed his head toward his companion, his eyes narrowing once more with confusion. "*I know you, don't I?*"

"*You do,*" his friend said, melancholy in his voice. "*And you have before. And you will again. And, sadly, sometimes you will forget.*"

———

"*You're back?*" the man asked, scrambling up from where he sat against his most protective tree. He wasn't sure how long since he'd last sensed the entity who called himself a friend, but it felt as if it had been an eternity.

"*I am back,*" came the reply. "*And I never left. And I was not here, and I will be again.*"

The man shook his head, furious. "*No! You've been gone for . . . I don't know how long. Days? A week? A year?*"

"*Yes.*"

Ignoring the confusion within and without as best he could, the human glared toward the horizon. "*He's here again. I know it.*" He turned in the other direction, then to the side, still searching, and quickly asked his companion, "*Don't I?*"

"*I can't easily know what you know.*"

"*You seem to know everything else! But you won't explain anything.*" Pivoting in a new direction, he tried to regain the "scent" he'd lost.

"*I know as much as you, I suppose, just about different things. My senses are quite dissimilar from yours.*"

"I've told you, I don't know what I know anymore." He stalked past his companion, looking into the air on the other side of him, then into a patch of trees, as if the answer might be somewhere inside, hiding among the dark trunks.

"Then tell me what you think you know."

The request came with a sense that this had been asked of him a million times, and somehow also that it would be asked that many more. Still, when he found the answer and gave it, he felt insulted that his "friend" didn't already know. *"I'm in pain!"*

"You're more than just a thing in pain, I hope."

"A piece of me is missing, that's all I know . . ." the man said slowly. *"No, I—I know more. I know . . ."* He hit his temples softly with the heels of his palms. *"What? What do I know? What do I know?"*

The entity shuffled forward and put an arm under the man's elbow. *"Tell me anything you know, no matter how insignificant."*

"I . . . I know the human skull is made up of twenty-two distinct bones," he said, suddenly confident. *"And the Vulcan skull has twenty."*

"Interesting."

"Of course, the Andorian skull has thirty-three," he said, growing more self-assured.

"Go on."

"Nerve impulses in the brain," the man continued, *"can move as fast as 430 kilometers an hour. Human brain impulses. Human brains. I'm a human. From the planet Earth."*

"Yes. You remember that again. This is progress."

"Yes. I—yes. How do I know all this?" he asked, perplexed. *"How do I know over thirteen hundred enzymes are active in a human cell, but for Vulcans it's far fewer?"*

"How do you know?" his companion pressed, fully knowing the answer.

"I'm a doctor." He looked pleadingly at the figure. *"Am I a doctor?"*

"You are. So what piece of you is missing? Wouldn't a doctor know?"

The man rapidly shook his head. *"No, no, that's not science. That's . . . That's . . . Paul."*

"You always remember his name," his companion noted. *"Do you still remember yours? You have before."*

"I . . . yes. Of course, I do remember," he said slowly. *"It's Hugh."*

"Hugh what?"

"Hugh . . . C-Culber." He straightened with pride. *"Doctor Hugh Culber."*

"And do you remember my *name?"*

Turning toward his companion, the doctor observed him, much as he might a new alien patient whose race he'd never encountered. Which in the other one's case would likely be common, as Culber had only ever known one tardigrade life-form. *"Y-you're . . . R-rip—. . . No. It's you! You're Ephraim!"*

"Yes, my friend," Ephraim said cheerfully, and the mere presence of that emotion from him helped to steady Culber even more. *"The clearing approaches, I promise. You will regain yourself."*

"I will? You'll help me get to him? And I will be free of this place?"

"You will. And you won't. And you are. And you aren't."

3

"Sequence complete."

Once the shunts retracted from his arms, Stamets stumbled toward the door. As it slid open, his mind cleared and he pushed himself to awaken further. "Yes, fine," he said, assuming someone had asked him how he was, though he wasn't sure anyone had.

"Um, okay," Tilly said, and he felt a hand on his elbow, guiding him out of the cube. Or did he? Was that his hand? His elbow?

Wait, didn't I come out already?

It *had* been Tilly's hand on him and her face was now in front of his. He felt the deck beneath his feet as the mental fog lifted. He was here, standing before her, as others worked quietly around them.

"Welcome back . . . ?" she said.

His shoulders tightened, reminding him that he had muscles. Which wasn't a thought that should randomly occur. "What does that mean?" He wasn't asking Tilly, but himself, about his realization that he hadn't felt his own body until a moment ago.

"You had that faraway look again," Tilly said, handing him his small, white water bottle, which this time he eagerly took. "Another spore dream?"

He drank, almost swigging, and only then realized how thirsty he was. As soon as Stamets finished, he asked for more.

Tilly handed him another bottle and she and Enav watched as he drained it quickly.

"Why did you rush out of the spore chamber?" Enav asked. "Did something go wrong?"

"Wrong? No. And we call it a reaction cube." He was feeling better now, and though it seemed to him like an eternity since the jump completed, it was clearly only seconds. He handed the empty bottle back and bent over a bit, taking in deep breaths to steady himself.

"It's okay. We sometimes call it the spore chamber," Tilly whispered to Enav as she moved back toward her current tasks on the upper level.

"We're at the destination?" Stamets asked, trying to steal a glance at Tilly's station as he pushed himself upright.

"Yes, sir. Cygnia Minor colony." The ensign moved to let him at the console as he gripped its edge, pulling himself to it. "And you're sure you're okay?"

Verifying their coordinates, Stamets felt calmed and released a tight breath. As if a switch flipped, he felt fully himself once more, and was stronger when he said, "I'm perfect. If we get to work on your mycelial communication idea, will you drop it?"

Tilly gave an ear-to-ear grin. "So hard it'll break."

"How long have we got before the next one?" Stamets asked.

"Depends on when we get word of another outbreak," she said, checking the schedule on the console. "If we run low on antivirals and supplies here, we'll need to stock up again, but the Arcturian system is close enough at warp speed so the captain may not order a jump."

With some effort, Stamets suppressed a feeling somewhere between dread and foreboding as he motioned toward the station. "So we don't unnecessarily cover the same ground

Straal and I did three years ago, why don't we review our findings . . . and failures?"

"Oh, I did that already," Tilly assured him, far too chipper for his liking, especially after he mentioned the failure part.

"I see." Stamets pulled up the files anyway, at least to remind himself. It all seemed fresh in his mind, but after the brief brain-fog he'd just experienced, he didn't want to chance he'd forgotten something. "Give me a moment to catch up and we'll talk about next steps."

As they did, he found that several of those steps forward led only to almost the same number back, and by the time Enav returned to look over their shoulders, she only shook her head with a fleeting comment that what they were working on made no sense to her.

"Is this quantum physics or biology?" she asked as she passed them.

"They're really the same—" Stamets began to call after her, but Tilly waved him off.

"I already tried. She's one of those *normal* engineers." She crinkled her nose. "Very little astromycological background."

"I'll put her on report," Stamets quipped, then pointed at the holographic simulation as it completed. "See this? That's not working."

"I know," Tilly said. "But if we had a nanoparticle regulator that could adjust quickly enough—"

"Even if we were to design one, we can't produce something like that from the ship's fabrication units." Stamets didn't want to sound defeatist, but their first stumbling block was a big one. "And I promise you there's nothing close enough in our stores."

Tilly's shoulders slumped a bit. "You're sure?"

He glared at her.

"Of course you're sure."

He could see a frown beginning to form, but he didn't like to sugarcoat anything. "I told you, Straal and I—"

"But that was different," she explained. "You were trying to make it work with *subspace*. This is basic radio."

Stamets agreed, but that fact didn't encourage him. "Yes, we never got to this point in our simulations, but that doesn't mean we can get further. We're still trying to get a signal into the mycelial network without an energy wave that disrupts the frequency. That just may not be possible."

He watched as Tilly focused her disappointment into cognitive action. She was trying to will a solution into realization. He'd been there, and sometimes even done that. But he feared not this time.

"Well, let's think about it," she said, "before we give up."

When did I stop doing that? he wondered. *Didn't I used to believe the impossible could be made possible?* "Hey, I'm not giving up." Her passion was pulling him out of his nosedive. "I'm just frustrated."

"Yeah, me too."

When the display flashed a new schedule change, he nudged her out of the way and took over the console. "I'll save our work. You call it a night. Bridge just flashed that we have an early jump to Cestus III in the morning."

Tilly glanced at the monitor and the new order. "Oh, this is before my watch. I'll assign Orna to cover. I'm an ensign now. I can assign people."

"I know, I know," he said dismissively. "Where will *you* be, though?"

"PT." She moved her arms as if running, but kept her feet in place. "I applied for the Command Training Program, remember? Gotta be ready if it's approved."

"Right. Well, okay."

Tilly clearly sensed dissatisfaction, though in fact he was

mostly surprised. "Do you want me to switch it? I mean, I can— I just—"

"I'll manage somehow. I'm used to having you there, but it's not like we chat while I'm jumping." What if they did? Would he choose Tilly for that? He could see positives and negatives. She was rarely at a loss for words. Would finding a way to talk him through a jump keep him from having a spore dream? *Do I even want to lose them?*

"If you're sure, sir."

"Positive." Stamets forced a smile. "Good night, Tilly."

"Thanks. You too." She bounded up the stairs and as the doors opened, she turned back and said brightly, "Hopefully, I'll dream up some options for us."

"That'd be nice."

And also nice to always look forward to dreams.

———

"Missed you at lunch," Joann Owosekun told Tilly as she placed her tray on the table and slid into the empty seat. Gen Rhys scooted closer to Keyla Detmer, offering Tilly more space.

Opposite her, Airiam nodded her customary greeting. "Ensign."

"I ate with Mister Stamets," Tilly explained.

"We saw that," Rhys said.

"I didn't." Detmer spooned what smelled like pea soup onto a crostini and took a dainty bite. "I had lunch with Bryce— *and* the captain."

"Ohhh." Tilly took a sip of her drink. "Exciting or scary?"

"Neither. Just a working lunch. The only scary part," Detmer added with some annoyance, "was that I was late because I couldn't find the padd I left on my bed."

"Oh," Tilly said.

"I had to scrounge another one to present my report." She leaned toward the ensign, her blue eyes bright and sharp. "That's the problem with having a roommate who would organize the dust bunnies under the bed by size and shape, if she could. Who's so tidy I can never find half of the—"

"We don't get dust bunnies on the ship," Tilly interrupted, trying to defuse the tension.

"Someone's missing the point."

"Last time I was in your cabin and had to use your sink," Owo tactfully interjected, "I did see a lot of eyebrow pluckings left behind. Maybe someone who leaves those all over the sink *needs* someone cleaning up after them?"

"You saw a few, *maybe*," Detmer said, suddenly defensive.

"Sure. From each eyebrow. Built up daily over a week."

"So, uh . . ." Tilly took a bite of her breakfast burrito, breakfast-for-dinner being one of her favorite things. The pause as she chewed gave her cover to change the subject, since this was a pet peeve of Detmer's that everyone present had heard her complain about at least once a month. "Where's Bryce?"

"Quarantine," Owo replied.

Tilly gasped. "No! What happened?"

"It's just precautionary," Detmer told her, then chided Owosekun. "Don't make it sound like he's going to die."

Owo shrugged. "I said one actual word. One."

"True. Sorry." Setting down her spoon delicately on the plate under her bowl, Detmer leaned toward Tilly and quieted her voice. "Bryce went down to help boost the colony's subspace array. Turns out one of their blood-burn cases worked the same facility."

"And they didn't sterilize it?" she asked, aghast.

"They did, but the captain wants to be sure and beamed Bryce right to quarantine."

"Something like that gets on this ship," Rhys said, "and . . . I don't want to even think about it."

"Gen, we have the proper antivirals on board." Airiam turned from him to Tilly. "Keyla and I are going to visit Bryce when she is finished eating . . . whenever that might be." She cast a frown toward Detmer.

"Are you making fun of my eating habits, again?" the conn officer asked.

"Yes," Airiam said.

In response, Detmer slow-motioned another sip of her soup and then made an exaggeratedly slow dab of her lips with a napkin.

"I don't have to wait," Airiam said as she rose, her empty tray in hand. "I can meet you there."

"I'm coming, I'm coming," Detmer said as she quickly gathered her things. "I was nursing it just to stay eating for Tilly's sake."

Tilly smiled in appreciation, then looked to Rhys and Owo. "You guys'll stay, right?"

"Sure," Owo said. "I've got nowhere to be."

"I was going to learn the rules of *Ket-ma Tah*," Rhys said, taking a fry from his own plate despite the fact he'd already covered it with a napkin. "But I've been putting that off for weeks, so another night won't matter."

"What's *Ket-ma Tah*?" Even though her burrito was lovely, Tilly suddenly wanted fries as well, but she pushed that craving away. He had the thin-cut ones and she'd want crinkle anyway, she told herself. And with cheese. Not the soupy cheese that tasted like it came from some weird powder, but real *melted* cheese that probably had come from an actual cow or bovine creature.

"It's like an Andorian mancala," he said. "If that helps."

"It doesn't," Owo teased, and Tilly was sure she saw

her eyes roll upward. Tilly had always sensed a big sister/ little brother vibe between Owo and Rhys, which made her think having a sibling might be a wonderful thing, except she wouldn't have wished her mother on anyone. "It's like someone asking what your alligator sandwich tastes like, and you say it tastes like dinosaur."

"Probably tastes like chicken," Rhys said playfully.

"It was a hypothetical," Owo shot back.

"What's mancala?" Tilly asked, only mildly interested, as she was feeling a bit left out of their fun.

"I wanna say it's like ancient checkers, but I could be wrong," Rhys said, and grabbed another fry, running it through what was left of his gravy.

Gravy, Tilly thought. "Now I want poutine."

"Huh?" Rhys asked.

"Poutine. Never mind."

"I'm guessing two players and the object is to get the other person's pieces," Owo said.

"I still need to read the rules," Rhys told her. "I got it as a gift."

"Who gave you Andorian checkers?" Tilly decided to call it that instead of *Ket-ma Tah* or mancala.

"Tactical officer from the *Kerala*." He winked at her. "She's Andorian. We met at a Starfleet training seminar about the new phasers."

Owo laughed. "She got you a strategy game you won't know—so she can *beat* you."

Rhys smiled ruefully. "*May*be. But it's not whether you win or lose—it's how you play the game."

"I'm sure the captain would appreciate that being the motto of the ship's tactician," Tilly said.

"I should start closing all my after-action reports with that line." Rhys slurped up a last french fry and finally pushed his plate far enough away that it wouldn't be within reach. "I was going to give the game to Landry, but I think you're not supposed to regift, right?"

"Oh yeah, that's bad. Don't do that." Tilly thought how much easier this meal was in comparison to her lunch with Stamets. Then again, while his brain could be intimidating and his manner could be condescending, sharing a meal with him didn't usually put her on edge. But she was worried about him, and while she'd liked to have sought counsel from her friends, she didn't want to gossip. If Saru or the captain learned Stamets was having issues, it could put the spore drive, and therefore their mission, in jeopardy.

At the same time, if her worry became more than a feeling, she would have to report it up the chain of command. They both knew that . . . but had avoided talking about it. It all weighed on her.

"What've you been working on?" Owo asked, pulling Tilly from her analytical anxieties. "Other than kangaroo-level jumps?"

"Starting something that could be big or could be a big fat zero, but we'll see." Tilly then leaned closer and whispered, "We think we might be able to use the mycelial network for communication." She leaned back smugly and let them form their own conclusions as to how cool that would be.

"We won't tell," Rhys said as he stood and began to clean up.

"Tell?" Tilly said, suddenly nervous. "Tell who what about what? It's just a hypothesis so far."

"Won't tell Bryce you're trying to make him obsolete," Rhys said. "Wouldn't be right to get him worried about one more thing while under quarantine."

"He's teasing you," Owo said, also rising and removing her tray.

Tilly looked down and realized that she, too, was done with dinner. She took a last, too-loud sip of her tea and gathered her things as well. "Oh, right. Ha! Funny!"

"She okay?" he asked Owo.

"She's just Tilly," she replied as they moved off.

It was the kind of comment that could be disapproving, but from Owo it was a compliment. *Just Tilly* felt right, and as her friends turned back, she met them with a smile to say *Thanks for getting me.*

"Sequence complete."

When Stamets exited the reaction cube, Tilly was waiting for him. "Sorry I wasn't here when the jump was initiated."

"I already told you," he said. "You didn't have to come in early." He rolled down his sleeves, avoiding eye contact with her. Instead, he absentmindedly viewed the screen across from them. But he wasn't really reading the data, and if she'd quizzed him on it, he'd have failed. What really troubled him was that there'd been no dream this time, and while that meant on the one hand this was a "normal" jump, somehow it also felt unresolved. What happened to the voices? Especially the one who called him by name and told him *it's you*? Did the frustration he felt from the presence when Stamets didn't respond properly mean their contact was at an end?

"I know I didn't have to come. I wanted to." She handed him a water bottle.

Once, after a relatively long jump, he had complained about his mouth being dry. Now Tilly had a fresh bottle of cool water ready for him, every damn time. Sure, he could always use a sip, and yesterday he could have had three full bottles, but she was always ready, just in case. He took a quick drink and handed it back, thanking her.

"Any dreams?" she asked.

"Nope. Nothing this time."

"Really? You think it's because I wasn't here?" The splash of a grin told him she was being playful, but for a moment he considered it. What if the tardigrade DNA gave him some sort of low-level, close-proximity psychic connection?

No, that made no sense. The presence he felt was surely not Tilly. It seemed like someone he knew, however, but had somehow forgotten. "It doesn't always happen," he told her. "This time it just didn't. It's called a coincidence."

"Well, I have something, I think." She held up a yellow, translucent data card. "*This* might work."

He took the card, slid it into the console next to them, and let the information scroll by. "That's . . . actually pretty clever. And we can test it with what we have on board."

"Just needed to think on it," Tilly replied as if her brilliance was nothing.

"No, this . . ." He struggled to find the proper accolade. "It's extraordinary. Why didn't *I* think to open a link to the mycelial network *first*, and *then* form a quantum tunnel to protect the EM frequency from distortion?"

She demurred but she shouldn't, he thought. Why not show off her skills? He always did. "I just kept thinking how the network connection was like the barrier itself, and what can let you breach a barrier like this better than quantum tunneling?"

"Yeah," he said quietly. "Yeah." But why did Tilly have to connect the dots for him? Had he been intellectually compromised?

"Sometimes my brain's 'random mode' kicks in," Tilly explained. "Sometimes *A* leads me to *C* and I forget about *B* but look: Isn't *L* pretty? And I think I left *K* over there. And by the way, sometimes *L* and *K* have nothing to do with *A* or *C* but *B* reminded me of them."

" 'Sometimes'?" He gave her a rueful smile but was on the edge of choking up. Rarely had Stamets met someone who was as positive a person as Tilly. Whether she knew it or not, he needed that right now. "Okay," he said, and pointed toward the display. "Run with it. I'll check in with you later."

"Later?" Her expression turned quizzical, but maybe there was also a bit of disappointment.

"Got a thing I need to do." He moved up the stairway toward the corridor.

"A thing? Okay. Is it a long thing?" she asked as he sped away.

"Won't take long at all."

———

"This is taking forever," Stamets said, not attempting to hide his annoyance.

"Mm." Doctor Pollard ran the handheld scanner over the astromycologist's body, but slowed over his shoulders and head as she glanced at the screen. "There are some minor anomalies from your last exam."

"And?"

"Nothing to worry about. How have you been feeling?"

"I assume people who say 'with my fingers' are immediately sedated."

"I generally order a vivisection when my patients decide to be smart-asses." She put away the scanner and gestured for him to lie down. "Cuts down on the smart-assery."

"Is sarcasm terminal?"

"Yours is chronic. Just don't see me on a bad day." Pollard

did give a small grin to suggest she enjoyed their exchanges. That was how Stamets chose to read it, anyway.

But he did sense an extra layer of tension between them, and he realized it was their current mission. "You've been leading some of the landing parties, I guess?"

"Yes."

Offering no elaboration, he assumed the doctor had seen firsthand some of the infected the *Discovery* had been brought in to help. He'd probably not want to talk about it either. "I'm sorry."

Padd in hand, Pollard used a stylus to check off what he assumed were findings from her examination.

"All good?"

"You have a tension headache. Are you taking the vitamin D supplements I gave you?"

"Sometimes," he admitted. Which usually meant only when he remembered.

"Shall I have it programmed into your meals? Because you're still low." Shifting through the screens, she landed on one and wrote a new note. "Your spore jumps drain your D levels."

That seemed a stretch. "Are you suggesting forgetting the supplement will jeopardize my project?"

"You're very light skinned . . ." she began.

"Am I? Hadn't noticed."

"The ship's lighting replicates natural ultraviolet emissions, but not everyone needs the same amount. That means one of us"—she indicated his pale skin with her stylus—"is going to be producing too little vitamin D."

"Isn't there a pill I can take to just fix it?"

She pursed her lips. "Yes. Your vitamin D supplements."

"I meant just one time."

As Pollard pulled a hypospray from her cart, she cast an

annoyed glance. "You think a once-in-a-lifetime pill I could prescribe just slipped my mind?"

"Like I said, I forget." Why did talking to one's doctor always feel like being scolded by the elementary school principal?

She jabbed the hypo into his neck—more harshly than she needed to, Stamets thought.

"Uh, ow?"

"This will help in the short term." Pollard returned the hypo to the tray. "We can alter the UV levels in your quarters to compensate, but unless you want me to treat you like a pediatric patient, do as you're told."

"Berating me isn't how you'd deal with a child?"

"It's when I'm not berating you that you should be worried," she said coolly, and indicated that he could stand. "Anything else?"

He sat up, but remained on the table, hesitating to broach the entire subject. Still, he knew he should. Especially after that morning.

"Lieutenant?" she prodded. "There's a lot I need to do if—"

"I, uh . . . feel a little . . . mentally out of it."

She studied him, her gaze softening with concern. "Can you elaborate?"

Stamets shifted uncomfortably on the exam table. "I can try, if allowed to sit in a real chair."

Pollard smirked and gestured toward her office. "Sure. Step into my parlor."

Like the sickbay, the office was austere, bordering on spartan. Because more than one doctor used it, personal touches were absent. A desk and a couple of cold chairs didn't inspire intimate discussion.

Stamets paused, standing to the side of the patient's chair. *Where do I even start*, he thought, *and how deep should I go?*

Doctor Pollard positioned herself in the seat behind the

desk, placed her padd in front of her, and must have sensed his reticence. "Two real chairs," she said gently. "No waiting."

"Thanks." He gingerly lowered himself down, as if into a vat of too-hot water. "Is this off the record?"

Pollard's expression was one of empathy mixed with concern. "I am a doctor—it should go without saying that our discussions are confidential. If there's something that affects the performance of your duty as a Starfleet officer, however, I have an obligation to report that, just like you would about someone under your care."

"Of course." He rubbed his chin and then placed both hands on his lap. "Okay."

"Okay." She waited.

"So . . ." he began slowly. "I had an episode where I couldn't think clearly."

Pollard nodded, encouraging him to continue. "When was this?"

He hesitated. He didn't want to be specific, to suggest it was linked to the jumps, so he left it vague. "In the morning? After waking up?"

She scribbled on her padd with a stylus. "Are you're asking me or telling me?"

Stamets leaned away. "Trying to remember, I guess." He gestured to the padd. "What did you write?"

"A note." She signaled with the stylus for him to continue. "How long did it last?"

Time being what it was—or wasn't—within the mycelial network traversal, he actually wasn't sure. "A few moments?"

"You're asking me again."

"I thought for a few moments, but later when working on a new idea, I wasn't able to make . . . certain mental connections."

"That you usually would make?"

Why did doctors always ask questions that sounded so accusatory? "I'd like to think so, yes."

"I see." Her comment was noncommittal but he felt she was arguing with him—and winning.

"It took Ensign Tilly to point out to me what I missed," Stamets muttered.

Pollard pursed her lips.

"What's *that* supposed to mean?" he asked.

"Are you upset that a younger officer, of lower rank, and less experienced, came up with something you couldn't?"

Insulted, Stamets jumped to his feet. "No, that's not—" But would storming out achieve what he came here for? "No, I don't think so," he said more calmly, but remained standing.

"Okay," Pollard said. "Would you like to talk to Doctor Yankey? He's a licensed therapist."

"No. I . . ." He started toward the door. "You know what? Never mind."

"Are you sure?" Again, her rather innocuous question annoyed him.

"Does he have a better bedside manner?"

"Than me?" she scoffed as she rose. "Big ask."

As they moved toward the doorway back to sickbay, Pollard took his elbow and gave it a soft squeeze. "Paul. Your tests don't indicate anything out of the ordinary. Some fatigue. And your tension headache? Doesn't even merit a report. I'm sure a lot of people in your position would feel the same. I understand you've been breaking new ground. I still don't approve of the genetic alterations you and Doctor Straal undertook—"

"It was an emergency situation, and we did what we thought was right."

A slight frown creased Pollard's lips. "And because of that, Starfleet may have given approval retroactively, but there's a reason there are strict limits on human genome manipulation."

Unwilling to relive that gone-but-not-forgotten argument, Stamets slid into the main sickbay. "Well, I have to say, this has been fun."

"It was," Pollard said. "I'm giving you a prescription for your headache, but it's a short-term measure. You need to confront the source of your tension."

Yeah, he thought as he exited into the corridor. *Easier said than done.*

4

"Should we be hearing something?" Enav brushed a few strands of dark curly hair away from her left ear. "I feel we should be hearing something."

"You would be," Stamets said, indicating a painfully blank status screen, "if it was working."

"Don't you need someone to be broadcasting?"

"With subspace radio, yes," Stamets said. "Have you ever listened to the EM band?"

"Not outside a classroom," Enav said.

"Normal radio has a sound. Static," Tilly said. "You can scan the EM spectrum and hear something. We assumed that would be happening here."

"Hopeless." Stamets shut down the program. He was disappointed but, had it worked, he wasn't certain he'd have been elated, either. What if they'd heard that disembodied voice during his jumps? What if that presence wasn't only *his* anymore? And why was the thought of that connection not being special to him so unsettling?

"It worked in simulation." Tilly was deflated, but still searching for an answer. "Maybe the tunneling isn't the solution."

"No, I think it's necessary, but something else is obviously still missing," Stamets replied. "Listen, we'll—"

"Bridge to Stamets." Airiam's voice broke in over the comm.

"Stamets here."

"We need an emergency jump to Vega IX, Lieutenant. FHO reports possible outbreak."

They all froze a moment. The entire quadrant had been on alert. Planetary and Federation health organizations had issued warnings through every government body and media outlet. The early symptoms of the disease mimicked half a dozen less deadly illnesses, but if they'd waited to see which cases were the blood burn and which were not, by the time they knew, even the *Discovery* would be too late. That's why some outbreaks they'd investigated hadn't been the disease at all, but meeting them head-on hadn't been a waste of time.

This case, however, was more chilling than the others they'd chased down. Vega was only ninety light-years from Earth. If this was an actual case of Symbalene blood burn, it was being carried into the more populated sectors of the Federation, despite all the travel precautions.

"Understood. Stand by." Stamets ordered Tilly to the console. "Pull up the coordinates." He hurriedly rolled up his sleeves as Enav loaded the console with a full spore container.

Rushing into the reaction cube, Stamets didn't have time for his usual meditative moment. As he lined his arms up and leaned back into the support sled, he knew he had to concentrate solely on the task at hand. Part of him had been hoping for another spore dream, but now he dreaded the idea of being at all unfocused or unprepared for another emergency jump.

He glanced to Tilly once the biomechanical connection was made to the ports in his forearms. "Ready."

"Bridge, we are go."

"Black alert."

When they jumped, sparkle was all Stamets saw. A wonderful, dreadful silence soaked into him. It was an eternity that lasted a moment, and a moment that lasted an eternity, but that was the network. As it flashed through him, though, he realized he finally understood at least one missing piece.

"Sequence complete."

"Bridge acknowledges destination," Enav called out.

"Spores!" Stamets exclaimed breathlessly as he half exploded, half stumbled out of the cube. "We need spores!"

Tilly wrinkled her nose as she moved toward him. "We have a lot of spores. I mean, more spores than you can shake . . . um, at spores. You were just covered in them."

"No," Stamets gasped, pushing away the water she offered. "That's what's missing from the mycelial communications system!"

"We already inject spores into it. Enough to conduct EM transmissions."

"It's *not* enough though. Not even close." He moved to her station to key in the changes for their simulation. "Because we added quantum tunneling to the process—still brilliant, by the way—we need to increase the spore ratio a million-fold." Before them, her holographic screen displayed the explosion of mycelia he was calling for.

"Ohhh! We shouldn't be injecting spores in the receiver. We should be housing the receiver"—she gestured to the reaction cube—"in *here*."

"We gotta go bigger." Stamets beamed at her. "We were thinking small. *I* was. But we don't have to. We just pretend we're building an *enormous* communications array. Because the mycelial network is, in fact, enormous. *Ginormous*, even."

"You used a made-up word!" Tilly gripped his arm. "He used a made-up word," she told Enav. "That's my influence."

"You must be very proud," Enav said dryly.

———

"He was here," Culber excitedly told Ephraim. *"I felt him! Did you?"*

"My sensitivity is different from yours," the tardigrade replied, *"but yes, to your understanding, I did."*

"I always forget what he feels like . . . until I get to feel him again." He ran his hand along the nearest tree, not only to collect more of the bark dust, but to have some tactile experience that wasn't just the burning air.

"Understandable."

"Why do I forget everything? Why can't I hold on to myself?" Culber pleaded with his companion.

Ephraim nonchalantly rolled his upper body. *"You are in this place and of this place, but your mind is incompatible. You are here, but cannot be."*

Culber didn't understand, but didn't care what the tardigrade meant, other than if they were friends, Ephraim should want to help him be free. *"If that's true, then help me get home,"* he said, rushing forward and thrusting his arms around Ephraim in a tight hug. *"Can't you?"*

"I can, and I will. And I can't, and I won't."

Angry again, Culber pushed himself away and lurched back toward the yeel trees that the painful JahSepp avoided. *"You make no sense! You never make sense, but you know I forget and so you tease me with your riddles over and over!"*

"You forget because your mind cannot properly attune itself in this plane. My contact with you does not help this, but when I connect you with those of your kind, clarity can return for a time. Your beacon—your anchor to your plane—they are the only mind I can bond to yours." Ephraim shuffled closer and raised his arms to the sky, indicating the network or perhaps existence

itself. *"Sadly, they flit about and are open to this only fleetingly. But there will come clearings. I am planting the seeds to help you. I have and I will bring them to you. I promise."*

"I don't want promises," Culber cried. *"I want Paul!"*

"Yes. They are who I mean."

———

"Sounds like a lot of nothing."

Stamets frowned at Enav as he adjusted the settings. "It's static. It's not supposed to sound like anything."

Covering her ears, Tilly cringed. "Then why do you have the volume up so high?"

Gesturing his apology, Stamets turned it down to a background hum. But to him, there was something helpful about *listening* for a pattern. Even if the computer found a signal repetition before he might, it was a necessary part of the experiment.

"When the computer *does* find a pattern—" Tilly began, but Enav cut her off.

"You mean *if*."

Through gritted teeth, Tilly replied with an exasperation Stamets had rarely seen from her. "I'm choosing to think positively, Orna."

"Right," Enav said, unconvinced.

Tilly didn't reply as she suddenly bounced on the balls of her feet and pointed to the screen. "Look!"

Wide-eyed, Stamets fine-tuned the controls, tightening the frequency reception to focus on the bandwidths that triggered the pattern alert.

He turned the volume up slightly again. "If we'd been listening more closely, we might have caught this first," he told them as beeps, sputters, and a high-pitched whistle filled the room.

"That is a definite signal pattern," Tilly said. "Across three different frequency ranges!"

Then it was gone, abruptly becoming dull static once again.

"Did we lose it?" Stamets asked, readjusting and calibrating the receiver. "Dammit. We lost it!"

"It's recorded, we'll analyze it," Tilly said, but Stamets was still trying to find the transmission.

No amount of signal manipulation or frequency jiggering was bringing it back. The speaker mocked them with random noises and Stamets angrily switched everything off.

"It works," Tilly told him, her hand awkwardly on his shoulder a moment before she pulled it quickly off.

He wasn't convinced and met her eyes with skepticism. "Does it?"

——

Hours passed, and Tilly wanted to delay their report, but Lieutenant Stamets was adamant they get feedback before the next jump. While his nerves—and his headache—may have played into his reasoning, he made it clear to Tilly his "vote" was the only one that mattered.

Saru moved down the steps toward them, his gait effortlessly graceful. "Good morning, Ensign, Lieutenant."

"Commander Saru," Tilly bubbled, in her half-nervous, half-chipper way.

"You said you have something of interest?" the Kelpien asked.

Stamets gestured Saru closer so he'd be able to see the console's display.

Watching the data stream across the screen, then sneaking a glance at the first officer for a hint of what he might be thinking, Stamets found only a blank stare.

"I'm not sure I understand." Saru indicated the frequency graph. "This is an EM radio band."

"Yes," Tilly said, as if that were a new and wondrous thing.

"That's not the point," Stamets assured the first officer.

Saru waved his hand toward the console, spreading his fingers wide. "Forgive me, but I believe I'll need some illumination, then."

"*This*," Stamets said, pointing at a particular flashing data strand, "is a recording of signals we picked up from inside the mycelial network."

Saru merely blinked, apparently waiting for more information.

"We think it's a distress call," Tilly said before Stamets could speak.

"I was getting there," he grumbled to her under his breath, then continued to Saru. "It *could* be a distress call. There's a pattern—"

"I see the pattern, but don't see how it's a distress signal." The Kelpien again motioned toward the display. "Is there evidence this is not naturally occurring?"

During their analysis, Tilly's certainty had encouraged Stamets that their conclusion was correct, but he felt less confident now that he had to explain it. "This, and this, repeats with one frequency, and then another." He indicated two consistent burst patterns across the different frequencies they were monitoring.

"Such patterns do present similarly in nature," Saru pointed out.

"Like Izarian moon-bats?" said Tilly.

Saru tilted his head. "An apt example, Ensign."

Frustrated, Stamets huffed out an annoyed breath, silently begging Tilly to shut up.

It didn't work. "Well, they chitter at two alternating frequencies," she explained.

"We're not talking about moon-bat chitters," Stamets said. "This transmission may even be encrypted, and moonbats don't do that."

Likely in an attempt to defuse the tension, the first officer spread his arms wide and bowed his head. "I'm open to examining any evidence you have."

Over the next few minutes, Stamets and Tilly shared their proof. The Kelpien listened intently and at one point took over the station and ran his own analytic algorithms.

"Interesting," he murmured.

"Then you see it," Tilly interjected, clearly unable to let Saru form his own conclusions. "Starfleet regulations—"

"I'm aware of the regulations." Saru stepped away from the console. "What you've done is extraordinary, and evidence does suggest you've recorded some kind of transmission. It may even be from a technologically advanced life-form. But without knowing what the message says . . ." He shrugged, which for him was somehow an elegant, almost musical movement. "How can we determine it's a distress call?"

"Distress calls in most cultures repeat a signal in an alternating pattern." Stamets indicated the console's readout, hoping the data still spoke for itself. "Human Morse code or Vulcan cautionary ciphers are very similar to what we're seeing."

"Has the universal translator suggested this is a distress call?" Saru asked. "The database should contain any number of mathematical lingua-codes."

Tilly actually snickered. "Did you just make a math joke?"

"Did I?" Saru may have been smiling, or may have been

pursing his lips—it was hard to tell. "In any case, I must ask: Why would someone encrypt a call for help?"

It was a good question, and off their shared, defeated look, Stamets and Tilly made clear they didn't have an answer.

"I can't bring this to the captain until you have something more definitive. But, if you believe this is an encrypted communication by an intelligent species sent over the mycelial network . . . decode it."

"That's not our area of expertise," Stamets said. "Could we use Lieutenant Bryce?"

Saru shook his head. "Given the importance of our current mission, we cannot have the lieutenant chasing what would likely be referred to as 'wild mycelial geese.'" With that, he moved toward the exit. "I have the utmost confidence you can resolve this yourselves."

"Thank you, Commander. We'll do it, sir!" Tilly called after him. "I mean, I'm sure we will. We just need some time."

"Let me know when you do," Saru said.

When the doors closed behind the first officer, Stamets turned to Tilly and glowered. "I thought you were going to work on having more unexpressed thoughts?"

———

"Back to the drawing board." Stamets pulled his tray from the food dispenser and turned toward Tilly, who already had hers—minus any Rigellian mayo.

"What? No—we found something. We heard something real," she told him. "It worked." She was leading them to an empty table, and he nudged her with the edge of his tray.

"No, let's . . ." He hesitated. "Let's open this up to more people." He took a pensive step toward Tilly's usual dinner companions. Why should her life be so segmented? He could fit in, couldn't he?

"You *want* to sit with us?"

"I *work* with fungi, I'm not one myself," Stamets dead-panned. "I can mingle with others."

"No, I didn't mean . . . I'm just surprised. Usually you don't want to be . . . you know . . . talky. We all talk *a lot*. I know it can get annoying."

"I work with you," he said. "I'm immune."

Tilly wrinkled her nose, but marched quickly toward her usual table, Stamets in tow.

"I'm sorry," he said softly, catching up with her. "That was me being playful, I know it doesn't always sound that way. You remind me of my sister . . . sometimes."

"Kid sister?"

"She's older, but—"

"Ah, so you're the baby of the family," she said, as if confirming for herself some deep insight.

His brows rose skeptically. "Hard to still say at my age, but I guess so."

As they took the last two seats at the table, Stamets greeted the group and they all replied more warmly than he expected. Owo was on his right and Tilly sat to his left. Rhys, Detmer, Bryce, and Airiam fanned out in front of them.

"Is anyone actually left flying this ship?" Stamets asked, motioning to what seemed to be the entire bridge crew.

"Autopilot," Airiam said dryly.

With her somewhat-tinny artificial voice, Stamets wasn't sure if she was kidding. Thankfully, Tilly leaned toward him and whispered, "She's being funny."

"I got that," he replied, as if he fully had, then said to the group, "Does anyone ever do a double shift?" In his field he was used to pulling all-nighters if need be, but only since his role developed into "mycelial network navigator" had he begun to worry that fatigue could impact his performance.

"It depends," Rhys said. "If something important is happening we usually work straight through."

"On the *Shenzhou*, Captain Georgiou had coffee and sandwiches brought to the bridge in a crisis," Detmer added. "Everyone took the coffee, but she had to order us to eat."

"Couldn't eat because the situation was too tense?" Stamets took a bite of his salad.

"Couldn't eat because the sandwiches were horrible," Detmer said. "Who even orders liverwurst?"

"I like liverwurst." Owo lifted the sandwich from her plate. "This *is* liverwurst."

"Sad," Rhys said. "We used to be friends."

"You've probably never even tasted it."

"I don't have to taste something to know I don't like it," he said.

"You and my three-year-old nephew have a lot in common," Stamets said.

"I'm glad you're joining us," Bryce said. "But why don't you more often?"

The astromycologist considered the question a moment, and decided he'd really just felt he needed some connection to those around him. Maybe because his spore dreams and the link to their mystery voice had disappeared of late, and he was seeking a replacement. "Sometimes I isolate myself unnecessarily," he said finally, and took a forkful of his eggplant parmesan so he wouldn't have to add anything deeper.

"You're always welcome," Airiam said. "Tilly speaks very highly of you."

"You do?" Bemused, he leaned his chin down on one hand and stared at her.

"Oh, no, I don't. I—it's not like I blather on about you."

She uneasily turned to Bryce. "How was quarantine? Glad you're back with us."

He took a sip of whatever was in his mug and squinted sheepishly. "I'll admit, I was worried for a couple hours." Seeming not to want to discuss it further, he gestured toward both of them. "Tilly said you two are working on something special?"

Stamets looked at Tilly, and she quickly explained, "I needed his sign-off to secure the parts we needed for the receiver."

"Right. Thanks," he told Bryce.

"How's it coming?"

Before answering, Stamets took another bite of his main course that had neither eggplant nor parmesan, yet managed to come amazingly close in taste. He then described the experiments he and Tilly had done, the data they received, and the conclusions they had drawn, including that they thought the transmission they received might be a distress call. He wondered if any of them actually cared, despite their listening intently as they continued to eat.

When he was finished, Bryce was the first to comment. "Why do you think the transmission is alien? Maybe the *Glenn* is playing with mycelial communication."

Taken aback by the thought, Stamets hadn't considered that. It certainly was possible. The *Glenn* and the *Discovery*, by Starfleet directive, were not to compare notes except on a preset schedule. The idea was they wouldn't cross-contaminate their experiments or hypotheses. Of course, it also meant they couldn't cross-pollinate either. Stamets always felt that worked to create a healthy competition. It led to Straal finding the tardigrade and taking his experiments as far as he could, then Stamets realizing it was the creature's DNA that would help them navigate the mycelial network.

"If it's the *Glenn*, why an encrypted mathematical code and not a Starfleet standard hail?" Airiam asked. "My left hand doesn't encrypt what it's doing from my right hand."

Stamets covertly made sure everyone else had considered that a joke, and decided it was safe to do the same. He didn't know much about Airiam, other than that the cybernetic augmentations were due to an accident.

"Maybe it's just a transmission test," Bryce suggested. "It could be encoded because they don't want anyone actually getting a message. Hell, maybe there *is* no message. Maybe it's just telemetry from a test probe."

"What if it's some kind of warning?" Tilly wondered aloud. "From an intelligence that inhabits mycelial space the way we do normal space, and . . ." She glanced over to Stamets, who was staring at her uncomfortably.

Without saying anything, he hoped his annoyed look suggested: *Mention spore dreams and you're done working with me.*

"Never mind," Tilly said. Clearly, message received.

"You don't encrypt a distress call *or* a warning," Owo said.

"It could be coded rather than encrypted. Maybe the key is either at the beginning or the end of the broadcast," Bryce said.

"I like him," Stamets said, gesturing to Bryce with his fork. "He's smart."

"Comms," he said, and tapped at his own temple with an index finger. "Gotta have brains."

"Wish the rest of us were just as smart," Detmer said with an eye roll. She moved a strand of red hair over her ear, suppressing a grin.

"Gosh," Rhys said, tidying up his tray, "all I do is lock phasers on the other ships and make sure it's not one of ours."

"I press 'go,'" Detmer said.

"I help too," Owo reminded her.

"Sometimes." Detmer winked and they all laughed—even

Stamets. He realized he'd needed that as much as he needed answers to his various problems. For the first time since the dreams began, his tension headache wasn't even noticeable.

———

"When I was two, I thought chickens could talk, and that they just used chicken words we couldn't understand." Tilly was running new calculations and Stamets gazed up from the opposite console where he was rerunning his first analysis, verifying he'd not missed anything.

"You actually remember when you were two years old?" he asked, skeptical that was humanly possible.

"Yeah. I know that's a little weird."

"*At least* a little. Is there a point to this chicken story?"

"Maybe these are just chicken words," she said, waving at the screen in front of her. "Maybe we can't decode it because it's not encrypted *or* coded. It's just that the universal translator doesn't speak chicken."

Stamets stopped what he was doing. "It's not enough that people think I make this ship fly on mushrooms? Now you want them to think we're making first contact with sentient chickens?"

"Well, if they're *sentient* they're not really chickens, are they? Just—chicken shaped."

"So, I should say poultry?" Before she could answer, he motioned for her to join him. "Tilly, look."

She rushed to his console and, judging by her expression, she saw the same thing he did.

"Coordinates. Those look like mycelial coordinates." She eyed an extra set of values that blinked, as the computer was unsure what to do with them. "But these? I don't know what this is."

"Neither do I," Stamets said with a chuckle. "But this—it's real progress. Whoever sent this . . . maybe they're giving us their location."

A boatswain's whistle sounded. *"Bridge to DASH lab."* Airiam again. *"Stand by for spore-drive activation."*

"Acknowledged." Stamets had lost track of time, but invigorated by their discovery he cheerfully rolled up his sleeves. For the first time in quite a while, he wasn't even partially dreading stepping into the cube. They still had to figure out what the extra data meant, but at least Saru would be able to go to the captain and explain that Stamets and Tilly had received and transcribed a message from within the mycelial network.

As he leaned back onto the support sled, the navigational shunts moved smoothly toward him, connecting to the ports in his forearms.

"Ready," he told Tilly through the chamber wall.

"Black alert."

5

"B-b-black alert. Red alert. R-r-red alert. Bl-black—"

"Silence that, please." Saru's visual spectrum was wider than a human's, but he could tell the bridge was suddenly bathed in what most would call darkness. "Emergency lights."

Dimmer than normal, the emergency lights that flickered on would brighten slowly over time, to give crewmembers' eyes time to adjust. Despite seeing into the ultraviolet band, Saru needed them as well, but he got his bearings more quickly than others. "Lieutenant Airiam, what happened?"

"Before my console went dark, it read an incomplete navigation sequence."

"Understood." Seeing the captain's-chair command-access panel was offline, Saru turned to Bryce. "Contact engineering. We need their status."

Bryce's expression was a fusion of frustration and annoyance. "Internal and external comms are down, Commander. I'm trying to get a channel for you."

The first officer moved toward Owosekun. "Ops?"

"We've lost main power, sir. Auxiliary is sluggish."

"That I can see." He gestured to the relative console darkness around the bridge. "Batteries?"

"Coming online now." Each console had its own backup system, but the deck-wide one could be slower to respond.

"Where are we?" He eyed the blank main viewer that

usually crackled with information. It was darker than it should be, even without its normal informational overlays, meaning protective shutters must have engaged, closing off the outside view. To have it so dark was unsettling.

"Sensors are down, sir," Rhys said. "We're blind."

His hand instinctively reaching toward the back of his head, the Kelpien felt his ganglia emerging in protest. They weren't fully extending—just poking out their end tendrils, which was disconcerting enough.

"Airiam?" Saru twisted toward her.

"Spore-drive computers are not responding." She stabbed at her now active if unhelpful console. "I cannot verify jump completion."

Detmer chimed in next. "Same, sir. Negative helm control. No status on warp or impulse. Without sensors, I'm unable to confirm our position."

"Thrusters?" Saru asked as he angled toward her and watched over her shoulder.

"I can't tell," Detmer admitted with an exasperated tone. "For all I know, we're at warp twelve and about to fly apart."

"No," Saru corrected, one long finger in the air. "*That* I would feel." He strode to the aft bridge to an auxiliary engineering station. "Crewman Barnetta, find the captain and report our status. Ensign Hams, coordinate runners. I want damage-control teams reporting from all decks via communicator, with priority on engineering. Also, find Commander Landry and have her report in."

"Aye, sir," both men said in unison as they moved to the lift, which had its own backup power. But when the doors did not open for them, Saru motioned them toward the emergency egress hatch.

"Clearly the lifts are offline as well."

Barnetta reached down to the deck-plate access panel in

front of the door to the captain's ready room. He anxiously felt for the manual release and had to try it twice before it opened.

As the hatch slid out of the way, he expected to see the ladder down to the next deck. Instead, Michael Burnham pulled herself up and out.

Barnetta's voice crackled with nervous surprise. "Captain on the bridge."

She gave him an encouraging look. "At ease, Mister Barnetta."

He turned to Saru. "I found the captain, sir."

"Well done," Saru said with a hint of sarcasm.

Once the captain was past him, Hams quickly disappeared through the hatch as Saru gestured for Barnetta to return to his station.

"Fill me in," Burnham said, moving with Saru toward the command chair.

"We're on auxiliary power and possibly adrift," he began. "Sensors and communications are down," Saru continued as Burnham swiveled the seat toward herself and tapped at the arm panel, which was now working. "We're unsure about the status of propulsion."

"Scanners prior to this?"

"Clear of other vessels or astrometric anomalies. I've sent Hams to organize reports from the damage-control teams via hand communicators."

"Good call," Burnham said, and went to a storage compartment to the left of the inoperable turbolift. Opening it manually, she pulled out a communicator and flipped it open. Once it chirped to life, confirming an open channel, she closed it, took another from storage, and handed it to Saru. She also pulled two type-1 phasers. "Let's go."

"Go?" Saru asked as he took the equipment and smoothly stored them in opposite pockets.

"I'm not waiting for answers to come to us." She motioned him back to the hatch through which she'd appeared just a minute ago. "Commander Airiam, you have the conn. Mister Saru and I are going to engineering."

"Of course," Saru said, hesitant.

She stopped and looked up at him. "With lifts offline, it's going to be a trudge. Especially for you," she said, glancing toward his booted hooves.

Congenially, he tilted his head to one side. "I shall endeavor not to slow you down."

Her eyes crinkled at the corners, ever so slightly, and for a moment it felt like one of their old competitions. On a track he'd always been faster, and would get a certain gratification in reminding her. But traveling up and down a ladder not built for Kelpiens would always slow him down.

Once the hatch closed and they'd worked their way down out of earshot of the bridge crew, Burnham gravely asked, "Do you believe we're under attack?"

"It is not my impression, Captain." Saru wasn't sure if his threat ganglia agreed, and he made another involuntary, habitual motion to check them. "Commander Landry, when she is located, may have a different opinion."

"Saru, when we're alone and you call me captain, it's a clear sign you're worried but don't feel you have enough evidence to tell me why."

The Kelpien felt his face tighten in what others of his kind might have perceived as a sheepish expression. "Observant, as always."

"We've known each other a long time. Longer than most captains and first officers."

"Indeed." Saru focused on placing each foot carefully on the descending ladder rungs, convinced that toppling onto his captain would only exacerbate their problems.

"Tell me what you're thinking," Burnham prodded, with a warmth she would not use if they were on the bridge. "You know I trust your instincts."

That was the truth. While their relationship *had* been contentious and quarrelsome, it had since grown—nurtured by their former captain—into something quite familial. With time, Burnham truly became like the sister Saru had left behind on his homeworld of Kaminar, and he believed he'd become a surrogate brother to her.

"Lieutenant Stamets and Ensign Tilly have been investigating the possibility of mycelial communications. Although I trust their skill . . . I fear their enthusiasm may have led to a series of consequences . . ."

". . . that occurred during this jump," Burnham said.

"A jump Airiam said registered as incomplete. Until sensors are restored, we cannot be certain where it left us."

"It would help if the main port wasn't shuttered."

"I shall add that to our list of priorities." Saru grunted as he nearly slipped off a rung.

"Careful." Burnham reached up to steady him. "You all right?"

"They could make these passageways less tight," he grumbled as they continued descending.

"I don't remember you being claustrophobic, Saru."

"The taller they are, the harder they fall."

"I don't think that's the saying."

He huffed his acceptance of that, and for another deck's passing they were silent, until he asked, "Should we contact the bridge for an update?"

"Negative. They'll let us know if there's anything to report. You hated when I micromanaged you. I trust them to do their jobs."

"That," Saru replied, "sounds like Captain Georgiou talking."

"I'll accept that as a compliment."

"That's certainly how I intended it."

After another brief silence, the captain pointed out: "Mycelial communication . . . didn't Stamets and Straal try that at some point?"

"They did, to no avail," Saru said. "Lieutenant Stamets and Ensign Tilly believe they can overcome whatever previous problems had plagued the project."

"Given our current mission, I'm not sure *plague* is the best term to use right now."

"We can only hope the situation reported on Benecia Colony is another false positive."

Burnham didn't sound as hopeful. "Benecia is within range of the other actual cases. I don't think we'll get as lucky as we were on Vega. Can you think of any reason this communications experiment would cause a ship-wide systems failure?"

"I cannot."

"Then I hope Mister Stamets can. And damn well better know how to fix this."

After a few more rungs of silence, the captain suggested, "Now it's been long enough to contact the bridge. See if there's an update to our status."

He stopped, gingerly took out his communicator, and flipped it open. "Saru to Airiam. We are on deck seven, descending toward engineering. Please acknowledge."

"Airiam here, sir. We read you. Damage reports are slowly coming in. Sickbay reports a number of serious casualties from structural integrity failures and coolant or plasma leaks. Commander Landry is one of them. A subdural hematoma. She's in surgery. We still haven't heard from engineering."

"Thank you, Commander. Please keep us informed. Saru out." With that he returned the communicator to his pocket, made sure Burnham was moving, then resumed his descent.

"Casualties," Burnham grimly repeated. "Landry."

"Yes. Doctor Pollard is a skilled physician. I trust her implicitly." Saru's tone was equally dark.

A sudden sound from below, unidentifiable. He motioned for the captain to stop. "Michael—listen."

She cocked her ear toward the bulkhead to her right. "What do you hear?"

"It's . . . people coughing. Choking."

"Where?"

Saru could sense the captain's entire body tense and her endocrine system skyrocket. "Two decks down," he told her, and they hurried toward that level.

Burnham swung the hatch open and she and Saru moved out to the deck. They were met with a billow of smoke that instantly stung his lungs and eyes.

On the deck lay three unconscious, wheezing crewmembers, and one alert but choking ensign who leaned against a damaged bulkhead.

"I've got you," the captain coughed as she helped Shanna Gilkeson into the arms of the first officer, gesturing for him to get the ailing astronomer clear of the acrid air.

"This way," Saru told his crewmate.

"Structural integrity fields failed," Burnham grunted as she stretched her arm between two fallen support struts. "Got to vent this section . . . but can't . . . reach manual controls."

Saru lifted Gilkeson onto the exposed access ladder from where he and the captain had entered the area. Helping her wrap her arm around one rung and her hand around another, he made sure she had enough strength to secure herself. "Can you hold on?"

Her throat rough from smoke inhalation, Gilkeson hacked out a sharp "yes." She wiped her soaked forehead against her uniform sleeve and pushed a damp shock of red hair from her eyes.

"Saru, I need you," the captain called. "Can you pull this away?"

When he returned to Burnham, she was trying to move an immensely solid composite metal strut. He searched for something he could use as a lever and found a fallen piece of conduit that would likely be strong enough. He slid it beneath the beam and with a long grunt, used all of his strength, hoping the piping would last. Slowly, the opening between the strut and the bulkhead began to widen.

Burnham snaked her hand through and opened the hidden manual vent with a quick tug. The fans clicked on and smoke was pulled out of the corridor.

As the haze cleared, Burnham spied several other crewmembers sprawled across the floor. Gilkeson stepped off the access ladder. "I'll take care of them, Captain," she offered through a cough.

"Mister Saru will help you. Get them to sickbay," she ordered. "I'll continue to engineering." As she pulled herself onto the ladder, she glanced back to them. "Be careful. Both of you."

———

"Paul? It's me, you."

Stamets tried to move but one of the articulators that connected the navigational shunts to his forearms hadn't drawn back and he had to pull it loose.

"Find you, Paul," the second voice told him, and through the shine that filled his eyes so brightly, Stamets had to feel for the door to the spore chamber.

Why can't I really see? Paul wondered as he trudged forward, feeling the voices on him. He saw Tilly, barely. She was bathed in a milky-white haze and he thought she might be voicelessly waving at him, but he wasn't sure.

"Come, Paul! Are you coming?"

Where? Stamets thought, unable to speak.

"To me," the more urgent voice said.

"To you," the other seemed to explain.

It didn't matter that the voices were vague. He *had* to follow them: up the stairs he could not see, but knew were beneath his feet; out the door that flew open for him, then closed awkwardly, limping behind him; through the smoky corridors that choked his lungs as he was pulled through them.

Coughing around each breath, Stamets almost instinctively found the EV suit that could give him the clean air he needed. He felt guided to it, though he still couldn't really see it through the gauzy haze. As he hurriedly put it on, he asked the voices, "Where am I going?"

"To me. Finally to me."

"To you. Go to him."

Stamets felt himself walk, seemingly aimlessly, toward wherever "he" was supposed to be, and was surprised when he heard the sound of the airlock hiss open. Moving forward, seeing only glimpses through the alabaster fog, he plunged forth, the voices still guiding him, somehow safely, toward them.

"Find me, Paul!"

"Yes, find you."

———

By the time she reached engineering, Captain Michael Burnham was breathing easier, but could still taste burnt data cabling and insulation in the back of her throat. Just as she stepped onto the deck, a young engineer stumbled around the corner and nearly bowled her over.

"Captain!"

"Ensign Chen, are you injured?" She steadied the man, grasping his shoulders to keep him from losing his balance.

"Captain!" he said again. "No, I . . . I just lost my bearings for a moment." He looked around, nervous and uncertain.

Burnham spoke slowly, clearly, trying to calm him. "You're fine, Hieu. You're good. You're a trained field medic, right?" She made a point of memorizing the crew's specialized training, commendations, and areas in which they excelled—and even problem areas where there might be room for professional growth.

"Y-yes." His breathing had become more measured, and she patted his shoulders. He was finding his center.

"Good. I need you to go up the way I came down, okay?" She guided him to the access hatch. "Up three decks. Commander Saru will need help with casualties, and you're the perfect person for that."

Chen steadied himself. "Yes. Aye, Captain."

"Hey, I'm lucky I found you here, aren't I?" Burnham asked.

Chen huffed out a breath, still a bit unsettled. "I think I'm lucky I found you, ma'am."

"We're lucky we found each other," she said, and pointed him up the ladder.

Once he was moving toward Saru, Burnham took a calming breath. Main engineering was to the right, but the mycelial bay was just to the left, and she headed for that.

The doors stalled as she approached them. A weak hiss told her the system had a rupture or fault somewhere, so she squeezed her hands into the slim opening and with a grunt pushed them apart.

Bounding down the steps to the lower deck, she found Tilly, unconscious near the spore control console.

"Ensign?" Burnham kneeled down and pulled Tilly toward

the spore storage bank. She slid her into a sitting position and searched for signs of injury. Concussed wouldn't necessarily show externally—she needed a medical tricorder.

"Captain?" Tilly asked fuzzily, squinting up at her. "What happened?"

"Stay there." Burnham pushed herself up toward where she knew an emergency medkit was stored by the spore canisters. She grabbed the case, and when she turned back, saw the spore reaction chamber was empty. "Tilly, where's Lieutenant Stamets?"

Dragging herself up to the console, Tilly stared wide-eyed. "In the cube? He—"

"Tilly, what happened?" Burnham demanded.

"I—I don't know," Tilly replied, incredulous and groggy.

"We need to find out, Ensign. Benecia Colony needs us, and to get there we need Lieutenant Stamets. Right now."

6

"Where am I?" Paul Stamets spun around awkwardly, shifting his weight from one foot to the other, and nearly lost his balance. That's when he realized he was unnaturally top-heavy—thanks to the bulky EV suit. Outside its confines, the mycelial forest spread out before him, just as it had in his dream: florescent biota, branching up from a dark plane of tightly packed material, and thick, shadowy trees that painted themselves in foreboding silhouette.

Was this a dream, too? It didn't feel like it—but then again neither had the other "spore dreams." *Still*, Stamets thought, *this is different even from that.*

He triggered the suit's built-in communicator. "Stamets to *Discovery*."

Silence.

"Stamets to *Discovery*. Are you receiving?" He turned again, looking to see what, if anything, was in view, other than the forest.

There was only the plane, which extended forever. All manner of technicolor fungi expanded around him: purple, cream, white, rust-brown, pinkish; all splattered against distant golden webs and spore geysers.

"*Discovery*, come in," he tried again, but was met with quiet rebuke. His frustration worked its way toward a zenith. "Computer, how long has this suit been in operation?"

"Three solar years, two months, fourteen days—"

"No, not since your service date. Today. How long has this suit been in operation *today?*"

"Thirty-three minutes."

"*Why* don't I remember putting it on? And leaving the ship?"

"Unknown," the computer replied.

Stamets pursed his lips and wondered if it was possible to internally rip the computer out from the suit. "I wasn't talking to you."

Chirping innocently, the system waited.

"Okay, let me think. What do I remember last?" Taking a few steps toward a particularly lovely ornate sprig of fungi, he touched it with a gloved hand and it recoiled as if from a gust of wind. He was an intruder here, he realized. A human anachronism among the fungi. "I was in the spore chamber. I remember that. Someone—something had called to me and . . . the jump felt wrong."

Who called to me? Flashes appeared in his mind's eye: a smoke-filled corridor, his EV suit in a rack, the airlock opening as the voices pulled him away from the ship and into the plane . . .

Where is that presence now? he wondered. *And if I am really on the mycelial plane . . .* "Computer, locate the *Starship Discovery*."

"Three point three nine kilometers from this position, bearing eighty-two degrees right."

He searched the horizon, but the forest was too thick to see that far in the distance. "Okay, that'll take a bit. Computer, plot a course back to the ship."

"Working." After a moment, the helmet's heads-up display blinked guidance information across his visor, indicating the proper direction. He rotated about as it suggested and the path forward flashed on the display.

"Warning: exterior integrity compromised. Loss of containment imminent."

"What!? When?"

"Suit breakdown began thirty-three minutes ago."

Computers were wonderful tools if one asked the right questions. "Explain why."

"Particulates in the external environment are caustic to the suit's material components."

Of course they were. The mycelial ecosystem fed on cellular regrowth, and part of that cycle was to *re*cycle. Elements of the forest had to break down and feed on what it determined was foreign, dangerous, or not a part of its biosphere. His EV suit most definitely fell into at least two of those categories, and so would the ship. They'd done tests years ago that confirmed it.

"How long until I reach *Discovery*?"

"At present speed, twenty-three minutes, fifteen seconds."

"How long before suit containment breach?"

"At present rate of decay, nine minutes, thirty-nine seconds." The computer's voice, of course, had no urgency to it. He knew that was by design. He wondered if an AI should be programmed to sense and mirror the anxiety of the person with whom it interacted. If nothing else, it might help ease the tension if one's computer was freaking out too. Maybe it would calm someone down as they tried to assuage the computer's fear.

His relatively slow gait first became a quick march, then as much of an all-out run as he could manage in an EV suit. "I guess I'd better hurry."

"Affirmative."

———

"Very wrong," Tilly said. "Very, very, *very* wrong." She retracted another spore container, verified it was spent, then returned it to its receptacle.

"I need fewer adverbs and more answers, Ensign," the captain said.

"Theoretically, a long jump could drain all the containers. Maybe it could happen—maybe—but there *is* no explanation for what happened to our forest. You saw it—we don't *have* a mycelial forest anymore. Not a spore! Where is it?" Tilly moved back toward the drive control station and braced herself against the console. "And where's Lieutenant Stamets?" Her tone teetered between fury and fear.

"Don't panic, Ensign," Burnham said as she shunted one set of relays past a burned-out circuit in the lower access panel just next to where Tilly stood. "You said you can scan for his implants anywhere on the ship, right? That's why we're getting your station working." Pulling herself up, the captain waved toward the inactive console. "Try it now."

"Aye, sir." Tilly activated the proper series of controls that lit up the console. "Or ma'am. I forget which you like. Sir or ma'am? Maybe it's ma'am?"

"It doesn't matter." Burnham's contact with Stamets's protégé had been limited. Usually they talked in her ready room for mission briefings, and while she was familiar with the ensign's predilection for verbosity, that quirky charm was only going to slow them down. "We don't have time, Tilly. Our task is finding out what happened to Stamets, the spores, and the ship."

"Sorry, sir," Tilly said, quickly adding, "And/or ma'am."

"'Captain' works if you can't decide," Burnham said. "Focus on the work. Ignore me."

Tilly tittered nervously. "Well, *that's* not happening." With another uneasy giggle, she added a swift, "Captain."

They both worked together and finally the displays began flashing with partial data as internal sensors came online. "Lieutenant Stamets is not on board," Burnham said.

"His last location was airlock fifteen-gamma." Tilly pointed to a data point on the screen.

"This deck," Burnham noted.

"Let me check . . ." Tilly ran her hands along the console controls, then she scrolled through the screens until she found what she wanted. "Okay, this is good. An EV suit is missing." Frustrated, she then added, "Wait, this isn't making sense either."

Burnham didn't have time to dissect the data display. "Was the jump completed?"

"Um, um, um." Tilly impatiently reviewed the information that seemed to be flowing by too slowly for her. "We jumped. Yes. We *did* jump." She pointed to a set of coordinates. "But this is wrong—these aren't the coordinates I confirmed. These are the coordinates we were decoding from the mycelial message we got."

"From the what?" Burnham asked sharply. Apparently Saru had left out that minor detail.

"Captain . . ." Tilly looked her directly in her eyes, the first time she'd made such long eye contact. "We're *not* supposed to be here. We *can't* stay here."

"Where is '*here*,' Tilly?" the captain asked, and from the ensign's grave tone she was dreading the answer.

"We're in the mycelial plane. Someplace we're supposed to be only while we jump. We jump *through* the mycelial network. We're not supposed to be inside it for more than a moment."

"Then how the hell did we get here?" the captain asked, a growing knot of tension in her shoulders pushing its way up her neck. "And how do we get out?"

"We can't." Tilly stared at the empty reaction cube. "Not without Lieutenant Stamets." She crooked a thumb over her shoulder at the hollow spore containers and empty mycelial greenhouse beyond them. "And definitely not without spores."

"Where would he go?" Burnham asked. "Why would he leave the ship?"

"I don't know," Tilly replied nervously, "but we are really going to die here without him."

Had Michael Burnham not been raised on Vulcan, she might have snapped at Tilly to get her to focus. Instead, she shut off the display screen to limit the ensign's distraction. "Explain."

"A tritanium hull can't maintain integrity in mycelial space. We run a check after every jump for any damage or weaknesses, and that's with just milliseconds of exposure."

"How long do we have?"

"An hour?" Tilly guessed. "Maybe less. There are fungi whose sole purpose is to break down matter—not just in mycelial space but anywhere fungi exist. But here, it's just as likely to break down a starship as it would a plant or animal." Suddenly Tilly's eyes grew wide. "Wait: Lieutenant Stamets had the presence of mind to wear a suit despite there being a breathable atmosphere. If he's off ship, he's alive."

"We need external sensors," Burnham said. "If a tritanium hull might last an hour, how long would an EV suit?" It wasn't just Stamets she had to worry about, but anyone in an area that might have a hull breach, since Tilly's guess of an hour was only just that. She flipped open her communicator. "Burnham to the bridge."

"Bridge. Airiam here, Captain."

"Alert all decks. We need all crew away from any section with bulkheads exposed to the ship's exterior."

"Understood. Do we have an external radiation problem, Captain?" Airiam's artificially processed voice vibrated with concern.

"No," Burnham said. "This is a little different. When the crew is out of those designated areas, we need emergency bulkheads to—"

Tilly put up her hand to interrupt Burnham. "Captain, please leave airlock fifteen-gamma open. We have to get Lieutenant Stamets. His suit won't last much longer."

"Airiam, did you get that?"

"Affirmative. Access to airlock fifteen-gamma."

"Acknowledged. Batten us down, Commander." The captain snapped her communicator closed and headed for the door.

"Captain, I want to go," Tilly said as she hurried behind Burnham and they marched up to the exit. "There's no need to put yourself in danger."

"If *Discovery* can't make it out of here . . ." The captain let the thought lie there, unwilling to give it voice. "How long before another ship can get to Benecia? More than just my life or yours is at stake. Those people are counting on us."

As they rounded the corner near the airlock, Tilly gave that quick consideration. "Understood, Captain," she said softly.

Burnham approached the inner airlock and entered her access code into the manual controls. When the doors drew apart, she hurried in and Tilly tentatively followed.

The captain marched to the EV suit storage, but sensed Tilly's anxiety. "You don't have to be nervous around me, Ensign."

"Begging the captain's pardon, but I kinda do."

"I'm telling you that you don't." Without the computer fabricating a suit to personal specifications, they were going to have to choose from those readily available.

"Is the captain ordering me not to be uneasy around her?" Tilly asked, probably trying to be amusing. Or, perhaps seriously asking. Burnham wasn't certain which.

"No." Burnham found a suit she thought would be close enough to her size. "I'm simply telling you . . . I remember being an ensign. Just, don't worry. At least about me."

"I do appreciate that. I really do," Tilly said as she searched the alcove. "I just don't want to be the one who gets you killed or—"

"We're *all* in danger right now," Burnham said. "Mister Stamets more than the rest of us. What happens when his suit fails?"

"I—I don't know. It'll probably hurt?"

"People can survive pain." The captain pulled on the last piece of her suit, secured it, and powered it up. "You're sure the atmosphere is breathable?"

"Yes." With a soft grunt, Tilly pulled a suit down and quickly began to secure it. "If it breaks down the suit, it'll start to break *him* down."

"Come on," Burnham said, grabbing a case from the bottom of the alcove. "We'll take a suit repair kit."

They approached the hatch to the outer airlock and again the captain had to enter a manual code to open it. "You know," Burnham said as they walked through, "my mother had a solution for tense situations."

Each hit the Starfleet insignia on the front of their suits, and their helmets coalesced around their respective heads. A hiss confirmed the containment seal as they began breathing filtered air.

"I'm guessing it wasn't to giggle incessantly," Tilly said, *"living on Vulcan and all."*

"No," Burnham replied with a calming tone as she closed the internal airlock and pressed open the external hatch. "She told me that there was nothing wrong with being nervous. Nerves remind us we're alive. Nerves tell us we're in pain, or when we're experiencing pleasure, or when we're in danger. It's an important part of who we are."

"All in favor say 'Ow'?"

The captain chuckled. "Ow."

"You laughed," Tilly said, seemingly shocked. *"That's very cool."*

"My mother was the cool one," Burnham said. "But I'll take the compliment."

The hatch fully open, they stepped out onto *Discovery*'s hull. Ahead of them, the ship extended deep into what appeared to be a black, dead forest. Trunks and branches stretched every which way, some broken, some bent, and still others curled around the hull as if they'd grown there—or as if *Discovery* just popped into existence amongst them. There were no leaves—just a flaky bark, and a dark dust that floated everywhere, blocking the horizon in a carbon-colored fog.

"Which way?" Burnham asked.

Tilly held out her tricorder, moving it right and left, then back, until her display flashed. *"Distance: point two seven kilometers. Bearing: twenty-six degrees right."*

"Let's go."

"Wait, it's really twenty-six point four degrees, so we should skootch this way a bit. Actually, I guess over a quarter of a kilometer, four-tenths of a degree won't matter much."

At ease, Tilly, Burnham thought. At the same time, the captain didn't want to suggest that she shouldn't be proficient and thorough in her duty. "I appreciate the accuracy," she assured the ensign.

As they trooped forward, the powdery substance on the hull shifted under their boots, making the surface slippery and compelling them to gingerly proceed.

While Tilly tracked Stamets, the captain used her tricorder to study their environment. The atmosphere was high in oxygen and carbon dioxide, which made sense, as they knew that mycelia inhaled and exhaled those gases. There was a higher oxygen content in the dark forest around them, which suggested that this biota therefore provided the mycelia the oxygen it needed and in return processed the waste gas it expelled.

"I have him locked in." A touch of disappointment creased Tilly's voice, as if Burnham didn't trust her and was double-checking her readings.

"I'm surveying the landscape," the captain said, giving the tricorder a turn. "We could be the first people to walk in the mycelial plane."

"Second and third," Tilly said. *"Lieutenant Stamets."*

"I stand corrected." She hoped that gave Tilly some confidence.

"They sent in probes, of course, which eventually broke down," the ensign said softly, even more quietly adding, *"Which was sad."*

The silence that followed was based on worry rather than personal discomfort, Burnham decided. Tilly worked closely with Stamets and by now his EV suit must be close to compromised—if not worse.

Oddly, their own suits' computers hadn't reported decay. The captain aimed her tricorder first on her own suit, then on the ensign's. "Tilly, there's no decomp." She swung the tricorder wide, focusing it on the ship. "In fact, *Discovery* is showing fewer signs of hull degradation than you estimated."

Burnham showed her the tricorder readout and they both shared a mystified look.

"Nothing here is as it should be," the captain said. "Why?"

———

"Computer, how long until suit failure?" Stamets huffed out the question as he ran around stalks, through spores, and occasionally into a large fungal branch or stump. Finally, he entered a dark jungle where he could barely see the ground. If what he was standing on even *was* ground.

"Containment failure in three minutes."

Stopping short and skidding into a fall, he stayed where he landed, needing time to catch his breath. "But . . . b-but you said that over a minute ago," he breathlessly choked.

"Affirmative. Containment stable for the last one point one-three minutes."

"Would have . . . been nice . . . to know . . . before now. Been . . . running . . . for . . . my . . . life . . ." He tried to get up but slipped in the sooty, mushy dust all around him. He grunted and twisted upward, but was too weak to free himself.

"G-give me your hand." The shaky voice, muffled by his EV suit's helmet, was raspy and he almost couldn't make out what was being said. "Paul! Give me your hand!"

Dark fingers gripped Stamets's forearm and heaved him to his feet as a man stepped into view.

Covered in the same black powder as Stamets, the un-kempt man suddenly embraced him in a bear hug.

"Paul!" the man cried, tears streaking down his soot-caked cheeks.

Stamets allowed the embrace—and in fact found it strengthened him. He fell into it, rested in it, and only after a long moment did he pull back to see just who held him. "You . . ." he said as he regarded the other man head to toe: tattered clothes, disheveled hair, and a frayed, scraggly beard. Stamets laughed, giddy at the sight of the figure standing in front of him.

"Yes, it's me," the man sobbed happily, and hugged him again, so tightly that even through his EV suit Stamets gasped.

He felt light-headed, and his faceplate fogged his view. "I can't—I can't . . ." Stamets struggled to catch his breath. Maybe the suit had been compromised in the fall. "Computer, retract helmet," he rasped.

With a mechanical whoosh, the protective panels disengaged and retracted into the back of the suit. Warm, musty air flooded into his lungs and Stamets coughed, gulping it in.

"Are you okay?" The man tenderly, tentatively drew his hand down Stamets's face. "Are you here? *Really* here? He said I'd find you here. He said he'd lead you."

"How can *you* be here?" Stamets asked, incredulous, tears welling and beginning to roll down his own cheeks. The other man's touch was unexpectedly comforting and surreally natural.

"I'm still not sure." He lowered his forehead onto Stamets's and held them together a long moment. "But I've found you. I've finally found you."

Drawing back a bit, a grin pulling at his lips, Stamets gazed into the other man's eyes and asked sincerely, "But . . . who *are* you?"

7

The man fell, his body losing all slack, with the powdery dust all over them causing him to nearly slip through Stamets's arms. Grunting, he struggled to keep his grip, only to have his footing give way and together they collapsed to the forest floor.

"Over here, I found—him?" Tilly's voice called over his suit communicator.

"Down here!" he called out.

Suddenly the man was lifted away, then two hands under him helped Stamets to stand.

"Who is this?" Captain Burnham had come with Tilly. She'd hefted this mystery man in a fireman's carry.

"It's really hard to shrug in one of these suits," Stamets said, and thanked Tilly for helping him up. "Captain, I'm not sure exactly. It looks like he's been here awhile. We need to get him to sickbay."

"And you, too," Tilly said. Then hugged him.

"Yes," Burnham said, rearranging the unknown man on her shoulder, *"you too."*

———

"We scanned him," Tilly told Doctor Pollard once they'd gotten the man to sickbay, "and he's human according to my tricorder. We didn't find any head trauma. I think he's malnourished and—"

"Yes, thank you, *Doctor* Tilly." Pollard had put the unconscious man on the only free biobed. There were still several crewmembers being helped by a nearly overwhelmed medical staff. She remained calm and professional, but she clearly wasn't in the mood for Tilly's excess verbiage.

Still in their EV gear, Burnham and Tilly watched as Stamets peeled off his suit, while a nurse scanned him.

Burnham surveyed the area, noting the number and severity of injuries, before giving her attention to the astromycologist. She didn't know how many people had already been through sickbay. The more serious cases would have been in surgery or recovery, not the exam bay.

"Is it less bright in here than usual?" Stamets asked.

"We're on auxiliary power," Tilly told him. "Reserve batteries on some decks."

"Can you explain yourself?" Burnham demanded.

"Explain?" He gazed up at her, then glanced past Tilly and Pollard at the man they'd found.

"Lieutenant," she said, calling his attention back to her, "what the hell's going on?"

His expression was still confused.

"I want to know why you left the ship," Burnham said, more sternly than she'd wanted. "Why are we where we are? What happened to our spore reserves?"

Bewildered, his eyes narrowed. "What happened?"

"*I'm* asking *you*," the captain said, her tone perched between frustration and concern. She glanced at Tilly, tacitly asking for the ensign's help.

"Paul," Tilly began softly, as if she were talking to a child, "not only are all the storage canisters empty, but—the forest is gone."

"We just were in—"

"Not that forest," Tilly said. "*Discovery*'s forest. The cultivation bay is empty. Though I guess it's hard to call it a forest compared to what's out there. Greenhouse, maybe."

"Flowerbox," Stamets said, still looking and sounding dazed.

"Yeah, that works."

"No, it doesn't," Burnham protested. "None of this works." She put a hand on his shoulder and angled him toward her. "Lieutenant, wake up. I need answers."

Pulling in a deep breath, Stamets confessed, "I don't fully remember leaving the ship, Captain. Honest. Everything was a blur." He watched the man he found, lying in a restless sleep on the biobed next to them. "I just heard this stranger call to me . . . and found myself pulled toward him. And then I found him. Or he found me, I guess."

Burnham gestured toward their guest. "Stranger? You look at him with recognition."

"Do I?"

Studying his face more intently, the captain watched Stamets's gaze draw back toward the unknown man again, with only brief glances to Tilly or herself. "Yes, you do," she said finally.

"Paul?" the mystery man called out as he shifted back and forth beneath a protective force field. "Paul? There are others. See them?"

"Can you explain that?" Burnham asked.

Uncertain, Stamets faltered. "Not . . . exactly. I feel like . . . he seems familiar. I . . . ."

"Doctor?" The captain called Pollard over.

Leaning toward Stamets, Tilly whispered, "Is he the voice in your spore dreams?"

"You're dismissed, Ensign!" he said loudly.

"No, you're not," Burnham told her. "Doctor, tell me about your patient."

Pollard gestured to the screen above the biobed. "His biosigns are all over the place. He's malnourished, in a state of shock, and his cortisol and adrenal markers suggest he's been in fight-or-flight mode for an extensive period. He has epidermal damage covering more than ninety percent of his body: some new, some old, and there's scar tissue that suggests some *very* old."

"How very old?" Stamets asked.

"Months. Maybe years."

The captain studied the unknown man's face. How could a human have been in mycelial space for years? The *Glenn* only made its first successful spore jump a year ago, with *Discovery* soon after.

"Can you rouse him?" Burnham asked.

"No," Pollard replied. "The body often knows what it needs. And I won't force him awake without knowing why he's in and out of consciousness in the first place."

As if to punctuate the doctor's point, the stranger thrashed back and forth in bed, moaning. "Paul?"

Burnham noted the sparkling containment field that jittered every time the man's elbow or knee touched it. "That's unconscious?"

The doctor indicated the bed's readouts. "According to his brainwave pattern, it is."

Edging toward the bed, Burnham flattened her lips into a thin line, and wondered if this man had something to do with their current predicament. "If he's *not* human, can you trust those readings?"

"Oh, he's human, though some findings are a little off." Pollard handed the captain her padd. "I can't confirm that it's not because of his exposure to the space we're in, however."

"The mycelial plane," Stamets said. "I guess it could be. I don't know."

"Whatever you call it, being here doesn't seem like a good thing." Pollard took her tablet back from the captain.

"It's not," Tilly said.

"What about him?" Burnham asked, crooking a thumb toward Stamets. "He doesn't remember how he got outside."

"Well, I . . . not fully. I remember some . . ."

"You followed a voice that called to you," the captain said frankly, then spoke to Pollard. "Is he mentally compromised?"

After a moment of sorting through the screens on her padd, the doctor said, "No . . . well, we should do some testing. I see increased neurotransmitters, and some odd white brain-matter changes that could be from what he was breathing out there."

"Does he have similar readings?" Stamets asked of the mystery mycelial man.

"Actually, he does. But you were *both* breathing that at-mosphere." Pollard turned to Tilly and the captain. "You have tricorder data on what was going on out there?"

"Yes." Tilly handed over her tricorder and the captain did the same.

"Is he going to be okay?" Stamets asked of the man shift-ing and groaning on the biobed.

Pollard frowned. "I don't even know how he's alive. You just found him out there?"

"With Stamets," Burnham said. "The lieutenant happened upon him on his return to the ship."

"Outside of his being in shock, I also can't tell you why he's unconscious," Pollard said, then faced Stamets directly. "Or why he keeps saying your name."

"I was first to see him . . ."

"Paul?" the man said weakly. "Look—others. Look."

"If he's unconscious," Tilly asked, "why is he saying . . . things?"

"He sounds delusional," the captain commented.

Pollard pointed at the readings on the screen above his bed, rather than the stranger himself. "Whoever he is, he's been out there some time. It might drive one into a dissociative state."

"Do what you can for him," Burnham said. "Once we can get our computer systems back online, see if you can find him in any Federation databases."

"Of course, Captain." The doctor moved off to another patient.

Stiffly pivoting back to Stamets, Burnham realized she and Tilly would need to get out of their EV suits. "Mister Stamets, you and I need to have words."

Tilly backed up, clearly sensing a tension to which she didn't want to be privy. "Am I dismissed?"

"Yes," Stamets said.

"Great." She spun on a heel. "Leaving."

"Belay that." Burnham lightly tugged the ensign's arm, guiding her back.

"Oh," Tilly said uneasily as she spun back around. "Okay, then. Staying instead."

"Is Mister Stamets released?" the captain asked Pollard, who was examining an injured Yeoman LaPlante.

Pollard waved a dismissive hand. "For now. We've got our hands full."

"Landry?" Burnham asked.

"She'll pull through," the doctor said. "You can't have her for a while, though."

Burnham turned to the door. "Both of you, with me."

Once they were in the corridor, Stamets edged toward the nearest turbolift, but the captain gestured him back. "Lifts are inoperative to engineering," she told them. "Damage-control teams are making progress, but the number of affected systems are slowing them down."

Stepping onto the access ladder, the captain beckoned them on.

"How bad off are we?" Stamets asked as he moved down the ladder. "What about casualties?"

"No fatalities—yet. As to how bad, you'll need to tell me," Burnham said. "Astromycology isn't my area, but I'm certain neither our spores nor our mycelial forest can just disappear. So—"

"Apparently they can," Stamets interrupted.

"*Mister Stamets*. We need to know what happened, and we need spores." Pausing, she looked up at him. "Is that why you really left the ship?"

"Something pulled me outside, Captain . . . someone— I think that man—called to me and I felt I needed to go." Stamets sounded honest, even contrite. "I didn't know about the spore loss, but I couldn't just take a cup and go out to scoop up some extra mycelia."

"Well, you can, but they won't be the *right* spores," Tilly said. "*Prototaxites stellaviatori* is what we'd need to find. Kinda rare, which is why we had them growing in the cultivation bay."

"I'm aware, Ensign." The captain stepped onto the deck and out of the way. "What I don't yet understand is how we got here."

"I don't know," Stamets said, joining her as Tilly followed.

"That isn't an acceptable answer." Burnham let annoyance crackle in her tone. Her first command was stuck in a dangerous and little-explored realm, her expert in the matter didn't have the resolutions she wanted, and it didn't help that she was still in her EV suit.

Stamets met her glare. "Michael, if I knew, I'd tell you."

Burnham sighed. She'd not known Paul Stamets as long as some others on board, whom she'd requested from the

Shenzhou, but they'd worked side by side frequently over the last year. She was new to her captaincy, and he to Starfleet, and there was no doubt their early days together had been bumpy. Over time, however, she'd come to trust and respect him. And despite an occasionally churlish attitude, she'd come to like him. "Okay," she said as they made their way toward the spore bay. "Let's talk it through."

"'Michael'?" Tilly whispered to Stamets as they pushed open the lab door. "Since when do you call the captain 'Michael'?"

"This is why I wanted to dismiss her," Stamets said.

"I do understand." She gave Tilly a slight smile.

"Can *I* call you Michael?" the ensign asked, hopeful.

Burnham ignored the question and focused her attention on Stamets as they trudged down to the lab's lower deck. "Why didn't we make it to our destination? Instead, Tilly told me we're at the coordinates from a mycelial message you decoded."

"That's . . . interesting." He slowly traced his left hand along the edge of the reaction cube.

"So all this is an accident, then?" Burnham wondered what the lieutenant saw when he eyed the empty compartment. Stamets spent a great deal of time communing biologically with the ship she commanded. She wondered what that must feel like. Captains often had close emotional bonds with their vessels, and *Discovery*, being her first command, did hold a special place in her heart. Sometimes an engineer might have similar feelings for their assigned ship, but would anyone be as close as the person whose job it was to become biochemically attached to it?

"Well," he finally began, turning toward her. "I didn't bring us into this on purpose. But maybe subconsciously?"

A cold chill moved down the captain's shoulders and

spine, and not just because she finally began to unwrap herself from the EV suit. "If your subconscious thoughts can take us so far off course—"

"'Maybe,' Captain. It was just a maybe."

"I need more than maybes," she said, standing only in the blue jumpsuit one wore beneath an EV suit. "And a uniform."

Tilly picked up what Burnham had taken off, and gathered parts of her own suit she'd begun to remove. "I can get our uniforms," she told the captain, who nodded her approval and appreciation as the ensign exited the bay.

Moving to the console behind them, Stamets tried to bring up the data from their mycelial communication experiments, but the computer responded sluggishly. "Can we get more power routed to . . ."

Off Burnham's head tilt and pursed lips, Stamets let his request trail off.

"Okay then," he said, waiting for the screen to fill with the data he requested. "What if Tilly was right from the start? What if this was a distress call? Could it be the *Glenn*? Maybe they're having the same spore-loss problem."

The captain couldn't help but wonder why their sister ship wouldn't provide more detail than a set of coordinates. "Why not a clear distress call? Starfleet regulations—"

"Aren't necessarily applicable to an emergency transmission on the first-ever mycelial-network-radio call."

She could accept that, but still felt the person they found outside the ship somehow figured in. "'There are others,'" Burnham said softly. "Your mystery man. He seemed to be telling you to look for 'others.' Could he be from the *Glenn*? The others being survivors of a . . . shipwreck?"

Stamets didn't reply. It was unlike him not to have an opinion on whatever she might throw at him. They were in uncharted territory, to be sure.

"If the *Glenn* has a way to communicate via the mycelial network," the captain thought aloud, "*Discovery* needs to figure out how to do so as well."

"Which is the higher priority?" Stamets asked. "That, or finding our spores?"

Burnham felt the weight of that question, but didn't give her answer more than a moment's thought. "You know how fast the disease we're supposed to be fighting can spread, Lieutenant. And I've seen firsthand what blood burn does. I'm afraid the only answer I can give you is 'both.'"

8

"You've been looking at that screen a long time," Tilly said. "Are you blinking? I don't think you're even blinking." She turned to Lieutenant Nilsson, who was running a bypass ODN cable to bring normal power to the engineering consoles. "Have you seen him blink?"

"Not recently," Nilsson said.

Stamets spun toward Tilly and blinked hard. Twice. "Better?"

Taken aback, Tilly laughed and covered a snort with her hand. "Yes." Stamets usually found a way to calm her when panic scratched at the door.

"I'm fine," he assured her. "I just don't know how we do any of this without our spores." Stamets dropped his head as if studying his boots, and said, "Tilly, I think we're going to die here."

Enav poked her head up from behind the opposite console where she'd been connecting the other part of Nilsson's cable. She cast a sideways glance at him. "Begging your pardon, sir, but your pep talks suck."

"This is my fault," he said, looking up. "And unless I find a solution to all of this"—he circled an index finger in the air—"eventually the hull is going to deteriorate and we'll be trapped here, like . . ."

"Like the man in sickbay," Tilly said.

"Yeah." Stamets jabbed at his console. "And even if we find a way to replenish our spores, this is where it ends."

"Where what ends?" She watched Stamets pull up a sensor report that was far too limited to be useful. Was he doing busywork to clear his mind, or was he too distracted to notice?

"The spore drive," he said. "Mycelial transportation. All of it."

"Why would you say that? Don't even think it." Tilly realized that since becoming his protégé, astromycology had grown as important as her desire to someday be a starship captain. "This work is too critical—"

"Do the math, Tilly. Maybe we find a way to replenish our spores. *Maybe* I get us out of here. But just the fact that we ended up here in the first place is the death knell of this project." Defeated, Stamets's shoulders slumped. "I'm . . . a random factor in displacement-activated spore-hub-drive travel. That's not good. If I'm unpredictable, and I take us who knows where, for who knows what reason . . . Normal warp drive may be slower, but there's nothing random about dilithium crystals."

Tilly bounced on the balls of her feet, excited to rebut at least one of his dour points. "Well, damaged dilithium crystals can cause unexpected problems. I mean, I wouldn't call them random, but—"

"A bad crystal's not going to send you somewhere you didn't expect. Nor will you run aground in subspace." Stamets pointed to a graphic on his screen that showed the *Discovery* trapped in a section of the mycelial forest.

"Actually, a crystal with a surface you didn't adjust for *could* cause an engine imbalance that would create an artificial wormh—"

"Tilly, you know what I'm talking about." Stamets pushed a button and the screen went blank.

"I do," she said.

He turned his head to one side and gazed past her. "Do you see that?"

Tilly followed his line of sight, but saw nothing.

Having finished the cable bypass, Nilsson looked up as well. "I don't see anything."

Enav switched on the extra power to the console before she moved away. "This is set," she told them, seemingly uninterested in whatever they were all trying to see. "You'll help me in main engineering?" she asked Nilsson.

"Happy to," she said, and both women headed toward the corridor.

"That!" Stamets seemed to ignore their exit. He pointed to the reaction cube as he spun back to Tilly. "You didn't see . . . ?"

She checked again, noting no difference in the chamber from when they entered. "I just see the empty spore chamber."

As he edged around one side of the cube and then the other, looking for whatever it was he'd seen, the door from the adjacent engineering section opened and Airiam entered.

"Commander!" Tilly called out, hoping that Stamets would be distracted enough to say hello, and maybe stop acting so strange.

"Ensign. Lieutenant." Airiam greeted them both with a cordial head tilt. "The captain asked that I deliver this, since intraship comms are still subject to disruption." Airiam held a data card out to Tilly, who took it from her.

Finally looking up from his close examination of the empty cube, Stamets asked, "What is it?"

"A data card," Tilly said.

"No—" Stamets began, his face creased with annoyance.

Airiam cut him off. "Yes, it is a data card," she said, clearly playing along. From their frequent lunches, Tilly knew this was her sarcastic "robotic" mode. "A duotronic-circuit-compatible storage device that encodes information into a long string of molecules that—"

"Uh-huh." He grabbed the card from her hand. "What's *on* it?"

"She's pulling your leg." Tilly snickered.

"It's irritating." Stamets slid the card into the slot on his console. "And not in the delightful way *I* annoy people."

"My apology." Airiam bowed her head a bit. "I was just trying to lighten your mood."

Turning toward her, thumb and forefinger together to form a fine point, Stamets sneered. "My mood is at the center of the gravity well of a black star."

"Heavy." Airiam's facial prosthetics didn't allow for much overt expression, but Tilly could tell she was amused. "The data is a navigational scan of the mycelial area we're in. I didn't find *Prototaxites stellaviatori* spores, but I did discern several energy signatures with which you may be more familiar."

Stamets called up the data from the card and his screen filled with information from her scan. "If it's not what we're looking for—" He stopped, and stared at the cube. "Okay, *now* tell me you didn't see that!"

Airiam shook her head ever so lightly. "I didn't."

"Is she being funny again?" Stamets asked Tilly.

"Airiam, are you being funny again?"

"No. And according to Lieutenant Stamets, I wasn't funny before."

Frustrated, Stamets spun toward them and Tilly braced for the brunt of the coming storm. Instead, he suddenly gasped, his eyes rolled back in his head, and he collapsed to the deck.

———

Underneath him: a slightly uncomfortable but supportive biobed. Visible even through his closed eyelids: sickbay's bright lights. As his eyes fluttered open: the glare of the exam room's shimmering white walls.

Stamets sat upright, expecting a buzz of activity, but there was none. He was not met with an assemblage of doctors or nurses, but instead saw the mycelial mystery man, also sitting up in the biobed across from him.

Standing next to the man's bed was the creature Stamets knew to be *Tardigradum galaktos*: a giant, grayish-brown space tardigrade.

"It's Paul," the man told the creature.

"Yes," the tardigrade agreed. *"I know."*

Palms down, slowly pushing himself forward, Stamets slid off the bed. His feet met the deck with more stability than he would have thought. *"You know me? My name?"* He took a few, uneasy steps. He should have been afraid, but wasn't. *"You remember me? And can understand me?"* His contact with the tardigrade had been brief, and he surely didn't remember speaking to it. Him? Her?

"You've met Ephraim?" the stranger asked, surprised.

Ephraim?

The tardigrade creature shuddered and let out what sounded like an almost joyful chitter. *"You remembered, Hugh!"*

Entirely perplexed, Stamets twisted toward the other man, this "Hugh." *"Ephraim? The tardigrade's name is Ephraim?"*

"I was surprised too," Hugh admitted. *"Didn't we call him Ripper?"*

"Ripper?" Stamets studied the creature, slowly circling it. Him? *"I never called him anything. Why Ripper?"* Slowly it dawned on him that this conversation was telepathic, that their connections were "more" than just speaking to one another, and in fact there didn't seem to be a physical element other than their respective forms, which appeared more ideal than he knew

them to be in reality. Hugh's eyes were bright, his skin undamaged, his hair well trimmed and neat . . . and very familiar.

"Names are confusing," the tardigrade said. *"But I'm not sure this is the clearing where I was called 'Ripper,' though even I have trouble keeping track. I much prefer Ephraim."*

"Ephraim." Stamets couldn't help but wonder how a giant interstellar water bear got an ancient Earth name. *"You don't look like an Ephraim."*

The tardigrade rolled his head about, seeming to indicate both men in the inclusive gesture. *"A name given to me by one of you, which I rather liked and kept."*

"One of us? A human? Then what's your actual name?" Stamets took another step closer to them, his eyes sliding over Hugh for a long moment. His face felt flushed, but he wasn't sure why.

"If you call me this name, and I answer to it, is it not mine?" Ephraim asked, and his mouth puckered in what Stamets thought might be a smile.

"I guess I've never thought about it that way," Stamets said, his mind whirling.

"You have," Ephraim said, then added, *"And you haven't. And you will again. And you won't."*

Taking in a long breath, Stamets tried to steady himself. *"I see."*

"You do?" Hugh scoffed. *"For me, he says a lot of confusing things."*

"Does he?" His mouth very dry, Stamets wondered, *Does this Hugh person have some symbiotic relationship with the tardigrade? Is that how he survived the mycelial plane? More importantly, how did he get there in the first place?*

Unless none of them were actually there, and it was yet another spore dream. Looking around the room, Stamets considered how long he'd have to live in that dream before he'd wake up. *Was* all of it *a hallucination?* Discovery *being stuck, the missing spores, and the empty cultivation bay?*

He closed his eyes. Several long moments passed. When he opened them again, he was still in sickbay, and both Hugh and Ephraim were staring at him. He couldn't discern the tardigrade's expression, but Hugh viewed him with some level of amazement and . . . perhaps oddly placed awe? *"It's not a dream, is it?"* Stamets asked. *"I think you're both real. All this is."*

His upper body rolling side to side, almost wave-like, Ephraim seemed to be trying to mimic a human shrug. *"I understand this is against your natures, but I assure you we are communicating and this is existence."*

"Okay," Stamets said, and so tried to attack his current circumstance as a scientist. *"Are you the reason we're here?"* he asked Ephraim. *"Well, of course you're the reason—your DNA— but did you do something to bring* Discovery *into mycelial space?"*

"I don't think so," Ephraim answered. *"But there is such a thing as serendipity, I suppose."*

Stamets chuckled with astonishment. *"You're sentient. Fully sentient."*

His form so alien, his body language so smooth and yet unfamiliar, Ephraim didn't seem to take offense at all. *"Wasn't that obvious?"*

"Yes, I suppose it was." Somewhat ashamed that he hadn't made more of an effort to learn about Ephraim, and had perhaps ignored the very real possibility that the tardigrade creature wasn't a creature at all, Stamets cast his eyes first toward Hugh and then the deck. *"Did we hurt you?"*

"We must have." Hugh also sounded embarrassed, but Stamets wasn't sure why. Had he been on the *Glenn* at the time? If so, why didn't Stamets remember him?

"This one didn't," Ephraim said, two of his right arms gesturing toward Stamets. *"And also did, and will, and also won't."*

Stamets looked at Hugh quizzically, hoping at least he understood Ephraim, but the other man just responded, *"See?"*

Something moved in his periphery and Stamets's whole body tensed. *"What was that?"* When he turned, however, whatever it had been was gone.

"The others," Hugh said. *"You see them?"*

Stamets pivoted back to him. *"Your crewmates? They're here, too?"*

"You're kidding, right?" A nervous, almost incredulous laugh lined his voice.

The outer sickbay door opened and Airiam and Tilly carried in a slack, unconscious man.

"We need help over here!" Tilly called out. "Doctor?"

Stamets saw Hugh tense and edge forward on the bed as Pollard came rushing to help Tilly and Airiam lift the man onto the biobed Stamets had been lying on when he awoke.

When they retreated, Stamets could see that the unconscious man was . . . himself.

Frightened, Stamets backed away and almost fell over, but Hugh was suddenly by his side, an arm across the man's back to steady him.

"What . . . is . . . happening?"

"I don't know." Hugh looked to Ephraim, so Stamets did as well.

"That's you," Ephraim said casually.

"I know it's me, but how the hell is it me?" Watching Pollard run a scan of his body, Stamets felt his face numb as he inched closer to his own unconscious form. He couldn't wrap his head around the concept. *"How?"* he whispered.

"Is he dead?" Hugh demanded of Ephraim, but kept his arm across the astromycologist's shoulder.

Stamets felt the man's warm touch and it was surprisingly comforting and supportive, both mentally and physically.

"I don't think so," Ephraim said, looking at the biobed's informational display, then motioning toward it. *"Is that dead?"*

———

Doctor Pollard rushed the hypospray into Stamets's neck. "How long has he been like this?"

"Minutes. We came right here." Tilly tried not to let the concern waver her voice too much, and she balled her fists tensely at her sides.

Pulling open one eye at a time, Pollard told her nurse, "Nonreactive to light and . . . whited-out?" As if the blue irises and dark pupils had been coated in a translucent film, Stamets's gaze appeared blank and unseeing.

Tilly gasped and covered her mouth. She'd never seen anything like it.

"What happened to his eyes?" Airiam asked.

Pollard indicated his readings on the screen above and attached a sensor directly to his forehead. "I'm more concerned with his brain activity."

———

"Tilly, I'm here. I'm fine." Stamets left Hugh's side and moved to her. When she didn't turn toward him, he waved a hand in front of her face. *"They can't see me?"*

"They can't see you, but they can see you," Ephraim said, his upper half rolling in the direction of the Stamets on the biobed. *"You can see you. I can see you."*

Inhaling sharply, Stamets suddenly speculated if it meant he wasn't really viewing Ephraim and Hugh at all. *"Can they see us standing here?"*

"*No,*" Ephraim said. "*They do not have the perceptive range.*"

"*Because,*" he said, "*we share a genetic bond now?*" Stamets then moved toward Hugh, contemplating how he fit into the equation.

The tardigrade wiggled his head, the spines on top waving as if moved by wind. "*I suppose we do, don't we.*"

"*Is that a nod?*" Stamets asked.

"*Perhaps.*" Ephraim did it again. "*Please show me a nod,*" he asked Hugh.

Stiffly, Hugh did so. He'd remained where Stamets had left him standing and seemed a bit lost, so Stamets gravitated back toward him.

"*Yes. I believe this is a nod, if it means a visual affirmation.*" Ephraim repeated the motion but added the mouth pucker that suggested a smile. "*Your bodies are very interesting. Very nimble.*"

"*Yours is very impenetrable.*" Stamets chuckled to himself, realizing he was literally talking to the creature he and Straal studied for weeks without actually being able to ask him anything about his nature. "*How did it get that way?*"

"*I don't know. This is how I am.*"

A thousand questions filled Stamets's head. At random, he picked two. "*Are you from a civilization? Do you have a family?*"

"*I don't think so,*" Ephraim said. "*Not if I understand these terms as you do.*"

"*You're just yourself? Alone?*" The notion saddened Stamets, and when he met Hugh's intense brown eyes, a flicker of that melancholy seemed to transfer to him.

"*I'm not alone,*" Ephraim said. "*I'm with you.*" His arms opened wide to include both humans.

"*I am so sorry,*" Stamets told him.

"*Why?*"

"Because it should have occurred to us that you were more than a test subject to be used." He bowed his head regretfully. *"At best, it was thoughtless. At worst, it was immoral."*

Rolling his wave-like shrug, Ephraim made a gurgling sound, which sounded more contented than annoyed. *"Aren't we all at times unthoughtful?"*

So fascinated by the interaction was Stamets that the din of Doctor Pollard working on his corporeal form as Tilly and Airiam hovered by began to recede into the background. He realized he didn't know if what he was hearing was Ephraim's voice or if he was listening to the tardigrade's thoughts. Was his mouth moving? Sometimes, but it wasn't as if it coincided with what Stamets thought he heard. And if people couldn't see him, and he didn't currently inhabit a body, then auditory sound waves needn't be involved.

And yet, Ephraim sounded almost cheerful to him. Did their shared DNA open him to the creature's telepathically broadcasted thoughts *and* emotions?

"This is just your nature?" Stamets asked. *"Your natural state of being is to exist in . . . our minds?"*

"I suppose. At least a part of me," Ephraim replied. *"What qualifies as natural?"*

"Nature is, uh . . ." He turned to Hugh for help, because a clear definition other than "what exists in nature" didn't quickly come to him.

"Anything that exists, I suppose." Hugh seemed pleased to be included in the conversation again and he gave Stamets a supportive look.

"Then everything you see is natural," Ephraim said, raising his top arms and strumming his fingers in the air. *"From this vessel to my claws."*

Hugh gave Stamets a wink but spoke to the tardigrade, and it was quite clear they had a previous rapport. *"Ephraim,*

I think he means naturally occurring versus something made by someone."

"*A very curious distinction,*" Ephraim said. "*So your ship is formed by beings and not what you deem natural, but my claw is of nature?*"

"*Yes.*" Stamets glanced back at his crewmates and realized they were distracting him less and less. Their voices had become low, distorted, and barely audible.

"*But if a being or creature is natural, why are their constructs considered unnatural? Is it always true?*"

Ephraim had asked a valid question and Stamets caught a wave of almost palpable curiosity from the tardigrade, but wasn't sure how to answer. "*I don't know. Maybe a beaver's dam would be considered natural.*"

"*What is that?*" Ephraim asked Hugh.

"*Beavers are animals,*" he replied. "*A dam is a wall they build that slows flowing water so their home isn't washed away.*"

"*Truly, very interesting,*" the tardigrade said. "*But you had a question, I think. What was it?*"

"*I don't even remember.*" Stamets bit his lower lip a moment. "*No, I do. Sorry: This is your nature? To be here? To show yourself to others?*"

"*I have. I do. I will. I won't.*" Ephraim gurgled at them happily. "*I find the clearings interesting, to see them and live them.*"

"*You do and will and won't?*" Stamets tensed at his own confusion. "*Are you saying you see the future, or possible futures, and then choose what you want to live out?*"

"*You make many distinctions of the same thing,*" Ephraim replied, laughing.

"*Did I mention he talks in riddles?*" Hugh asked.

"*No, I think I get it.*" Stamets pulled in a breath. "*Einstein said that past, present, and future were an illusion.*" He took a step toward the tardigrade, fascinated by his complex existence. *"To you, there's no such illusion, is there?"*

"This Einstein being sounds very clever," Ephraim said. *"Can I meet him?"*

Stamets chuckled as he slowly began to understand. *"You know, I wouldn't doubt it."*

"Neither would I," Hugh said. *"Ephraim is a unique being in a biologic network that connects an infinite number of universes."*

Ephraim demurred, shy. *"You're certainly feeling more yourself,"* he told Hugh.

"Yes. Being here, with Paul . . . I see it all more clearly now."

"As it always is," Ephraim said.

Twisting to Hugh, Paul couldn't shake the déjà vu or strange familiarity he seemed to have with this complete stranger. *"Ephraim . . . have Hugh and I met? Or, from your point of view, are we* going *to meet?"*

"Yes, I think you finally grasp it."

"No, no." Stamets frowned. *"That was an either-or question."*

"Why?" Ephraim asked sincerely.

Lost in the tardigrade's charm, Stamets's mind filled with other questions that came flooding out, unfiltered. *"Where do you come from?"*

"I don't know."

"Are there others like you?"

"Possibly, though not that I've experienced."

"Why are you here now, with us?"

"Where else should I be?"

Not one to give up, Stamets hoped to press further but suddenly saw an unclear form by his body on the biobed—an alien form, he thought. The wispy, fuzzy outline wavered as if stuck in a soundless transporter beam. *"That!"* Stamets called out and pointed. *"What is that?"*

"The others," Hugh said. The form twisted toward them, seeming to stare for a moment, before turning back to Stamets's inert body, which abruptly began writhing in pain.

9

"Captain, if I may have a moment?" Saru stood back from his station on the bridge, giving Burnham space to view the display.

Hoping this meant a positive progress report, she rose from the command chair and strode to his console. "Tell me something good, Saru."

Her Kelpien first officer tilted his head to one side and she could tell his jaw had tightened.

"Okay," Burnham said, "tell me something better than terrible."

"*That* I believe I can do." He displayed a schematic of *Discovery*'s structural damage, which, while extensive, wasn't as bad as their trudge to engineering had suggested. "All decks have reported in, and damage-control teams are effecting repairs. Estimating three hours to restore main power."

"Three hours is more time than we have." She didn't quite whisper, but kept her voice low.

"Perhaps not," Saru said more buoyantly than she'd expected. "Hull degradation is significantly less than Ensign Tilly suggested. Either there was an error in her calculations—"

"Doubtful. I saw the test data." There was a tone Burnham knew she had, shaped by her rigorous education, that made a correction sound like rebuke, and refutation come off as argument. She remembered to soften it when talking to her crew, but she dropped into old habits more easily with Saru.

Despite the problems this had caused their relationship early on, she knew he'd learned not to take it to heart.

"It is likely there is an unknown factor mitigating the rate at which the hull is being processed by the fungi attacking it."

The captain ran a hand quickly over her brush of cropped hair and eyed the navigation console past Saru's station. *Insufficient Data* flashed in the position where galactic coordinates usually sat. "We don't know where in the network we've become stuck. Could it be that the very nature of this space has caused our spores to disappear, but also slows the saprotrophic fungi from breaking down the hull?"

He clearly thought it a remarkable enough concept that he paused a moment for consideration. "An interesting hypothesis, Captain."

"Moot, if we don't survive long enough to gather data to test it." Pushing down a deep foreboding as best as she could, Burnham asked, "If *Prototaxites stellaviatori* doesn't thrive in this region of mycelial space, how do we escape?"

"We cannot." Saru dabbed at his console screen. "And I'm sure I needn't remind the captain that deceleration of our hull degradation isn't negation." He pointed to several points on the display where hull plates were slowly being compromised. "I believe we'll have enough time to restore main power, but after that, catastrophic breaches are sure to follow."

Sighing, the captain tried to knead what had become a constant knot of tension from her neck. "Even if we can find the right spores, what if bringing them to *Discovery* causes them to die, or disappear, or . . ." She let her sentence trail off.

"It *is* a conundrum, yes."

"And I thought Vulcans had a talent for understatement, Mister Saru." Burnham gave him a flicker of a smile.

Before he could respond, Bryce, earpiece in hand, called for her attention. "Captain, I've got sickbay for you."

"Landry?"

"No, ma'am. They report Mister Stamets has collapsed."

She twisted toward the lift that now would at least get her halfway there. "Saru, with me." As he followed, Burnham crooked her head toward Owosekun. "Owo, you have the conn."

———

Burnham and Saru made quick time to sickbay, the lift leaving them only one deck above. "Doctor, how is he?"

"Calm for now." Pollard pulled a bed restraint across Stamets's torso, and Burnham noticed another was already strapped against his legs.

"Are those necessary?"

"Until force-field containment is back online." She connected the secondary strip and gestured to the damage-repair tech across the room. "Mister Stamets has been prone to involuntary movements. Intense ones."

"What happened?" Saru's question was not directed to the doctor, but to Tilly and Airiam, who were standing close by.

"We don't know," Tilly replied, and Burnham tracked the concern in her voice.

For her part, Doctor Pollard just bit her lip a long moment. "Captain, this . . ." She seemed to lack the phrasing for what she wanted to say. "These are uncharted waters."

Stamets groaned. He looked at Burnham and she inhaled sharply when she saw his egg-white eyes. Only a hint of his blue irises bled through. "What happened to him?"

"Some kind of rapidly growing nictitating membrane?" Pollard offered. "That's the least of his problems." She motioned to the secondary display that had been rolled close to the biobed. "This is an unprecedented state of neurological dysregulation. A major reorganization of the tracts within the white matter of his temporal lobe."

"Your previous medical reports suggested *minor* restructuring," Saru said. "I believe your exact words were 'posed no risk.'"

Bordering on an annoyed grumble, Pollard muttered, "Clearly I was wrong."

"Clearly." Burnham leaned down trying to hear what Stamets was mumbling, but she couldn't make out anything above his shallow breathing. "What's he saying?"

"His lips move, but it's mostly noiseless." Pollard gestured toward the opposite biobed. "Much like our other patient."

Across from Stamets lay the stranger they'd found in the mycelial forest with him. Like *Discovery*'s astromycologist, he lay semiconscious.

"Could they be talking to each other?" Burnham asked, and while it might be an outlandish idea to some, it wasn't to someone raised on Vulcan. On a world where touch-telepathy was common, and where the inhabitants used a telepathic link to bolster one another's rational faculties, it wasn't such an unusual question.

"Come again?" Pollard glowered at the captain.

Burnham could sense Saru was about to reply for her. Curious as to what his answer would be, she held back and listened.

"One man," the first officer began, motioning fluidly to Stamets, "is often biochemically linked to the mycelial network. The other has been living within it for an undetermined period of time. How do we know he's not similarly a mycelial navigator? Perhaps the network links them."

"And that link would suggest some sort of telepathic connection?" the doctor asked, her eyes darting between Burnham and Saru.

"Is it possible?" the captain asked.

After a moment, Pollard said, "I don't know. I'll see if we can find out."

I don't know had been a common answer recently, and while it was no one's fault that they were stumbling around into unknowns, it was nevertheless frustrating. Burnham repressed the desire to frown as she stepped over to her remaining spore-drive specialist. "Tilly, I need you to get back to work. I'll give you any help you need. Airiam, or Bryce, if you need him, just ask. While Mister Stamets is here . . ."

Head shaking at a rate that seemed to make her red, curly locks almost vibrate, Tilly put up her hands as if to stop Burnham from continuing. "Captain, I don't have his level of knowledge. *Or* his skill. He knows this all so much better than—"

"Nonsense, Ensign," Saru said. "Your understanding, intuition, and innovation have also been exemplary."

Burnham put her hand supportively on Tilly's shoulder. "Listen to me. This is—"

"An order, yes, ma'am." Her nervous energy shrugged the captain's hand off her arm. "Or sir, but—I can't," she tried to almost desperately explain.

"It's not an order," Burnham said, then reconsidered that. "Well, technically, it *is* an order, but that's not the point. We *need* you."

Despite the captain's best efforts, Tilly was still anxious, tipping toward terrified.

Burnham made a half turn to Saru. "Commander, didn't the ensign apply for the Command Training Program?"

"She did," Saru confirmed. "And I have filed my letter of recommendation in her favor."

"Why?" the captain asked Tilly.

"Why? I want—" She hesitated. "Do I have to say? Out loud? To you?"

"I get that you want to be a starship captain someday. I'm asking *why*."

When Tilly's eyes moistened, the captain pulled back, but just a bit. This was important and there was a reason and determination within her that Burnham needed to access. *"Why?"* the captain asked again, but this time softly, just for her.

"I can do it," Tilly said quietly. "Be a starship captain. I mean, I could learn . . . how to make the right decisions." When she finished speaking, Tilly pushed out a breath as if it had been stuck. With it seemed to go a significant amount of her tension.

"That's a good answer," Burnham said. "I believe you, and I want you to take that journey. The CTP is a great way to begin. But one of the things I've learned is that command isn't just knowing when to make a decision. It's knowing how to inspire the people around you, encouraging them to do what they can, so you can do what you must." She put both hands on Tilly's shoulders and gave them an encouraging squeeze. "A crew may not be sure what heights they can reach. Their commanding officer has to have the confidence—in them— that they may lack."

"Y-you have that confidence in me?"

"I do." Burnham held her wide-eyed stare.

Tilly straightened and a proud glimmer shined in her eyes. "Okay. I won't let you down, Captain."

"I know you won't," Burnham said, motioning toward the door. "So let's get to work."

Once Tilly and Airiam were gone, Saru leaned down to his captain and whispered, "Michael, did not Captain Georgiou give you that same speech?"

"How could you know that?"

With a twinkle in his eye, he admitted, "She also bestowed it upon me."

Burnham smiled, remembering fondly their shared service under Philippa Georgiou's command. Looking back, that had been a time of personal growth they both sorely needed. Their former captain had taken great care to test them, individually and together. At times it even felt like they were being pitted against each other. In retrospect, Georgiou had instilled in them what Burnham had tried to nurture in Tilly: confidence in one's self and one's crewmates. "I really miss her, Saru."

"As do I, my friend."

10

Hugh Culber watched as Doctor Pollard situated the biobed on which his body lay so that he was sitting three-quarters up, then she hovered the scanner from his sphenoid to his occipital protuberance. It was surreal to view his own medical exam, especially since he was a doctor himself and would have treated his own patient in the same way.

Handing the scanner to her nurse, the doctor then flashed a light in his eyes, and finally waved her hand in front of them. Culber heard her talking, but only in vague muffles; something about never seeing eyes dart around so much but not react to pupil dilation tests.

Don't worry about me, Culber thought. *Worry about Paul.*

In the opposite biobed, Stamets's body languished.

Bending over his own form, the astromycologist felt both horrified and fascinated. *"I'm going to ask this one more time,"* he told Ephraim as he pointed at his own body. *"You're certain this is really happening? I am standing here talking to you, but also lying in bed."*

"You are and you aren't," was the ambiguous reply.

Culber let out a scornful chuckle. He was used to Ephraim's vague, equivocal answers, but that didn't mean he enjoyed them.

"If I'm real and you're real, what about that?" Stamets pointed to the insubstantial, incorporeal alien forms moving around sickbay. They moved this way and that, coming espe-

cially close to Ephraim, and collecting equally ethereal sparkles in cylinders similar to the canisters *Discovery* used to store spores.

"The spores?" Ephraim asked, moving in such a way that more sparkles appeared—or was he exciting those that were otherwise invisible? *"I suppose they are as attracted to me as I am to them."*

Culber watched Stamets squint, as if that might allow him to see them more clearly as he waded through the humanoid shapes that milled around the tardigrade. *"No, not the spores,"* he said, his gaze darting between Ephraim and the wispy forms. *"These . . . ghostlike entities."* He put up a finger. *"Though, at some point I'd like to get back to this seemingly symbiotic relationship you may have with* Prototaxites stellaviatori.*"*

Ephraim puckered his mouth and bowed slightly forward.

"You don't believe in ghosts," Culber chastised Stamets, then realized neither did he. Except, for some time he'd doubted he was alive and thought he might be a ghost anyway. A tortured one.

"Then what are they?" Stamets asked.

"Those are the others," Culber said. *"I told you I saw them. Or . . . I think I tried to."* He bit his lower lip, attempting to recall. Memories could sometimes be as transient and elusive as Ephraim's riddle-like answers. He knew who he was again, but he also remembered regaining and then losing that fact innumerable times. Parts of his memory were still fuzzy, and he wasn't sure why, now that he was in *Discovery*'s sickbay, it was easier to grasp it all.

Right! Discovery*'s sickbay*, he realized, putting the disjointed moments together. *I'm not just on any ship with Paul, I'm on our ship! I'm home!* Culber turned in a circle, taking in the familiarity of the location. *"I'm not just a doctor. I'm a doctor here."*

"Here?" Stamets asked. *"Not the* Glenn*?"*

Culber spun toward him, annoyance marbling his tone. *"Yes. You know that."* There was an odd logic that told him his own memories were malleable but other people's—especially Stamets's—should somehow be immutable.

Or maybe it had nothing to do with other people, and was only about Stamets.

Looking blankly at Culber, unnervingly so, Stamets pointed to his own chest. *"Me? So have we met? I mean, before today."*

Feeling unsteady, hands trembling with tension and nerves, Culber tried to balance himself against the bulkhead near his biobed. He braced one hand against the wall, and put the other to his face. He glanced at his own restless body, still sitting up in bed, then down to the quivering hand of . . . whatever it was he was looking at.

"Why don't you know me?" Culber whispered, eyes closed.

A moment later, he felt Stamets's touch on his arm. The sense was unmistakable and Culber's eyes snapped open to find that kind, curious face staring back at him.

"Maybe I forgot," Stamets said softly, his delicate brows raised warmly. *"Tell me who you are."*

Roiling in a kaleidoscope of emotion, from the indignity of having to say it to the elation of remembering it, he met Stamets's gaze and said, *"I'm Doctor Hugh Culber. A Starfleet lieutenant commander, ship's physician aboard the* U.S.S. Dis-covery.*"* He nearly added *and your husband* but on the back of Stamets's expression, decided it best left unsaid.

"You're sure . . . we've served together?" Stamets gestured back and forth between them. *"I think I'd remember that."*

Culber let out a long, wavering breath. *"So would I,"* he whispered.

"On this point," Ephraim said, and in doing so startled both men, *"perhaps it would help if you searched your recollec-tions, and feelings."*

Perhaps a bit taken aback by the recommendation—conceivably because it came from a giant, talking space tardigrade—Stamets looked away, likely riffling through his memories.

"In a bar," Stamets said finally, his eyes still seeming to look back through the years. *"We were rude to each other."*

"You were rude," Culber said, gathering himself, wondering if perhaps his mind was remuddling and he was remembering his own history wrong. But at least they recalled the same meeting.

"So were you. I remember now. I wasn't the one humming horrible opera in public." A playful curl tugged at Stamets's lips.

Taking some strength from his own memory of that day, Culber felt himself in that moment and reflected on his annoyance. *"You thought you were funny then, and you still think so."*

"No, no, actually I know I was rude then. And you were probably right to call me an asshole."

"That's—no!" Culber spat angrily. *"I didn't call—"*

"Pretty sure you did," Stamets interrupted, his face flushing red.

Ephraim waved his arms about, trying to calm them both. *"Show him,"* he suggested to Stamets. *"Live it with him."*

And suddenly they existed, together, in that critical memory.

Three years ago

Alpha Centauri City was not the most populous metropolis, but it stood as a hub of commerce, culture, and technology for the entire system. It was home to a large university, a Federation Research Council complex that rivaled Earth's, and an enormous monument and museum dedicated to Zefram Cochrane, its most famous adopted son.

But after his and Justin Straal's presentations to a joint FRC/Starfleet audience, Paul Stamets was pretty sure nothing in the city held any appeal to him whatsoever.

"'Prove it.'" Stamets glowered at his own drink, took a sip, then set it back on the bar. "It's so easy to say that, y'know?"

"Are you drunk?" Straal asked.

Stamets scoffed, but otherwise ignored him. "It's like they've never even been scienced." An exaggeration, especially for a body supported by the Federation Science Council. "I've scienced a hell of a lot more than most of those . . . carcasses."

With a rueful chuckle, Straal said, "We knew there wouldn't be open arms. We're mycologists, Paul. Face it, we've never been and never will be the cool kids."

"I don't need to be cool. I just wanted them to look at the data and not dismiss it out of hand."

"That Starfleet officer—the Andorian—he asked some pretty nonthreatening questions."

"Starfleet." Stamets snorted.

Straal pulled in a long breath and despite putting his hand on his friend's shoulder, the brief silence wasn't all that separated the two men. "Listen, Amelia wants to see me tonight. She's concerned that our STELLA research is taking away from the terraforming project."

"Well, I'm sure today's presentation changed her mind," Stamets said sarcastically, polishing off his drink in one gulp and motioning to the bartender for another.

"I've got another meeting." Straal moved toward the exit to the atrium. "Try not to drown yourself while I'm gone."

"No promises," Stamets replied as the new drink was placed in front of him and the empty glass was removed.

Now alone, he took a sip. "This one tastes less blue," he muttered too low for the barkeep to hear him. "I miss my mushrooms."

Two seats away, an irritating—and given the mood he was in, almost infuriating—humming began. He took another pull on his drink, but that didn't help, and the sound continued.

It emanated from a slim, precisely groomed gentleman in a casual and yet somehow elevated-to-dressy tunic, bolstered by the fastidious man who wore it so well. The man faced the other direction, reading or watching something on a tablet.

"Excuse me, is that Kasseelian opera?" Paul asked. He didn't hear his own words slurring yet, but another drink or two and they'd start to.

"Yes!" Culber twisted his bar stool around until they met each other's gaze. "You know it?"

"Mmm." Stamets downed a quick swig from his glass. "I hate it," he said. "My ears thank you in advance for ending your little concert before I have to report your disturbance of the peace to the local authorities."

"You're rude," Culber said. "Worse, you think being rude is funny. It's not."

His glass empty again, Stamets motioned for yet another as soon as he caught the bartender's attention. "I hear that, sometimes, from people who lack a sense of humor."

"Do you?" Culber's voice dripped with antipathy.

"Um-hmm." Another glass replaced, Stamets refreshed himself with a sip. He could feel the thickening of his own voice now. The numbness was appreciated. "I think people just don't understand how really amusing I am."

"It's a shame you don't help more." Culber stood, his body clearly tense with a visceral dislike for the other man.

"Oooh, but I'm the rude one." Stamets laughed derisively.

"You are." Culber twisted away. "And you have bad taste in music."

"You wouldn't know, because I don't do others the disservice of humming it in public."

Culber snaked toward the exit, dipping through the crowd. "Asshole," he muttered just before he was out of earshot.

"Aren't we all?" Stamets raised his glass to the man's back as it disappeared behind others near the exit. "Aren't we all," he repeated sadly, and mostly about himself.

———

"That's—just wrong." Culber felt confused and angry. *"That's not the way it happened. That wasn't me."*

"We all have off days. That was clearly one of mine." Stamets raised his hands in surrender. *"I'm not offended, I—"*

"No, I mean that's literally *not how it happened."* Culber began a slow pace of the sickbay deck.

"I hate when people use 'literally' incor—"

Culber cut the other man off. *"I'm using it correctly,"* he snapped. *"I'm telling you: my memory of that event is* literally *different."*

Eyes wide, Stamets took a step toward him, reaching out. *"Well, memories—"*

Stopping without backing away, Culber tensed and Stamets pulled back his hand. *"You don't understand. I didn't insult you, or call you anything. I said your lectures were better than your manners."*

"You heard my lectures?" Stamets straightened, seeming both surprised and complimented.

"No one goes to the university on Alpha Centauri for the night life." Culber calmed himself and took in a centering breath.

"Or the opera?" Stamets grinned. *"Listen, I'm sorry I was rude . . ."*

"Are you?" Culber asked the question without the hostility he saw in the memory.

"I am," Stamets said, sounding very sincere. *"I think at the time 'rude' was my default setting."* Self-conscious, he dropped his gaze. *"I was attracted to you, but was wallowing in such an ocean of self-pity that I didn't care and didn't even get your name."*

"So you . . . this you . . . we didn't see each other the next day?"

"This is my only me," Stamets protested, his left hand steepled against his own chest.

Culber swallowed hard. *"I'm asking if we met again on the orbital station. You were waiting for a transport to Deneva. I was heading for a posting on Antos IV to treat casualties from that disaster."*

Considering it a moment, Stamets rubbed the back of his neck. *"I remember the Antos IV massacre. Some psychotic starship captain rechristened his science vessel from the* Heisenberg *to the* Ares *and attempted genocide when the planet wouldn't bow to him."*

"Yeah, that's the one." Culber rubbed both temples with his fingertips. *"But you caught me before I left and we talked."*

"You remember *the event as Paul and you experienced it,"* Ephraim said with a clack of one of his claws toward Culber, *"but he remembers it only as what he and that you—Hugh—experienced."*

"Make sense," Culber snapped as confusion and frustration threatened to overwhelm him. *"For the love of starships and . . . and mushrooms—I am begging you to make sense."*

"I think I understand." Stamets twisted toward their tardigrade mycelial-astral guide. *"You're saying the Hugh I met isn't this Hugh. And the Paul he knows . . ."*

A deep sadness washed over Culber as Stamets's voice trailed off. *"Isn't you,"* he said.

"A parallel universe," Stamets gasped, then added in a whisper: *"Universes?"*

"From your point of view, myriad universes, yes." Ephraim rolled his upper body and the spines on top of his head twitched. *"Some are almost exactly the same, some very different."*

"Other Pauls." From other universes. *With other Culbers in most of them?* It was a concept that Culber had forgotten and remembered and forgotten again where Stamets was concerned, as he always focused on his husband. But it rarely had occurred to him that these other universes would also have versions of himself. *"I remember now."*

"You've met other mes?" The look on Stamets's face was a mix of fascination and dismay, but he must have noticed Culber's own bitter expression. *"Not all . . . happy experiences?"*

"No," he said, like it was some unscrupulous confession. *"One was like you in intelligence, name, and looks, but not at all in morality."* Culber was probably thinking more of his own Stamets than this "new" one, as he didn't really know the man long enough to know his values, and yet he sensed this Stamets was kind. Culber could see that in his eyes and he reached up and stroked softly along the man's cheek. *"He was like a mirror image of you . . . but warped."*

"A funhouse mirror," Stamets quipped, then seemed to suppress a shiver. *"I . . . I can't imagine that."*

"Then experience it," Ephraim suggested. *"To better understand."*

———

Culber had awoken on the forest floor, multicolored mycelia all around. Bright pink spore-geysers tinted the dark sky above. Just moments before, he had felt Stamets's arms cradling him, his warm, safe embrace all-encompassing.

But that was now gone.

Instead, towering above him, stood an angrier Paul Stamets in a black uniform trimmed with gold. If eyes were the window to the soul, Culber feared this man had none. Instinctively, he cringed.

"Well, hello," this Stamets menacingly said. "I must admit, I'm surprised to see *you* here."

Culber pushed himself back along the ground, trying to skitter away as the man drew closer.

Suddenly, instantly, Culber found himself no longer on the forest floor, but in a lab, strapped down to an examination table. He struggled to get away, but thick bands cut painfully into his legs, arms, and torso.

"Not exactly who I expected," Not-quite-Stamets said, turning away from an equipment tray.

"*Discovery?*" Culber asked, looking around at the odd yet familiar surroundings. "Paul?"

"Neither, really. Though I suppose 'Paul' qualifies as correct, but I don't think I'm the one you expected, either."

"Where am I?" Culber asked, confused. He tried to keep his voice even but a puzzled warble betrayed him.

Leaning down, a malevolent grin spreading across his visage, this darker Stamets pressed himself against his captive. "Well, not the *Discovery*. Yours or ours. It's not even my lab on the *Charon*." He straightened, grabbed what seemed to be the sharpest implement off the tray, and cuddled it close to his face. "Though I must say the network cleverly provides an amazing facsimile."

Still befuddled, Culber thrashed again against the straps that held him to the table.

"Yeah, it's just going to inflict more pain when you struggle." His captor smiled again mirthlessly and leaned forward. "The neat thing is that none of this is real—it's all . . ." He tapped at his temple with the blunt end of the instrument in his hand. "But the mycelial network knows me more than you, so can take my cues. Makes it real for both of us." Stamets laughed. "It's a much cleverer network than I thought."

"What do you want?" Culber relaxed his muscles against the restraints as best he could. They still cut uncomfortably into him.

Stamets frowned thoughtfully. "Oh, many things. Some peach cobbler. Someone to buy that useless trillium mine I bought. My aunt Sarah, dead. Oh, and to be free from this place before *I* die."

Aghast, Culber thought of Stamets's aunt—a delightfully harmless woman, even if she tended to be a compulsive organizer. "Sarah?"

"I can be as angry as anyone," Stamets admitted. "But even *I* wouldn't torture cats—and document it. That's beyond cruel."

"None of this makes any sense!" Culber pulled against his bindings again, instantly regretting it as they constricted tighter in response.

"Agreed," Stamets said. "You're not like me, but you're still here, which is incongruous. The question is why?"

Culber said nothing. Despite having Stamets's face, and even his mannerisms—and apparently an aunt Sarah as well— this couldn't actually be his husband.

"Uh-uh-uh," Stamets warned as he brought the business end of a bone-marrow tap to Culber's nose. "You *want* to help me, I promise."

"By getting you a new medical instrument catalog?" Culber asked, encouraging his inner snark to show. "That's an implement that went out of use over a hundred years ago. You can get a marrow sample a lot easier than that."

"True." Stamets bowed his head. "But neither as painfully, nor as much fun for a sadist."

Culber steadied his breathing. "Which bone?" he asked coolly.

Perplexed, Stamets straightened. "Excuse me?"

"Which bone first?"

"I—I hadn't—"

"Hadn't thought the threat through?" Culber sat up abruptly, his restraints dropping away, and he launched himself from the table and at his would-be torturer. "You shouldn't have said this was being created for you and it was all in our minds. That means you're not really in control." He grabbed the instrument from Stamets's hand and threw it across the lab. "You're an idiot."

"No," Stamets protested, backing away. "I'm a genius. Unfortunately, you're *not* an idiot, and clearly can't be bullied or fooled."

The lab dissolved around them, returning them both to the mycelial forest.

"Aww," Stamets said. "Bummer."

"Are we even here?" Culber asked. "What is this place? It looks like the cultivation bay, but on a scale—"

"Yeah, this is actually the mycelial plane." Stamets smirked. "Try to keep up."

"Why are we here?"

"Well," Stamets said with a wave of his hand through a fungal branch that sent spores swirling in all directions, "I'm in a coma—or maybe it's just a catatonic state—in my lab, on the *I.S.S. Charon*. So we're neither in your universe nor mine."

Universes. More than one. "Right. Alternate . . . *parallel* universes." Speculation, even scientific investigation of them, had been around for centuries, but there had never been conclusive proof until *Discovery* found itself in a universe not its own.

"I know, right?" Stamets made a soft *boom* sound and his hands mimed an explosion from his own forehead.

"*I.S.S.?*" Culber stroked his chin and felt his throat tighten around the words as he remembered the details in the ship-wide report that informed the crew it had found itself in a universe embodying the antithesis of their own.

"Imperial," Stamets said flatly. "Your universe doesn't advertise its Terran Empire? How do alien worlds know to cower in fear?"

"We have no 'empire,'" Culber said proudly, with a crack of disdain for this other-Stamets etching across his tone. "We're part of an egalitarian union. Hundreds of members, and thousands of allies. Billions and billions of sentient beings, all working together."

"Ha," Stamets scoffed, plucking an orange, tube-shaped fungi from the ground. "That's not sustainable." He slowly crushed the mushroom in his grasp. "Which is why you should be helping me. I need your version of me—the Paul from your universe—to help me find my way out of this . . . hell."

Culber pushed his clenched fists into Stamets's chest. The man staggered back into the mycelia behind him and a puff of spores filled the space between them. "You can *stay* in hell. The only Paul I'll help is mine."

11

"Captain?" Burnham couldn't remember Pollard's voice ever sounding so urgent. "Something's changed."

The captain and Saru were instantly at Stamets's bed. " 'Something' is a very vague term, Doctor."

"White-matter hyperintensity has increased," Pollard said, filling a hypospray, "in both of them. Does that help?"

It hadn't, and Burnham couldn't pretend to know biology the same way she understood quantum physics or xenoanthropology. "It will if you explain it," Burnham said. "Less attitude, more answers, please."

Pressing the hypospray into Stamets's neck, then handing it off to her nurse, the doctor watched the biobed's monitor for any changes. "I wish I had answers," she said apologetically. "Readings like these point to significant brain disease. But I can't find an underlying pathology. Both are headed toward complete neurological dysregulation if it continues."

"Are they in mortal danger?" Saru asked.

"Yes, Mister Saru," the doctor said. "They most certainly are."

———

"I could feel *his depravity,"* Stamets said of his warped doppelganger in Culber's memory. *"How could I feel it?"* he asked, covering his face with both hands.

"Because he *could feel it,"* Ephraim said, indicating Culber.

"This Paul doesn't feel evil," Culber told the tardigrade. *"His heart"*—he looked at Stamets—*"is good."*

"An interesting conclusion," Ephraim said.

"What does that mean?" Culber asked, agitated.

"Only that good and evil are curious concepts," he explained. *"Many have very concrete definitions of these notions. Yet there seems to be a variety of qualifications and temporizations that allow them to explain away exceptions."*

The oddity of Ephraim was that he could be completely comprehensible at times, and completely enigmatic at others.

"Are you saying I'm doing that?" Culber demanded. *"Or that he is?"*

"Neither," Ephraim said. *"Or both. It depends on the circumstance and types of you."*

Culber felt perplexed. Did Ephraim not see him as an individual but as a version of a Plato-like "perfect form"? To him, and his mycelial network–traversing, multiverse-spanning existence, were there no individuals? Only variations on a theme?

"I can promise you both I'm not evil," Stamets said. *"But I think we have a more pressing problem than machinations about my moral code."* He indicated the space near Ephraim. *"The spores around you? They're gone. And so are the wispy forms we've been ignoring."*

"That's a bad thing?" Culber asked.

"Yes, very bad, because all the spores we had aboard are gone too, so we need to harvest more. Discovery is stuck here without them, and people are waiting for us to deliver antivirals to stop an outbreak of Symbalene blood burn." Stamets turned to Ephraim. *"Will you be stuck here with us?"*

The tardigrade rolled his upper body in that neutral motion he made. *"I am not physically here, my friend."*

"Then where are you?" Stamets asked.

"I don't really keep account of where or when I am," Ephraim confessed with a nonchalance that defied reality.

Culber was used to being stuck in mycelial space, but Stamets clearly was not. He pivoted toward Culber, his expression and tone spiked with urgency. The same hurried tone Culber remembered from his own Stamets, when there was work to be done and little time for anything else. *"We need to wake up. Now. Or at least I do."*

"Then wake up," Ephraim suggested.

———

"Now!" Stamets yelled, bolting up in bed so quickly his forehead knocked Doctor Pollard's scanner from her hand and sent it clattering across the deck.

Burnham noticed his eyes were back to normal, and she glanced up at his biosigns. They'd also returned to expected levels.

Saru reached down and scooped up Pollard's scanner and handed it back to the doctor.

"Thank you. Knew I should have left him restrained," she muttered, checking the monitor above her patient. "I've never seen such a quick recovery."

Now seeming fully aware, Stamets surveyed sickbay and urgently asked the captain, "Have you seen the others?"

Burnham stepped closer. "Tilly and Airiam said you mentioned seeing something. Intruders?"

"I think so."

"I saw them too," the mystery man in the next bed said. The clarity of his voice shocked everyone, except Stamets, Burnham noted.

Also fully awake—his hair having been trimmed, his tattered clothes replaced with patient's scrubs—the stranger had a certain demeanor that the captain felt was familiar. As if he was used to discussions of aliens and intruders.

"Where did you see them?" Burnham asked.

"Here. Sickbay," the man said, and nodded to Stamets for corroboration.

"They're gone now, Captain. From this area, not from the ship."

He tried to swing himself off the bed, but Pollard pressed him back down. "Whoa, cowboy."

"Burnham's the captain?" the mystery man whispered.

Burnham's gaze flicked to him a moment, but she quickly refocused on Stamets. "How do you know that what you saw was an intruder and that it's still aboard?"

"You've been unconscious since first seeing them, have you not, Lieutenant?" Saru added.

"It's . . . more an impression they're still here."

"I got the same impression." Like a tennis match where people kept looking from one player to the other, Pollard, her nurse, the captain, and Saru all looked back to the mystery man.

"And you are . . . ?" Burnham asked.

"Hugh Culber," Stamets replied. "I'll vouch for him. We . . . we've met before. I just didn't remember."

"Pleased to, uh, meet you," Culber said, "*Captain*." He offered his hand, which she shook, but he seemed unsettled by it.

"I need more than a name." Burnham placed her hands behind her back in what she knew was a somewhat intimidating stance. At least that was how it felt when used by the Vulcan masters from her childhood. "How did you get here? We found you outside our ship. And we're currently—"

"Stuck in mycelial space. I know," Culber said. "I'm not sure how I got here either, to be honest."

"Honesty would be appreciated," she said. "Are you

Starfleet? From the *Glenn*?" It was a logical assumption. Stamets said he knew Culber, and the man's bearing seemed recognizable—like someone who'd been through Starfleet training.

Culber hesitated as Doctor Pollard approached, scanning him again, apparently finished with Stamets for now. "I'm a lieutenant commander."

The captain sensed he wasn't answering both questions with his reply. "But not from the *Glenn*?"

"Starfleet Medical," he said with a gesture to Pollard. "I'm a physician." He met the other doctor's eyes. Searching for some kind of recognition?

Burnham wasn't sure.

"And you have no idea how you found yourself, without environmental protection, walking through a fungal forest in mycelial space?" Saru asked.

"He doesn't know," Stamets said defensively. "I've already asked."

Burnham turned back toward her astromycologist and eyed him skeptically. "While you were unconscious?"

Stamets must have known how it sounded. He scratched the side of his head. "It's . . . hard to explain, Captain."

"Try. I excel at listening."

"Right." Stamets gingerly pushed himself off the bed, pinching the bridge of his nose between his thumb and index finger. "Where to start, is the question."

"Pick a fact. Something you know for certain. We'll build from there."

"He's from another universe," Stamets blurted out, indicating Culber.

Burnham and Saru exchanged a surprised glance, then looked at the stranger, before turning back to Stamets.

"Okay," the captain said. "Not where I thought you were

going to go." She paused a moment, uncertain she should take the time to hear out someone the ship's doctor had indicated had been having major brain-matter changes. By the same token, her own instinct suggested something different about Culber that intrigued her as well. "How do we know this?"

Stamets pursed his lips but said nothing.

"I know you," Culber said matter-of-factly, rising from the bed and joining them. "All of you. But you don't know me, it seems. I'm a doctor on the *Discovery*." He leveled his gaze at Pollard. "Just like you, Tracy. But not *this Discovery*."

"An alternate universe with each of us duplicated within it?" Saru asked, intrigued if somewhat incredulous. "Can you offer any proof?"

Burnham watched Culber's features as he struggled to find whatever it was he might present as evidence.

"I . . . I'm not sure," he said, sounding forthright enough. "My Tracy Pollard likes sushi and hates pickles and is an incredibly proficient surgeon. My universe's Commander Saru is one of the kindest, most empathetic people I know. And my Paul Stamets? Well . . . I more than knew him . . . he's the same here, but also very different."

"And I'm not in command of the *Discovery* in your universe." That wasn't a question—Burnham had already noted his apparent surprise at her position.

Culber seemed to look past her rather than meet her gaze. "No. You're on board as a specialist. You lost your rank after the Battle of the Binary Stars."

The captain stiffened but examined the man's face for duplicity, or even irony—anything to suggest he was being insincere. She found neither.

"What battle?" Saru asked, astonished. "While that confrontation has colloquially become known as the Standoff at the Binary Stars, the incident has yet to be declassified."

"In my universe, it sparked a war with the Klingons."

"The war we avoided." The captain nodded ruefully to herself. Perhaps in Culber's universe, that Burnham had chosen the desperate path she herself had considered, but instead had decided against, resolving to trust her values and her captain. "Again, how did you get here?"

"I don't know."

"The mycelial network," Stamets said, drawing his hands apart, "apparently connects not just every point in our universe, but every point—I suspect—across a multiverse of universes. We're stuck between it all. And I think we ended up here like this because somehow Hugh sent me some kind of message across the network with the coordinates to be here."

"How?" Saru asked Culber.

"I know that seems like a straightforward question, but I don't have a good answer," Culber said to Stamets. "Now *I* sound like Ephraim."

"Ephraim?" Saru asked no one in particular. "Ephraim who?"

"Ugh." Stamets grunted in frustration. "Okay, this is *also* going to sound insane . . ."

Reeling from the revelation of not only an alternate universe, but one in which her counterpart may have made a momentous choice that started a war, Burnham waited anxiously for Stamets to continue.

Saru seemed to as well, while Doctor Pollard stood and watched, but handed her padd to a nurse, who nodded and took her leave.

All eyes on him, Stamets was at a loss for words. "Ephraim," he began slowly, "is the name—believe it or not— of someone we've all met. Not with *that* name, or really any name, but—"

"Lieutenant," Burnham interrupted, "I appreciate you've

been through a trauma, but there's a clock ticking. Benecia Colony is waiting for us with a medical emergency, and we don't know if any other ship will be dispatched in time. On top of that, we have just hours before the ship's hull is irreparably compromised."

His face paled in recognition. "Right, right. How long has it been so far?"

"One hour, seventeen minutes," the captain said.

"Tritanium shouldn't last this long." Stamets started pacing. Burnham could see he was mentally running through the possibilities. *"Why . . ."*

"Fortunately, the local atmospheric composition seems to have a moderating effect on the decay rate," Saru said. "For now. Whatever elements are here have the ability to recycle—"

"The JahSepp," Culber said. He held his right elbow in his left hand and his right hand was thoughtfully at his chin. "That's what Ephraim called them. They don't like the yeel forests. Something in the bark repels them."

"Fortunate for us," the captain said, "but it doesn't solve the overall problem." Part of her wanted to ask more about the JahSepp and their nature, but the weight of not just their situation but their overriding mission bore down on her. "Mister Stamets, please tell me you have a plan to get us out of here."

"Not yet," he replied, "but I would bet my life that these other, 'almost-corporeal' forms we saw, collecting spores off Ephraim—"

"And again I must inquire, who is Ephraim?" Saru asked in frustration, turning to Burnham. "Forgive me, Captain, but we've yet to hear exactly who that is."

"Agreed," she said, leveling a very serious look at both men. "Who the hell is Ephraim? You both have to level with me here."

"Ephraim is the entity who guided me to Paul," Culber

said, "and I think who guided Paul to me as well." His voice softened and he put his hand on Stamets's arm. "I think he cares about us."

Smiling awkwardly, Stamets seemed to make eye contact with everyone present. "That was my sense too. And as odd as it seems, Ephraim is . . . the giant space-tardigrade creature whose DNA Justin Straal and I used to help solve the navigation problems of the spore drive."

Silence followed, except for an uncomfortable cough from Pollard.

Kelpien facial expression wasn't the most fluid, but when Saru looked to the captain, she knew him well enough to read baffled puzzlement across his visage. "Should I inquire further, Captain?"

Burnham shook her head and sighed. "If we survive this . . . presumably we can read it in the lieutenant's report."

"So you believe me?" Stamets asked, incredulous.

"Conditionally, I do." Burnham's logical philosophy taught her to have confidence in certain things—instruments, facts, people—based on one's experience. She thought of Sarek, her foster father: *The sun shines. Is it faith to believe when you awaken tomorrow, you shall see it again?* he would ask Socratically. *No,* she would reply. *Because I have evidence of previous patterns upon which I can base a logical prediction.* And yet, if any feeling in life had tempted her to call it faith, it was the trust she had in her comrades; chief among them had been Saru, whom she'd met when first coming aboard the *Shenzhou,* and Stamets, who was already on the *Discovery* when she was given it as her first command.

For the time being, his word was good enough to vouch for Hugh Culber, who she sensed had been equally trustworthy in trying to explain the situation.

"Thank you, Michael," Stamets said simply, and in his

body language the captain saw a passion she'd only previously noticed when her astromycologist was talking about his vocation. She had perceived some minor changes in him of late—a more composed demeanor, and perhaps some deeper introverted behavior, but this level of emotion she had never seen.

"Tell me about these alien forms you've been seeing," Burnham prompted.

"I first saw them in my lab, and then Hugh and I both saw them here. They may still be in the lab."

"Or elsewhere." The captain spun to Saru. "We need a complete sensor sweep, bow to stern. Have Airiam and Tilly report to the bridge. If there are intruders, let's find out."

"Yes, Captain." Gliding toward the sickbay exit, Saru opened his communicator and moved quickly to his task.

Burnham asked Pollard, "How is Landry?"

"Doctor Schanne is attending to her in recovery. Khal and Genego are there too. They were our worst cases, but all are now stable."

Burnham felt a wave of relief wash over her. "And are these men well enough to be discharged?" She gestured toward Stamets and Culber.

"To be honest, Captain, I'm not sure," Pollard said. "Scans show me the same tracks in their white matter, but the trauma and neural dysregulation are gone."

"I need a decision, Doctor," Burnham told her, "and please bear in mind that it is unlikely the ship will survive our current predicament without their immediate assistance."

"In that case, absolutely."

———

As Burnham, Saru, Culber, and Stamets entered the turbolift, Stamets filled in the captain and first officer about his "spore dreams," and what he could understand about his discussion with the Ephraim tardigrade.

"You should have reported the dreams, Lieutenant." The captain didn't meet his eyes until she felt his gaze and the silence between them endured too long. Eventually, her disappointed air impelled him to speak.

"I'm sorry, Captain," he said. "Sometimes when you're not sure what something is . . ." His shoulders slumped. "Clearly they weren't just dreams, because Hugh is very real. I just had no idea."

When this crisis was over, they'd need to speak in more detail about it all, Burnham thought. She'd not been sanguine about the genetic manipulations both Stamets and Justin Straal had employed. Both she and her *U.S.S. Glenn* counterpart had been concerned about side effects and repercussions, and this critical event seemed like those chickens were coming home to roost.

When the lift doors opened to the bridge, Owosekun rose from the command chair. Burnham nodded to her, accepting return of the conn. Airiam and Tilly were at the port science station.

As the captain and her officers filed toward them, Culber lagged behind a bit, uncertain where he should be. Keyla Detmer nearly ran him over as she quickly crossed back to her station from Bryce's.

"Oh, I'm so sorry." She gripped his elbows to jointly restore their respective balance.

Once they backed safely away from each other, Culber's expression was painted in surprise. "No implants," he whispered.

"Implants?" Detmer appeared confused.

"Right—that battle never happened." His gaze lingered on her a long moment. "Never mind, I'm sorry."

"Doctor Culber?" Burnham motioned for him to join them.

"Yes, Captain," Culber said, and again the odd tone in his voice when he called her captain gave Burnham pause.

"I need you to work with Mister Saru and Ensign Tilly to modify our internal sensors," she told both men. "We need a way to see what they saw," she told Saru before lowering herself into the captain's chair.

Burnham pulled up status reports on the arm displays. They were on track to restore main power, including shields, which might buy them time before *Discovery*'s hull was damaged beyond repair. *JahSepp* was how Culber had referred to those corrosive environmental elements, but knowing what they were called was little help.

She glanced back at Doctor Culber as he and Stamets conferred with Tilly and Airiam. If Stamets looked at Culber with some fondness, Culber reciprocated by a multiple of that. When he said he "more than" knew Stamets, Burnham suspected this meant a serious relationship. Would such an attachment compromise what she could trust from one or both of them?

By accepting the account of Culber's origin, Burnham had now opened herself to all manner of doubt she wished to silence in favor of the task at hand. Nevertheless, some of those questions persisted: If the Binary Stars incident had gone differently in Culber's universe, that suggested the mutiny she'd considered and thankfully avoided had put into motion a series of events that brought about a war and stripped her of her rank, and yet somehow she still wound up on the *Discovery*? If she wasn't the captain, who was? Philippa Georgiou? Saru? Someone else? What other similarities and differences did that reality have?

Perhaps it didn't matter. She had her own universe's ship

and crew to save. Pondering roads not taken wasn't going to make that happen faster.

After conferring with Owo on details of the damage-control reports, Burnham made her way back toward Saru, noting that Rhys had joined them all at the science station.

"Captain," Saru said, "as usual, your timing is inspired."

"You have something."

"I believe so." He drew his nimble fingers across the console, and the screen before them brought up a schematic of *Discovery*. "With the majority of our internal sensors back online, we've been able to adjust them to Ensign Tilly's specifications."

"I wasn't really sure what parameters to modify," Stamets said. "But given the changes in the white matter of me and Hugh, it made sense to look for something a human wouldn't *normally* perceive but could, given the changes we've undergone."

"Which sensors can be adjusted for," Tilly added.

"As much as I enjoy the technical details, can we limit this to information useful toward solving our current problem?" For Burnham, this was usually the part she found most fascinating, but they had to stay on track. The survival of the Benecia Colony and the incubation rate of the Symbalene blood burn weighed heavily on her every moment they weren't acting toward their primary goal.

"Unknown energy readings," the ensign said, as if she was cutting to the chase.

"Which are in flux, and have no known cause," Saru said. "The readings are similar to those generated by our missing mycelial spores." Gesturing toward the ship's schematic, he explained, "Sickbay shows some residual evidence, but sensors indicate engineering is where current activity seems to be centered."

"A sensor glitch?" Airiam asked. "These data are identifying places that had contact with mycelial space. The spore lab in engineering, which interacts frequently via the reaction cube, and sickbay, where people were being treated after being in the mycelial plane."

"Honestly, that still makes more sense to me than intruders," Rhys said. "How would they have come aboard?"

"We know what we saw. Both of us," Culber replied.

Yeah. A giant tardigrade life-form named Ephraim, Burnham thought.

"It's a valid question." Stamets turned to Rhys. "How *would* someone get on board unnoticed?"

"The same way we didn't know you left," the captain said. "When sensors were down and most systems were offline."

"But if we can't really see them . . . is it cloaking technology?" Rhys asked.

"Or just a mycelial life-form we've never encountered," Tilly said.

If there were truly aliens aboard, which form they were taking didn't matter. Burnham pivoted toward communications. "Mister Bryce, signal an intruder alert, all decks. Have tricorders issued to security details, calibrated to scan for the energy readings we found."

"I can help with the tricorders," Tilly said, and the captain nodded her approval.

"Intruder alert," Bryce announced over the intraship speakers. *"All decks: intruder alert. This is not a drill."*

12

"You're my canary in our coal mine," Michael Burnham had once told Saru. And while the Kelpien didn't understand the reference until she explained it, she was never sure if he was mildly offended, bemused, or perhaps even proud. Those alien eyes could hide as much as they wanted. However he felt about it, his threat ganglia could be a good indication of a figurative—or sometimes literal—oncoming storm. At the moment, they were not visible, which Burnham found reassuring.

"Doctor Culber?" The captain hoped her tone came across as sympathetic. "You said you're not certain how you arrived in the mycelial network. Do you know how long you were exposed though? Doctor Pollard said she found evidence of long-term, repeated epidural damage."

Hesitating, Culber caressed his neck and gazed past Burnham. What wounds had been visible, Pollard had treated. The unseen scars plainly lingered. "I don't know," he said finally. "But it felt like a very long time."

"It may have been, even if it wasn't," Stamets said.

"What do you mean?" Rhys asked.

"Time works . . . *differently* in the network, I think."

"Doctor," the captain said to Culber, "you were covered in that dust that protected you somewhat."

"From . . . the JahSepp, I believe you called it?" Saru added. "What language is that?"

"I don't know," Culber said. "It's just what Ephraim called them. They don't thrive in the yeel forests."

"Did Ephraim suggest you cover yourself in the dust from the yeel trees?" Burnham asked.

Uncertain, Culber ran a thumb along his jaw. "I know the air burns less when I use it. It's one of the few things I never forget. I either stumbled upon it or . . . I don't know."

"We think that's why the hull is degrading slower than I thought it would," Tilly said.

"The coordinates in the message we received brought us here," Stamets said, with an excitement that encouraged the captain. "We crashed or materialized or whatever, right in the middle of this yeel tree forest."

"What do you mean, *whatever*?" It wasn't like Stamets to be inexact. She noticed he'd been more equivocal since returning to the *Discovery*.

"I still haven't had a chance to determine exactly how we ended up here," he replied.

The turbolift doors parted and Commander Ellen Landry, *Discovery*'s chief of security, walked slowly, and a bit uncertainly, toward them.

"Should you be out of sickbay?" Saru asked.

"Depends on who you ask." A weary expression belied Landry's strong tone.

"I'm *going* to ask Doctor Schanne," Burnham said.

Landry glowered. "He lies a lot."

"Commander—" Saru began to chide her.

"I heard the intruder alert. The doctor said we're stuck in mycelial space. That means there's work to be done." Landry held up her right hand. "I promise I'm okay. I'm groggy is all. Schanne wouldn't give me a stimulant, so I'll get some coffee. Maybe a lot of it. I'll be five by five."

Burnham sniffed her disapproval, but given the circumstances, she saw no logic in fighting her chief of security on the point. "Fine."

Landry jerked her head toward Culber. "Who's this?" No one said anything, so she looked back to Burnham. "Captain?"

As concisely as she could, the captain explained. "Doctor Culber was found outside the ship, in the mycelial forest in which we find ourselves . . . beached."

"Human?" Landry asked, looking him over, likely assessing his threat level.

"Very," Culber said.

Burnham noticed a look in his eye . . . Did he know Landry? Plainly, she didn't know him. Did they have a problem with each other? Was he her doctor? What caused the ghost of recognition?

"Mister Stamets, I want the yeel dust analyzed," Burnham ordered. "See if there is something we can incorporate into our shielding that might help us stay in one piece if we are stuck here." She crooked a thumb toward the main viewer. "And might allow us to raise the port shutters."

He nodded.

"Ensign Tilly." The captain raised her voice a bit so it carried to the communications station. "You and Mister Bryce will continue to work on the mycelial radio. Get it running, please."

Bryce shared a glance with Tilly as he gave his console over to his relief. He motioned her toward an auxiliary station. Under their current conditions, the bridge had the most reliable computer access.

Burnham then rotated toward Airiam. "Work with Rhys. See if we can tune the internal sensors so we don't need to run grid searches with tricorders."

"Aye, Captain." Airiam and Rhys excused themselves to the tactical station.

"What about me?" Culber asked.

"Sickbay," Burnham said. "Commander Landry will escort you."

Culber started toward the lift. "I can find my way."

"Commander Landry *will* escort you." The captain waved her over to him.

"You don't trust me," Culber stated.

Burnham felt her jaw clench. "Doctor, I simply don't know you." She met her security chief's eyes, and Landry's narrowed gaze suggested she understood the captain's concerns.

Once Landry and Culber were in the lift, Burnham gestured Stamets toward the door to her ready room. "Lieutenant, a word, please?"

Burnham wished she had the time to be less blunt, but the people on Benecia needed them. When the doors closed, allowing them a measure of privacy, she asked, "Doctor Culber. You have feelings for him?"

Stamets seemed to search for the best way to describe it. "I . . . sense a connection. I feel I can trust him, I guess? That *we* can trust him."

That had been sufficient to keep the stranger out of the brig—which according to the status report didn't yet have power anyway—but it wasn't enough, given Culber's somewhat wanting answers, to inspire the captain's complete confidence. "I need to know who he is, and no offense, I can't simply take your word for it."

"Of course." There was a trace of offense in his tone.

Burnham straightened and flipped a switch on the desk console behind her. "Computer. Access service record, Hugh Culber."

"Accessing . . . Culber, Hugh. Serial number: G098-632MQB. Rank: lieutenant commander. Position: ship's surgeon and chief medical officer. Current assignment: U.S.S. Hood NCC-1703.

Commendations: Legion of Honor, Award of Valor, Asclepius Staff of Antos Aid Mission. Twice decorated by Starfleet Medical. Decorated by Starfleet Command."

"Impressive." She'd be lucky to have such a crew member.

"*Constitution*-class assignment," Stamets noted. "They only take the cream of the crop."

"I'm not dissatisfied with the *Crossfield* class, mister," the captain said.

They shared a brief smile, but Stamets motioned toward the port beside her. "It's not been great today."

Burnham didn't argue that point. She lowered herself into her desk chair and flipped the console's switch back off. "Thinking cynically, how do we know the Culber in sickbay isn't the one whose record we just heard?"

"If we reached out to the *Hood*, we could confirm this isn't our universe's Hugh." He took the chair opposite her when she motioned to it. "But we can't."

The captain leaned forward, noting Stamets always used Culber's first name. "Why are you certain he isn't the Hugh Culber in the database?"

Taking in a long breath and releasing it slowly, Stamets seemed to consider it. "I don't think I can explain it," he said, looking away for a moment. "In any case, I don't sense he means us any harm."

"Because his Starfleet record is exemplary?"

"That's the record of *our* universe's Hugh Culber, not his."

Her face tight with frustration, Burnham felt Stamets might lack the skepticism she was hoping he could manifest. "Okay, for the sake of argument, let's say he's unquestionably from a parallel existence to ours. There's nothing to suggest someone is the same in every iteration of an alternate universe."

As if he had tasted something unpleasant, his expression

soured. "Ephraim showed us a version of me that was . . . well, I'm not sure 'evil' fits but, immoral? Amoral? Arrogantly violent?"

"Ephraim. A unique name for a creature who looks like a giant tardigrade. Didn't you name him something else?"

"Straal did." Stamets chuckled. "Yogi the water bear."

"I don't recognize the reference."

"I think it's from an old book," he said, uncertain.

"Can you contact this Ephraim?" Burnham asked. "He may have insight or information that would help us in this situation."

"I don't think so, Captain. He appeared to us while we were unconscious. At least to the outside world. I got the feeling he was there for Hugh rather than me."

"Why do you believe that?"

"I don't know that, either. Hugh seemed better acquainted with him. I *did* get the sense he just wanted to be helpful."

Was he still referring to Culber, or did he mean Ephraim? Burnham wasn't certain, but sometimes it was better to just let someone talk than to interrupt for a clarification. "Go on."

"Nothing, I . . ." He hesitated. "I think Hugh and I . . . in his universe, we were . . . I think we're much closer."

"And that possibility excites you or confuses you?"

"To be honest"—he let out an uneasy breath—"it scares the living shit out of me."

She kept her eyes locked with his. "Why?"

Stamets broke the connection, stood, and moved toward the screen opposite the desk. "Is this working?"

Burnham rose and followed him toward it. "Yes."

"Let me show you." Stamets activated the screen and began tapping at it as the captain leaned against the table and waited. "This is the data we've been accumulating from our jumps. Eighty-three in all."

He pushed the image to the holo-display above the desk,

so they could appreciate the full, three-dimensional view, and the captain turned to follow the map.

"Now, here're the *Glenn*'s," he continued, adding information to the electronic diorama. "This brings the total to over one hundred sixty-four jumps." He moved closer and pointed to several blank areas among the arcs and points of light. "See these scattered pockets of negative mass?"

"Yes."

"What if these aren't blank spots, but unseen, unknown pathways? It's what I tried to explain in sickbay. What if the mycelial network doesn't just connect places in our galaxy, in our universe, but also to *other*, parallel, alternate universes." He indicated the gaps in the map. "These could be markers of not just conduits to Hugh's universe, but a multitude of others."

Starship captains, especially those raised on Vulcan, tended to control their outward reactions. But amazement bubbled up as Burnham marveled at the possibilities. "This is far beyond the conventional conception of spacetime."

"Exactly!" Stamets said. "Doesn't that terrify you?"

The captain didn't answer, not because it would have been inappropriate to admit, but because the truth was . . . she wasn't. Astonished and a touch disconcerted, but mostly she was fascinated.

Nevertheless, she could see where this discovery could push one toward existential chaos. If people knew there were other, perhaps better—or worse—versions of themselves in existence, what might they do? And even if there was no action they could take, what would the psychological effects be? Some might be thrust toward greatness . . . others toward madness.

Even worse, what would the mere fact of alternate universes do to those who had lost someone they loved? If one was grieving a child, a parent, or a partner, and believed they could find them existing elsewhere . . .

More specifically for Michael Burnham, it meant somewhere another version of her parents were still alive. She was sanguine about that possibility, and could in fact gain strength from it, because she knew that while *her* parents were dead, some other Burnham had lived a different, perhaps better life. Or not. How was she to know? Maybe her best self was raised by Sarek and Amanda on Vulcan. She could be contented in that belief and find satisfaction in her singular existence. But she also saw where others might not.

"I *do* understand," she said eventually.

"There's a lot of baggage to unpack," Stamets whispered, slumping back into the chair.

"Let's get home first. We can unpack it there."

He looked up wearily. "Yeah. It can wait."

"I hope so. People are expecting us to get to Benecia. The *Republic* was the closest ship by conventional warp, but that was going to take two days. I need to be sure not just of your impartiality regarding Doctor Culber, but your ability to remain on task." She searched his visage, hoping to see the more certain Paul Stamets she was used to.

"I can."

"I know you believe that's true. I just hope you're able to assess yourself reliably."

"I'm okay," he told her. "Meeting Hugh feels like the road not taken. That's something I have to deal with, but like you said: home first."

"Good. Let's get on that."

He stood to leave but twisted back before reaching the exit. "Thank you, Captain."

As the doors opened to the bridge, Saru let Stamets pass, then entered the ready room.

Surprised, Burnham rose to greet him. "Am I getting a status report?"

"If I may be frank, I was hoping for a captain's report." He glanced momentarily at the holograph floating above the desk behind her. "How are you?"

"Looking for grounding, Saru." She returned to her chair and indicated the mycelial jump map Stamets had left hovering. "The Matrons of Vulcan Philosophy had little to say on the topic of parallel universe theory."

"Perhaps Professor Gill's alternate-history theory, then," Saru said.

"I beg your pardon?"

"Historian John Gill has a theory about like planets sharing traits and patterns of historical development. Not multiple universes, but perhaps the theories might be applicable."

"I'm not necessarily doubting the theory. But there *is* a Doctor Hugh Culber on the *Hood*. Occam's razor requires me to ask how I know the man in sickbay isn't really him."

"More to the point, if he *isn't* the Doctor Culber from the *Hood*, and *isn't* from another universe, then who or what is he?"

"That, my friend, is an excellent question." She marched back to the computer console. "Computer, access records on Culber, Hugh, ship's surgeon on the *U.S.S. Hood*."

"Records available."

Pacing back and forth along the desk, Burnham formulated the right questions to ask. "Computer, search Doctor Culber's medical records for results from any psychosimulator, engram, or hyperencephalogram testing."

"Working. Results found."

"Transfer to Doctor Pollard in sickbay."

The computer beeped to acknowledge the command.

"A logical enough course to take, Captain," Saru said,

"but if different, what would the results indicate other than that he is not the Hugh Culber from the *Hood*?"

"I don't know, Saru. I can't make decisions in an information vacuum. We need facts. Have Doctor Pollard do a deep dive, now that main computers are processing again. Every test she can think of, above and beyond those to compare with what we have in the records."

Burnham moved past her first officer and toward the door, ready to retake the center seat.

Before they exited, his tone quiet, Saru asked, "Michael, if he's not who or what he says he is . . . Well, I had noted Mister Stamets seems rather attached."

She met his eyes, and reflected in his gaze saw the worry she felt. "That he does."

"Enough that it's a concern?"

"I don't know, Saru. I don't think he does, either."

13

"Gen, please recalibrate lateral starboard sensors." Lieutenant Commander Airiam was polite, but because her voice was a bit mechanical, anything she said sounded imperative. As if there might be a massive overload if the lateral starboard sensors were not adjusted *right now*.

"Stand by," Rhys said. "I'm almost finished with the forward ones." He was inputting a set of metrics the sensors had never used before, and he feared they might reject them. "You ever get so frustrated with technology that you imagine retiring to a beach somewh—" He stopped himself, mortified. Airiam's last beach vacation ended in a shuttle accident that killed her husband and required all the technological augmentations she now dealt with every day. "Oh . . . I-I'm sorry."

"Please don't be." She put her warmer-than-you'd-think hand on his arm a moment, then removed it just as quickly. "People seem so afraid to engage in frank conversations with me. Even my friends." She grinned, as deeply as the construction of her face would allow. "I relish such connections."

"Oh, okay." He was relieved that he hadn't offended her. After he entered the recalibrations she'd wanted, he asked, "See anything on the port scan yet?"

"I do not." Airiam barely glanced at that screen. "But I believe our preliminary, less attuned, scans suggested that area would be clear."

Rhys was still considering what she'd said about her

friends. "May I ask a personal question I've never wanted to bother you with?" Before she could respond, the lateral starboard sensor recalibration finished and a blip of data appeared, and just as quickly disappeared. "Did you see that? Deck eight, section twelve."

Airiam checked the screen, then reran the scan. "Whatever was there no longer registers."

Another flash appeared on the screen and Rhys moved to zoom in on it, but again it disappeared. "That one was deck nine, same section." Rhys forced out an annoyed breath and tightened a fist against the console's edge. "Something must be wrong with the relays. A rolling glitch."

"I shall check." Airiam brought up the diagnostic screen. As she started running tests, she said, "What was your question?"

"The Starfleet database just lists you as *Lieutenant Commander Airiam*." Rhys kept glowering at the sensor display for the decks where the anomaly had appeared, searching fruitlessly for the blip to return. "Why just the one name?"

"Ah," she said knowingly. "On the *Europa*, people always asked me that, but you are the first on *Discovery*." When she noticed Burnham close by, she leaned toward him and whispered as best she could. "Not even the captain has inquired." Straightening again, she continued her diagnostic. "Airiam is a badge I wear, as much as this." She touched her hand to the Starfleet insignia on her chest. "It is an homage to the old me, but a symbol of the new."

"How so?" Still paying attention, Rhys wondered if what the sensors picked up could have been a type of transporter signal, but when he scanned for signs of such use, found none.

"As I recovered from the accident," she said as they worked, "with much of my old self replaced with my new self, my visual, aural, and vocal augmentations needed attuning. Before extensive configuration, Airiam was all I could say of my name. Due to how my new systems are connected, for a time it was also all that I would answer to. My given name had become foreign to my fresh ears."

His throat closing in empathy, Rhys only managed to croak out another "Oh."

"I chose to stay with my new name, as a symbol of the different person I had become. It was an attempt to keep myself from looking too far—and too often—backward."

Perhaps because he found her positivity so dear, or because he realized he might not be so lovely a soul as she, had he gone through the same ordeal, Rhys felt his chest tighten with emotion. He kept it from his voice as best he could, not wanting to embarrass her. "Do you recognize your birth name now? I mean you can say it, and answer to it?"

"Yes, of course."

"I'd like to know it. If that's okay?"

"Miriam." Her lips turned up in the closest he'd ever seen her to a beaming grin. "Rhymes with Airiam."

With a laugh, he choked up and wiped at his eye before an actual tear came out right there on the bridge. "Both are lovely."

"Thank you, Gen Rhys. I like your names too." She closed the diagnostic screen and returned to the sensor calibration controls. "I can find no errors in the lateral starboard sensor arrays on decks eight or nine."

"Damn," he said. "Then what did I see?"

"Not a sensor glitch," Airiam assured him.

"I'm not sure which bothers me more: the idea we've been boarded by intruders we can't scan for, let alone see, or that Mister Stamets and someone who says he's from another universe are the only ones who can."

"Do you disbelieve their claims?" Airiam asked.

Rhys shook his head. "No, but from a tactical point of view, what they say is disconcerting."

"If it was an intruder, they can traverse the ship with a speed our scanners have difficulty following. I will inform the captain that those decks need security attention and suggest tricorders may still be of more use."

———

When Paul Stamets returned to engineering, the damage-control team had nearly finished. Nilsson, he noticed, had been tidying up those sections the teams had yet to get to.

"Thank you, Lieutenant," he said as he scooped up a toolbox that had been removed but not returned to its compartment. "Damage-control teams seem to repair one kind of damage and create another."

The toolkit back in its place, and the damage-control personnel filtering out, Stamets approached the cultivation bay. The doors parted for him and beyond lay the stuff of his nightmares. Not merely sporeless *Prototaxites stellaviatori*, but *no Prototaxites stellaviatori* at all.

Nilsson stepped in behind him, the expanse of the empty bay shocking her as well. She muted a gasp that barely escaped. "Damn."

With a twinge of pain, Stamets shuddered. It wasn't cold—in fact the cultivation bay was humid and warmer than the rest of the ship. And yet, the instinctive overwhelming sensation he had sent a shiver down his spine.

"Do you sense anything?" he asked, narrowing his eyes as if he might see the shapeless wisps again.

She looked around the bay, then back to him. "No. Should I?"

He motioned her back toward the lab. "Get your tricorder." Stepping forward, Stamets searched for . . . what? He wasn't sure. He cocked his head, as if to hear something, but other than the normal ship sounds, the empty chamber was maddening in its silence.

By the time Nilsson was back, the feeling was gone. Resisting the urge to pull the tricorder from her hand, he let her scan the room. Waiting was a slow climb to annoying.

"Just those same residual energy flux patterns we recalibrated for." She showed him the readings.

"Where? Specifically."

"All over," she said, encompassing the empty bay in one arm wave.

Nilsson curved toward the door but Stamets grabbed her arm and pulled her back in. He would have described his feeling as eerie, but the sensation was more than that. "Scan it again," he told her in an urgent whisper.

She activated the tricorder and after a moment its humming changed in pitch, then an alert flashed on the screen.

"They're here," Stamets said, his voice quiet as he glared into the hollow compartment that once housed his personal mycelial forest.

Nilsson whispered back, "Who?"

"The 'others.' " He twisted around and gestured for her to join him in the lab again. As the bay door closed, he said, "Alert the bridge. Send them the tricorder data."

Nilsson hailed the bridge and reported what they discovered. Captain Burnham's singular order was to get "more answers," so she returned to Stamets with a shrug. "You heard the captain. Now what?"

He thought a moment. "I'll need a sample of the dust from my EV suit—"

Nilsson held up a small vial. "Collected and ready to be processed." Off his puzzled expression, she added, "From the EV suits, before they hit decon."

"Perfect." He grabbed the vial and placed it in the analysis bay. Keying in a sequence on the console, Stamets reminded himself to breathe as they quickly began their investigation to figure out what the dust from the yeel tree actually was.

As the information slowly played across the screen, Nilsson drew close. "That's interesting. Looks like some of the properties I've seen in Basidiomycota samples."

Taken aback, Stamets felt a wave of pride wash over him. "You read the mycology books I gave you? I like you just a little bit more today than yesterday."

"And," Nilsson added, "without trying to be teacher's pet, I'm pretty sure I remember that some species of Basidiomycota are pathogens."

"Not all," Stamets said, continuing to be impressed, "but yes, some. To both plants and animals. I wonder which the JahSepp qualify as?" Suddenly he found himself distracted by the same feeling he'd had in the cultivation bay—a sense something wasn't quite right. Were "the others" back?

Almost as soon as the impression struck him, it was gone. Like a window had opened and then closed.

"What's wrong?" she asked.

"Nothing," he murmured. "Everything."

As Stamets buried himself in the data again, there was a pull on him that was inexplicable. He wanted to talk with Culber. He didn't believe in fate, but his connection to the doctor was undeniable. He wasn't sure how he had missed it the first time they met. *Except they hadn't, really.* He had met the Culber who belonged to this universe and never got past that brief encounter . . . so he never knew what he was missing. Now that he did, he wondered if given a second chance he would make the same choice again.

14

"*You're here, aren't you?*" When Culber turned, Ephraim the tardigrade was by his side on the biobed. At a significantly smaller size than usual, though, so he could sit easily beside him.

"*To you, I am, yes.*"

"*How do you do that?*" Culber asked, indicating his size by dropping a leveled hand from one point to another.

"*A mental projection of my physical form is still just a mental projection.*"

Culber pointed his chin toward Commander Landry, who stood—refusing to sit—next to the biobed opposite them. "*Why not to anyone else? Other than me and Paul.*"

"Our *connection,*" Ephraim said, moving his topmost arms in a circle, "*is more than they can perceive or conceive.*"

"*I get why Paul can see you—or maybe feel you is more accurate—but how can I?*"

"*This plane connects us all.*" His arms spread wide. "*You are of this.*"

Blowing out a frustrated breath, Culber bent back his neck, then twisted back and forth, trying to stretch out its tension. "*I don't know what that means.*"

"*I know you don't,*" Ephraim said with great sincerity. "*But you have and you do and you will again.*"

Culber chuckled ironically. "*I would give anything if you never said that ever again.*"

His puckered mouth seemed to emit a chitter, an Ephraim laugh. *"I know you would. And—"*

"Stop."

"It wasn't my intention to cause you anxiety." Rolling his upper body, Ephraim seemed to demure. *"I thought I was being humorous."*

"Most people do." Culber pursed his lips, and noticed that Landry was watching him, her expression quizzical.

"Am I people?" the tardigrade asked.

With much of his Starfleet career spent on deep-space missions, Culber didn't hesitate to answer. *"Of course. 'People' doesn't necessarily describe only human beings. It's a word that just means sentient beings, really. Generic, if you know what I mean."*

"I believe I do." Pausing to consider it, Ephraim tapped his claws against themselves, alternating arms in a pattern that didn't seem random. *"I do not communicate with words, as you conceive them, but they're an interesting concept."*

"Ever?" Culber felt confusion play across his face, and thought Landry must have noticed that as well. *"How do you know you like the name Ephraim if you don't use words?"*

"I can hear. I like its sound."

"Do you like music?"

"All things," Ephraim said, spreading his arms wide again, seemingly to suggest the universe.

"That's not an answer," Culber said.

The spiky protrusions on Ephraim's head vibrated softly, and because he wasn't actually there, his bewilderment was more felt than seen. *"What is not music?"*

"Do you mean, 'what is music?'" Culber asked.

"What is not music?" Looking around, from the sickbay bulkheads and consoles to the sleeping, recovering patients, and even to Landry, on whom he didn't linger, Ephraim said, *"All of these are expressions of music. Are they not to you?"*

"No." Culber shifted his weight and reached for his training. *"But, there are people with something called synesthesia. They perceive the data from sense experience as . . . more. They may hear something as anyone else would, but also see it as colors."*

"Do you have this quality yourself?"

"No, I don't see music. I just enjoy its sound. It can make me feel things, think about things, but that's about it."

"But everything is music," Ephraim insisted.

Culber realized this was the most pleasant, calmest discussion he'd ever had with the tardigrade. Then again, he didn't really remember the vast majority of them. *"Nice music, I hope."*

"Often." Ephraim curved slightly, toward Landry. *"Not always."*

Recognition? While it was a different Ellen Landry than Culber had known, there was only one tardigrade they knew of. Therefore only one Ephraim, he assumed. *"In my memory, she hurt you and you killed her,"* Culber whispered, despite no one being able to hear him.

"I know this moment." The tardigrade wasn't exactly dismissive, but it was clear that the "melody" of that event had been discordant.

"But here . . . she's alive." Culber searched Ephraim's expression for some reaction, or rather he tried to feel whatever emotion was being projected.

"She is alive," the tardigrade agreed. *"And she isn't. She will be again, and she won't."*

The more time Culber spent on *Discovery*, the more his mental faculties returned. He found he had a clarity that had been sorely lacking on the mycelial plane. Now, able to examine the tardigrade more clearly, the doctor began to understand some of the being's nature. If Ephraim traversed the multiverse, then he, as perhaps the singular being who could do so, would see other beings in a completely different way. *"You understand that to her, this is her life? Her only life. And the one you killed . . . she's just gone."*

"Are you sure?" The tardigrade's tone was thick with emotion, perhaps akin to regret.

"Yeah, pretty sure." There was a time he'd have replied that he was absolutely positive. But his experiences of late, the ones he could remember, had Culber wondering if he was dead, or had been and was now alive again and . . . very little of it yet made sense. If there was a linear progression of events that might help give him certainty, it was elusive to him.

"I am sorry for that one," Ephraim said after a somber pause. *"But not for this one."* He snapped a claw toward the Landry just meters away.

"As difficult as the concept of a multiverse is for us," Culber said, *"I think so is the concept of a single universe for you."*

"There is no single universe."

"But we can only experience one universe at a time."

"And this makes you sad?"

"No," Culber said. *"How could it?"*

Ephraim's upper body rolled around and the emotion he broadcast felt foreign. *"How could it not?"*

For a long moment, they sat in silence as Culber considered the question. *"I had a patient once,"* he finally began, *"who was born to a telepathic race, but didn't have the ability herself. There's a stigma among her people about such an inability. She could work, she could learn, she could laugh and love. But she was pitied."*

"This story is sad," Ephraim said.

"Yes, it is. When she was nine years old, she wanted to be 'fixed' with a procedure that was supposed to give people a limited telepathy. An implanted stimulator would trigger certain neurotransmitters that— Well, I suppose the details aren't important."

"*Did it fix her?*"

"*I advised against the surgery. But she'd had a friend who was going to get the procedure too, and her parents wanted her to try, and . . . she just wanted to be like everyone else.*" A wave of melancholy washed between them, creating emotional eddies that Culber could actually feel.

"*Did it work?*" Ephraim was almost childlike in how he listened to a story. Full of curiosity and hope.

"*It was . . .*" Culber took a shaky breath before continuing. "*She'd never experienced telepathy before, so her brain couldn't interpret the information it received. It was all noise. Had she had years of training and practice, maybe she could have made sense of it . . . but she was only nine and thought the operation would instantly make her 'normal.' Those who didn't have the ability rejected her because she'd turned her back on them. And those she wanted to be like still didn't accept her.*"

"*Then it didn't help her,*" Ephraim morosely concluded.

"*I wouldn't say that, either. What she ultimately learned is that she* wasn't *broken in the first place. She eventually deactivated the stimulator and never used it again. She lost her desire to be anything other than who she was.*"

"*But she isn't telepathic,*" the tardigrade lamented.

Culber shrugged. "*Neither am I. Most sentient beings* aren't. *We don't miss what we never had.*"

"*This person,*" Ephraim said, indicating Ellen Landry with a gesture, "*she is much the same as the one who hurt me.*"

"*Do you have feelings about that?*" Culber asked. "*Do you want to hurt her?*" As Ephraim was only telepathically present, the question wasn't a concern for Landry so much as a point of curiosity.

The tardigrade shuddered. "*I never want to hurt anyone. Like any living entity, I have instincts and I reacted.*"

"*Do you know what those instincts are?*"

Chittering thoughtfully, Ephraim seemed uncertain. *"I suppose only once they come into use."*

"I guess that's true of us all."

Ephraim's mouth puckered and he radiated happiness again. *"Then I am a people?"*

Smiling lightly, Culber nodded. *"You certainly are to me."*

———

"Uh . . . hello?"

Commander Ellen Landry was briskly waving her hand a half meter in front of Culber's face and he pulled back, startled. "Excuse me?"

"You look like you're in the middle of a conversation, but no one's talking to you." She stood, muscles tightly coiled, seeming ready to strike, and when he slid off the table, she backed up only enough to allow it.

"I was lost in thought," he said.

"That's not how it looked."

"You're not the doctor—I am."

"Are you?"

Her skeptical expression bristled him and he marveled at how similar she was to the woman he knew in his own universe. "Yes," he said firmly, and with a measure of pride he'd not felt for some time. "I am."

"I checked on you, now that the computers are up." She paced away a few steps, then spun back. Her dark hair was pulled into a neat ponytail that swung around as she did. "Hugh Culber is a Starfleet doctor, but he's stationed on the *Hood*." Her mouth a flat line, she motioned around the sickbay with her right hand. "This is not the *Hood*."

"Therefore I'm not Hugh Culber?"

Landry rolled her eyes toward the ceiling for a brief moment, as if in thought—Culber wasn't convinced—then quickly zeroed back in on him. "Yeah, Doctor Pollard told me the whole alternate universe thing. So, no."

"Hmm." As rude and distrusting as she was, the only thing Culber felt was pity. Not for this reality's Landry, but for his own.

That feeling must have been immediately apparent, because she cast him a curious glare. "Why did you look at me like that?"

Unwilling to explain his regret at being unable to save her doppelganger in his universe, Culber glanced away. "I wasn't looking at you any special way—I promise."

She marched around the other side of the bed, into his line of sight. "Have we met before?"

"I don't know," he said facetiously. "Ever been to the *Hood*?"

"Funny," she said mirthlessly.

He returned her sneer.

She closed the distance between them, but the bed still kept them apart. It didn't help the tension, just bisected it. "Maybe the captain is buying your story. I'm not."

Culber leaned in. "That's fine. I'm not selling a story, Commander. No purchase necessary."

Before Landry could answer, Doctor Pollard entered. She first checked on the two other patients in their respective biobeds, then moved toward Landry and Culber.

Watching silently for a bit, Pollard then said, "Seems like I need a laser scalpel just to cut the tension."

Without moving his glare off Landry, Culber smirked. "Second storage cart on the left. Tray two, fifth tool over."

The doctor was taken aback. She glanced over, making sure the drawer wasn't open. "That's . . . correct."

Culber's expression turned smug. "I know."

Landry still wasn't convinced. "Oh, come on. You're from another universe, but we all store our medical equipment in the same place?"

He grinned. "Even the one where you're *not* a pain in the ass."

Clearly annoyed, Landry twisted back toward the biobed she'd been standing near. Pollard followed, running a medical tricorder across her. "Why're you scanning me?" the security chief demanded.

"After that exchange? Making sure you don't need the burn unit." Pollard smirked and shared a quick wink with Culber before motioning Landry to sit on the bed.

"Don't piss me off any more than I already am, Doctor."

Unfazed, Pollard continued to run her scan. "You left without Doctor Schanne releasing you."

"I'm fine."

Reviewing the data, Pollard scoffed, "Didn't you say that three months ago *before* I patched up that phaser blast in your leg?"

"And?"

"And, since you're here, you will stay here until I say otherwise. That's an order."

Landry crossed her arms and grunted unhappily, but didn't get up as Pollard moved away.

"Be grateful I'm not tying you down," the doctor called back to Landry, but her tone was gentler with Culber as she then ran her scanner over him. "With the main computer back on line, we may be able to get some more conclusive"—she looked up at the monitor, back down at her scanner, then tripled-checked what she saw—"results."

The display above Culber's biobed made an odd *blip-blip* he'd never heard before, and he moved toward the screen. "It shouldn't do that."

"No, it shouldn't," Pollard said.

From across the room, Landry asked, "What exactly is it doing?"

"I don't know . . ." Pollard kept the scanner in one hand and grabbed a padd in her other, then scrolled through a rush of incoming data.

"May I?" Culber asked, looking to the padd.

She hesitated.

"I'm a doctor," Culber said earnestly, "and it's about me."

Still uncertain, Pollard pursed her lips and shot a look at Landry, who, without verbally disagreeing, seemed to say *don't* with every muscle in her face.

"Tracy . . ." he said.

"Sorry. We don't know each other well enough to be on a first-name basis." Pollard returned to reviewing the data.

"No," Culber said, deflated. "I guess we don't." He wondered if he could possibly fit into this universe, assuming they'd be able to exit the mycelial plane. It would be like starting his life all over again.

Could he?

When Pollard glanced up from the padd, he was still looking at her hopefully, and something in his gaze must have changed her mind. "Okay, you win. Here." She handed it to him.

Shocked, Culber felt his face flush and his neck tighten. "Huh."

Landry joined them. "Let me see." She held out her hand.

"No," Pollard replied. "It's not a security matter. It's just an anomaly."

Culber glanced at Landry. He respected her perhaps-too-healthy skepticism, despite its being leveled at him. "It shows an odd amino-acid sequence in my makeup," he told her. "That's all."

"He's not human," Landry said.

"Oh, yes he is," Pollard replied.

Landry folded her arms across her chest as she looked from Pollard to Culber and back. "Then what's it about?"

"Burnham will—" Culber began.

The security chief corrected him immediately. "*Captain* Burnham."

"*Captain* Burnham will want to know," he said. "Paul too."

"Why Stamets?" Landry asked, eyes narrowing.

"Stick around," he told her. "It's about to get interesting."

———

Doctor Pollard had requested that both Captain Burnham and Lieutenant Stamets come to sickbay, but Stamets arrived first. Were it possible to burst through a self-opening door, he would have. "What's wrong?"

"Nothing," Culber assured him. Stamets noticed Hugh had trimmed his beard closer and more defined than the sickbay staff had when they initially cleaned the biota out of his more scraggly appearance. And his hair was tightly buzzed as well. He looked good—damn good, as a matter of fact. Fit, healthier than before.

"There's something you need to see," Culber said, handing Stamets the padd with Doctor Pollard's results.

"Oh," Stamets said quietly, swiping through the data. "Oh. That's . . . yeah, that is interesting."

Commander Landry stepped toward them, her hand out. "I think this sounds like a security issue, Lieutenant."

Ignoring the comment, Stamets's focus was on the possibilities raised, and on Culber. "Doctor Pollard is sure about this?"

"I reran it myself before you got here." Culber turned toward Landry, but Stamets pulled his attention back.

"Hugh, it probably doesn't mean anything."

"Everything means something," Culber said.

"What means what?" Landry said, a note of exasperation creeping into her tone. Still considering possibilities for the readings, Stamets ignored her again. If Culber was planning to reply, she didn't give him the chance. "What am I, dead to you both?"

When Stamets finally glanced up from the padd, Culber seemed frozen as he stared back at Landry's narrowed gaze. Stamets didn't understand what was going on between the two, but Culber looked like he needed a life preserver thrown to him. Luckily, just the thing popped into Stamets's head.

"Hey, are you hungry?" he asked.

The question seemed to snap Culber out of his blank stare. "Right now?"

"No, I'm not asking you to dinner. Though I *completely* would," he said. Suddenly he flashed on a mental image of them both enjoying a meal somewhere. Casually, easily. Stamets could feel such a moment, and that same déjà vu washed over him. "What I mean is: When's the last time you remember eating when you were stuck in the mycelial forest?"

Bouncing a thumb lightly against his chin, Culber tried to recall. "Honestly, I don't know."

Pollard and her staff would have ensured their patient was eating properly once aboard, but that's not what Stamets was curious about. Before anyone could inquire further, however, the doors to the corridor parted and Michael Burnham strode through them.

"Captain," Landry greeted her, clearly wanting to have the first word.

Burnham held up a hand and focused on her astromycologist just as Doctor Pollard entered from the lab. "Report."

"We've found a potentially significant . . ." Pollard began.

"There are some amino-acid sequences in Hugh's cyto-chrome C that match what we'd usually find in certain fungal organisms," Stamets finished for her, handing the captain the padd and indicating the highlighted data.

Landry cleared her throat irritably. "I'm not familiar with that."

"Cytochrome C is a hemoprotein that usually conducts transfers between mitochondrial membranes," Culber ex-plained.

"Do you have a theory?" Burnham asked.

"What if Hugh has existed here as long as he has because he's absorbed certain amino acids present in the environ-ment?" Stamets said. "It could mean the yeel tree bark is just a salve, and his molecular makeup is what's helped him survive. We'd then need to investigate a similar combination for the ship." He gestured to Culber and hoped his growing excite-ment for the research and the time they could spend together wasn't too obvious. "With permission, I'd like to run some tests on him in the spore lab."

"Doctor?" Burnham asked Pollard. "You ran those comparisons I requested?"

"I did. Psychosimulator, engram, hyperencephalogram tests are all within human norms. However, they are not exact matches for the references on file." She let that sink in. "Inter-estingly, they fit the variable patterns found in identical twins."

Burnham considered the doctor's findings, then asked, "Any issue with Doctor Culber leaving your care?"

"None."

Either because Commander Landry's body English tele-graphed her opposition, or because the captain herself had reservations, Burnham asked her, "Any objection?"

"Actually, I don't." The security officer glanced affably toward Culber, the first expression of kindness she'd shown him. "I see no reason he needs to be confined."

One brow raised, Burnham was genuinely surprised. "Okay."

Somewhat taken aback himself, Stamets began to leave, but Culber tapped his arm lightly, holding him back.

"Why?" Culber asked Landry.

"*You* tried to answer my question," she told him simply, with a quick frown directed at Stamets.

Culber offered her a warm look. "Sorry if it didn't help."

"I'm more a physics type than a biology type."

"They're really the same—" Stamets began, ready to proselytize.

Culber gave the other man a short shake of his head. "Not the time."

"The point is," Landry said, her tone making it clear she didn't care to hear another Stamets science lecture, "people who're hiding things: they hide. You didn't. You're trying to figure it all out with us."

"Thank you," he murmured, then followed Stamets out of sickbay.

15

"You're different," Culber told Stamets. He kept himself from reaching for him, because in truth he'd only known *this* Stamets for a matter of hours. Still, his ability to separate the man in front of him from his own universe's version was proving difficult. Removed from his husband for so long—he just wasn't sure how much time had passed—there was a great temptation to convince himself this Stamets was the one he loved.

"I'm just distracted." Stamets gestured around the lab with the scanner he was running over Culber's torso. "There's a lot going on. On a *good* day, there are usually a hundred thousand and seven things bouncing around my head. Right now, I think it's a million and seven."

Culber found himself bathed in a radiated pleasure he'd not felt for so long. "That's a lot of thoughts."

Stamets glanced up, and their eyes met. "Many of them about you."

"You're a charmer."

Scanner still in hand, Stamets made a so-so hand motion. "Pretty sure the only context in which I could be called that involves my coaxing a snake from a basket with a flute."

An honest laugh bubbled from Culber's throat.

"Wait," Stamets asked. "Did you mean I'm different than earlier, or different than *your*—the other me?"

"Both." His cheeks began to ache from maintaining such

a cheerful grin. It was a pleasant contrast from the burns the JahSepp usually inflicted.

"*This* is interesting." Stamets studied the tricorder readings, then moved to the nearby console, pulling up the data.

"I assume you'll share." Culber stepped closer and studied the display. "Interesting? More like weird."

"Human genetically, but the body chemistry . . ." Stamets highlighted a section of the scan, pulling it forward and magnifying it. "Altered somehow."

"I see it. The genetics *are* right—"

"But the amino acid and enzyme ratios are off." Stamets tapped at the screen, then turned to Culber. "This may be why you don't remember eating. I think, like a mushroom, you were processing sustenance from the environment around you."

"The yeel bark?"

"Maybe. Maybe." He brought up his analysis of the tree's composition. It did have most of the nutrients a human would need, given the altered chemistry of Culber's biology. "What changed you? How *did* you get here?" Stamets asked.

"You," he replied. "You found me." Their eyes met again, this time more deeply, and even though the doctor's answer was metaphorical, there was a fundamental truth within it that he felt down to his atoms.

"Your eyes are very brown," Stamets said. "Almost black."

"Yeah." Culber's voice felt thick, barely above a rasp. Would a kiss be wrong? He just wanted to feel Paul, to connect with him. And yet Culber couldn't help but think it was a betrayal.

Was it?

It was always about the eyes for his Stamets too. And it didn't matter if it was the right universe or not—these were Paul's eyes he was gazing into.

Looking away, Stamets saw Lieutenant Nilsson working on

something at the alternate console. Instinctively, he and Culber backed away from each other, unwilling to share publicly what each must have sensed the other was feeling.

"I don't mean today—how you got to the ship," Stamets explained, his voice a wobble.

"I know what you mean." Culber shook his head. "You still found me," he whispered.

"That makes zero sense."

"I know. I'm sorry." Culber reached far back into his memory, as best he could. He found a jumble of images: fragments and flashes—some painful, some frustrating, many joyful and jubilant. But no memory of how he had arrived on the mycelial plane. "It might have something to do with you. Or rather *my* Paul."

There was an immediate change in Stamets's expression. A distance, a disappointment? "I assume you want to go back. To your Paul, I mean."

The question caught Culber off guard. He'd been so confused by the day's events, the recovery of his identity and many of his memories, that the thought honestly hadn't occurred to him. The allure of people being around him again—anyone, let alone familiar faces—had been such an overwhelming experience that he hadn't even considered there might be a path back to his own universe. "I . . . yes. Is that possible?"

"I'm not sure." Stamets looked away, shy. "It's not horrible, if you're stuck with me, is it?"

This was a Paul Stamets that Culber had rarely seen. It's not that there wasn't an insecure part to the man he'd married, but he didn't show it to most people. This Stamets . . . he was more unassuming. He could fill a room with personality without it crushing down on those around him.

"I can think of worse things," Culber said softly, and began to reach his hand forward.

Before he could connect, Stamets moved to a console Culber couldn't remember having seen before. Another difference between the universes?

Bringing up the mycelial navigation map, Paul pointed to the blank areas. "Just because I don't know a way to your universe today doesn't mean there isn't one to find."

Examining the intricacy and beauty of the map, Culber marveled at the work and the man behind it. Perhaps every Paul Stamets in every universe was brilliant, always looking to learn. "You're a devoted scientist," he said, just to have a topic that wasn't about leaving the comfort this place was beginning to give him.

"I love science. Not enough to snuggle under a blanket with it, mind you. Which isn't to say my enjoyment of it isn't part of the very fiber of my identity. But it's just the means to an end."

"Really?" Culber was pretty sure there were some nights his Stamets would've been content to snuggle with his work under a blanket. "Then what are you devoted to? What's the 'end' that science gives you?"

"Creating easier ways to explore? And just . . . figuring out life, and saving it? As much and as often as possible." The attitude was pure Paul Stamets, not the bitter-tinged man that Culber had watched him become after the Klingon War began. Stamets and Justin Straal had joined Starfleet to further space exploration on every possible level. They hoped to unlock the mysteries of the universe. Then all-out war twisted their research—their life's work—into a tactic rather than a tool of discovery.

Not here, Culber realized. *Not here*. "You joined Starfleet for very noble reasons. Perhaps nobler than mine."

"What were yours? You're a doctor, so I assumed it was to heal the sick."

"I could do that anywhere. I didn't have to be in Starfleet. I suppose I wanted adventure and saw it as a way to merge that with my passion for medicine." He pursed his lips thoughtfully. "Got more than I bargained for."

"I've noticed, especially lately, that events in life seem indifferent to my plans."

Culber realized that his husband's counterpart was so like the man he married that he, too, had found himself in Starfleet. *What if my own doppelganger had been less rude to him?* Would they be together, here on the *Discovery*, creating a very awkward circumstance for them all?

"Are you happy?" Culber asked, wondering what this Stamets's life was truly like. He was alone, just as *his* Stamets would be if Culber stayed in this universe.

Considering it a long moment, the astromycologist finally said, "Happy-ish? Happy-esque? Sometimes you don't know you're not as happy, until you figure out what's missing."

"And what's missing?"

Stamets took Culber's hand and squeezed it tightly. "Maybe 'the road not taken.'"

His hand. In mine. Here and now.

Except it wasn't. All the history Culber could remember with his Stamets hadn't happened here. Could that in any way be forgotten?

Stamets released his grip and returned both hands to the computer console.

"Have you ever been to the Met?" Culber asked.

"Metropolitan Museum of Art? New York City?" Stamets eyed the ceiling. "Hmm. Let me think . . ."

"I think you'd remember," Culber assured him, but was skeptical about what seemed like classic Paul sarcasm.

"Oh, I know I haven't." The other shoe dropped. "I'm trying to think of something more boring."

Culber smirked. "Having any luck?" In a tense situation, Stamets's penchant for acerbity could be nails on a chalkboard. Somehow Culber had missed that—it was as warm and comforting as his hand had been.

Except this isn't my Paul.

"A class on Vulcan calligraphy? Probably just as boring," Stamets said.

Culber accepted that *would* be dull. "Okay."

"Denevan worm farming?"

"That's a thing?"

"There's a kind of worm on Deneva where the larval form takes over a decade to gestate."

"Fun. Can't believe I called you charming."

"I'm charming in mysterious ways." He stuck a finger into the air. "Wait, I have it! Klingon mah-jongg."

"That's *not* a thing."

"But you can picture how it would be, right?"

Culber made a trigger motion with one hand. "Probably not boring."

"Point taken."

While the sarcasm was there, there was also a layer of vulnerable shyness that Culber couldn't deny had enhanced this Stamets's allure. A softer demeanor made him seem more emotionally present.

At least that was what Culber saw in the other man's face: friendly, bright eyes and . . . a look of hope.

"What are you thinking?" Culber wondered aloud, and assumed he might be told about the scientific data Stamets was working on.

Hesitating as he took in a deep breath, Stamets's tone was full of regret. "That I shouldn't have been rude to you when we first met."

Culber wanted to say that wasn't him, but it was in a way.

At least, Ephraim showed them that he and this universe's Culber were much the same.

That was a fascinating, chilling, exhilarating notion. How many universes were there? An infinite number? For every decision Culber made, was there a universe where a different but similar man made another choice, and another, and another, and sprouted a universe for each?

He suddenly realized that such speculation was less alluring than what he might learn about this universe's Paul Stamets.

"If you don't care for art, what about music?" Culber asked.

Continuing to run his computer simulations, Stamets sniffed. "I've never had much of a connection to either." He then pulled the data card from the console and offered a pleasant smile. "Can you excuse me? I need Nilsson to look this over."

Interestingly, in his own universe, Culber's husband also didn't have—prior to their meeting—much of a relationship with art or music. He'd found beauty mostly in nature and science. Which is why their visits to certain museums and various concerts had been some of Culber's most treasured memories. He'd helped his Paul find the connection between their respective notions of artistic expression. And that journey with the man he loved had been sheer joy.

———

"Then you remember those events?" Ephraim asked.

Culber curved around to find the tardigrade inside the reaction cube. *"You're back. Again."*

"I never left," Ephraim said. *"And I was never here."* He studied the cube and groaned. *"I remember this place."*

"Yes," Culber whispered, the memory of the tardigrade's anguish radiating from the chamber.

"But you also remember much of your life now, yes?"

"I do, yes. Strongly." He could see it clearly now, wide swaths of time, memories, more focused than even an hour before.

"I am pleased," Ephraim said.

"Paul can't see you?"

"He is not looking."

Stamets glanced toward them. *"He just looked over here."*

"You know it's not your eyes that see me. I am here," the tardigrade protested. *"But I am also not, and will be, and won't."* He made his rolling, shrugging movement. *"There is no other way to explain it."*

"So you're here, and not here?" Culber questioned.

"Yes, you understand."

"No, I really don't."

Ephraim stepped through the closed reaction cube door. *"This is our home. We are of this place."*

Culber shook his head. *"I am not of—"*

"We are of this place," the tardigrade insisted.

"'We' as in you, and the spores? Or you and Paul? Or as in you and me?"

"I do not understand." Ephraim crooked his head askew, a gesture he may have learned from humans. As with most of his mimicked mannerisms, it seemed too purposeful and a tad off.

"Sometimes I think you're not really here at all."

The tardigrade moved toward him. *"Then what am I?"*

"Maybe my brain created you as a sounding board. Maybe all this"—Culber waved his hand to indicate their surroundings—*"is that too. The network can create images to make us more comfortable, can't it?"*

"Yes," Ephraim agreed. *"If you are embraced."*

"Am I?"

"You are of this place," the tardigrade said again. *"You were brought to this place and are of this place."*

Culber clenched his teeth. *"How can both be true?"*

"It is true, and not true, and—"

"Okay, I shouldn't have asked."

"I did not come to unease you." Ephraim sidled up beside him and seemed as if he was about to put his head on Culber's shoulder.

The doctor backed up a step. *"Then why did you?"*

"The opposite."

Culber took in a steadying breath. *"Okay. So, set me at ease. Give me your advice: Am I wrong to feel guilty? This Paul . . . I know he's not* my *Paul, but in many ways he is the equal of the man I love."*

"Completely?" Ephraim asked.

"No. There're a few ways in which this Paul is more . . . I can't describe it. Emotionally accessible, I guess." He sighed. *"Did fate put me in a situation where I'd find a Paul like mine, but . . ."* Culber couldn't bring himself to say *better*, but it was the word that came to mind. *"Did I die in my universe, only to end up in this one, with a gentler, kinder Paul?"*

"Explain fate.*"*

"That there's a set order that must occur." Culber hadn't believed in fate until he and Stamets fell in love, and then he decided it was the one thing in the universe that was meant to be.

But . . . that universe was gone to him. He was now in a new one.

"I do not understand, but I see things from a different perspective than you," the tardigrade told him. *"You are special. Your life-form type sees things singularly, linearly. I cannot. It is not my nature. Your existence, your perceptions . . . they are beauty to me. They are music."* He patted the man's arm with a claw. *"Muuusic."*

"*Thank you?*" Culber said, awkwardly appreciative of the admiration. "*That's not exactly advice, though.*"

"*I have studied you, and while I still have a great deal to learn, I think I know enough to impart this: Live your moments as you can, my friend.*" Ephraim puckered and lolled his head around. "*Accept happiness as you find it. Hold it as long as possible. Because for you, some moments have yet to happen, and some are gone forever. For this you have my pity, and my awe.*"

"*That's actually pretty cogent advice.*" He was warmed by the guidance, but that didn't mean it helped. He still felt the weight of guilt when he watched Stamets.

This Stamets.

This *other* Stamets.

How could being with him not be a betrayal?

———

"I think we've got it," Stamets said, waving a yellow data card in his hand. "I—" He stopped, suddenly, and stared at where Ephraim had been just a moment before. "What the hell?"

Culber turned, and saw it too. A hazy, misty sparkle, roughly the shape of two humanoid forms. They were more solid than last time. "I see it," he said.

"Nilsson?" Stamets called over to the lieutenant. "Do you see this?"

She looked around the lab. "No, still nothing, sir. Just like last time."

Pulling out his communicator, Stamets flipped it open and it chirped to life. "Stamets to bridge—intruders in the spore-drive section."

16

Captain Michael Burnham and her first officer arrived just moments after the security detail headed up by Commander Landry.

"Phasers on stun," Burnham told them, then waved them all through. Weapons in hand, she and Landry took the lead. The three remaining security officers went next, and Saru followed.

"Fan out," the captain ordered, motioning Landry and the others to positions around the upper level of the lab. She and Saru marched down the steps to Culber, Stamets, and Nilsson.

"I don't see anyone," Burnham said.

Nilsson held up her tricorder. "This does."

Holstering her phaser, the captain made a beeline for the lieutenant. "Show me."

Letting Burnham view the tricorder's display, Nilsson offered the entire device to her but the captain waved it off. The visual was enough: the same energy signature seen before.

"What do *you* see, Mister Stamets?" Saru asked.

"More than before," he answered. "Last time it was just one sketchy form of shadow and light."

"And now?" Burnham searched the room.

"More than we saw in sickbay," Culber said. "Many more."

She glanced up to Landry on the upper level. "How many more?"

Stamets said, "Seven? Maybe ten."

"And yet, we've not been attacked," Burnham said, mostly to Saru. "And you sense . . . ?"

"No danger." He put up a lithe finger. "That does not mean there is none. Merely that I don't sense any."

Most days, his intuition was good enough for her. "Positive news, Mister Saru."

"I think I have more of that, Captain," Stamets said, his face an odd mix of excitement and trepidation. "With the tricorder adjustments, we're also reading our mycelial spores."

This time Burnham took Nilsson's tricorder when it was offered. She confirmed the reading: their spores weren't gone . . . just mysteriously inaccessible. "Explain this in a way I'll understand."

Stamets took the tricorder from her hands and placed it on the console next to them. The data transferred from the unit, filling the display. He pointed to three different data streams, moving too quickly for even Burnham to follow. "These power signatures are expressly—exquisitely—from the *Prototaxites stellaviatori* spores. Since external sensors have found none of that variety in this area of the mycelial plane, they *must* be the spores that we had, or *have*."

"Fascinating." Burnham accepted that, but it wasn't the explanation she'd asked for. "Now, tell me how."

"Something has—I don't know how to describe it— tweaked their energy signatures on a quantum level." Punctuating the idea with a gesture, he moved his thumb and index finger together, then slowly pulled them apart. "Separating them from our visual spectrum, and in fact out of normal sensor frequencies."

The captain glanced around the room as if a hard look might reveal the now invisible spores. She was staggered by the thought of how much power it would take to manifest that change. "I don't believe that's possible as a natural occurrence."

"It would be new to me. You?" Stamets asked Nilsson.

"Nothing I've heard of," she said, and looked at Culber.

"I'm a doctor. Theoretical physics isn't my thing. Sorry."

The captain pulled out her communicator. "Burnham to the bridge."

"Bridge, Airiam here."

"Have you and Mister Rhys completed sensor modifications for the DASH lab and cultivation bay locations?"

"No, Captain—a burned-out relay in that section has caused a delay. We've dispatched a damage-control team to replace it. We were completing modifications on the tricorders, given the sensor data we previously experienced."

"Understood, Commander." Burnham paced from the console to the reaction cube. "Give Owosekun the conn and join us down here. I'd like you to modify the sensors yourself, on site." Waiting for a repair team wouldn't be optimal.

"Acknowledged."

"Burnham out." She flipped the communicator closed. "Nilsson, work with Airiam when she arrives, please. We need those upgrades." Both officers were more familiar with the complex circuitry than any repair team would be. Hopefully it would speed things along.

"Aye, Captain."

"Is it possible," Burnham asked Stamets, "that *all* the readings we're getting are the spores?" She didn't want to insult the sensibilities of her astromycologist, but noted that Culber was the first to mention *others*, and perhaps his influence was at play. That was why the captain needed the internal sensors fine-tuned. While instrumentation was fallible, it was either showing something or it wasn't—it didn't interpret the data through a human brain, which by its nature sought patterns in all manner of otherwise random elements. "Could your impression of humanoid forms be mistaken?"

Stamets reflected on the question a moment. "Let's try this." He strode to the upper level and opened a storage compartment next to Landry. Removing a cylindrical handheld device Burnham didn't recognize, he pushed buttons on it for a moment.

The captain watched, but also noticed her chief of security was tensing, regripping her phaser a couple times. *One too many coffees*, Burnham thought.

The doors from the corridor opened and Airiam walked in. The captain gestured her down to join them.

"This," Stamets informed them, stepping back down to the lower level, "is a luminal resonator." He pointed it toward the drive control console. "We use it to check for leaks in the spore injection conduits. I've reset it to change its resonance wavelength on a looping cycle. Hopefully it'll find the right one." He waved their respective gazes away with his free hand. "Don't look at me." He thumbed the device's trigger. "Look everywhere else."

Once activated, several bursts of energy emanated in a series of now-visible white rings around the circumference of the instrument. Stamets held it high above his head.

Illuminated by the annoying strobe that stung her eyes and forced everyone but Airiam into a painful squint, Burnham saw several flashes that revealed a thick mist of spores shimmering through the air. Higher concentrations lay in meter-high tube-like shapes along the deck. More importantly were the areas without the sparkling spores: humanoid shapes seen in silhouette against the luminescent backglow.

Her eyes beginning to water against the strain, the captain shielded her face with a forearm. "That's good," she said, her voice a little louder than probably needed. "Shut it down."

Stamets flicked the switch and the forms disappeared.

"Okay," Burnham said, looking to the deck where she'd

seen the tube-shaped mass of spore-sparkle. "Hypothesize with me: If aliens are here, but we cannot see them, can't experience them perceptually—at least naturally—is this their normal state or did they create it to hide themselves from us?" She looked around the lab, making eye contact with each crew-member, welcoming input from all. This wasn't the first time they'd asked that question, but now they had new information.

"You know my vote," Landry grimly said.

"I'm not looking for votes," the captain said calmly but with a firm edge. "I want suppositions we can test, not conclusions set in stone."

A slight nod was the security chief's apology. "Suppose it's purposeful. We get a message Mister Stamets thinks is a distress call, maybe sent by them. They need the same type of spores we use. The call is the trap. As soon as we arrive, they pull our spores into their perceptive range."

Them. There were two ways to see any *them*, either as a threat or an opportunity. And Starfleet captains were supposed to turn the former into the latter.

"To what end?" Saru asked. "To steal them?"

"It *would* explain the cylindrical collections of spores I saw," Burnham said, eyeing the deck where she'd seen the columns of sparkle. She'd witnessed the beauty of the cultivation bay, and the mycelial forest now outside their ship, but the resonator device, even if painful, illuminated every spore, not just those naturally energized. It was like the physical manifestation of light, right before them. "I've never seen anything like it," she breathed.

"I have," Airiam said.

The captain spun toward her. "You have?"

"My ocular implants at times require adjustment. Fine-tuning them will occasionally make anyone I see look the way Mister Stamets and Doctor Culber described the humanoid forms."

"Why did we only see them in silhouette?" Saru asked.

"It's a luminal resonator I designed for a specific task," Stamets replied. "It's only made to interact with our spores, not *any* organic material. It's not some alien black light."

"Perhaps it would be possible to adjust my implants to see them," Airiam said.

Before Burnham could offer her opinion, Culber spoke: "Yes, it might."

The captain leveled her gaze at him, prompting him to continue.

"I would need Paul's—Mister Stamets's help," he added. "But I don't see why it shouldn't be possible, given the capabilities of her implants and neural interface."

There was a silence that followed as Burnham mulled over the offer. Her glance at Airiam suggested that, if nothing else, she wasn't against the idea. What else played on her features was hard to say.

"It wouldn't hurt her," Culber said, perhaps if only to break the quiet consideration.

"I am willing," Airiam said.

The captain wasn't sure she should be.

Apparently neither was Lieutenant Nilsson, who asked, "Begging the captain's pardon, but how is *he* aware of the capabilities of Commander Airiam's implants?"

"I, uh . . ." He hesitated and looked to Burnham.

She gave him a look that said *it's up to you.* If Culber wanted to offer his alternate universe explanation to a wider audience, she wasn't going to stop him.

"I'm familiar with the technology in use," he said finally. "There would be no danger," he told Airiam and the captain more explicitly.

"We can try it," Burnham said. "You and Mister Stamets can confer with Doctor Pollard, who'll perform the actual procedure. She's *more* familiar with Commander Airiam's augmentations."

"If I am to go to the sickbay," Airiam said, indicating both men, "who will help Lieutenant Nilsson with sensor repair and modification?"

Burnham glanced to Saru.

"I would be delighted to assist the lieutenant," he said, gliding toward her.

As Stamets and Culber followed Airiam up the stairs toward the exit, the captain made eye contact with Commander Landry. "I want you to stay here."

The security chief waited until the doors swished closed again. "It's one thing to trust him walking around." She jerked her head toward the general direction of the corridor and Culber. "But do you trust him *this* much?"

Burnham rubbed her forehead and scratched at an eyebrow. "Let's say I don't *distrust* him."

"What's the difference?"

"He hasn't given me reason to doubt him, but 'I don't know' is sometimes cover for 'I don't want *you* to know.' Why don't you give me your gut opinion." The captain skimmed toward where the other woman stood on the upper ring.

"My gut trusts him, but only so far." The security chief leaned down on the rail, her expression more mellow than usual, which alone said a lot. "But you don't always listen to my gut."

"I always listen," Burnham said. "I don't necessarily act on it."

"Rank hath its privileges." Landry made an acquiescent shrug.

"And its burdens," the captain reminded her, worrying again about how far the blood-burn outbreak had progressed on Benecia.

—

Upon entering sickbay, Culber noticed the recovery room had only three patients, and the inner exam/treatment room was empty. Comforting, in that it meant casualties were well enough they could be released, but also because it had pained him to see them and sit by, unable to help. Since remembering he *was* a doctor, that had been the most powerful reminder he was out of place on this *Discovery*; he wasn't allowed to treat anyone.

Until now. At least if he could assist in reconfiguring Airiam's augmentations, he might feel even more like himself.

The three of them met Doctor Pollard in her office.

"Doctor," Stamets began.

"I know. The captain already informed me."

Pollard looked to Airiam. "You're sure about this? Stuck here, should something go wrong, I don't have replacements."

"If it can help," she told Pollard, "then I must."

"Not if you're being pressured."

"It was my idea, Doctor," Airiam assured her. "I appreciate your concern, but I'm convinced I'll be in good hands."

Culber could see why she would have confidence in Stamets and Pollard. But her trust in him was interesting. Intuition? Faith? He'd talked often with his version of Airiam, and she was a woman of interesting beliefs. Not in mystical or superstitious ways, though. Culber had told her once that his parents were going through a difficult stretch, as he understood all marriages did. She'd said, *I hope it works out.* He'd told her she needn't worry, that he was sure they'd stay together, and he was just worried about the stress on them all.

But Airiam had explained, *"Works out" can also mean they don't stay together. It just means "what's best for all."*

That was her brand of optimism, and maybe it grew from her

personal trials, or more likely was what saw her through them. Of course, that was his universe's Airiam, not this one . . . and yet was there really a difference? If they'd had the same general lives, give or take this or that incident, weren't they fundamentally the same? Perhaps he was beginning to see it as Ephraim did.

"Since you're sure . . ." Pollard led them to the main treatment bay.

Culber went directly for the cart with the tools he'd need and removed the proper tray of devices. "You don't need to be sedated. Just relax. But you will feel a bit of a vibration or a buzzing, prob—"

Pollard took the tray of medical implements from his hands. "No."

Annoyed, he tried not to glare at the woman who'd been his friend and colleague for almost— No, from her perspective, she'd only met him today. "I'll need to configure these before you perform the adjustments," Culber explained. He understood Pollard's uncertainty, even though it grated on him. The only person who accepted him fully . . . was Stamets.

Releasing the devices back to him, Pollard's expression softened. "Of course."

She guided Airiam to a biobed and situated it into a sitting position as Culber showed Stamets the first of three devices to adjust.

Usually, when he was working so closely with Stamets, it was to treat him after some harebrained mushroom scheme that had gotten him injured or ill. *This*, Culber thought, *is a nice change of pace.*

Once Stamets was finished, he placed them on the tray, which Culber brought to Pollard.

"I assume this is like a normal adjustment process?" Airiam's tone sounded a bit uneasy.

"It's just a little different. Nothing you need to worry

about. You'll be fine." Culber brought up the diagnostic monitor on her upper body, then centered it on her head.

"I'll be in charge of the procedure," Pollard reminded him. "Captain's orders."

He nodded, and handed her the first of the instruments. "It's your show, Doctor."

Taking the first of the manipulators, Pollard placed it at Airiam's left temple. "Usually this is a thirty-second procedure."

"It's further along the frequency band, so it may take a little longer," Culber told her.

Above them, the biobed monitor displayed the slow modulation of her left ocular implant input. Once out of expected range, the indicator began to flash red.

"That alert is expected," Culber told Airiam as much as Pollard. "It's just not within your usual parameters. It's fine."

"If it helps," Airiam said, "I can't see the screen."

Culber and Pollard shared a small smile. Sometimes patients as easy as Airiam were hard to come by.

"A little more," Stamets said, closely watching the wavelength. "Do you feel anything?"

"Hungry?" Airiam said.

Culber knew she'd had more than her share of medical procedures and that another one was not a big deal to her. Still, a doctor tended to treat each time as if it were the patient's first.

Often, when he'd had to treat his husband, Culber had left his bedside manner out of the equation. It was why a physician wasn't supposed to treat relatives. On a starship, that could be a difficult ask.

As Doctor Pollard completed one eye and began on the other, Culber took Airiam's hand. The more time he spent with these people he knew so well (even if they did not know him), the more of a connection he felt.

Looking at the Paul Stamets next to him, Culber found it hard to imagine them having cross moments. Then that heavy pang of guilt struck again. These weren't his friends any more than this was his ship, or his universe.

But he could see it all becoming his, given time. And he could *feel* Stamets—more than his physical presence, but the same palpable aura of kindness, humor, and honesty he fell in love with. That sharp edge of wit, which could cut tension as often as it stoked it, was also there, if a bit softer.

It wasn't just his relationship that felt fresh. Maybe it was Captain Gabriel Lorca's absence, or Michael Burnham being in command, that offered an invigorating lack of tension. The captaincy suited her. In this universe, she'd never mutinied and destroyed her career. *Standoff at the Binary Stars*, Saru had called it. What happened here was so different. If he stayed, would he be forever playing catch-up on such small details?

He could live with that.

"I think we're done?" Pollard said, placing the last instrument back on the tray.

Culber gave Airiam's hand a last squeeze before letting go. Pollard helped her off the bed. "How do you feel?"

"Fine. I don't see anything out of the ordinary." She blinked a few times, looking around the room. "Well, I do see a few sparkles. Spores?"

"Probably," Stamets said. "Let's get back to the lab."

———

In the months since Airiam had served under her, Michael Burnham had never heard her gasp in shock. Until now.

"What do you see?" The captain forced herself not to uselessly look around.

"I think I see what Mister Stamets did." She moved down

the lab steps to the lower deck, lightly waving her hands, fingers trilling through the air as she did. "Definitely mycelial spores here."

Burnham had never seen Airiam move so fluidly, so ethereally. "What about the intruders?"

"Fragmented . . . globular . . ." She rotated around slowly, looking everywhere but seemingly focused on nothing in particular. "They're here. Like blobs but . . . segmented into humanoid—if ill-defined—forms." She spoke breathlessly, amazed by it all, and yet the reverberated sound of her vocal processor made her tone sound harsher than her words indicated. "Canisters are being gathered." She bent at the knees and felt around the floor. "It's like pushing through a hologram. I see it, but I can't feel it."

"They *are* gathering the spores?" Stamets asked.

"I believe so," Airiam said, still fluttering her fingers through thin air. She looked like a child trying to catch a dust mote in a sunbeam. "They, and the spores, are absolutely outside our tactile and visual range."

"They somehow pulled the spores out of phase with us, and our own containment apparatus . . ." The captain gestured to their empty storage rack. "Which flooded the ship with spores we now can't see or collect."

"They," Airiam said, presumably moving her hand through one of the alien forms, "are definitely collecting them."

"We need to find a way to pull the spores back into our quantum wavelength," Stamets said. "Or we'll be stuck here until we die."

"Trust me," Culber mumbled, "the last thing you want is to be stuck *here*."

17

Captain's log, supplemental. *With modifications to internal sensors complete, Commander Saru and Lieutenant Rhys have verified we have intruders on multiple decks. Given her modified implants, Lieutenant Commander Airiam has been dispatched with Commander Landry on security detail for a deck-by-deck search. The question foremost on my mind: Are the intruders here to sabotage our vessel, take our spore supply, or both?*

"Captain?" Saru approached Burnham with his usual aplomb. "Engineering reports no signs of sabotage. Remaining repairs are proceeding; however, we are beginning to register more degradation of the outer hull."

Burnham rose and circled around her chair, hands clasped behind her back. When she had more questions than answers, that seat was more the center of annoyance and anxiety than authority and control. Sitting in it could feel like she was waiting for events to unfold, which she didn't have time to do. "Percentage?"

"Twenty-one percent and climbing." He offered her a padd. "Hull sections still covered by yeel-bark debris show significantly less damage."

"Still covered?" She took the padd with one hand, and tried to massage a tight knot from her neck with the other.

"Those external sensors we have working suggest wind patterns are moving the protective dust off large areas. Sometimes this covers other sections that have been previously unprotected, but the net effect is that we are being exposed to increasing harm." He took the padd back as she held it out for him.

Burnham understood the concept of saprotrophic recycling. If it didn't occur, every ecosystem would be kilometers high in waste. Normally, this didn't include starships with tritanium hulls. "Progress on shield modifications?"

"Mister Stamets informs me they're nearly complete, but the shields themselves are still inoperable. Engineering reports it may be another forty minutes."

"That's cutting it too close. Already on priority?"

"Yes." The Kelpien bowed his head affably. "I assumed that would be your directive."

"Thank you." Burnham wondered if she'd have been as good a first officer for Saru, had their roles been reversed. He knew her well enough that he could anticipate her orders or questions with an almost spooky regularity.

Walking back to Saru's station, the captain wondered aloud, "What we need to figure out is how they shifted our spores, and our entire cultivation bay, into a different quantum existence, so we can reverse it."

"I have been giving that considerable contemplation," Saru replied, ordering up a diagram to his display. "The reaction cube *does* assure the spores injected into it are all quantum aligned. Lieutenant Stamets tells me any misalignment can throw off his course calculations, therefore the injectors have multiple filters to stave off such an occurrence."

"Could they be modified to accept the spores that are in a different quantum phase?" Burnham asked.

"*That* would not be possible, since the filters are unable to react to the spores in their current state." Pulling up another schematic of the workings under the reaction cube, Saru continued. "However, I believe the process could be modified to send out an energy wave that would have a cascading effect, which would realign our spores back into our own quantum wavelength."

She tapped at a data point on the screen. "Again, the power necessary—"

"Would have to come from the warp engines," Saru agreed. "We cannot create a warp field in mycelial space. But, the power output should be enough for the necessary pulse."

As usual, he'd thought of everything, so Burnham knew her next question likely had an answer. "What will this energy wave do to our own quantum wavelengths?"

Tipping his head to one side, a Kelpien hedging that he fused to a more human shrug, Saru said, "That is where the filters come in. There should be no negative effects."

"'Should be' is an unsettling equivocation."

He spread the fingers of his right hand toward an uncertain future. "It isn't possible to foresee every unknown, but I have high confidence this plan will work."

Still, Burnham wished there were time to test it. But the hull damage, and the colonists on Benecia, couldn't wait for an excess of computer simulations and laboratory experiments.

"Who do you need?" she asked her first officer.

"If Ensign Tilly can multitask with Mister Bryce, that will be enough."

"Might be hard to *keep* her from multitasking," she said with a wistful smile. "Get started."

———

"You're sure they're here?" Landry asked again.

"Positive, Commander." Airiam normally didn't become frustrated with her crewmates, but the security chief was putting her nerves to the test. "Do you want bearing and azimuth, or will two meters forward and along the corridor wall suffice?"

"You're not even looking at your tricorder."

"Cybernetic enhancements do have their advantages."

"Hard to get lost, I bet."

"Anyone can be lost if they lack points of reference."

"Hmmm." Landry's gaze moved from her own tricorder to the wall in front of them. "What're they doing?"

"They appear to be studying something." Across from them, Airiam watched as drifting, bobbing forms made of light moved around an access panel in the corridor bulkhead. Their "arms" and "legs," for lack of a better description, moved through both the walls and the decks. "They can't interact with the ship in a conventional way. They appear to be floating."

"They can't stand on the deck?" As if punctuating her point, Landry thumped her own boot on the floor. "Interesting."

"It would account for the sensor readings Mister Rhys and I saw, which seemed to move too quickly from deck to deck. Even the canisters I attempted to touch in the lab seemed disconnected from the ship's structure." Airiam reached out toward them, and just as before, her hand went through. "Like ghosts."

"Not a fan of ghost stories. You?"

Airiam hesitated, a bit surprised at such an unexpected question from the security officer. "Not really. But I like any story, if well told."

As they patrolled, Landry remarked, "You say there are advantages to your augmentations. I'm guessing there are disadvantages, too."

Airiam stopped and looked Landry in the eye. "Yes, there are."

"I'm blunt, I know that. I'd like to say it's a chief-of-security thing, but I think it's really an Ellen Landry thing."

"I don't mind blunt." Resuming their patrol, she leaned toward Landry as if confiding a secret. "You'd be surprised how refreshing it is when people are direct. It's one of the things I admire about Captain Burnham. She's very frank."

"Vulcan schools will do that." Off a blip from her tricorder, Landry pointed with her phaser. "Over here, in this alcove."

"Checking." Her own phaser holstered, Airiam surveyed the recess, which provided access to a Jefferies tube into the inner bulkhead. She hesitated, watching two wispy forms curled around each other. "I think they're . . . I could be reading into this."

"What?" Landry tensed, her weapon in hand. "Tell me what you see."

Like looking through a fog, Airiam could only make out the most obvious of motions. "Kissing, perhaps?" She glanced over at the commander, eyes wide. It could have been more than that, of course. Or something completely different. She had no way to be certain.

Landry peered down at her phaser. "I've never shot anyone for that."

"Good to know. I'll pass the word along to the crew."

"Send the section coordinates to the bridge to continue to monitor this"—Landry motioned toward the alcove—"whatever this is."

Airiam tapped the location into her padd and sent the report. "What do you expect to do with the phaser?" she asked as they continued their patrol. "You can't hit them. They're on a different quantum wavelength."

"Security blanket. Pun intended," Landry said. "So, you said there were disadvantages?" When Airiam glanced quickly at her, she added, "Blunt, remember?"

It was an old story, but since she hadn't told it to the

security chief, and her personnel file had only the relevant information included, Airiam was willing to be accommodating. "In my accident, my brain suffered significant trauma to its memory centers. While my neural augmentations do not store most of my old memories, more recent engrams are facilitated and stored cybernetically." The deck patrol complete, they stopped at the turbolift and when the doors opened, Airiam boarded and turned to face her crewmate. "We met nine months and four days ago. A Thursday. Eleven hundred thirty-six hours. That memory is stored artificially." Looking toward the lift indicator, Airiam told the computer to move to the next location on their route.

"Forever?" Landry asked.

"If I don't delete it."

"Why would you?"

"Storage is not unlimited." Airiam wasn't sure what she saw in the security officer's face. Not pity—she'd received that from many but rarely from her Starfleet comrades. She'd seen it from her in-laws, soon after the accident, for example. But in time, she had demonstrated that pity was unnecessary. "Some content is deleted on a regular basis."

"You say that like you're cleaning out a closet."

"An apt analogy." Airiam shrugged, but knew the up-and-down motion of her shoulders was not as refined as it used to be and probably appeared . . . robotic.

When the lift doors opened, they resumed their task.

"How do you decide what to delete?" Landry asked after a short time.

"With great care," she said as evocatively as possible, then added, "I keep that which is meaningful."

Gesturing toward the way they'd turn, Landry asked: "You don't keep the good and delete the bad?"

"Our memories, positive and negative, are what make us,"

Airiam said. "I remove that which won't inform my future actions."

"Yeah."

"Would you delete your bad memories if you could?" Airiam didn't just appreciate frank discussions from one side; she was capable of engaging in them herself. Landry could be a bit of a mystery as well, and she was curious to know her better. Now seemed like an appropriate time.

The silence churned between them as the security officer contemplated an answer. "I don't know. I probably would. And then regret it later."

"What bad memories would you consider deleting, Ellen?" Airiam felt calling her by rank would be awkward considering the very personal question.

"My mother was emotionally abusive." Landry paused and her eyes darted away a moment. "And . . . my father let it happen."

It was a more direct answer than Airiam had expected, and even though she eschewed pity, she felt a pang of it for Landry. "Would you delete them from your life?"

"They're both dead now, but no. I loved them." Landry twisted away as if looking for something up the corridor, but perhaps it was just to hide her face. "They were my parents. And . . . realizing they were human only came after I lost them. I knew my mother was damaged beyond fixing from about the age of five. I endowed my father with sainthood until he died."

"What changed that?" Airiam asked quietly.

"Things that told me he wasn't as selfless as I thought." Landry's voice didn't falter but there was a vein of emotion through it. "I'd always run to him for protection, and it wasn't until after his death that I realized he wasn't protecting me, as much as he was preserving the status quo of their relationship."

"You felt betrayed."

Landry turned back, her lips a flat line of forced stoicism. "In the greater scheme of things, it didn't matter. It was what it was. I'm here all the same."

Airiam reached out, sympathetically putting her hand on Landry's shoulder. "I embrace my painful memories for the same reason: because they're mine."

Not meeting her eyes, the security officer buried her nose in her tricorder. "This section is clear." Her voice was strong and didn't betray the rawness it might cover.

Purposely sounding more upbeat, Airiam let the connection they'd shared rest. "Then on to the next."

—

Tilly finished bringing the data up on the secondary lab console. She didn't think she'd forgotten anything: all the equations, a list of the tools needed and where they were stored, and a list of tools that probably weren't needed, and where *they* were stored—*and* a shorter list of tools Bryce would never need but, just in case, where they, too, were stored.

Lists helped to control her anxiety. They didn't have to be necessary.

"Okay, I have to work with Commander Saru now. Do you have this?" Tilly asked.

"I do," Bryce assured her. "It's a transmitter, Tilly—stop being a mother hen." He smiled and his neatly trimmed beard made it seem like a wider grin. Did he have to trim it every day to look like that? Or did he apply something to suppress hair growth in specific areas? How did that work for beards?

"Yeah, no. You're good." She moved toward the reaction cube.

"If I have a question, you're right here," he reminded her.

She pointed to where Saru had opened an access panel to belowdecks. "Underneath the deck, but yeah."

"Ah, Ensign. I've already removed the main plate," the first officer told her from his kneeling position. "The multi-stage safety processor should be here."

Tilly grabbed the nearby toolkit and lowered herself to her stomach near the open panel. "Ready to get your hands dirty, Commander?"

Eyes wide, Saru put up a finger. "Should either of us get our hands dirty, I believe we will have made incalculable errors."

Tilly blinked at him, uncertain if he was kidding. "Oh, that's just a figure of speech, sir." Shouldn't he have known that?

"Ensign, I have learned over ninety languages. Among my lexicon is the colloquialism about getting one's hands dirty, along with, dare I say, thousands more you've never heard."

"Of course, sorry, sir."

He reached for the toolkit and pulled it closer in one fluid move. "Also, I *do* have a sense of humor."

"Oh, agreed, sir." She leaned over and whispered, hoping she didn't sound patronizing. "You're very amusing."

"No need to be condescending, Ensign." He sounded at least mildly exasperated, perhaps more.

"No, sir, of course not, sir." Opening the housing above the power conduit that led to the processor, Tilly pointed to the spool of ODN cable Saru had opened. "Sir?"

He pulled a section off the spool and pushed it toward her. "Do you believe this will work?"

She stopped heaving the line in midpull. "You're asking *me*?" This was his idea—his plan. Was he testing her?

"You spend the bulk of your time in this lab. You know this equipment second only to Mister Stamets."

True, and it was nice to be recognized, though she often

felt self-conscious about the kudos. Tilly could track that back to her mother, but knowing the source of one's anxiety didn't necessarily help alleviate it. One of the things she was working on was accepting compliments without reticence. "Thank you, sir. I think it will work. I just wish we had a chance to test it."

"So does the captain," Saru said. "As do I and Mister Stamets."

Connecting the ODN cable to the safety housing, Tilly reached out for the harmonic sealer that was just out of her reach.

Saru placed it in her hand. Mister Stamets might have only pushed it toward her.

"How is he, to you?"

"I beg your pardon?" The Kelpien looked over to her. "Whom?"

"Mister Stamets. I mean, how does he seem to you, sir?" Running the sealer around the circumference of the cable, Tilly waited the standard three seconds, then made a second pass. "He's been different today, you know? Look how he is with Doctor Culber."

Reaching out for her to pass the sealer back, Saru said, "I'm not sure this is an appropriate discussion to have about your superior officer."

She handed him the implement. "Sorry, sir."

Mirroring Tilly, Saru sealed his end of the cable. After a silence that Tilly could only endure for so long, she considered a number of things she might say to nevertheless draw him back into that topic. *Anything's better than an eternity of taciturnity*, she thought, and inwardly giggled at the rhyme.

Finally, he was first to speak again. "On a strictly personal level, I share your concern for the lieutenant." He reached for another processor. "But, I also trust his sensibilities."

The ensign pointed to a different area. "Oh, no, not there.

We need to modify this one." Correcting a superior officer's mistake or miscalculation—or anyone's for that matter—was never comfortable. Not because she feared some retribution, but because there was an inherent dread her mind was moving too quickly and that he wasn't wrong because she was two steps ahead.

"Yes, thank you." Saru's kindness at being corrected, or just in general, was comforting.

Tilly recognized that on the path to being a captain she'd someday be a first officer, and Saru was the finest she knew. Her sample size was small, but still . . .

"Why're you doing this, sir?" She gestured to indicate their work.

"Hmm?" Saru asked. "To get my hands dirty, as you said."

She smiled slyly, believing she knew the first officer's real motives. "I think you're here to see that Mister Stamets is okay too."

Saru shook his head. "Focus on your work, Ensign."

"Aye, sir." One day she'd have to be just as measured in her responses to subordinates, though it seemed impossible from where she sat.

"We have it, Mister Saru," Stamets called out.

Saru drew himself up to a standing position. It was an unusual movement for him, less graceful than Tilly was accustomed to seeing, almost like a baby doe standing from a prone position.

"We, Lieutenant?"

Stamets motioned to Culber. "Hugh was invaluable."

The doctor self-consciously waved the notion away. "I'm not sure how true that is."

"The harmonics we need to use are biology based. You're a doctor." Stamets's exuberance was not only writ on his face but appeared to wash over Culber as well.

He seemed to bask within it. "You're the astromycologist. I only—"

Saru lithely gestured toward the exit. "Gentlemen, while I appreciate the mutual admiration, I ask that you get these changes to Mister Rhys."

"Aye, sir." Stamets also motioned toward the doors, allowing Culber to precede him.

Tilly watched them leave and when they were safely into the corridor, she spun her head toward the first officer. "See! You saw that, right?"

His tight brow drawn down, Saru chastised her. "Ensign . . ."

"Sorry," she said, remembering herself. "Can you hand me the microcoupler, sir?"

He stretched toward the toolbox, and in one fluid motion moved it from the case to her hand. "If I'm not mistaken, this is the last step."

Tilly pushed the small coupler onto the two conduit ends and locked it in place. "It really *should* be tested . . ."

"We have very limited time, I'm afraid. I am returning to the bridge." He smoothed out his uniform. "I will run an additional simulation and consult you on the results. Please attend to the cleanup and then continue to assist Mister Bryce."

18

Looking over her tactical officer's shoulder, Michael Burnham seemed to scan through the data as quickly as Stamets entered it. "This is good," she told him as Culber watched them both. "This may buy us a few more hours."

"It will mimic the yeel bark as well as some of Hugh's own makeup," Stamets said, giving the doctor's arm a squeeze.

"I appreciate your contributions as well," Burnham told Culber, and he sensed she was more accepting of him.

Still, he knew he'd done little. "Some scans and a few blood samples I didn't mind giving up. Mostly I just kept him company."

"He's too modest." Stamets was being defensive on Culber's behalf, and while it was probably unnecessary, it did feel good to see.

"Paul's the one who knew what to look for. And how to make the shields trick the JahSepp into sensing there's a thick layer of yeel-bark dust covering the *Discovery*."

"It was good work," the captain said.

As familiar as it all was to Culber, the vibe on this *Discovery*'s bridge was far different from his own. Captain Lorca extracted a certain attitude and demanded a demeanor among his crew that created a militaristic aura. Granted, there *was* a war on in his own universe, and peacetime in general shaped a distinctive atmosphere, but he suspected that compared to

Lorca, a Captain Burnham in his universe would have interacted quite inversely with her crew.

The doctor watched her easy manner as she issued orders
across her bridge. She had a command style that pulled the
crew in, and Culber could tell she was the kind of leader under
whom he could proudly serve. Would he be allowed to? There
already was a Doctor Hugh Culber in this Starfleet. Would
they permit two?

He looked at Stamets as he discussed shield power levels
with Rhys.

Yes, it wasn't his Paul, but in so many ways he seemed to
be the Stamets for him. If he could have a wish, would Culber put himself back in his universe, with his Paul Stamets, or
would he wish to have been born into this one, so that his fit-
ting into a life with this man wouldn't be a problem?

"Some of these changes have to be made at the emitters,"
Rhys said, pulling Culber's attention back to the discussion at
hand.

"Lifts are still achingly slow. Are transporters working?"
Stamets asked.

"I wouldn't trust transporters just yet," Saru replied.

Burnham pulled a blue card from the tactical station and
handed it to Stamets. "I'll let engineering know you're on
your way."

He snapped up the data card and motioned Culber to join
him in the lift.

Once they were gone and the lift was on its way, the captain spun to Saru. "Landry and Airiam should be done with
their sweep, correct?"

"I believe so."

She pulled out her communicator and flipped up the
antenna grid. The device chirped alive. "Burnham to Landry."

"Landry here."

The captain watched the frequency oscillations on the communicator's display. The very nature of mycelial space disturbed the bulk of their technology. Even something as simple as the device in her hand. "Commander, I want you to meet Lieutenant Stamets and Doctor Culber in engineering."

"Aye, Captain. Airiam and I were just finishing up."

"Have Airiam report to the spore lab to assist there."

"Acknowledged."

"Bridge out."

When the captain returned to her chair, the first officer followed. "You have concerns?" he asked, in a low enough voice that only she could have heard him.

"My concerns have concerns." She motioned to a *Discovery* schematic on her chair readout. "Where have intruders been most localized?"

Without glancing toward the display, Saru instantly answered: "Sickbay, the spore lab, and its adjacent cultivation bay."

"Again, we've already noted these are locations where one generally finds Mister Stamets and his new friend. But we may be focusing on the wrong man."

Surprise widened Saru's eyes, and his voice also expressed astonishment. "Your concern isn't Doctor Culber?"

"Like I said, concerns on top of concerns." Burnham lowered herself into the command chair. "I don't need to understand the why to foresee possible complications."

"What do you suspect may happen?"

Drawing in a deep, slow breath, the captain looked toward the main viewer. Though she couldn't see past the viewport's protective shutters, she knew that outside their ship expanded the mycelial forest. A different plane of existence they'd forayed into constantly but minutely, and so it was still entirely alien to them. "I wish I knew. But we'll probably find out."

—

When the lift doors closed, Hugh pressed his thumb against the control panel, but also used a verbal command, just to be sure. "Computer, halt."

"Lift halted," replied the unimpressed mechanical voice.

"What's wrong?" Paul spun toward him, his pale brows upswept. "We need to get to engineering."

Hugh grabbed Paul's empty hand and drew it into both of his. "It can wait five minutes, I think."

"Yeah, sure." Paul nodded, and his features conversely comforted and complicated the doctor's feelings.

"I don't know how to . . ." His voice trailed off. How did he even begin this discussion? When he stopped the lift, he figured he could wing it, but inspiration didn't follow. He was wasting time they didn't have, so he simply pulled Paul closer.

"What's wrong, Hugh?" Paul didn't pull his hand away. "Tell me what you need."

"I need *you*. But you're—" Closing his eyes, but still able to see his dilemma, Hugh pulled Paul's hand close to his chest and pressed it there. "You're not *you*, you're nicer than you. And I want that but I also want him and . . . Maybe I don't know which is which anymore. Maybe you're just the 'you' I need, but he's the 'you' I married." He felt his face flush and his eyes begin to well. "I don't know," he said, and it almost became a sob. "None of this makes any sense and the more I try to figure it out, the less sense it makes."

Rather than pulling away, Paul stepped closer. "We'll figure it out, I promise." His encouraging voice was hushed but husky.

His data card clattering to the deck, Paul wrapped one hand tenderly around Hugh's neck, and as they embraced, put the other behind his head.

They kissed, and Hugh's own hands fell to Paul's torso and hung on for dear life, as if he'd instantly be returned to the mycelial plane in which they'd found him should he let go.

Lips as soft as the real Paul's, the same electrical pop of excitement thumped Hugh's heart. Was it even stronger than he remembered? That made it all the more bittersweet. The man was the same, but *not* the same. The connection was right, but wrong. How could Hugh ever reconcile the Paul-not-Paul dilemma?

"Tell me what you're feeling," Paul said when Hugh pulled away, ending the embrace.

Hugh closed his eyes, then opened them to find that beautiful face, so kind and comforting that it almost jarred him. "You . . . are an oasis," he said, feeling his own voice betray the emotion beneath. "Water in the desert."

"Yeah, I know what an oasis is." Smiling kindly, Paul quipped, "Is it cool water, though? Because in a desert it would probably be warm, and that's— I mean you still need to drink it, but ugh."

"Cool water," Hugh said with a shaky lilt. "A little too cool, sometimes."

"Too cool? No such thing."

"I see that no matter the universe, you don't know when to—"

Paul took the other man's face in his hands again, caressing his neck and jaw tenderly as they kissed. When they pulled apart once more, he said, "Listen to me, Hugh. I feel the connection. I *know* it's there. I don't doubt it, not for a minute. And, yeah, maybe I'm not the man you married, and you're not the one I once met, but does it matter now?"

"I think so. Because, you're him"—the face *was* Paul's, and the touch was too, and somehow seemed more loving, more attentive, and so just a tinge off—"but *not* him."

"I don't care." Paul put his forehead against Hugh's, like the moment he first saw him only a handful of hours before. "I know it's insane and surreal as hell, and . . . I guess 'insane' probably covers it best, but . . . it's . . . it's science."

Hugh's voice broke through a sob and a snicker. "Oh, it's science, is it?"

"Chemistry. Kismet—whatever you want to call it."

The lift controls started beeping. If they didn't resume, it would eventually sound an alarm.

They kissed again, three times, one after another, softly but deep. More than pecks, but less than either man needed.

Beep beep.

"The lift can't be stopped this long," Hugh said around another soft kiss.

"I know." Paul closed his eyes and just laid his cheek against his.

What if I never feel this touch again? What if this is a dream, or a lie? Worse: What if it's real?

Beep beep.

"Computer," Hugh croaked out, not wanting it to end, but knowing it must. "Resume."

The system whirred to life as Paul reached down with one hand and picked up his dropped data card. He clasped his other hand on Hugh's arm and gave it a long squeeze. "This'll be okay."

Hugh wasn't sure, though he wanted to be.

"Let me be your confidence," Paul said, sensing his doubt. "I can be strong when you're not."

That's what Hugh wanted. To fall into that pool of affection and tenderness and just bathe in . . . "It doesn't seem fair."

Paul turned to him, his gentle eyes puzzled. "To whom?"

"Him." It was an absurd, ridiculous conundrum, but it crushed down on him. "I don't think he knows . . . that I'm alive."

The doors opened on the engineering deck. They both stood there, unwilling to move forward.

Finally, Paul stepped out first. "I don't know how to get you back to him." Making his way toward engineering, he cast back a singular, passionate glance. "And to be perfectly honest, I don't want to."

———

"Captain?" Saru's willowy fingers danced over his station, and Burnham amused herself by calling it a Kelpien hand ballet. "Engineering reports shield emitters have been reconfigured."

She swiveled her chair toward tactical. "Mister Rhys?"

He flipped a switch and checked the screen above him. "Green lights across the board, Captain."

Hands pressed into the arms of her chair, Burnham steadied herself and turned toward the main viewscreen. This was one slice of a multipart process that would hopefully allow them to jump back to normal space. Once there, they needed to either be intact enough to make it to Benecia themselves, or contact Starfleet so another ship could be dispatched to help thwart the Symbalene blood-burn outbreak.

All lives aboard *Discovery* were in her hands, but as members of Starfleet, the crew accepted any danger as their duty. Her responsibility as their captain was to get them home at the end of every mission.

The colonists on Benecia lived a relatively safe life in comparison to the complement of a Federation starship. They were already home, and likely living an unimaginable fear they'd not expected.

Burnham had a duty to them as well, and the number of problems that needed to be solved before that obligation could be satisfied weighed down on her.

A deep breath in, the captain ordered a hopeful, "Raise shields."

Owosekun nodded her head and seemed to steady herself as well before activating the console. "Raising shields, aye."

A warbling sound reverberated through the deck plates and a field of energy bubbled forward. The viewport's shutters immediately retracted and they watched as the wave pushed the surrounding air into the mycelial biota. It crashed against hyphae trunks and smaller fungal sprigs that whipped back and forth. The noise became a dull hum as small sparkles sizzled against the shields. Not constantly, but enough to make it seem there was a wind sending debris and other microorganisms into the barrier around them.

"I've never heard shielding make that sound," Owosekun said.

"Feedback, but nothing severe," Saru said off his readings. "It appears to be working. I believe the impact against our shields are the JahSepp organisms. Some remain on the ship's hull, but degradation is down by seventy-six percent."

The captain pushed herself from the command chair and stood between Owo and Detmer. "Good. How long can we maintain?" She watched as another wave of JahSepp crashed into their defense bubble, sending tiny jolts of lightning crackling across the screen.

"At this rate," Saru said, "I estimate two and a half hours."

The captain glanced at a similar readout on Owo's console. *Two point six hours*, she thought, *but who's counting?* "Let's hope that's long enough." Turning back to the command chair, she bent toward its controls. "Are internal comms working?"

Saru bowed his head to one side. "Communications are restored."

Burnham sat, leaned forward a bit, eager for the next stage to begin. "Bridge to the DASH lab."

"Airiam here, Captain."

"Are we ready for the quantum calibration wave?"

"We are."

———

"Initiate," Burnham ordered.

Airiam slid the screen control forward. "Initiating, aye."

An almost imperceptible flash winked into existence, then dissipated as quickly as it formed. When it was gone, the lab was crowded not just with spores, but alien intruders.

Tilly's gasp might have become a scream if she'd not self-muted with a hand over her mouth.

No longer the wisps and blobs of light she'd seen before, the aliens were fully formed. Basically humanoid, but with long, slender digitigrade legs and squat torsos. Their relatively dark orange skin was smooth and unmottled where she could see it, but they wore protective gear not dissimilar to Starfleet's own EV suits. Their faces, neither avian nor reptilian, suggested an evolution along those branches. Of the seven that appeared, three had collapsed to the deck, writhing in what she assumed was pain.

Airiam was as shocked as Tilly, but she didn't show it.

Judging by the looks on the faces of the aliens that still stood, they were just as stunned at what happened. They didn't make a sound, but across from her at the alternate console, Bryce wasn't as silent.

"Tilly, move!" he called out, just as one of the aliens pulled the ensign's phaser from her hand as she drew it from her holster. Holding Tilly's right hand in a tight grip, it aimed the phaser threateningly at the others.

"What's going on down there?" Burnham demanded.

"Captain," Airiam said, "we see the spores, but also the intruders. They are fully corporeal now." She spoke evenly, calmly, not wanting to further alarm anyone. "One has taken Tilly's phaser and is holding her hostage."

———

Burnham leaned down, one hand against the tactical console, the other on the back of Rhys's chair. "Scan for alien signatures. All decks." She pointed to Saru's station. "Monitor results and dispatch security teams, starting with engineering deck." Twisting back again, she watched the display as the internal scan data flooded the screen.

"Security en route," the first officer said.

Burnham was about to order another security detail to the spore-drive section, when the unmistakable sound of phaser fire crackled from the speaker.

"Airiam, report!"

Ensign Merrill, Bryce's relief, called from communications, "Captain, I've lost them."

"Closed?"

"No, sir. Cut at the source."

"Manual override," she ordered. "Rhys, help him." She stalked toward Saru's station. "What happened?"

"I am at a loss, Captain," Saru admitted, continuing to work his console and so glancing up at her only momentarily. "I can only imagine that, because we configured the pulse for organic material, it had a wider effect than we believed possible and therefore brought not just the spores, but their would-be thieves into our quantum phase."

She huffed out a frustrated breath, less at Saru and Tilly for their calculations than herself for not allowing the further testing they both requested. "We need to get a handle on this situation. And fast."

19

"What happened to him?" Commander Landry was bent over Culber even before Stamets had dropped to his knees beside him. He'd been closer when the doctor fell to the deck, but Landry got there in time to cup his head and lower him safely down.

"He collapsed," Stamets said.

Of all people, Landry understood frustration expressed as sarcasm. "No, I mean he dropped after the realignment wave. Why?"

"I'm not a doctor," Stamets snapped. Culber's eyes fluttered, and he started to get up. "Are you okay?"

"I'm fine, I'm fine." Culber pulled in a knee to steady himself. "Help me up."

Landry put one hand under his armpit and let him use her other hand as a push-off point, but when he got his legs under himself halfway, she pulled both and he stumbled into Stamets.

"Hey!" the doctor exclaimed.

She drew her phaser and aimed in the direction of the movement she'd seen peripherally. "We've got hostiles."

Three space-suit-clad aliens looked back at her, then around at the others in the room—mostly engineers who appeared as stunned as the intruders, but who had the forethought to pull their own weapons. Two additional intruders were slumped over, struck similarly as Culber.

The standing aliens mouthed something, but it came more

as clicks, pops, and a few oddly placed tones—almost tweets. Which perhaps fit, as they had an almost avian-like quality about their demeanor. And yet, their legs looked more rabbit-like.

"They're trying to say something," Stamets said.

"It better be, 'We come in peace.'" Landry moved her phaser to encompass the tightly packed five, suggestively conveying that if any of them moved they would be fired upon. "I'd also take, 'Oops, didn't mean to invade your home and steal your shit.'"

Culber leaned against a console, watching as Stamets pulled out and opened his communicator. When it activated, making its usual squeak, the aliens peered quizzically at one another, then at him. "Go ahead. Say it again," he told them softly, laying the device on the lip of the console that separated them from the intruders.

The ones who seemed unharmed pulled the other two close, shared what was perhaps a concerned look with one another, as well as a series of chitters, clicks, and whines. They then motioned to the communicator with an expression that could have been interpreted as caution or suspicion.

"Does that sound like, 'We surrender'?" Landry appreciated Stamets's attempt to communicate, but so far it had been futile. It wasn't the first time the universal translator couldn't cope, but it was admittedly rare.

"I don't think the UT has enough for a framework. We need to keep them talking," Stamets said. "They don't seem to have any weapons."

Standing up, Culber asked, "How do we know they recognize the phaser as a weapon?"

Landry kept her aim on the intruders. "I could stun one as a demonstration."

"Is this how you manage first contact?" the doctor asked, motioning in the aliens' direction.

They chittered and popped at Culber's gesture.

"I like first contacts that begin with friendly hellos, not intruder alerts!" she barked, and it sent one of the aliens toward the door. "Stop!" Landry aimed her weapon directly at it.

It chattered back at her, but didn't halt.

Moving her aim quickly to the door, she squeezed the trigger and fired a stun charge that sizzled through the air and slammed into the metal just a meter in front of the intruder.

"What the hell are you doing?" Stamets demanded.

"Containing the problem." She leveled her phaser back at the alien and motioned for it to rejoin its comrades, which it did, albeit slowly. Hearing her own communicator beep, she took one hand from her weapon and pulled the device out, flipping it open. "Landry here."

———

"We need security at Stamets's lab, Commander," Burnham said, checking that the phaser Saru just handed her was set to stun.

"We have our hands full in main engineering, Captain. Five hostiles."

Suppressing an impulsive twist toward the turbolift, Burnham felt her muscles tighten. Every instinct told her to race down to the action that instant, but she was a starship captain, not a first or second officer anymore. She had orders to issue before joining Landry. "Everyone okay?"

"No casualties."

"Then why describe them as—?" Saru began.

"Landry, leave part of your team there. Take the rest to the spore lab. We'll coordinate a deck-by-deck search from the bridge. Go now."

"Understood. Landry, out."

Burnham closed the channel. Holstering her phaser, she said, "Mister Rhys, we need simultaneous scans with and without the sensor enhancements."

"Both?"

"Both. There's no way to know if we got them all in the quantum wave."

"Aye, Captain."

"We did not intend to 'get' any of them," Saru said.

"I am aware." The captain gave him an empathetic look as she headed for the turbolift. "You have the bridge, Number One."

"Are you headed to engineering?" Concerned, the first officer began to protest, but the lift doors were already closing.

"That's where the party is."

———

The alien held Tilly's phaser in one hand, and her neck between its long arm and squat torso. Airiam and Bryce were separated from Tilly and her captor by the smoking console the intruder had fired upon. Amongst the smoke and the occasional mote of spores that wafted back and forth, it was more difficult to see the players than Airiam desired.

Chirping erratically, the lead intruder seemed irate and disoriented. He or she clicked and popped to the others, and they chattered back. One of those who'd collapsed was on its haunches, and the other two were leaning against the bulkhead. The rest stood tensely, waiting.

"Tilly, remain calm." Airiam kept her left palm up in a *halt* gesture, but her right hand held her phaser.

The young ensign's eyes bulged. "Begging the commander's pardon, but you—" Catching herself, she switched to a sharp whisper: "*You* remain calm!"

"I am calm," Airiam said. She rather hoped the absurdity of a lighthearted response would keep Tilly grounded.

Judging by the ensign's expression, it didn't work. "Well, *you* don't have an alien wrapped around your neck, do you?"

Airiam lowered her phaser. "We don't want to hurt you," she told the intruders. "And I don't think you want to hurt us."

"What makes you think they don't want to hurt us?" Bryce asked.

"When they got Tilly's phaser and grabbed her, they used it on the console, not us."

"Maybe they wanted to see what it would do," he replied.

"Wouldn't you?" Airiam asked, then looked back to the intruders. "It's okay. We will all be calm." She was telling them to relax, but only Tilly really understood, and that's what she wanted of the ensign.

"You keep saying be calm," Tilly said, her frustration turning to anger. "But my phaser is *not* set on stun anymore, so it's really *really* extra hard to stay calm!"

"Noted." First contact was one of the most dangerous missions for a Starfleet officer. The Academy had simulated situations with countless variants, but Airiam could not remember one where the alien subjects didn't understand you and were holding a friend captive at the point of a phaser. "Mister Bryce, please check the console and tell me which systems are offline."

Without moving, he said, "I'd have to put down my phaser."

"That's why you have a holster."

"Airiam—"

"Ronald."

Exasperated, he pursed his lips and ground out, "Aye, Commander."

Holstering her own phaser, Airiam showed the intruders both palms. "He's not going to harm you. No one will. He's just checking our systems."

Popping and chittering, the lead alien gripped Tilly tighter and moved a step back.

"They *don't* understand you," Tilly complained.

"I realize that. We need to find a way to communicate with them." Even when there was a communication barrier, it was a rare culture where screaming suggested calm and soothing tones conveyed anger. "One step at a time, Ensign," Airiam said. "We need to earn some trust. Bryce, what do you see?"

"Looks like an overload," he said. "Doors work manually, if we can get at them. Comms are down but we have communicators. Lights are on bypass."

Still watching the aliens intently, Airiam told Bryce, "Lock the doors."

"Are you kidding?" Tilly whispered harshly.

"We don't want the intruders or the spores getting out."

"Right. Okay." Tilly closed her eyes as if she simply decided to wait until she was released.

Bryce, making only small movements on the section of console that still worked, finally said, "Doors locked."

"The overloaded circuits?" Airiam asked.

"Fixable. But one of the panels we'll need to access is behind them."

"Let's not get behind them just yet, okay?" Tilly asked, her eyes still jammed shut. "Agreed, people?"

"Agreed. And no sudden movements," Airiam said. First Contact 101: there was no telling what random gesture might be taken the wrong way.

Backing away from the console, Bryce raised his hands slightly.

Airiam could tell that he wanted to reach for his weapon again. "No phasers, Mister Bryce. What we need right now is our communicators."

———

"It's locked," Landry said. "I could override it, but this is Bryce's code. And the blast doors are jammed shut." Frustrated, she smacked her hand against the door's controls.

"Is that helping?" Burnham asked.

"It hasn't yet."

Landry's expression was jointly glum and annoyed. Every emotion Burnham tried to conceal, her chief of security freely displayed. "What do we know?"

"Before we lost sensors, visual logs showed seven aliens. Three unconscious. One of them had a phaser in its hand and its arm around Tilly's throat. A console sparked, I assume by the phaser fire. That's all that recorded. I'm not sure if that's a deliberate act or a lucky shot."

"From intruder alert to hostage situation," Burnham said. "But we can work with that," she added. "It suggests their thinking isn't *too* alien."

"There are five more in main engineering. I'm waiting for the report on the deck-by-deck search. I sent Stamets and his friend to sickbay."

"Why?" Burnham felt another worry settle across her shoulders. What new problem was there with Stamets and Culber?

"The doctor collapsed like the aliens when the wave came by," Landry explained.

"That's interesting."

"It just seemed a lower priority."

Pulling out her communicator at the tonal prompt, the captain flipped it open. "Burnham here."

"Captain, it's Bryce. I'm with Airiam, Tilly, and seven very real, very nervous aliens."

Placing her free hand on the door, Burnham wished she were on the other side. "We're here, Lieutenant. Is anyone injured?"

"No, though Tilly is close to having kittens." Bryce's voice was unruffled but sounded forced. A self-imposed composure he didn't truly feel.

A bit more faintly, the captain heard Tilly in the background: *"I'm allergic, actually. I mean, I just need a shot and I could have them. Not give birth to them. That would take more than a shot."*

"She's fine," Airiam added.

"Universal translator's no help?" the captain asked.

"Useless," Bryce replied. *"And without knowing what they want, it's a stalemate."*

"Understood. Everyone stand by." Burnham closed the communicator and looked at Landry. "Okay, we have their people, they have ours."

"Should we be worried about a ship?" she asked. "Where did they all come from?"

That was a good question. "External sensor range is limited, and I've had it focused on the hull."

"You ever get so frustrated you want to chew neutronium?" Landry asked.

Burnham offered her one arched brow.

"I'm going to take that as a no."

With a slight smile Burnham said, "Growing up with Vulcans didn't turn me into one, and even they have emotions—much stronger than most humans. They just decided logic and reason were easier than neutronium gum."

"Think they're right?" Landry asked.

"Most days." The captain curved toward the turbolift.

"Keep a tight hold on our uninvited guests next door, and work on getting a look into the lab here. Take resources from where you need." As the lift doors parted for her, Burnham added, "I'll be in sickbay."

———

"How is he, Doctor?" Burnham asked Pollard as she approached the biobed where Culber lay and Stamets waited. It looked as if they'd just finished with the full-body sensor array, and Pollard moved the unit back into place at the touch of a button.

"I think I know why he fainted," she replied.

"I didn't faint," Culber said. "I felt light-headed."

Whichever it was, he seemed no worse for wear, Burnham noticed.

"*Scans* show brief unconsciousness, even if you didn't notice. Syncope." Pollard handed Culber a padd. "You fainted."

"Did anyone else on the ship?" Burnham asked.

Pollard took back her padd and searched through it quickly. "Not that's been reported, no."

Culber raised his hands in faux surrender. "Captain, I promise you, I'm not some alien intruder wearing a human suit."

"No one said you were." Despite her early misgivings about his true nature, Pollard confirmed his humanity and Burnham had no doubts.

"I did find something, however," Pollard said. "His quantum signature isn't consistent with ours." She frowned in self-disappointment. "I wish I'd thought to check before now."

"That proves it, then," Stamets said. "Hugh is from a parallel universe."

"Does it?" Culber asked.

"It does," the captain said, at least being able to put that matter to bed. "All matter native to our universe would resonate with the same quantum signature. Unlike a quantum wavelength, nothing can change it."

"The wave that changed the phase of the spores," Stamets said, "bringing them into tangibility with us, was geared toward matter native to our universe."

"It staggered Doctor Culber, who has a different quantum signature." Burnham added, "Perhaps did the same to some of the intruders, who we may find not only had a different wavelength, but signature as well."

"Are you suggesting they're not only from a different quantum phase, but a different quantum universe?" Pollard asked, fascinated. "I'd love a good look at their physiology."

"The mycelial network . . ." Stamets began, even more captivated by the notion, "connects it all. Just like the gaps in my map suggest." His face glowed, giddy at the possibilities. "We could spend the rest of our lives studying this."

"It'll be a short life if we don't get out of here," the captain reminded him. "I need you back in your lab. Unfortunately, it's currently under alien control, with Tilly, Airiam, and Bryce held hostage inside."

Culber slipped off the table to stand with them as Pollard asked, "What do they want?"

"Unknown." Burnham disdained pacing in front of the crew, but her legs tensed as if she were about to waltz around the room. "The universal translator rarely needs this much time to examine a language before giving at least some indication of meaning."

"Math," Culber suggested. "Paul said the distress call you received was mathematical. Maybe that's how you get through to them."

Smirking, Stamets affectionately gripped the other man's shoulder. "Why didn't I think of that?"

Equally impressed, Burnham wondered why she hadn't either.

Stamets spun to the captain. "You know who loves math like it was a warm puppy?"

"Tilly," Burnham said.

"Tilly."

20

Pantomiming on Bryce, Airiam demonstrated to the alien how she wanted Tilly released. Starting with her arm around the communication officer's neck rather awkwardly, she straightened it to release him, but then bent it back to again hold him to her torso. By the third time, Bryce whispered, "I don't think this is working."

"No, it's helping," Tilly told them, realizing the alien had neither phasered a hole in her head nor tried to cut off her air supply. She'd managed to reset her anxiety to an acceptable level and appreciated that the intruders didn't seem to want to harm anyone. "He's relaxed his arm. I don't think he wants to hurt me."

Airiam demonstrated again, and Tilly softly patted the intruder's hand. "It's okay if you want to let me go now," she said soothingly. His exposed hand felt as smooth as his face appeared. Almost as if it were a polished surface. "Standing this way is starting to hurt."

He popped a few clicks, and vocalized a tonal sequence that wasn't quite a chirping bird sound.

Suddenly, as if some switch had flipped, the alien released her. Tilly gasped in surprise and backed into the reaction cube door, but froze when the intruder aimed her phaser at her. In a motion she could interpret well enough, he gestured toward Airiam and Bryce.

"He wants your phasers, I think," she told them.

"Are we going to do that?" Bryce asked Airiam, his voice creased with a track of tension.

Rarely did Airiam hesitate, but evidently she was thinking it through. Tilly was nervous about the idea, but she understood that first contact held difficult and unexpected challenges and rarely went as planned. It was two different peoples introducing themselves to each other, often unexpectedly, or accidentally.

What would Captain Burnham do? Tilly asked herself. *Captain Burnham would do what she had to to keep her crew safe*, she thought. *And further the mission.* "I think we should."

"Tilly, *you're* the one they attacked," Bryce said.

"I know, but think about it—if you're an alien intruder, which people do you send into a lab?" She motioned to the one with the phaser, then quickly pulled her arm back, hoping it didn't take it as an aggressive gesture. "Scientists, right? I mean, wouldn't I be on a landing party that involved collecting mycelial spores?"

Silence ensued as her two crewmates regarded her just as quizzically as the intruders did.

"Well, it makes sense to me," Tilly said, quietly defeated.

"Me as well," Airiam said finally as she slowly pulled her phaser's power pack from the handle and set both on the console in front of her. "You too, Mister Bryce."

Plainly not thrilled with the decision, he complied. "Aye, aye." Breaking down his phaser took the same amount of time, but his hand lingered a moment longer than Airiam's had. Eventually, however, he set the components on the console as well.

Looking at the items, then the humans, and then their own comrades, the aliens clicked and hummed to one another.

The intruder's phaser slid downward from Tilly to the deck, and the ensign released a breath she'd been holding.

"That's progress," Airiam said.

Relieved, Tilly mouthed a *thank you* to their captor.

"I notice he hasn't let go of it," Bryce said through gritted teeth. "Meanwhile, ours are in pieces."

The console in front of Airiam started flashing and she quickly looked down. "A message from the captain," she said. " 'Try math.' "

"Math?" A feeling of excitement washed over Tilly. "I love math."

———

"Red alert. Red alert." The lights already informed Burnham of the threat. The klaxon had too. She didn't need the computer's monotonous voice adding to the din. "Silence that, please," she told Merrill as she exited the lift and marched to the command chair.

"We are under attack," Saru reported as the captain lowered herself into the center seat. The ship quaked around them and it felt unlike any attack she could remember. Grounded in a forest, butting up against trees, dirt, and other fungal biota, their vessel vibrated awkwardly in place.

"Tactical."

The main viewscreen filled with data Rhys had collected and collated, which the captain quickly scanned. In one corner of the screen, a small, hazy dot spat forth a shot of energy that made its way into the *Discovery*'s shields.

"Magnify."

The image warbled as it zoomed in, showing only a slightly larger but still blurry opaque gray-and-white cloud firing on them.

"Is that a ship?" Burnham asked, gripping the arms of her chair as the vessel shook around them again.

"I believe it is. And presumably as out of phase with us as the intruders and spores were," Saru said, his long fingers curling around his console to steady himself.

"Not so out of phase their weapons aren't hitting us," Rhys said. "Shields down to eighty-six percent."

One hand tapping at his controls, the first officer checked a readout. "I believe it would be worse if they *weren't* out of phase."

The captain pushed off the arms of her chair and joined him at his console. "Show me."

"Here," he said, pointing to one set of data, "and here."

"They modified the wavelength of their weapons." Burnham met her first officer's gaze. "*After* we brought their people into our perceptive range."

"So it would seem," Saru said.

The captain noticed his ganglia peeking out. "What about our own weapons? Photon torpedoes would have a devastating effect on this plane, but what about phasers?"

"They're just out of our range. And I'm afraid weapons systems have *not* been a priority. Available power is being rerouted to shields. We could bypass back to phasers and try to increase our reach, but only at the expense of our own protection. Not only from the weapons fire we're taking, but the organisms that wish to devour our hull."

"Have we tried hailing them?" the captain asked, edging toward communications.

"Universal hails on all bands," Merrill reported. "No reply."

Another salvo shook the ship.

"Shields down to eighty-four percent," Rhys said.

"Interesting." Saru checked his console a second time as Burnham turned back toward him. "Captain, their last volley was half the power of their first."

Sharing a curious look with her first officer, Burnham then stepped toward the viewscreen, studying the indistinct blur that was supposedly another vessel, sitting with them in mycelial space. "Are they losing power?" she asked. "Perhaps in the same situation as we are? Or are they simply trying to warn us against harming their people?"

"It is possible their boarding party has been in communication with them," Saru offered.

"How? No conventional signal has left this ship. Telepathically?" Burnham wondered, more to herself than Saru. She continued to watch the other ship as it sat motionless.

Pondering that a moment, her first officer agreed, "I suppose that is a possibility."

Nodding both her understanding of the problems that would present, as well as her own realization of how to proceed, she pivoted back to the command chair. "Call Mister Stamets to the bridge."

———

When Tilly had tentatively started tapping the console to signify prime numbers, the alien with the phaser motioned her away from it. He then herded Bryce, Airiam, and Tilly together, which took from her a measure of the calm she'd regained. Now the three stood at the base of the steps that led toward the doors at the back, all contained by the phaser the ensign foolishly let be taken from her grasp.

Soon after they were grouped together, the ship began rocking.

While two aliens cared for their weaker, lethargic friends, the lead intruder kept the weapon on the *Discovery* crew, and click-chirped at his subordinates—about what, the Starfleet officers didn't know.

"What's happening?" Tilly asked.

"The ship is being fired upon." Airiam made a small hand motion to indicate the aliens opposite them. "They don't seem to care."

"I wish we could get at a console or a tricorder," the ensign said. This was *her* lab they'd taken over, and it felt invasive. Well, hers and Stamets's, and . . . okay, it was more his than hers, but she spent most of her time there. Still—it was wrong for her to be a hostage in her own workspace.

"We shouldn't have given up our phasers," Bryce said. "He's not lowered his aim since he moved us over here."

"It was," Airiam agreed, "possibly a mistake." She shrugged sharply, in that over-exaggerated way she had. "Still, it resulted in Tilly being free of his grasp."

For that the ensign was very grateful. "I don't actually know if he's a she or she's a he. I guess it's not important. To us, anyway. Probably he cares. Or she does."

"This would be a lot easier if they'd let us near one of the consoles again," said Bryce. "We could display symbols that suggest a mathematical progression."

"I am not sure that would make this easier," Airiam said as they felt another shudder. "Faster, perhaps."

Math had always been Tilly's best friend. The beautiful harmonies that numbers sang, the elegance of mathematical geometry—many people didn't see the pure esthetic nature that mathletes did, but there was joy in it. Growing up, reveling in that beauty had eased the lonely days.

"I once did a paper on the Elisurians," the ensign said, biting her lip absentmindedly.

Bryce waited. After too long a pause he said, "Who are the Elisaurians?"

"*Elisurians*. They speak in melodic quadratic equations," Airiam explained.

Tilly twisted toward her, excited. "That's right! You know them!"

"I've never met one personally. How are they important here?"

"I wanted to learn their language for my presentation. Maybe . . ." Tilly rotated toward the aliens and sang them one of the three song/phrases she still remembered. When there was no response, she tried the other two.

Their reaction was to stare at her, though one did seem to mutter something to the intruder holding the phaser. She hoped it wasn't *Shoot her first.*

"That didn't seem to work," Airiam said. "Do you know any more?"

"No, not really." Her shoulders hunched over in defeat.

"Hope your presentation went better," Bryce said, probably in an effort to bolster her spirits.

It hadn't. "I guess their clicks don't sound very melodic." And yet, they still reminded her of the Elisurian communications she'd listened to. "You know what we need?" she said, index finger tapping her chin. "We need pi. Not pie like P-I-E but pi, P-I, as in the ratio of the circumference of a circle to its diameter."

"Thank you for not expressing that calculation as far as you remember it," Bryce said.

"Oh, yeah. No." Tilly jabbed him with her elbow. "We don't have that kind of time."

Still watching the alien with the phaser, Airiam asked, "You think if we can express pi to them, that will give us the basis of an understanding?"

"There's always room for pi," Tilly said.

Lowering his head into his palms, Bryce groaned.

The alien across from them watched closely, moving his body back and forth, perhaps wondering if the human was injured. And, considering Bryce's dislike of puns, he might have agreed he was.

"I wish Rhys was here," Tilly muttered.

"Because of his tactical skill?" Airiam asked.

"He just appreciates a good pun."

"You were right," Bryce told Airiam. "Best if I don't have a weapon right now."

Ignoring him, Tilly mused that if the intruders wouldn't let them back near the control consoles . . . "We have to improvise, because I have no way to express pi tonally," she said, and began to hum. "Hmmm hmmm mmm mmm mmm . . ."

The aliens' attention focused on her, occasionally looking at one another quickly, but then all eyes were back on Tilly.

"Tilly, what're you doing?" Bryce asked.

"Music is really just math, expressed aurally. Or in my case, orally." She waved toward the intruders. "Because I'm singing."

"That is a mathematical tune?" Airiam asked.

"Yes." She hummed it again.

"What is that?" The give in Airiam's brow was minimal but her eyes narrowed. "Those five notes sound familiar."

"From a very old movie," she explained. "Where aliens come to Earth and this is how the scientists greet them. No universal translators back then." Humming again, Tilly repeated the notes.

"You're using a fictional story as the basis for attempting first-contact communication?" Airiam asked skeptically.

Bryce deadpanned, "We are dead."

"I don't know what else to try," Tilly confessed, singing the five notes again.

Airiam pursed her lips in thought. Off yet another reverberation that shook the deck, she gestured toward their captors. "It doesn't seem to be alarming them. You may continue, Ensign."

Trying something new, Tilly crooned a different melody.

The intruders popped and clicked at one another, then the one who'd been sitting against the bulkhead rose and made a deep note that ran the scale up in tenor until it became a screech. Tilly and Bryce shielded their ears, while Airiam turned her head away and seemed to cover a wince.

"What did you sing to them?" Bryce asked. "A threat?"

"It's something my aunt sang to me when I was three."

The aliens, now all standing, though the weakest two still appeared fragile enough to need support by leaning on the wall or the others, watched the ensign as she continued to hum.

"What's the song about?" Bryce asked. "They seem interested, at least."

"Lemurs," she said. "But that's not the point. It's just a very mathematical tune."

"What would that mean to them?" he mused.

Tilly hoped it was something nice, but couldn't fathom a guess. "I have no idea. Right now this is like barking at your dog and thinking you're speaking dog-ese."

"They're more intelligent than dogs," Airiam said. "But don't seem to have their own version of a universal translator."

"Or, they do," Bryce suggested. "But theirs is as useless in communicating with us as ours is with them."

"Try again, Tilly," Airiam ordered. "They don't seem really aggressive. If you've elicited any response at all, beyond confusion, it's curiosity."

Thinking adding actual words might muddle the path to their goal, Tilly vocalized a popular tune she'd been listening to on her daily runs, but left out the lyrics.

Very slightly, very gently, the aliens before them were swaying with the tune.

"Can you get to your communicator?" Airiam asked Bryce.

He motioned to the intruders, who were now looking like some odd set of backup singers to the weirdest alien band. "They seem more enamored with Tilly."

"I'm distracting them," she sang to him, miming a dance that the weird music group in her imagination would have used. "You let the bridge know."

"What exactly am I letting them know?" he asked.

Airiam's lips pulled into a light smile. "Music hath charms to soothe a savage beast?"

21

"Suggestions?" Burnham and Saru had brought Stamets to the secondary science station, and showed him the data on the attacks, which continued unabated, though were considerably weaker than when they first began.

What's the point of it all? the captain thought. *Just to wear down our shields to where they can beam out their crew?*

"These weapons," Stamets said, stabbing at the scanning controls, "are mycelial-spore-based armaments." He seemed both amazed and angered. "This is *exactly* the kind of technology we didn't want to come from our research."

Burnham shared an annoyed glance with Saru, then took Stamets's elbow in her hand, as much to shock him as to steady him. "Get a grip on yourself, Lieutenant. These are neither our weapons, nor your technology." She directed him toward the main viewer as another charge exploded in sparkle against their shields. "*We* are under attack."

He pulled from her grasp, but his expression told her that the message had been received. "Sorry, Captain."

"I do understand. But every time we solve one problem, another arises. Assuming the one blood-burn case on Benecia was the Symbalene strain, in the time we've spent here, that single infection could be dozens by now. Even with the most stringent quarantine procedures." She let that settle on him, then said, "I need to know if we can bolster the shields against this method of assault."

Stamets scanned the data again, and the captain could see his wheels beginning to turn. "Maybe. Maybe."

"You have an idea?" Saru asked.

"I'll, uh . . . do a thing." He shrugged. "I'll, you know, I'll be me and figure it out."

"You'll be *you*?" the captain asked. "That's your plan?"

He paused self-consciously. "Yeah."

Saru put his left hand to his side and leaned away from the astromycologist. "I am hoping," he told Burnham, "the lieutenant also has a plan B."

"So am I," the captain said dryly.

But when Burnham looked back, Stamets was already running a simulation on the console. "It's all very funny until I come up with an idea to modify our shield frequencies." He poked again at the console, then swiped a graph toward the display. Motioning to it proudly, he just smirked as if to say *voilà*.

The screen presented an esoteric shield modulation that Burnham had once seen in school, but wouldn't have thought to use here. "This is generally used to control fungal disease outbreaks in aeroponics gardens or modern greenhouses."

"I know," Stamets said. "There's a similar decontamination procedure in the cultivation bay."

Suitably impressed, the captain tilted her head to Saru. "He'll just be him."

"Well, I wouldn't release the confetti just yet," the astromycologist said. "We have two problems."

"Two *more* problems," Saru pointed out.

"Right." Stamets tapped again at the console. "One: the shield emitters don't have the frequency range we need. We can cannibalize the decon equipment—"

Burnham cut him off. "We don't have access to the cultivation bay right now."

"I know. Alternatively, if we can find a quarter of a kilo of rubindium crystals to realign the particle matrix of the emitters, we will be able to do what we need."

"I believe we do have that much." Saru took a padd from the console, checking ship's stores.

"What's problem number two?" Burnham asked, and as another blast skittered off the shields above them, she hoped it wouldn't be a hill too high to climb.

When Stamets hesitated, a twist of tension worked its way up from the captain's lower back and spread across her torso.

"Mister Stamets?" Saru prompted.

"I'm afraid the shields will have to be dropped to make this work."

The tension Burnham held now pushed itself into a headache. "For how long?"

"Twenty-three seconds."

"That is a very exact calculation," Saru said with admiration.

"I know the captain would want exact."

She did, but that didn't make the number more palatable. Without shields, it was possible the damage done to *Discovery*'s hull—not just by the alien weapons but by the JahSepp organisms—wouldn't be reparable in their current location and state. In fact, it was likely to hasten their deaths.

"Twenty-three seconds," Burnham said solemnly as she stalked toward the main viewscreen, watching the blur of a vessel spitting fungal charges at them, "is a very long time when someone is firing at you." Lowering herself into the captain's chair, she swiveled toward tactical. "Mister Rhys, current shield status."

"Seventy-four percent, Captain." He loaded the available data to her chair and she glanced at it. "They've been maintaining the attack, but the charges are relatively weak."

Burnham studied the alien ship as another charge spat forth, punching energy against the shields with a crackling snap.

She moved to Saru, back at his own station, while Stamets worked on the opposite console. "Correct me if I'm wrong, Number One, but the timing of their firing is even and metered. I count sixteen seconds between salvos."

Saru checked his console. "Sixteen seconds is accurate. Mister Stamets needs seven seconds longer to reconfigure the shield emitters."

"Even at their weakened power levels," Rhys said, "without shields, a blast from those weapons against our naked hull would create a breach we couldn't seal."

"Why?" the captain whispered to herself. "Why weaken their charges at all?"

Saru overheard and offered a possible answer: "If they were gathering our spores, and are using spore-based weapons, they may be low on their own reserves."

"Let's say the distress call *was* theirs," Burnham replied. "Low on fuel, they lure in a ship with the technology to intercept their message, and covertly try to take their spores." She rose, and walked toward Saru. "We interrupt that. They take some of our crew hostage, and we take some of theirs."

"They realize we have found them," the Kelpien added to her narrative, "either by sensor scan or communication with their people."

"Then they fire on us," Burnham said. "Have they lowered the charge because they don't want to harm their people? Or us?"

"We cannot know," Saru said. "Not without the ability to communicate with them."

"Captain," Ensign Merrill called, "I have Lieutenant Bryce on the comm."

She tapped the screen on her chair's arm. "Go ahead, Mister Bryce."

"Captain . . ." Bryce's voice was calm, but the sound behind it was . . . inexplicable.

Burnham spun slowly toward Saru and caught his eye. "Is that Tilly? Humming?" she asked Bryce while also confirming with the first officer that he heard the same.

The Kelpien's expression suggested he was equally perplexed.

"Yes, sir," the comm officer replied. *"As an attempt to communicate."*

"Is it working?" Burnham imagined that could have gone wrong in so many ways.

"It doesn't seem to be doing any harm, Captain. We think mathematical progressions, expressed tonally, is the way to go. They won't let us near the consoles. I doubt I would've been able to get a communicator if Tilly wasn't distracting them."

It hadn't occurred to Burnham to consider music as math, but there was a certain brilliance to it. "Understood, Lieutenant. Commander Landry is just outside . . ."

They heard a sudden crunch of static, then silence.

"Bryce?" The captain thumbed at the comm control again. "Lieutenant?" She spun toward Ensign Merrill.

"Signal's gone, Captain. The communicator is no longer transmitting."

Burnham frowned and pushed herself from the seat. "Check in with Commander Landry. I want to know when she's ready to enter the lab." Off his silent acknowledgment, she turned back to her first officer. "Saru, pull up the universal translator. Let's see if we can build off Ensign Tilly's idea." She then paced to Stamets at the auxiliary science station. "How soon on your shield enhancements, Paul?"

"Engineering is getting the rubindium in place. Ten minutes, tops."

As the captain paced back, she felt the vibration of another contact against their shields. She had known it was coming and physically steadied herself for it. Mentally, she could not. *They are pounding the life out of my ship.*

———

I feel so alone, Culber told himself. And before he could complete the thought, there was Ephraim.

"You are hardly alone," the tardigrade said. He was closer to what Culber considered the creature's full size, but once again, as he moved toward the biobed across the room, he seemed to visually lose mass.

"Well, I feel that way," he said.

"Why?"

"This isn't my place." Culber sighed. *"The only time I feel right is with him. And that feeling is a lie."*

"A lie is a nontruth," Ephraim explained, probably to himself. *"What about any of this is a nontruth?"*

Fists balled on his lap, Culber bounced them on the top of his thighs, struggling to put into words—or rather thoughts—what he wanted to convey. Not just to Ephraim, but to himself. *"This isn't my universe. It's his. And another Hugh Culber's."*

"You are Hugh Culber. You have remembered that."

"But somewhere, on the Hood, *is another version of me."* Culber stood and motioned around the sickbay. *"A Constitution-class's medical facilities are much the same. At this very moment, in a room similar to this one, maybe that other Doctor Culber is caring for a patient. So where am I meant to be? There's already a version of me here."* He tapped an index finger on his own chest. *"I don't fit in here."*

"Why?" Ephraim's sincerity in trying to understand wasn't as frustrating as it once was, but it didn't help.

"*I can't take another man's life. What if* this *Paul*"—he crooked a thumb behind himself to indicate wherever Stamets might be—"*is supposed to be with* that *Hugh?*"

Clacking his right claws as a human might snap a finger, the tardigrade seemed to understand. "*Then you do believe in fate, as you described it.*"

"*Maybe.*" Culber looked down at his left hand. He held it out in front of himself, flexing it. "*I . . . think I know I died . . . and I know I'm now alive.*" He turned the hand over and stared at his palm. "*And those two facts are in contradiction with each other, so one of them can't be a fact.*"

Ephraim's mouth puckered in his odd alien smile. "*Or . . . can they?*"

"*They can't,*" Culber assured him, more bitterly than he wanted.

"*Or . . . can they?*"

"*Stop it,*" Culber angrily told him. He pushed himself from the biobed and stalked away. "*Just—don't.*"

Ephraim awkwardly followed, skittering in an odd half gallop across the deck. "*If two things seem to contradict and both are believed true, perhaps one is just not as true as you think.*" He paused, possibly for impressive effect. "*You could call it almost true.*"

"*I have no idea how a thought can be so clear and so muddled at the same time.*"

"*I am not the confused one,*" Ephraim said, without a hint of acrimony.

"*No, you're the confusing one.*"

"*I admit I am confounded by your anxiety. Has your being here not calmed you? Brought back to you who you are?*"

"*I feel at home here more than any place I've been in a long time.*" All those he'd met on this *Discovery*, reflections of the people he knew, were here. And because they were unhampered by the Klingon War, they were the same . . . but better. *"But these aren't my people . . ."* Culber told him, feeling some sort of reverse, warped survivor guilt. *"I know I shouldn't exist here."*

Ephraim's form seemed to collect itself in front of him. *"Do you know what I have learned from you? From your kind?"*

Culber didn't answer, but merely waited.

"You are composed of moments. You live in them." His short arms drew in as if he was holding himself. *"You are not like me. I see the whole forest. You live in one clearing."*

"What?" Culber felt his face drain of blood. *"Are you saying I'm not capable of your level of abstract thought? What are you trying to tell me?"*

"That your *nature is not of this place, but you are of this stuff. This is a conflict. And this ship is a moment—a clearing in the forest. Yes, you can survive the forest—barely—but you need to be in the clearing."*

" 'There's a clearing in the forest.' " Stamets had said it once, and Culber whispered it now to himself.

"You need this moment," Ephraim told him, and put one claw on the human's arm. *"Live here. Just for your now. Your now . . . is your way."*

Awkwardly, but with deep feeling, Culber took Ephraim's hand and held it tightly. *"You really do care about me."*

"I caused you," the tardigrade said, and the emotional state he broadcast was a mesh of pride and regret.

Why, the human couldn't guess. *"You caused me?"*

"And I didn't. And I won't. And I will."

"Of course," Culber said, exasperated. But he couldn't be too frustrated. Ephraim's frame of reference for reality was so different from his, so much more fluid and overarching than a linear existence. . . . The human *did* understand. Somewhat. And also knew that he had before, yet sensed he would forget again. Someday.

As that dawned on him, the tardigrade was encouraged by his expression of recognition. *"You understand now."*

"And I have before. And will again. And I won't?"

Excitedly, Ephraim said: *"Yes. This is not your clearing, but your mind* needs *a clearing. You cannot master the forest as I can. You must seek your moments!"*

"There's a clearing in the forest. That's how they go." I'm the *"they,"* he realized. Ephraim's conception of a being like Culber was too different to say it another way. *"You brought me to this place . . . this clearing, to restore me? My memory? My mind?"*

The tardigrade deflated a bit and the spikes on his head rustled. *"When I can, I guide you. When you allow it, I will. But I also won't guide you. And I also cannot guide you."*

"Are you saying you want me to stay here? Is that it? Stay *in this 'clearing'?"*

The tardigrade made some sort of movement that Culber didn't recognize—a shrinking deflation that felt like disappointment or sadness. *"In this now, let this be your clearing."*

Culber didn't comprehend, but he did appreciate the effort the tardigrade made to help him. *"By far, this is the strangest relationship I've ever been in."*

"Is strange good?" Ephraim asked hopefully.

Moving his head side to side uncertainly, Culber smiled guiltily. *"Sometimes strange is just strange."*

———

Stamets finished as if he were a concert pianist ending a concerto with a flourish. "Captain," he said formally, "we're ready."

"Stand by," Burnham ordered, curving toward tactical. "Mister Rhys, we want to time this just after their last shot hits. Assuming they keep to their sixteen-second rate, there should be only one raw strike against our hull before we raise shields again."

The thought of that didn't sit well and Lieutenant Rhys masked most of the dread from his voice. "Understood."

Burnham felt the same trepidation and turned to the first officer. "Mister Saru, one more idea, before we commit to lowering our shields. How difficult would it be to polarize our hull plating?"

"Captain?" His Kelpien features slanted toward puzzlement.

Burnham crafted her hands around an imaginary miniature of their vessel. "An old Starfleet method of bolstering the outer hull to attack."

"Yes, I'm familiar with its use, but our hull plating—"

"Vastly different in composition, I get that. But if it can carry any sort of electromagnetic charge, it may help."

He poked at his controls a long moment, then looked up, his expression mildly surprised. "I believe we can route power to the hull that would perhaps charge it enough to hamper their aiming sensors—a small amount—but they are not so distant they'll lose target lock. How much it will disperse a concussive blast, I cannot say."

"I'll take whatever I can."

He dabbed at his screen before placing his hands at his sides. "Then we are ready, Captain."

Burnham stepped toward the main viewer. "Please confirm all nonessential personnel are secured from any possibly exposed areas."

"Confirmed," Saru reported.

Through the forward view, beyond the primary hull that spread itself into the mycelial plane, past the forest into which they'd been pitched, hovered the translucent blob-wisp of an alien ship.

Two seconds remained . . . then just one.

A white bulb of energy shot toward them. When the charge had fully dissipated into harmless sparkle, Burnham twisted back. "Shields down," she told Rhys, and gave Stamets a quick look. "Paul, go."

The main viewport's shutters dropped again, but with sensors and circuits mostly restored, the tactical overlay remained. Burnham watched the passive blink of the reticle that signified the alien ship's location.

Moment to moment, every ship's bridge had a dominant emotion that radiated across its crew. Calm persistence, dedicated frustration, eager hopefulness . . . they were all par for the starship course. As they waited now, the overwhelming feeling was an unreasonably thick tension that pressed in on them like the humid night before a crashing storm. The captain felt it most of all.

Four seconds had slogged past. Twelve more to suffer.

"Polarization field standing by." Saru's voice was calm despite the trepidation Burnham knew he must feel. Whereas his people, by his own description, let their fear influence them greatly, the Kelpien first officer had learned to govern himself with rational aplomb.

"Polarize the hull plating," the captain ordered as she returned to the command chair. She wondered how long since someone had ordered *that* on a starship.

After Saru acknowledged it had been done, Burnham checked the time again, hoping that at least fourteen seconds had passed. Only eight actually had.

Now she just watched her display and counted: *Ten, eleven, twelve* . . .

"About halfway there," Stamets said. When she glanced back at him, his hands were a flurry between console and display.

Fourteen seconds. She tightened her fingers on the edge of the arms of her seat.

Fifteen . . . sixteen . . .

Nothing happened.

Plus one, plus two . . .

She exchanged a look with Saru, whose eyes widened as they waited.

Plus three, plus four . . .

Owo and Detmer glanced back at their captain. All Burnham could offer them was the expression Saru had given her.

Plus five, plus six . . .

"Twenty-two seconds," Saru said. "They *are not* firing."

The captain rose toward the first officer's station. "The question is why?"

"Perhaps, between lowering our shields and polarizing our hull—"

"That could act as a sensor mask," Owo said, swiveling toward Saru.

Hands up, Stamets backed off the secondary science console. "Modifications complete. Shields up!"

"Belay that," the captain said, holding up a hand as she returned to the command chair. "I'll thank you not to give command orders on my bridge, Lieutenant." She pressed the comm control. "Bridge to Landry."

"Landry here, Captain."

"The intruders in main engineering. Any activity?"

"All quiet. I think they know not to make a move on us."

Burnham took in a slow breath. "Interesting. And in the lab?"

"Sensors are still down," the security chief said. *"Restoring those circuits is difficult without internal access. We've been monitoring for more phaser fire as we work on the doors, but it's been quiet."*

"Understood," Burnham said. "Proceed as planned. Bridge out." She thumbed the comm off and began a slow pace to the main viewscreen, stopping just between the helm and ops stations. "It's one thing not to fire when we dropped shields for a few seconds, but it's been almost a minute." She put her hand on the back of Owo's chair. "Raise the port shutters."

Owo coded in an override and the main viewport was again revealed.

Burnham watched the alien ship a contemplative moment, then slowly turned to Saru. "Did they stop as soon as it became apparent an attack would damage us?"

"So it would seem," the first officer said.

"We've missed four salvos now," Rhys reported.

"Opinions?"

"They don't want to destroy our ship because their people are aboard," Saru said.

"Or they don't want to destroy our ship at all," Owo said, gesturing toward the vessel on the main viewer behind her. "They may see us dropping our shields as a good-faith act."

"That's a hell of a hunch," Detmer said quietly, perhaps only wanting Owosekun to hear.

The captain disagreed. "No, it's reasoned speculation: the aliens on board have no weapons we've seen. And we're here because of what Ensign Tilly and Lieutenant Stamets believed was a distress call."

"That wasn't intentional," Stamets pointed out, finger in the air.

"Not relevant," Burnham said, arcing toward him. "If it was a distress call, then the aliens were hoping for one of their own vessels to bring them spore replenishment. Being out of phase with us limited them from seeing the *Discovery* or her crew at all, and they may be as surprised by us as we've been by them."

Chiming in, Stamets took a step toward them. "Right—they may have scanned our spores, assuming their sensors are calibrated to look across quantum wavelengths specifically for *Prototaxites stellaviatori*, but totally missed they were ours—because to them, *we* didn't exist."

"Until we accidentally pulled some of their people into our quantum phase," Saru added. "As fascinating a topic of discussion as that may be, if we do not raise shields very soon, our hull will be eaten through before we have a chance to finish such a debate." To emphasize his point, he motioned toward the section of his display screen that showed hull degradation statistics. Several places flashed in red.

"A valid point," Burnham said as she retook the center seat. "Mister Rhys, I want to extend the shields around the alien ship as well."

"*Captain?*" Her Kelpien first officer leaned toward her from his station.

"That will limit the time we can protect ourselves," Stamets advised, quickly running the calculations. "The few hours we were supposed to buy will be cut in half."

Now at her side, Saru kept his voice to a near whisper. "Polarizing our hull plating will *not* protect us from a charge fired from within our own shields." He leaned down, his threat ganglia playing peek a boo behind the hand he used to cover them. "Michael . . . if you're wrong, we will be at *extreme* risk."

The captain was sympathetic to his concern, but didn't lower her own voice. It was fine for him to point this out, but she wanted her answer to loudly resonate. "I know, Saru, and I understand your reasoning. But if I'm right . . . maybe this enemy can become an ally, and we can help one another escape this place together."

"Begging the captain's pardon, but you say this isn't a

hunch . . ." Stamets took a few steps toward her as she turned in his direction. "Yet this feels really hunchy."

"You're free to frame it any way you choose, Lieutenant." She swiveled around to tactical. "Mister Rhys, reconfigure our shields to protect the alien vessel."

"Aye aye."

Accepting her decision, Saru and Stamets retreated to their respective science stations as she turned forward again. Settling in against the back of the command chair, Burnham hoped her hunch would be right. "Raise shields."

22

Captain's log, supplemental. *Ensign Tilly's suggestion that pi was a starting point for the universal translator has proven fruitless. Extending* Discovery's *shields around the alien ship, however, has stopped attacks on our vessel, and at least one method of communication seems open to us: actions, proving the proverbial cliché, are speaking louder than words.*

As a junior officer, Michael Burnham had sworn that should she get her own command, she would never use the captain's ready room. As she sat now, she smiled ruefully at her foolish, younger self. The solitude gave her the stillness she needed to center herself in her search for answers. She wasn't looking for Vulcan meditation or even human zen . . . just a personal moment of calm.

Which was broken when the door chime sounded.

"Damn. Come in."

Commander Saru entered, followed by a very distracted Lieutenant Stamets. Her first officer took a seat opposite her as the lieutenant motioned to the screen on the wall. "Engineering?"

"Just keeping an eye on our guests," Burnham said.

The aliens in main engineering were talking amongst themselves. Data scrolled down the left side of the screen and a very frustrating *Unknown Species* designation flashed along the bottom.

"They have four digits on each hand," the captain noted. "Have we tried base eight?"

"I tried bases one through ten," Saru replied. "Unfortunately, to no avail."

Of course he had. Saru could think outside the box . . . around, on top . . . the box had nothing on her first officer.

As she monitored the aliens, Burnham noticed that when they clicked their unknown language to one another, sometimes their fingers moved. Each seemed independently opposable to the other, like a robotic grappling claw. If there were nails, she couldn't see them, though the overall shape suggested talons, even if the sharp parts weren't present.

"Try sixteen," she said suddenly, looking at the aliens' booted feet.

"Toes?" Saru asked.

"It's a possibility." Stamets finally sat with them at the captain's desk. "If they have four toes on each foot, totaling sixteen digits between hands and feet . . ."

"There were sixteen seconds between attacks," Saru added. Truly intrigued by the idea, the Kelpien rose. "With permission, I'll attempt to prepare the mathematics and linguistic algorithms the translator will need."

With Burnham's tacit wave of approval, he exited, leaving the captain not quite alone. "Mister Stamets, to what do I owe the pleasure of your company?"

"May I?" Stamets moved to the screen, opening a stream of data with which she wasn't familiar. "Internal sensors show our cultivation bay full again, and—"

"Commander Landry said she couldn't get the sensors online." Burnham leaned forward, wondering how he'd managed to outsmart her security chief.

"The cultivation bay has certain unique horticultural scanners that check for the proper environmental conditions. From that, I could see our forest was back in phase with us." He indicated a relevant part of the data. "While a third of our spores have already been lost from the ship—being out of phase, they simply escaped—I think the bulk of our reserves are available."

"Enough to get us out of here?"

Stamets hedged, squinting uncertainly and lowering his head to one side. "To know that, I'd have to chart a course out of here, which means I need to see where we entered the mycelial plane. I can't do that from here. I need to access the spore drive's navigational computer."

The captain sighed, deflated. "Which is both offline and not in our hands. What about the hull?"

Changing the display to external sensors, he seemed more encouraged. "We've slowed the rate of decay by thirty-two percent. But extending the shields around the other ship means we can't maintain it for long." A smug expression broadened across his face. "I can't be sure, but I think I may have invented the galaxy's first antifungal starship shielding."

She patted him on the back as she moved toward the door. "If we survive this, I look forward to reading your paper."

———

"You were correct, Captain," Saru said as Burnham took the captain's chair. "A hexadecimal mathematic system seems promising. I believe we have enough of a lingual map to at least transmit *something* that to them would not seem like gibberish."

She turned toward the communications station behind them. "Mister Merrill?"

The ensign readied his console. "All hailing frequencies open, Captain."

Burnham deferred to Saru. "Please do the honors, Number One. Universal peace and hello greetings, or as close as you can come."

Saru worked his console and then motioned to Merrill, who slid his fingers across his screen and tapped a virtual button. "Transmission sent."

Two seconds became ten and the captain counted silently to sixteen.

"No reply," Merrill said.

Saru began, "Perhaps—"

Lieutenant Rhys cut the first officer off. "Captain, I *am* reading an energy buildup on the alien vessel."

Letting the command chair spin wildly as she turned and launched herself toward tactical, Burnham leaned down and looked over Rhys's shoulder. "Specify. Communications frequencies? A weapons signature?"

"I can't tell." He tried to tune in on the wave, applying different filters just as the captain would have. "The patterns are too irregular." He let out a frustrated huff. "Like . . . choppy."

"Saru?"

"Scanning." He was quiet a moment as he analyzed the data. "Indications are imprecise, as the ship is not entirely in our quantum phase, but"—his gaze narrowed—"these readings are building to critical levels."

"Engine breach?" Burnham asked.

"I'm unable to discern what or where their ship's engines are," Saru confessed. "It is possible."

Unexpectedly, Stamets called out from the auxiliary science station. "Captain, if their engine is as mycelial based as their weapons, which we have to assume it is or they wouldn't be here, our shields *might* defend us from a blast at this range, but not if they're *inside* our protection."

"I believe," the Kelpien said in a metered yet anxious tone, "we should cease extending our shields around them."

Burnham wasn't convinced. She studied the detailed energy readings on the viewscreen. The ship was still a blur, despite the computer enhancement. "This makes no sense. Peaceful greetings don't send alien vessels into self-destruct."

"Not generally," Saru said, "but we have seen how cultures like the Klingons take to them."

"This doesn't feel like that," the captain said.

"Maybe they're in trouble," Owosekun noted from ops, sharing first a look with Burnham and then Detmer.

"Speculation, Captain," Saru said. "But even if we make that assumption, the problem remains." His right hand spread across his chest, the first officer lowered his gaze. "My recommendation stands."

After protecting the alien vessel with *Discovery*'s shields, removing them could be seen as an aggressive act, which wasn't how Burnham wanted first contact to proceed. At the same time, Benecia was waiting. Her crew and even her ship were being held hostage.

She met Saru's eyes and despite his misgivings, asked, "Could this be their attempt to communicate?"

He swallowed hard and his jaw tightened. "I suppose it *is* possible, but, Captain . . ." She could feel his concern add to her own.

Her ship, her crew, her mission . . . especially her mission. First contact wasn't more important than that.

"Captain, a message!" Ensign Merrill called out before she could order Rhys to drop the shields.

"Put it on screen," Burnham ordered.

"Text only: 'wait.'"

Too suddenly for Burnham to order a reply, a bright, agonizing flash of white light overwhelmed the bridge crew. They all turned away, shielding their eyes as the main viewer struggled to compensate.

When the captain heard Saru grunt in pain, she forced her eyes open just as the overpowering brightness dissipated. The Kelpien collapsed toward the deck, but she caught him, steadying him until he regained his footing.

"Are you okay?" Burnham asked.

Eyes still closed, Saru groaned and leaned into his console. "Yes, yes. Everything's just *very* bright." One eye squinted open to check the ambient light level before he slowly blinked both back to normal.

Burnham twisted toward Stamets. "Did it explode?"

"Amazingly, no."

She turned back and watched as the alien vessel loomed close, now fully formed and no longer a translucent swath of foamy light. The captain was astounded by the sheer beauty of the ship. Fashioned like an hourglass, the vessel had no nacelles or outward signs of engines. It did have some of the same trappings as any starship: viewports, docking ports, and what appeared to be a deflector array. The hull was smooth, with significantly larger hull plates (perhaps armor?) than a Federation starship, but the seams between them were barely visible.

"Oh my," Saru said, standing sluggishly, still leaning on his station. "The craftsmanship is astonishing."

"They have brought," Stamets said slowly, "their entire vessel into our quantum wavelength."

"It's magnificent," Burnham breathed.

"Is it . . . biological?" The Kelpien studied the alien ship with focused intent as he returned to his scanners.

"Captain," Merrill said, his voice a reverent whisper. "They're hailing us—ship-to-ship visual."

Feeling the blood drain from her face, Michael Burnham stood in front of the command chair, straightened her shoulders, and smoothed her uniform. "Patch them through."

A rectangular window opened across the main viewer, showing what was probably their bridge. Three of the same alien species as were in engineering greeted her. The lead one, perhaps their commander, spoke first, his or her arms raised, almost in a surrendering stance, but more formally. Their cultural equivalent of open arms, Burnham supposed.

"Greetings of peace also to you, Great Angel of Science Sailing House. I am Breytik, humble, nonrival angel twin of the Maligonq Familial Consideration."

Signaling for their audio to be muted, the captain turned to Saru. " 'Angel of Science Sailing House . . . nonrival angel twin'? Little help?"

" 'Captain of the *Starship Discovery*,' I believe." He tapped at his console and reviewed part of his monitor. "Yes. And it seems 'nonrival angel twin' means he also is in command. This translation matrix is twelve minutes old." One hand making a circular motion, he assured her, "It will catch up. It always does."

After a motion to Merrill to resume transmission, she looked forward again.

"I'm Captain Michael Burnham of the *Starship Discovery*, a representative of the United Federation of Planets. We have several of your personnel aboard our vessel. I want to assure you, they have not been harmed."

"Your sailing house wavered, Captain. We were innocent of your lives or home." Already "great angel" had been replaced by her proper title. Not that "great angel" wasn't nice too. Still, she glanced back at her first officer for some context.

"The computer suggests," Saru said, "that our natural quantum wavelength led them to believe we were not present."

"Thank you."

Burnham noticed the Maligonq dressed similarly to their crew aboard the *Discovery*. Their uniforms appeared to be more casual, comfortable versions of the EV suits, but all a pale blue. Each had symbols that could be rank or insignia, but what they meant she couldn't guess. "Commander Breytik, we also didn't understand your natural phase was out of sync with ours. We're here by accident. Our contact with mycelial space is generally brief and we cannot maintain our hull's integrity for very long."

"Saga twin, Captain Mykkel Burn-um. Coincidence is our contact." Her first name came out of the translator sounding more clicky, as the UT tried to approximate the Maligonq commander's enunciation as best it could. His arms now at his sides, his fingers flexing and clenching, he seemed sincere.

"We believe you travel using a mycelial-spore-based propulsion system. Is this new to your culture?"

"We are old," Breytik said. *"Many dead and born since beginning."*

"I see." It sounded like they'd been using mycelial travel for generations, though "born" and "dead" could refer to something other than people.

"Your use of this method is fresh?" he asked, seeming as curious about them as she was about the Maligonq. Thankfully, more and more frequently, the translator was giving them a normal syntax.

"Yes, this is new for us," Burnham said, stepping closer to the main viewscreen. She was trying to seem both open and relaxed, and she casually gestured to the helm. "At least, relative to our usual matter-antimatter warp engines."

"Warp?" Breytik scoffed, with a popping sound that may have been a laugh. *"Matter-antimatter!"* He seemed disgusted but not aggressive, per se. More like when Sarek would sniff at her and Amanda's occasional need to visit an Earth-style roller coaster.

Another voice was heard, more distant: one of the other

Maligonq speaking to Breytik. *"Commander, the chief edict may be of import."*

Turning toward the voice, Breytik snapped a hand in the other speaker's direction. *"No, no, they have breached the mycelial barrier. Their science is elevated. Their culture is relevant."*

"Do you think they're discussing their version of General Order One?" Saru asked.

Burnham smiled. "I think so."

"Amazing," Stamets whispered. "They see mycelial travel the way we do warp." He then added, "See? I elevated your science."

Startled by his presence, Burnham found Saru suddenly at her side. "Captain," he said quietly, "our scans show their hull has more extensive damage than ours. I believe they need to extricate themselves from mycelial space as much as we do."

"Affirmative, Captain Mykkel," Breytik said, clearly hearing Saru's report. *"The JahSepp do not tolerate intruders. They will transform those they can."* As the translator improved, the alien commander seemed more authoritative. It gave his warning gravitas.

Burnham wondered if the Maligonq, as more frequent visitors to the mycelial plane, had given those organisms their name. "Is JahSepp *your* word for them?"

"Our word?" Breytik's eyes blinked quickly, two sets of eyelids that closed and opened in tandem with one another but opposite their counterparts. Apparently this was meant to convey a negative reply. *"No, no,"* he said. *"This is their word."*

Saru and Burnham shared a curious look.

"A disease of ship stranded us here," the Maligonq commander continued. *"We sent out a message, but it was too weak to penetrate to our realm."*

"We picked up your distress call," Burnham said. "And"—

she gave Stamets a fleeting glance—"accidentally found ourselves here."

Breytik stooped over a bit, perhaps an apology. *"We saw what we now know are your fuel spores. We thought it a . . . fortunate coincidence and brought them into our perceptive range."* Glancing at someone offscreen, as if the act had been taken at that person's recommendation, Breytik seemed annoyed. *"It would never have been our intention to commit piracy."*

"You've done this before?" Burnham asked. "Brought spores from one quantum wavelength to another?"

"Yes, when needed." He clicked a long, thick sound that didn't translate, maybe a vocal tic or an idiom. *"It is not preferred, as it takes a great deal of energy. We do find a need to reap these fields occasionally and have found that some spore fuel lives across a wide range of wavelengths."*

"Your realm . . ."

"We know our realm is not yours," Breytik said, sounding a bit disappointed. *"Differing quantum variance and wavelength separate us."*

"Interesting," Saru said. "All of these alternate universes have a unique variance, but some may have a different wavelength as well." He glanced back to Stamets. "This is an astounding discovery, Lieutenant."

As Stamets had suspected, the mycelial network linked not only places in their own universe, but myriad alternate universes, even those in a different perceptive phase. How many? There was no way to know. They may as well try to count the stars in the sky.

And someone *was* going to try . . . someday. *Discovery* was there at the beginning of it, and Burnham couldn't help but be filled with an incredible surge of pride.

"Captain Mykkel," Breytik said, standing on one foot, *"we deeply apologize for our mistaken appropriation of your*

fuel. I have attempted to alert my crew aboard your ship of this misunderstanding. But, I believe their communications equipment has failed."

Was standing on one foot akin to a bow? As a trained xenoanthropologist, Burnham wanted to study the Maligonq. Perhaps, she mused, standing on one foot put one purposely off balance, and therefore it was like showing a weaponless hand, kneeling, or bowing one's head.

Stamets approached now and addressed both captains. "It's possible that accidentally pulling the Maligonq crew into our phase fried their comm equipment."

"They are also in your perceptive range?" Breytik asked.

"Yes," Saru said. "That was an error on our part."

"You didn't know?" Burnham asked the Maligonq commander. "Then why did you bring your entire vessel into *our* quantum wavelength?"

"It was the only way we could communicate with you," he replied. *"All other attempts failed."*

The captain of the *Discovery* grinned broadly. *He's truly my counterpart*, she thought. *Just as eager to solve a problem through communication.*

"Commander, may I suggest you join me here on *Discovery*?" Burnham stepped closer and indicated the spot next to her, as if inviting him to stand at her side. "It may help us solve each other's problems."

His hands flexing eagerly, Breytik seemed most excited about the idea. *"Captain Mykkel, I should be delighted."*

23

"Energize," Burnham ordered, eagerly awaiting Breytik's arrival.

The transporter chief activated the console, slid his fingers slowly down the controls, and a lone pad swirled in a sparkle of light.

When the hum of the transport faded, the Maligonq leader looked around nervously, until he met his fellow captain's eyes.

Burnham motioned for him to step off the transporter dais. "You said you were familiar with matter-energy transport technology."

"I am," he assured her as he gathered his composure. "Your process is significantly slower than ours." The translation of his vocal clicks and whistles was now smooth, the universal translator having learned at least enough to make it seem as if the language they heard were coming from his own lips.

With a slight bow, Burnham greeted Breytik more formally once he was at her side. She introduced her crew, indicating them in turn. "My first officer, Commander Saru," she said, "and our mycelial navigator and astromycologist, Lieutenant Stamets."

The Maligonq commander turned to him. "Ah, you understand our science well!"

"I didn't know it was *your* . . ." Stamets stopped when Burnham glowered at him. "Yes. I try."

"Is he pink?" Breytik asked Burnham. "He's very pink." He turned back to Stamets. "You're very pink."

"Thank . . . you?"

"I hope you feel better soon," the Maligonq told him, just above a whisper.

The captain motioned toward the doorway. "If you'd come with us, Commander?"

Burnham and her Maligonq guest exited first, followed by Stamets, who muttered to Saru, "It's not easy being pink."

Once in the corridor and on their way to main engineering, Breytik ran his four-fingered hand along one bulkhead as they passed—carefully not touching any control surfaces. "This is all manufactured?" He rubbed the opposable fingers together, then brushed them clean against his tunic. The idea of a nonorganic ship seemed to unnerve him.

"All Starfleet ships," Saru explained, "are manufactured."

"No wonder your transporter is slow," Breytik said.

Inside main engineering, Landry and the Maligonq "intruders" seemed to be enjoying one another's company, now that the universal translators had made that possible.

"You really should carry some kind of weapon, even a small one, if you're going to be on a landing party," she was telling one of the five, showing him how a type-1 phaser slid out of a type-2 to make a more concealable, if slightly weaker, energy weapon.

"I will suggest it to our— Oh! There he is! Commander!" The alien getting the armaments lecture nearly leaped toward Breytik. With all eight fingers, they instantly embraced each other's heads, then the other four did the same with their commander.

"You are all well?" the Maligonq captain asked his crew. "Dofchi? How is your back?"

"There were some moments of fright," Dofchi said, blinking toward Landry in a way Burnham wasn't sure was a wink or side-eye. "But all is well. My back is as it has always been. Too old to be away from home."

The clicking/popping sound they released, Burnham could tell from their expressions, was clearly laughter.

Their good humor was infectious and while it was difficult for any of the *Discovery* crew to keep themselves from smiling, Burnham knew there was still a tall hill to climb to get both vessels home.

"Where are the others?" Dofchi asked. "They were harvesting fuel."

"They're close," Landry said.

"In our spore-drive section." The captain glanced to Landry, who shook her head. "We still don't have access."

"It's a protected area, and there was a, uh, an accident that has jammed the blast doors." Burnham didn't feel it useful to go into the details that the cascade of failures began with a phaser blast from Breytik's crewmember. Not only because that served no purpose, but because the captain was sure she or one of her people might have reacted similarly to an alien vessel—and crew—suddenly appearing around them.

"Is there no way to reach them?" Dofchi asked the Maligonq captain. Burnham couldn't discern his expression; the tone the translator imparted might have been either regret or concern. If Dofchi had been lead on the landing party, perhaps it was guilt.

"Momentarily," Burnham said, and looked to Landry. "Correct?"

Her security chief nodded. "The engineers are almost done replacing the manual override circuits," she assured the captain.

"That's only going to unlock them," Stamets said. "We'll still need to use antigravs—very *gentle* antigravs—to move them because if they shift alignment and we can't easily close them again—"

"It's all in place, Lieutenant," Landry assured the astromycologist. "I read your parameters and I know my job."

Either because they were hosting an alien captain and his crew or because the multiple coffees were wearing off, Burnham noticed her security chief was far more placid than usual.

Stamets was caught off guard by it. "Well, okay then."

Burnham motioned him forward. "Lead the way, Lieutenant."

As he led Breytik and the others down the corridor, the captain hung back with Commander Landry for a moment. "I'm impressed," Burnham said.

The security chief gave her captain a discreet wink. "I know more than one way to disarm someone."

———

An eager group of engineers hopped to attention when the captain appeared with her alien guests. "Status?"

Orna Enav closed the panel nearest the door and gave Burnham a thumbs-up. "That's the last of the bypass circuits. It'll open now."

As Stamets double-checked the settings on the antigrav units, his brow remained furrowed. "Phasers should be automatically deactivated in sensitive areas. Have I ever mentioned that?"

"You have," Burnham said. "This entire vessel is a sensitive area. Ready?"

Reluctantly, he keyed the initiator and stood back as the antigravs steadily lifted the heavy blast doors.

It was a slow process, but once complete, only the normal doorway stood between them and the spore-drive lab.

Burnham moved toward the door but Landry put her arm out. "Captain, I think it would be best if Commander Breytik took the lead. Let his people see him first."

A prudent idea. "If you're willing," she said to her Maligonq counterpart.

"Yes, of course," he said.

When the blast door finally opened, Burnham heard something she couldn't place and crooked her head to try to localize it.

"Is someone screaming?" Landry asked, her hand on her phaser again.

"No," Saru said, "I hear a buzzing."

Seemingly without such worries, Breytik, true to his word, entered first, holding up his arms as the inner doors parted and he descended into the lab. Burnham and Saru followed behind, with Landry and Stamets the last to enter.

The odd sound they'd heard before the doors opened was now instantly recognizable: music. Had Burnham thought about it, it would have been obvious. What she never would have imagined was Tilly standing on the damaged console, singing into a phaser power pack as if it were a karaoke microphone. And her Maligonq "captors" acting as backup singers.

"With an oink, oink here," the ensign sang, bouncing awkwardly on the control station.

"And an oink, oink there!" the Maligonq scientists answered.

"Here an oink—" Tilly continued.

"There an oink—" the alien backup singers called out, swaying behind her.

"Everywhere an oink, oink!" Hopping down, Tilly conducted her chorus.

"Old MacDonald had a farm—" Airiam sang, getting into it as she gathered the parts to reassemble her phaser.

"E-I-E-I-O!" the lead Maligonq crooned into an imaginary microphone.

Tilly twisted around, finally seeing that the lab door was open. "And on that farm she had a— CAPTAIN!"

"E-I-E-I-O!" the aliens sang.

Flustered, Tilly handed the phaser's power pack to Bryce and rushed forward, anxiously smoothing her uniform jacket as she did. "Captain, you're here! It's good to see you!" She motioned to those behind her. "We were singing."

"I can see that," Burnham said, sharing a bemused look—she hoped—with Breytik, then shooting a quick look to a rather stone-faced Saru.

"They really like 'Old MacDonald,'" the ensign explained with a nervous titter.

"A little too much." Bryce folded his arms defiantly.

"I tried to get them interested in *your* music," Tilly snapped. "They hated it."

Bryce looked away, rolling his eyes. "Back off already, Ringo."

"That's the Beatles!"

"Lots of people like Martian Punk," the lieutenant retorted.

"Yeah, but anyone with taste?" Tilly muttered snidely. "Martian Punk scared them, Captain," she explained to Burnham.

"I assume," Saru said, "that the universal translator began working in here."

"We noticed once Kittik here started singing with the lyrics." Tilly moved her head toward the Maligonq who'd been holding the imaginary microphone. "Kittik, this is Captain Burnham."

Kittik raised his hands and a friendly clicking radiated from his throat as he turned to Burnham. "Greetings, Old Mac-Donald. What else is on your farm?"

The captain hesitated. "I don't . . ."

"Oh, no." Tilly pulled Kittik back a step and tried to get between them. "Songs aren't always about people." She looked to Burnham. "We dedicated that to you, Captain, but it wasn't *about* you."

Turning to the Maligonq leader, the captain introduced her crew. "Commander Breytik, may I present Ensign Tilly, Commander Airiam, and Lieutenant Bryce."

Tilly giggled. "Hi."

Burnham said, "Tilly is very enthusiastic."

Commander Airiam silently greeted the Maligonq commander, but seemed to be working hard to hide a smile.

Lieutenant Bryce was still fuming, but managed: "Commander Breytik."

"Captain, Kittik told us his people thought our spores weren't ours." Tilly motioned to where the Maligonq containers had been. "They'd been trying to gather what they could because they're also trapped here."

"We're aware, Ensign."

Breytik put up his hands. "Greetings, Till-lee. I like the color of your hat."

"Thanks," she said cheerfully, then added with a whisper, "It's actually hair."

Noticing that Stamets was checking things on the damaged station, the captain edged around two of the Maligonq to get his impressions. "How bad?"

He ran his hand along the console and rubbed soot between his fingers. "Charred—"

"We can fix it." Tilly was clearly eager to make up for being found singing atop it.

Stamets moved to a working console and began pulling up sensor readings. "Captain, I can confirm we have seventy-two percent of our spore reserves available in the cultivation bay. But that won't be enough to get out of here, let alone share them with the Maligonq." He turned to the alien delegation who now filled the lab. "How did you lose your reserves anyway? And why are you even here?"

Burnham gave the lieutenant an annoyed look. However,

even though she wasn't thrilled by his tone, the questions were valid. She wanted the answers as well.

"We detected an infection in the network and were dispatched to cure it," Breytik replied forthrightly. "In doing so, our own fuel spores were accidentally infected."

"I had warned of that possibility," Kittik said.

The Maligonq captain shifted back and forth, one foot to the other. "Yes, yes, my friend, you did. But a bit too late. That's why we sent the message."

"We got it," Stamets said, "but didn't understand its meaning."

"It was not for you." Kittik's throat popped loudly. "We were warning our earlier selves."

"Warning . . . yourselves?" Stamets shared a look with Burnham.

"To not make the mistake that infected our spores," Breytik explained.

"You sent a message back in time? Doesn't that create a paradox?" the captain asked.

Kittik's expression teetered toward bafflement. "What is that? Pay-row-docks?" Clearly the universal translator didn't yet know a Maligonq word for the concept.

"Contradictory events," Tilly said. "At least in time travel. I can't go back in time and stop my parents from meeting before I'm born, because then how could I go back in time to do that."

None of the Maligonq's expressions suggested they knew what she was talking about.

"Fascinating," the captain murmured.

Stamets held up a finger. "A moment, please. Just to be sure I'm getting this: The message we intercepted, that accidentally brought us here, was for your edification, *in the past?* You have no problem breaking causality? Without consequence?"

"Causality?" Breytik communed silently with his comrades and then they all click-laughed for an extended period. "A child's notion of things," he said more to them than to Stamets.

Burnham gave her astromycologist a wry look. "It's the tortoise."

"I beg your pardon?" the Maligonq captain asked, confused.

The captain noticed Saru's features had tightened into a Kelpien smirk and she offered Stamets the chance to explain. "Tell them what I'm talking about, Paul."

Vacillating a moment, Stamets pursed his lips, seemingly unwilling, but he finally acquiesced. "It's something I used to say when people told me the mycelial network theory was ridiculous. I suggested they still thought the world was a flat plate on the back of a tortoise."

"What is a tortoise?" Kittik whispered to Tilly.

"Like a turtle."

"Oh. What is a turtle?"

"It really doesn't matter," Stamets assured them. "It's just a reminder that as much as we think we know, there's at least as much we don't. If not more."

Patting his shoulder as she stepped to the center of the lab, Burnham called the room's attention to her. "I appreciate the feeling of camaraderie we suddenly have, and my hope is that this is a great beginning to more formal first contact," she said. "But we still have a problem if between the two of us, we don't have enough spores to get even one of our vessels, let alone both, out of the mycelial network."

"But you grow your own," Kittik said. "Which I admit is an ingenious plan to keep your stores filled."

Stamets bowed his head appreciatively. "Still, our cultivation bay needs a minimum of twelve hours to replenish, and it's more time than we have."

Burnham stepped toward Kittik. "If we can help you communicate with your previous selves, sending your warning fully back in time as you planned, would saving your spore reserves be enough to get us both out of this plane?" It would be a wild scheme, at least to a logical mind. How could they tell themselves to avoid a mistake, avoid it, and still have the foresight to send the message back? *I suppose after it's been avoided, there's no longer a need to send the message, because the circumstances never arise in the first place,* she thought. *But then you're left with a message from a future that no longer exists? No wonder the Vulcan Science Directorate denied the possibility of time travel for so long.*

"It may be possible," Kittik said. "Show me how much you would need."

Stamets worked the console in front of him and pulled up the data. Behind him, Burnham noticed Saru was directing Airiam and Tilly in repairs of the primary console.

When the Maligonq spore engineer saw the information provided, he balked and reacted almost angrily. "No, no, your spore-energy ratios are primitive." He looked from Stamets to Breytik. "Horrible. Horrible."

"I'm sorry?" Stamets said.

"You waste power." Kittik motioned to the display. "You waste spores."

"How?" Tilly asked from across the room.

"Yes, can you show us how?" Stamets was equally intrigued.

Kittik's nasal ridge did seem to crinkle at the idea. "Not with this antiquated, nonorganic ship."

"Antiquated?" Stamets nearly choked on the word.

Burnham tried not to bristle as well. It was odd to hear her state-of-the-art ship described in such terms.

"I mean no insult, Stah-mets." Kittik glanced over to

Tilly and motioned toward the lieutenant. "This is the Stah-mets, yes?"

"Yes."

"He's very pink."

She waved the comment off. "You get used to it."

"Maybe Justin Straal was right," Stamets said. "He said my mycelial forest was a mistake, and that a hold filled with spore reserves was more reliable. The *Glenn* would have enough spores for us all."

"Would they?" Burnham asked. She caught Stamets's gaze and held it. "Enough for *three* ships?"

Stamets didn't think on it long, nor did he need to consult the computer. "Yes, it would, Captain."

Burnham smiled. "Then let's hail them and show them the way."

Doubt creased the astromycologist's features. "Captain, I admit it's a good thought, but I don't think we have the time."

"Lieutenant, Bryce and I did get the mycelial communications array working," Tilly said. "It would use a lot of spores to make it work, but it could get a message to the *Glenn*."

"You're missing the point, Tilly." Stamets stepped toward her, his voice marbled with guilt. "I got us here by accident. Now, I've worked out how to get us *out*, but telling them how to get *in* the network—and stay here long enough to deliver the spores? That's another animal."

"Is it a tortoise?" Kittik asked.

"It's a unicorn," Stamets told them before turning back to Burnham. "Because it's not possible, Captain. Maybe I could tell the *Glenn* how to modify their systems, but that would be the easy part. Retrofitting their circuits so it doesn't inca-pacitate them like it did us? That would take at least an hour longer than we have. By the time they arrive, the JahSepp will have eaten through our hulls, and then our bodies."

As brilliant as he was, it amused Burnham that he seemed to be the only one in the room who wasn't putting all the pieces together. "Mister Stamets, I believe *you're* missing the point."

When his blank look told her that he still didn't understand, she turned to Saru, who seemed to be itching to explain.

"Lieutenant," the Kelpien began, "the Maligonq were sending themselves a message in *the past*. Are we correct in assuming that you could craft the temporal coordinates of your message so that it reaches the *Glenn before* we arrived here?"

Bouncing on the balls of her feet, Tilly seemed to want to answer that question. In fact, she had raised her hand.

"This isn't a classroom, Tilly," Bryce said.

"I don't know about that." Stamets smiled contritely. "I think I just got schooled." Bending back over the computer console, he ran some calculations, then straightened, deflated. "We don't have enough spores to send the signal." He turned to Kittik and Breytik. "Would you?"

The Maligonq commander glanced to his scientists, and they all wrinkled their noses. He then turned again to Stamets. "I'm afraid not."

A pall dropped over them, and somehow Burnham now felt responsible not just for her own ship but for Breytik's as well. On top of that, she couldn't forget that Benecia Colony still needed them, and were by now calling for help, wondering what had happened to their medical support.

Suddenly jumping to his console, Stamets began tapping quickly at the controls.

"You have an idea, Lieutenant?" Saru asked, edging toward him.

While Stamets furiously worked, Tilly answered for him. "Oh, he has an idea."

Throwing up a power calculation on the display, the astro-mycologist motioned to it with pride. "We only need spores to open the network path. To *send* the broadcast . . . our 'ancient' warp-power tech will have to do."

"You can do this with your primitive matter-antimatter process?" Kittik drew close to the screen, studying the data. He looked back to his fellow Maligonq scientists in shock.

The tension that had been twisting tightly around Burn-ham's spine released mildly. She put her hand on Stamets's shoulder and gave it a cautious, encouraging squeeze. "Let's make a call."

24

Justin Straal watched as Captain Deb Underwood brushed the side of her hand across the ready room table for the third time. If there were any crumbs left from her Andorian spice-bread toast that hadn't already been pushed to the floor, all would be shocked. Nevertheless, it was a habit of the *Glenn*'s captain that her crew knew too well.

One of the few things about which Straal and Underwood could always agree was that food was the best way to get through tedious scheduled briefings. But given the message they had received and he had just relayed, he had no appetite.

"Explain it again," Underwood ordered.

Straal stifled a sigh and reset the holographic. A blue map of the mycelial network sprouted and grew above the table. Certain areas glowed brighter than others, some in white, some in green. "The distress call we received from within the network," Straal said, "shouldn't be possible—on many levels." He motioned to a white blip. "This is our last reading on the whereabouts of the *Discovery*, approximately twelve parsecs from the Denobula Triaxa system." He then pointed to another small, flashing icon. "This also indicates the *Discovery*, sitting within the network itself."

"And you got it the moment they last jumped?" the captain asked, resting a hand on her teacup.

"Yes," Straal said. "But judging by the relative time codes, the message is coming from the future. Our future. Their present."

"I hate time travel," Underwood grumbled.

"Everyone does," Straal said.

"You've authenticated the call?"

Straal deferred to the spore-drive ops officer. "Freddy?"

The young lieutenant hesitated, scratching his beard thoughtfully. Straal knew he didn't like being put on the spot, but it was Kovalik who had first received the transmission. "It's how I read it, Captain. Once we decoded it, it was pretty clear."

Turning to her chief of security, Underwood pursed her lips and grunted softly. "Opinion?"

Lieutenant Commander Henry Sieber pushed away his mostly empty plate. He removed the napkin from his lap and dabbed at his mouth lightly before answering. "We're obligated to pursue it, sir. It is not standard operating procedure, but I'll certify it's genuine. Won't be easy, though, from what I saw."

"It'll take over an hour, yes," Straal said. "But it's not outside our wheelhouse."

Underwood sucked her teeth a long moment, then decided. "Very well, Commander. Get to work. Dismissed."

———

Even with Kovalik's and Sieber's help, and an extra engineering detail, the work took closer to two hours to finish. They might have been completed a few minutes sooner had Underwood not gotten on the comm every quarter hour to ask how much past the time they'd be delayed. "It doesn't matter," Straal explained. "We'll get there when we're supposed to."

But the captain didn't mind being too careful.

When they were ready to jump, Sieber was there to see Straal off. "You're ready for this?"

As Straal rolled up his sleeves and slid the biomonitor cuff onto his own wrist, he winced, then shook off the too-tight feeling.

"You okay?" Sieber asked.

"I don't like the cuff, but it's not the first time we've needed it."

"Sorry. Doctor's orders, at Stamets's recommendation."

"They're both worriers."

Snorting, Sieber patted the man on the shoulder. "No offense, Straal, but you're a pretty pessimistic guy yourself."

His eyes narrowed defensively as he pulled his arm away. "Please. I have the most upbeat, positive outlook on life of anyone I know."

Sieber crossed his arms and just stared at the man as he ran a last check on the spore-injector console.

"I do!" Straal protested as he met his friend's eyes.

"Justin, last month I told you my cousin's cat ran out of the house and they couldn't find her."

"So?" Straal brushed past him to check something on the other console. "I said it was too bad, didn't I?"

"No," Sieber said, his arms still crossed. "You suggested they shouldn't have a cat because they're too much of a bother."

Stopping midstride to the reaction cube, Straal turned back. "Oh. Sorry. I'm usually nicer than that."

"You're fine," Sieber told him, slapping him on the back. "*Nice* isn't a term I'd use to describe you, but you're at least . . . friendly. Most of the time."

Lowering himself against the seat that held him at an incline in the chamber, Straal laid his forearms in position for the biomechanical shunts that would momentarily link him with the spore drive's nav system. "Glad I can be easily labeled with such pet-like terms. Next you'll tell me I'm well groomed."

"You are." Sieber laughed as the door closed with a hiss.

Straal rolled his eyes, and wiggled his hips uncomfortably against the sled. "Aren't you heading to the bridge?"

"You want me to stay with you?" the security chief asked. "I could make up a reason."

"Ritkowski is here," Straal said, nodding toward his position at the main station.

"I don't mind," Sieber assured him.

"You worried you might lose me doing this, or lose the *Glenn*?"

"Yes," Sieber said, acknowledging both.

Perhaps admiring the honesty, the astromycologist laughed with some amusement. "You're the one who told the captain you agreed this was from the *Discovery*."

"Because it is," Sieber said. "Look, you're uncertain, I get that. And it does concern me that you're maybe distracted. We've never done anything like this before. Are *you* thrilled about shutting down and isolating half our systems?"

"Not really," Straal replied. "But I trust Paul."

"And if you trust him, I trust him," Sieber said. "Just stay focused. Please." He patted the glass between them. "That's a security directive, my friend."

"Yeah." Straal tried to take the moment lightly, but he found he couldn't. He watched his friend march up the steps to the exit, then called to Ritkowski. "Initiate."

———

"Are the shield adjustments online?" Captain Underwood asked tactical as she paced the bridge.

"Yes, Captain," Lieutenant Mikhailov replied as she checked her screen. "No problems."

The captain pivoted toward the spore-drive console.

Kovalik saw her coming and promptly reported, "Spore drive is online and engaged."

Just as the lift doors opened and Sieber took his station to the left of her, Underwood lowered herself into the command chair. Settling in, she punched the intraship control on its arm. "All hands, this is the captain. What we're about to attempt might be a rougher ride than usual. But you are skilled, you are strong, and our sister ship needs us. We will be there for them, just as Captain Burnham and the crew of the *Discovery* would be for us." She took in a breath. "Black alert."

"Black alert. Black alert," the computer announced as alert screens flashed and the bridge's lighting took on a bluish hue.

Glancing one last time at Sieber, Underwood squared her shoulders into the back of the chair and steadied herself more than she normally would have. "Jump."

Previous leaps began with the sound made by the cavitation of the modified saucer section, but that odd squealing, unique to the *Crossfield* class alone, was over rather quickly. Usually. This time, it seemed to last interminably, and as the captain turned the center seat toward Sieber, she could feel her chair and her bridge shaking beneath them.

"Report."

"Modified shields are holding." Sieber's voice needed to be louder than a typical jump, just to carry over the din of the reverberations around them. He swiped one hand across his station, while steadying himself with the other. "Sheer climbing, but within tolerance."

After what was perhaps the longest fifty-four seconds of their lives, the vibrations around them didn't slow—they stopped.

"Jump complete," Kovalik said, sounding out of breath. "Computer is reading this as an incomplete navigation sequence."

"That's expected," Underwood said, and it made sense, since the mycelial network wasn't a destination—it was the road. "It just means the coordinates aren't in the nav system's database." The captain leaned toward Lieutenant Viswanathan. "Ops?"

Akila Viswanathan's voice had a bit of a rasp, likely from tension tightening her throat. "Systems *are* responding—sluggishly. Shielding held."

The captain nodded her approval and activated her chair comm. "Bridge to spore drive."

"Straal here."

"All well, Commander?" Underwood asked.

No immediate reply came, but that could have been because he was removing himself from the reaction cube. *"Not a trip I'd like to make every day,"* Straal said finally. *"But yes. I'll be fine."*

"Good. Get your gear. The job's only just begun."

"Acknowledged."

"Bridge out." Rising, Underwood clasped her hands together, rubbing some warmth into her fingers. Mycelial jumps always made her fingers cold. "All right, people. We're in one piece. Let's bring it all back online. Report status to the first officer."

Sieber was in charge of gathering the status reports and when the crew had reported in, he came to the command chair to confirm. "All systems back online, Captain."

She gave him a slim smile and motioned toward the main viewscreen. "Lieutenant Viswanathan, let's see where we are."

"Onscreen," Viswanathan said, but there was a delay as the computer slowly parsed what must have been a voluminous amount of sensor data.

When the shutters retracted and the main viewer flashed to life, Underwood felt her jaw slacken. "Oh, my," the captain breathed out, her eyes widening. She took a step forward.

Beyond their starship, the saucer section jutted forward into an organic fungal landscape: the mycelial plane. It extended as far as they could see, where a vibrant horizon met a dark, starless sky. The entire color wheel of fungi stretched out in every direction, bright and glowing against the black background of the dark forest. Distantly, a spore geyser exploded, and yet it seemed coordinated and not chaotic. The beauty of a nature heretofore unseen, until Straal and Stamets had opened it to them.

Only once since *Discovery* launched had Deb Underwood seen their cultivation bay. Either Stamets or the young ensign who gave her the tour had called it their mycelial forest. In comparison to this, it was a sparse garden.

"Get Straal up here," the captain ordered Sieber. "He needs to see this."

Underwood heard her first officer on the comm, but she couldn't take her eyes off the main viewscreen. She took another two steps toward it.

"Are we in position?" she asked, still somewhat breathless.

"Thrusters autofired at the proper coordinates," Garrison confirmed off his console.

"Two vessels nearby," Mikhailov called out. "One is the *Discovery*."

"Give me that visual," Underwood ordered.

The viewscreen now showed their sister ship, which was covered in black soot. Wind brought motes of dust or debris into contact with its shields, causing cascades of sparkle and color as the tiny fragments sizzled against the deflective screens. Underwood could see the starship had, in fact, extended its shields around another ship, which appeared less like a vessel than it did some spacefaring creature. The alien ship looked far more like it belonged in the mycelial plane than either of the Federation vessels.

The captain heard the lift doors open, but it was only when Straal inhaled sharply that she turned to face the astro-mycologist.

Straal just stood for a long moment, a few steps out of the turbolift, his jaw quivering.

Underwood watched him, enjoying vicariously the man's joy. Obviously his route to the bridge had avoided any other observation ports. "Nice view?"

Overwhelmed, Straal was uncharacteristically speechless. He finally moved forward, stretching a hand toward the main screen as if he might reach out and touch the realm that for him lived mostly in dreams.

The captain was pleased. Not only had they gotten there, but she could see it had reenergized her mycelial navigator. Proudly, she turned to communications. "Hail the *Discovery*. Tell them we're ready to bring them home."

———

"Captain Underwood of the *Glenn*, Captain," Lieutenant Bryce said. "Pretty amazing, since we literally just sent the message a moment ago."

"Temporal mechanics doesn't always have to hurt," replied Burnham. "Patch her through." As she rose from her chair to greet Underwood's hologram, it flickered with static and garbled into a knot of light and lines. She turned back to Bryce. "Lieutenant?"

Bryce worked at his console and after a moment shook his head, frustrated. "Shields are disrupting the holographic signal."

"Switch to screen," she ordered, and turned back to the main viewer.

"Switching, aye." A tap on his console and Bryce sent the image of the *Glenn*'s bridge to the viewscreen.

"What'd you get yourself into this time, Michael?" Underwood teased, breaking the pretense of protocol.

"It's been," Burnham said frankly and with a weary smile, "a very interesting day. We're glad you're here. Any update from Benecia?" She'd made sure to add her overwhelming concern of the medical emergency in a personal log for Underwood to read.

"They've been informed of your delay. It's not as long as it feels to you. They still only have the three cases and they're all in quarantine."

"At least there's that. What's your status?" Burnham asked. "Rough ride?"

"Thanks to your specifications, far smoother than yours."

She met Underwood's eyes, somehow easier to do on the solid image of the viewscreen. "Thank you for coming, Deb."

"Anytime, Captain. Now let's get you out of here."

25

"Energize," Paul Stamets ordered.

Tilly stood at the cargo bay's heavy-transporter console. "Aye, sir." She moved its sliders down.

The central plate with the giant Starfleet insignia, just meters in front of them, hummed to life as the sparkling columns formed. When the light show was finished, Justin Straal stood there with a dozen large stasis containers behind him.

Leaping toward Stamets, he rushed forward into an excited mix of handshake and embrace. "Paul, have you seen it?" He held the other man by the shoulders. "We scanned it. It's bio-organic. Its capacities for meiotic sporogenesis must be immense."

"Kittik tells me they are." Stamets gently untangled himself. He couldn't remember seeing Straal so enthusiastic about . . . well, anything. Even their first jump hadn't inspired him to this degree. "But their entire stock became diseased and they had to purge everything. The whole lot."

"I want to meet them. Where are they?" Straal looked around the cargo bay, searching for the Maligonq.

"Kittik is here. But the others beamed back to their ship. We'll have Tilly beam what we need to the cultivation bay, and then send the Maligonq their share."

Suddenly realizing the ensign was even there, Straal said, "Oh, hi, Tilly!"

"Hi, Doctor Straal." Tilly waved, but quickly got back to working the transporter controls.

"This'll be all we need?" Stamets asked.

Straal motioned toward the canisters. "It's all there. Should be more than enough. Forty percent for you, the rest for them. But you'll get only one shot, because we need to get out of here too."

"Got it." Stamets motioned toward the corridor. "Come along, my fungal friend. Meet their chief engineer. *Mycelial* engineer."

Straal was ready and eager and strode so hastily that he had to slow down to wait for Stamets to catch up. "You say everything is spore based?" he asked.

Moving quickly, they had to dodge around various crew going to their stations, or still cleaning up from the damage when the *Discovery* hard-landed into the mycelial plane. Even thinking about that mishap couldn't minimize the excitement Stamets felt from getting to show this to Straal. "I mean, I've not seen it all, but it's the basis of their vessel—which, did you say is at least eighty percent bio-organic?"

"Yes! Can you imagine us pitching that?" Straal laughed as they boarded the turbolift.

Stamets snickered. It had been hard enough to sell anyone on a new method of propulsion. "What if we suggested that you could grow a starship? Would anyone believe us?"

"No," Straal said. "We'd get more sea-monkey kits than we could count. Remember someone signed up the lab for a mushroom-of-the-month club?"

"I'd forgotten. Who was the joker behind that?"

"If I had found out . . ." Before Straal could finish his threat, the turbolift doors opened and he was back on their first thought. "An organic starship. Do you think we could ever?"

"For us, no," Stamets said. "The Maligonq have been traveling the mycelial network for hundreds of years."

Once in the lab, Stamets rushed him to the Maligonq scientist, introducing him with excited formality. "Justin Straal, this is Kittik. Kittik, this is my longtime friend and colleague. We discovered how to access the mycelial network and together helped to build this." He spun a finger in the air to include all they saw.

When the Maligonq turned to Straal, Stamets watched, rapt. They'd both met many different species. But this was a first for them: a being who could teach them both on the ins and outs of their life's work. Others might feel intimidated upon learning they were the small fish in such an intellectual pond. Even Stamets had at first. But Straal was quicker to see how much more there was to learn.

Rushing into the lab and bounding down the stairs to the lower deck, Tilly returned. "Breytik reports they received our transport of the spores to his engine room," she said a bit breathlessly. She must have run and taken ladder access to avoid slow lifts. "I beamed ours directly to the cultivation bay, but we'll need to process them into the empty canisters."

A finger to his lips, then toward Straal and Kittik, Stamets tacitly urged Tilly to join him in watching their meeting.

What Straal was thinking wasn't clear, but his eyes welled with tears as Kittik greeted him, arms raised. "Greetings, Jus-tan Stra'al. You have come far in a short time. I commend your efforts."

"Oh, wow," Straal whispered, focusing only on Kittik. "I cannot tell you," he said around the lump in his throat, "how happy I am to meet you."

Grinning so widely his face numbed and began to twitch, Stamets watched giddily as Straal took Kittik's hand and shook it awkwardly.

"Justin, you okay?" Stamets leaned toward him and quietly asked, "Are you crying?"

Straal giggled. "I don't even know why."

"I do." Stamets put his left arm around Straal's shoulders and pulled him close. "It's validation. And amazing. And just . . . makes the universe more beautiful."

Looking between the two men, Kittik obviously thought there was some important ritual being performed, and he put an arm around each man's shoulder and pulled them both toward him.

Unable to resist a group hug, Tilly rushed in as well.

They all stood a long moment, until finally Stamets pulled away when he heard Hugh Culber clearing his throat.

They looked up to find the doctor standing a meter away, a playful twinkle in his eye. "I hope I'm not interrupting."

———

Stamets laughed. "No, no, Hugh, come in." Motioning Culber down the steps, he said, "This is who I've been telling you about."

Taking Culber's arm, Kittik held it perhaps too tightly and the doctor pulled away. "You have?"

"This is the Hugh?" the alien asked. "Kul-bur?" Kittik studied him head to toe, running his wrist just centimeters from his sides, perhaps scanning him with some hidden tricorder.

"Yes, I'm Hugh." Culber tensed. "What's going on?" he asked.

"Well, I told Kittik about your condition . . ."

Seeming to be reviewing data on a screen only he could see, Kittik stepped away, his hands moving as if manipulating invisible objects hanging in the air.

Culber moved toward Stamets. "Now I have a condition?" He glanced at Straal, then did a double take. "Justin," he murmured.

Straal held out his hand for Culber to shake. "Yes, Justin Straal, Paul's counterpart from the *Glenn*."

"Yes we— I've heard." Slow to take Straal's hand, he was unnerved by the awkwardness of meeting yet another person he'd known who was, to him, dead. *I guess I'm dead, too, to my universe.* How often, though, would this happen? It was always an overwhelming feeling: that crushing, foreboding reverse-déjà vu he'd now felt a dozen times.

"I'm guessing you know me in your universe, but I'm different?" Straal asked. "Paul filled me in too."

"Yeah, a little different," Culber said. *How about turned inside out by a navigational mistake?*

"Different good or different bad?" Straal was trying to be charming, but didn't seem very skilled in that area.

Mustering his best bedside manner, Culber hid his discomfort with a smile. "Neither. Just different." When Straal seemed to want more, he added, "I didn't know you that well."

"That makes sense."

"I showed Justin and Kittik your scans," Stamets told Culber, and used the nearby console to bring up the data.

Straal put up his hands. "I've not had a lot of time to go over anything."

"This is you." Kittik touched the screen, making it blip, then seemed to be looking at his own internal display again. There was probably some implanted device that fed information to an optic-nerve interface. "You are these data?"

Stealing a glance, just to be sure the readings were his, Culber said, "Yes, taken today."

Kittik's nose crinkled. "You are of this place."

Ephraim had said the same and Culber got a chill along his spine. He still didn't know what it meant. "Not by choice."

"Yes," Kittik said, as if making some internal realization. "You are also *not* of this place, aren't you?"

Wondering why having both of them examining his biology was necessary, Culber remembered how single-minded his universe's Paul could be.

Unexpectedly, Stamets asked Straal and Kittik, "Do you see a problem with Hugh coming back to our universe with *Discovery*?"

Neither the alien nor the human scientist answered immediately, but Straal was the first to reply. "This is guesswork, but despite the mycelial-based enzymatics, his DNA is human, and the quantum signature shouldn't be a problem. And it's certainly not safe to be here. Look at his subdermal scar tissue." He pointed toward the display above the console.

"Would you agree with that?" Stamets asked Kittik.

He made a motion that suggested he was weighing things in either hand but couldn't decide which was heavier. "You are unique life-forms to me. His situation is unique. We would never have met you had you not accidentally changed our quantum wavelength. We did not know beings existed like this."

If that's his way of saying I don't know, *it's the long way around*, Culber thought.

Kittik turned then to Straal. "Will you help me, Stra'al?" He motioned toward the reaction cube. "I need a few more readings from your modifications to assure we can easily return to our natural phase."

Unable to contain his enthusiasm, Straal practically leaped to Kittik's side. "Happy to!"

When they were alone, unnerved by what felt like an invasion of privacy, all Culber could ask Stamets was, "Why?"

"I wanted to make sure that when we jumped, there wasn't something that would kill you in our universe." Collapsing the screen, Stamets closed the data file, and knowing him, he probably assumed the uncomfortable discussion would go with it. "Everyone agrees the quantum signature is meaningless. The odd enzymes we found? Maybe we just have to supplement your diet or . . . I don't know. But it's nothing serious. I just wanted to be sure."

Was it that easy? Culber thought. "Don't you have to know what you're looking for, to find it?"

"Hmm?" Stamets moved toward the wall of spore storage containers and picked one that was full. Most were still red. "We were just looking for possible problems. And found none." He placed the container into the console and injected it into the system. "You'll be fine."

"Will I?"

Looking up, a faint shadow of unease fell over Stamets's face. "You *do* want to come back with us? With me?"

A nervous chuckle gurgled in the back of Culber's throat. The mycelial plane was no place for him. Although the day-to-day of survival was a blur, and really always had been, the recollection of his JahSepp attackers—the air that burned—was seared into not only his memory, but his skin. "I know I can't stay here."

"Exactly." Removing the empty spore container and replacing it with a full one, Stamets continued to work. "Starfleet will want to debrief you, and probably they should be the ones to let *our* Hugh Culber know . . . but I'm sure it will be fine."

"That'll be a hell of a day for him."

Watching Stamets move, Culber searched for a difference between this universe's Paul and his own. In manner and mannerisms, they were identical. In presence and charisma, the same. And Culber wanted him—yearned to stay with him, to be with him . . . except he'd known the man mere hours.

"What's wrong?" Stamets asked, perhaps seeing Culber's doubt play across his face.

Everything.

It was the one question Stamets probably shouldn't have asked—and as a result, Culber was able to solidify his feelings into a thought that could be articulated: "How do you know that *he's* not the one for you? Your universe's Hugh Culber?"

"I don't even know him."

"Paul, you don't know *me*." Culber let his hand fall against the lip of the console. "What has it been? Three hours? Four?"

Taking Culber's hand in his, Stamets turned from his work and held the doctor's fingers against his chest. "Ephraim showed us each other's memories. That . . . connected us. I admit it all sounds like mystical nonsense, which I'm so allergic to it gives me hives." He leaned his head to one side and with his free hand pointed to his neck. "See? Hives."

"There's nothing there." Hugh wished he could give Paul the laugh he clearly sought, but only an uneven, emotional breath came out.

"No, I can feel it. Help me. I need a doctor."

"Head doctor."

"Agreed." He leaned in and whispered, "You're making me crazy."

Finally Culber laughed, and Stamets did as well. It was the easy, near-surreal kind that people who'd known each other forever could share.

"Come with me," Stamets said. "You know you wanna."

Culber felt his face numb and he pulled back his hand. He rubbed his cheek and chin just to feel himself, to make sure he was still real. "You don't only mean come out of the network. You mean *be* with you."

"Yup. And, listen, this—for me." He wagged a finger between them, suggesting their relationship, their connection, and the feelings they both clearly had. "A difficult, implausible, *asinine* leap of faith. Which I don't do for just anyone."

"Believe him," Straal said, breaking the moment between the two. "Sorry. Didn't mean to eavesdrop. But it's true. I've never seen him like this before."

I have, Culber thought.

And I haven't. And I will again. And I won't.

26

Captain's log, supplemental. *The arrival of the* U.S.S. Glenn *has refueled our own mycelial drive, as well as the Maligonq ship. With fourteen minutes of shield power remaining, it is imperative we get under way. Needless to say, we shall miss our newfound friends, and hope we'll be able to make contact with them from our respective universes, once back in normal space.*

"You're certain you'll be able to return to your normal quantum wavelength when you jump away?" Burnham asked the Maligonq commander.

A line of static bisected Breytik's image on the main viewscreen. *"Yes. We have all the data we need to assure that our people, who were aboard your ship, will change phase with us as we exit the network. Your openness, your assistance, and your forgiveness have been an inspiration, Captain Burnham."*

Finding it difficult to fully focus on Breytik's words, the captain marveled at the alien bridge that mixed bioengineering with holographic and physical controls. Burnham wished they had more time for the scientific and cultural exchange they'd begun. She envied Lieutenant Stamets, who had spent the most time with the Maligonq's chief mycelial engineer. Once they got home, she'd be poring over his report, and likely recommend to Starfleet they investigate a way to confer with the Maligonq on ways to improve the spore-drive technology.

"I'm only glad we were able to help one another, and forge what we hope is a long and edifying relationship."

"Do you need us to stay in this realm until you return to yours?" Breytik asked. *"If there is a problem, we may be able to help."*

Sharing a quick glance with Saru, the captain did consider it and could see her first officer was doing the same. "As agreeable as that would be," the Kelpien said, "extending our shields is a drain we could do without."

Burnham raised both arms, mimicking the greeting Breytik had made when they first met. "Thank you for the offer, Commander. We have the *Glenn* here. We'll be fine."

Raising his hands in the same manner, Breytik crinkled his nose. *"Fair travels, Captain."*

"And to you."

The communication ended with a flicker and Burnham watched as the Maligonq ship spun on an axis, slowly at first but quickly building up speed. With a crackle of sound and a flash of bright blue light, the ship seemed to melt into a ball, then vanish. It was lovely, and awe-inspiring, and somehow even a bit frightening.

Only the *Discovery* and her sister ship remained. *One down*, Burnham thought. *Two to go.*

———

"I better be getting back," Justin Straal told them, closing his communicator. "Captain Charisma's getting antsy."

"I'd say you should transfer to the *Discovery*, but then I'd have to transfer to the *Glenn*. No, thanks," Stamets said.

"She's definitely an acquired taste," Straal admitted. "Someday I might get there."

Stamets grabbed his friend, gave him a warm hug with a

clap on the back, and then pushed him to arm's length, still holding on. "Thank you for . . . well, everything. The whole deal. Starting this journey, and getting us out of this mess."

Straal smiled a bit as Stamets released him. "Brave new universe."

"Universes," he corrected. "See you on the other side."

When Stamets turned away to resume his tasks, Culber noticed the *Glenn* mycelial navigator hesitated. They both watched Stamets, working excitedly with Tilly and Nilsson, and Culber wasn't sure what was etched into Straal's face.

"You okay, Justin?" Culber asked the man as he climbed toward the exit.

Pausing when he got to the upper level, Straal peered back at Stamets again for another quiet moment. "I used to think Paul would never be happy until I was as dedicated to our work as he was. I thought he was missing out on life because he'd never fully let someone else in. Hell, I didn't even think there was anyone for him." He leveled his gaze directly at Culber. "Now I see I was wrong . . . and I don't think I'll be happy until I find what he has with you."

Stifling a protest, Hugh shuffled his feet and looked away.

Straal hung there briefly, then finally pivoted and left.

As Culber turned back and saw Stamets in his natural element, the illusion of this man being exactly like his husband was irresistible. The shame of that continued to haunt him, however. Was the love he had for his universe's Paul fungible? Could it so easily transfer from the original to the . . . well, not copy, but "new and improved"?

Perhaps this Paul Stamets only seemed a bit more caring and more together than the one he left behind because he'd been without him for what seemed like an eternity.

Is this heaven, or hell? he mused.

Heaven was in his husband's arms. Hell was in his doubt: *How could you throw* him *aside?* The guilt radiated across Culber's psyche like a toothache—throbbing everywhere but difficult to localize.

Tilly at the main console, Nilsson at the backup, Stamets rolled up his sleeves as he strode toward him. "We'll be putting into Starbase 46 for repairs once we get home. I'm taking leave with you. There's a moon—"

"With a Kasseelian opera house. I know." Culber found himself unable to meet Paul's eyes without choking up. "But you hate it. Why—?"

Stamets's fingers lightly pushed Culber's chin up until he was looking at him. "I'd rather hate something you loved, with you, than love anything else, without you."

Falling into a tight embrace and a deep kiss that was brief and yet more intimate than what they had shared in the lift, they stayed together, vise tight, until either Nilsson or Tilly cleared her throat.

"Get a room, you two," Tilly teased as Stamets turned toward the reaction cube.

"Soon," he told Culber as the door closed him into the chamber.

Nodding to the ensign once the arms of the biomechanical shunts popped into place, Stamets leaned back. "Ready."

She hit the comm button, then worked her console to confirm all levels one last time. "Bridge, spore drive primed. Green lights."

"*Acknowledged,*" Burnham said. "*Black alert. Mister Stamets, take us home.*"

"*Black alert,*" the computer warned. "*Black alert.*"

Connecting with Hugh a last moment before he closed his eyes, Stamets looked blissfully happy. He settled comfortably into the sled and murmured, "Aye, Captain. Home."

From the captain's perspective, a normal jump through the mycelial network was brief. As this protracted jump dragged on, however, the captain couldn't help but worry about the hull damage. Was *Discovery* holding together? The ship rattled around her too long, but eventually there was a crackle of electricity, and a subtle lightness of being akin to artificial gravity going offline, and it was finally over.

Burnham took a breath and waited for Airiam to confirm arrival. "Sequence complete."

"Confirming," Saru said, and the captain swiveled in his direction. "According to astral navigation beacons, as well as stellar locale scans, we are"—he looked up happily—"within orbital range of Benecia."

Detmer and Owo smiled at each other, then glanced back to Saru.

"Starfleet Command is hailing, Captain, requesting our status," Bryce called from the communications station. "As is the *Glenn*."

"Key systems are functional," Saru said. "Many are on bypass or backups. I recommend we limit warp speed factor to six."

"Send that report, Mister Bryce, along with my regards to Admiral Cornwell and Captain Underwood, respectively." Lifting herself from the center seat, Burnham stepped toward the viewscreen and took in the swath of starscape laid out before them. In the corner of the image lay Benecia. To their perspective, *Discovery* was barely late. "Standard orbit," she ordered, and turned to Saru. "Have Doctor Pollard coordinate delivery of antivirals." Striding toward communications, she told Bryce, "Lieutenant, please get an updated database from the Federation Health Organization and confirm any new blood-burn outbreaks."

Her crew responded appropriately, offering their respective acknowledgments, and for the first time in what felt like days, but had only been hours, Burnham felt relieved. The mycelial plane had been fascinating scientifically, but clearly was not a safe place.

"Captain . . . you're needed in engineering." From Bryce's grave tone alone, the captain instantly felt a steel cable of tension tighten around her.

"Saru, take the conn."

———

The sizzle in the air was short-lived. The musty smell he would never forget pressed down cruelly until it felt like a part of him. When he sunk to his knees, a puff of yeel-tree dust billowed up to choke him. Despite that, the air still burned. The memory of how painful that could be spurred him toward protection. He dug his hands into the bark around him, covering himself quickly, sloppily, as best he could.

He continued until exhaustion came, then sobbed and curled himself into a fetal ball.

"I am sorry, my friend." Ephraim's voice was quiet at first, and Culber had difficulty focusing on it. *"I empathize with your anguish."*

"You knew this would happen, didn't you? You knew I would be left behind."

"I didn't, and I did. I will, and I won't."

His jaw clenched, fists at his sides, Culber's eyes burned with anger, hate, and yeel dust. *"You son of a bitch—"*

"You needed this," Ephraim said sympathetically, *"but that makes it no easier."*

"Why? Why did I need to be tormented into believing I would be free of this place?"

"You will be free. And you won't—"

"No, no, NO! Stop! Please go away! Just go away!" Culber pounded the ground until his fists stung, scraped either from the roughness of the forest floor or from the JahSepp that snapped at them. When he stopped, sniffed in the foul air again, and searched the plane, Ephraim wasn't there.

The distant, empty horizon laughed at him. The angry air branded his skin. And the fungal forest welcomed him "home" for his eternal torment.

———

"Paul!" The voice was muffled, faint: a nightmarish shriek into a pillow.

"Paul?" That voice was different. Distant. "Can you hear me?" *Yes.* It grew louder, clearer. *"Lieutenant?"*

"Yelling my rank isn't really the best way to rouse me," Stamets said groggily as he tried to raise his head. He couldn't quite manage that, so he blinked his eyes open instead. "Where am I?"

Tilly and Captain Burnham stood over him, and Nilsson lurked somewhere in the background. He was just outside the spore cube, and judging by the angle, on the floor. . . . Was he leaning against Tilly?

"What happened?" He sat up weakly, searching the room through squinted eyes. "Where's Hugh?" He should have been there.

Kneeling beside him, the captain took his arm in her hand and gave it a supportive squeeze. "He's gone, Paul."

His eyes widened in fear. "Gone *where?*"

"We don't know," Tilly said. "He disappeared during the jump."

Pushing himself up, gripping first on to Burnham and then

using Tilly's shoulder to bolster himself, Stamets staggered toward the reaction cube. "We have to go back for him. Now!"

"Lieutenant, we can't." The captain yanked on his arm, keeping him from entering.

"No, we know we can do this!" He pulled from her grasp and burst into the chamber. "Tilly, load—"

Tilly stood stock-still, arms at her sides, eyes glistening in empathy.

He turned to Burnham. "Captain . . . Michael . . . *please*."

"Paul . . ." She looked at him with more woe than he could remember her expressing. "We don't have the reserves. You know it'll take at least twelve hours. *Discovery*"—Burnham motioned toward the overhead, the bulkheads—"can't take the strain."

Huffing through his nose, stifling a sob with each breath, Stamets felt his knees weaken and he bent into the reaction cube doorframe. He pounded a fist weakly into the glass and jammed his eyes shut. "No . . ."

Hugh. What happened?

———

"Do you at least have a theory?"

Burnham wished she had. "Lieutenant Stamets is in no condition to sift through the data. He's trying, but . . . Tilly and Saru are working on it. . . . But if anyone is going to figure it out, it will be Paul."

Fleet Captain Philippa Georgiou leaned back and took a slow sip from her glass. "Are you going to look for him?"

Burnham pushed her food around the plate, though she'd made little headway eating it. The captain's table on the *Shenzhou* had always been a haven. But there was little comfort tonight. "I'll recommend it to Starfleet. There are scientific reasons, of course. The *Glenn* already tried. They were in better shape to make the attempt. They found nothing."

"Maybe it's not *they* who need to do the looking," Georgiou said. "Your report suggested Mister Stamets had a special bond with Doctor Culber. They were both able to contact this tardigrade entity." She took a small bite of her salad. It always took the captain a long time to finish any meal, and while Burnham didn't eat like a speed demon, she had to pace herself to not be sitting in front of Georgiou with an empty plate while her dinner partner had barely begun. Tonight that wasn't a problem.

"I'm not sure 'contact' is precise. From what Mister Stamets said, Ephraim just appeared to show them how neither was who they knew from their own respective universes."

Georgiou nodded contemplatively. "Ephraim."

Stabbing a cherry tomato with her fork, Burnham said, "That was my reaction too." She took half a bite and rested the utensil on the edge of the plate. "There's so much we don't know. This is not my area of expertise."

A smile slowly spread across the *Shenzhou* captain's lips. "That's why you have a good crew under you. That's why I had you."

"Did you ever feel like a person from a thousand years ago who somehow found a shuttlecraft and all she could figure out was it was meant to hold people?"

"I think I'd also know which direction it should point." She took another sip of her wine. "But yes, I do know that feeling."

"I can't help him," Burnham said, and while she wouldn't let her crew see her despair, she was more open with her former captain and friend.

"Of course you can. You can't solve his problems, is what you mean."

At that, Burnham only grunted. She ate the rest of her to-mato, then took a long drink of water.

"You are despondent," Georgiou told her. "Do not wal-low in it. That will help no one, least of all your crew."

"I'm not despondent. I am . . . unnerved."

"Hmmm." Her former captain took another small bite of food, but didn't take her eyes off Burnham.

"I don't wallow."

"Of course not," Georgiou replied, suddenly checking the antique clock she kept on the bookshelf. "I thought Saru was going to join us. It's not like him to be late." The brown Bakelite Art Deco case and faded off-white clock face hid an internal mechanism that had been updated so it would synch with the ship's chronometers.

"Why did you move that from your quarters?" Burnham asked. The clock had been her gift to her captain when she was promoted. A way of thanking Georgiou for all the time she'd invested in her.

"Here, people get to see it."

"I'm glad you like it." Art Deco's clean lines always spoke to Burnham. She liked the order of its geometry and the smooth curves that hinted at a less chaotic nature than she knew to exist.

Waiting for the last of their dinner party to arrive, Georgiou asked, "Tell me, is Saru the first officer I believed he would be?"

"I don't know what you believed," Burnham said. There was a certain pleasure in a pedantic response.

As was her habit when met with one, Georgiou waited calmly for a proper answer.

"He's certainly the best one *I* could hope for."

"Good. I'm not the least bit surprised." Georgiou took a longer sip of her wine and sighed contentedly. "Certain people just work well together, even if they don't think so at first.

Sometimes," she added, with that mischievous twinkle in her eye, "*because* they don't."

The door chime rang. "Come in."

When the doors slid open, Saru entered. "My apologies for being late, Captains." He bowed slightly to each in that graceful way he had.

"Speak of the Kelpien in question . . ." Georgiou said, motioning toward the empty seat between them.

"He's got ship's business to discuss," Burnham said. "I can tell."

Georgiou poured Saru a glass of his favorite juice. "No business tonight. Just family. My wayward children returned."

"Wayward?" Saru seated himself, placing a napkin on his lap as he did. "Nonsense."

Leaning toward her former captain, Burnham whispered, "If we *really* upset him, he'll say 'poppycock.'"

"A perfectly fine word when used in a proper context," he protested. "Was I a topic of conversation?"

Georgiou motioned toward them both with her glass. "Yes, in regards to how you two work together."

"We *were* recently reminiscing about how far we've come." More comfortable eating with his fingers, a trait Burnham noticed Saru shared with their fellow crewmate Linus, he plucked a few berries, one by one, from his plate, eating each in turn.

"Sometimes strong personalities, as you both have, mix caustically," Georgiou said. "In the beginning, you did to a point. But I knew you would be rocket fuel, harnessed to reach great heights, and not a bomb that would explode . . . in my face."

Burnham tilted her head to Saru. "I *think* that's a compliment."

"It is." He bowed his head toward their former commanding officer. "And it is appreciated."

They sat silently for a while as they ate, before Georgiou asked Burnham, "Are you ready to tell me what's really bothering you?"

Willing to talk in front of Saru, she shared a moment's glance at him over her glass as she stalled with a drink of water. Finally, she began, "There are days I've wondered if I'm ready for my own command—especially of such an experimental vessel."

Georgiou leaned back in her seat and asked, "Do you doubt yourself, or the mission?"

"Sometimes both," Burnham said, and glanced out the ready room's ports. Orbiting the starbase opposite the *Shenzhou*, the illumination from the spacedock painted *Discovery* in alternating strips of light and shadow. "Should we be playing with this method of travel? The mycelial network opens up paths to other universes. And given the message we were able to send the *Glenn* in our own past . . . Is this a safe place to be experimenting?"

Georgiou looked to Saru and seemed to find something in his Kelpien features that suggested he could answer Burnham's concerns. She gave him silent approval to try.

Reaching out, Saru placed his hand on his captain's. "In all candor, Michael, I'm not sure we can have those answers today. But because you are willing to ask such questions, that suggests to us both that you are the right captain for our vessel and her crew." As he removed his hand from hers, he gave it a pat. "And for me."

Hiding any possible moistening of the eyes, Burnham reached out and gave Saru an equally loving touch on his arm. She then leveled her gaze at Captain Georgiou. "Why do I get the feeling the *Shenzhou*'s arrival at Starbase 46 isn't a coincidence?" She turned to her first officer. "You sensed my mood and called in the cavalry?"

Unashamed, he pinched a spinach leaf from his plate and, before placing it in his mouth, said, "Isn't that my job?"

"I suppose it is," Burnham admitted, and silently returned to her own appetizer.

"What are you thinking about?" Georgiou asked when the silence lasted too long. "I know you too well not to realize there isn't a more specific thought burdening you."

"'The Battle of the Binary Stars,' Doctor Culber called it," Burnham said after a moment's hesitation. "In his universe, I was far from being *Discovery*'s captain."

"That bothers you?" Surprised, Georgiou's brows jutted up.

"I am . . . understandably curious."

"Any decision we make could break a thousand different ways," the *Shenzhou* captain said. "Perhaps there's an alternate universe for every alternative."

"So what choice did I make that ended so badly that a stalemate became a battle?" Burnham asked. "In our universe, it created a cold war. In his, the choice I made—"

"I'd have liked to have asked Doctor Culber about the differences," Saru said, his plate now empty. "But why do you assume whatever choices your counterpart made were integral to the outbreak of the battle?"

Burnham had no logical answer for that, and yet it was difficult not to delude one's self into thinking so much of one's life was under one's control.

"What happened in another universe matters only to that universe." Georgiou pushed her plate away, apparently finished, though much of it was untouched. "Here, in our reality, I took a promotion to fleet captain yet kept my ship. You respectively became captain and first officer of a wondrous vessel of your own."

Tipping her water glass toward Georgiou as if it were a

more potent beverage, Burnham offered her appreciation. "You have our thanks for that."

"Oh, please," Georgiou protested, "let's not pretend I swung around my weight to get you a command. That was your own hard-won success, for which you should be immensely proud."

"Indeed," Saru agreed, and lifted his own glass. "The merit rests squarely on our own shoulders."

Appreciative, Burnham grinned at them. "Well, your counsel has always been of the highest quality and value."

"I think I should thank *you*, actually," Georgiou said, pulling one more tiny bite from the plate she'd already pushed away. "Your achievements are often said to reflect favorably on me. Perhaps I owe *you* for being such an attentive student."

"What we have here," Saru said as he sniffed at his plate and delicately poked his meal with a finger, "is I believe colloquially known as a 'mutual admiration society.'"

"No," Burnham said, "Philippa had it right: family." She raised her glass.

Georgiou and Saru followed suit. "To family."

27

"Tell me how to help you."

Tilly had entered the cultivation bay saying she was checking on internal sensors, claiming humidity readings were off. Stamets knew it was a ruse. A rather weak one, since she hadn't checked anything. And hadn't brought a tricorder. And had no instruments in case she *had* needed to adjust something.

"You could leave me alone," he suggested. "That'd be a nice change of pace." He hid his face behind a hyphae and ran a scanner over the long branch.

Curling her head around the stalk, Tilly met his annoyed visage. "It's been two months."

"Yes, I'm painfully aware how long you've been a pain in my ass." He waved her away. "On *this* topic anyway. The historical statistics are much longer."

"Aaaand you shouldn't shut everyone out."

Moving to the next row of *Prototaxites stellaviatori*, Stamets made another *shoo* gesture at Tilly before initiating the next scan.

"I know it's not easy," she said.

"To get rid of you? Yeah, it's looking impossible."

"Can I give you some advice?" Tilly peered over his shoulder, pretending she was reading his tricorder. "I think I have some really good advice."

"Everybody thinks they have good advice." Just to see if she was actually reading the tricorder's screen, he switched it to an unrelated information display. "Also, everyone asks if someone wants advice, determined to give it whether the person says they do or not." Since she didn't at all comment on the nonsense data on the screen, he turned it off and spun toward her quickly enough she was caught off guard. "I get it. You see me in pain, and you don't want that for me. Message received, Ensign. But what you want—or *I* want—is unrelated to what I'm feeling."

"I know." She looked down and he thought he was making some headway with her, so he continued.

"I found . . . and then lost . . . love." He gazed past her, losing himself in his mycelial garden. "All in one day."

"But, you could *call* him. I mean our—*this universe's*—Culber. How do you know he isn't the same man? What've you got to lose? The *Hood* isn't far. There wouldn't even be a comm delay." She waited and watched him turn to continue his scans. When he didn't reply, she prodded: "Lieutenant?"

He stopped, pushed out a frustrated breath, and marched toward the exit. "I have considered your advice, and filed it appropriately."

"Ugh."

He spun around. "I'm sorry, did the ensign just *grunt* at the lieutenant?"

"No, n-no, sir. I would never."

Tilly backed away, but he closed the distance between them. "Sounded like a grunt."

"So, uh." She pulled a stalk toward her and held it between them. "Where did you file my advice? Because you said you filed it 'appropriately.' But is that like alphabetically, or circular file, or like under 'not a chance'?"

He took the branch from her hand and placed an appreciative hand on her shoulder. "Under 'probably not, but thanks for trying.'"

Working his way through the fungal patch toward the entrance back into the lab, Stamets could hear Tilly following him.

"We're just . . . all worried about you, you know?" she asked as the bay doors opened. "The captain, too."

Returning the tricorder to its storage, Stamets then activated the main console and tossed her a sideways glance. "When exactly did you become buddy-buddy with the captain, Tilly?"

She leaned her head toward him, a small line of red hair pulling itself slightly from her tight bun. "We have a good friend in common."

"Is it Saru?" he asked. "I think it's Saru."

"Ha, ha," she deadpanned, but said nothing more.

Hoping for continued silence, he ran through the data from the tricorder, but wasn't really paying attention to it. As much as he didn't want Tilly to worry, he understood her reasons. Had the roles been reversed, he'd have felt the same. But he wasn't lying when he told her he'd be okay. He knew he would. "These things take time, is all," he told her quietly. "I promise I'll be fine. Eventually."

"How long is 'eventually'?"

"Three years, two months, nine days, fifteen hours, forty-six minutes, and twelve point eight seconds." He tapped at the screen as if it were proving the answer—which it wasn't. "Ask a ridiculous question . . ."

"How is he today?" Enav asked, indicating Stamets as she descended the stairs into the lab.

"Stubborn." Tilly was beginning to pout.

"I am not stubborn." He eyed Enav suspiciously. "Are you just here to check on me?"

"Recalcitrant?" Enav asked, ignoring the question but turning back toward the exit as quickly as she entered.

"Headstrong," Tilly said.

Thinking about it a moment before she left, Enav said, "How about obstinate?"

"How about determined?" Stamets muttered.

"To be sad?" Tilly asked. "What are we even talking about here? Why stay miserable if you don't have to?"

"This conversation is over." Shutting down his console, Stamets twisted past Tilly and headed to the stairs to the corridor exit.

Tilly followed, ready to protest.

He spun to face her, waving a finger in the air. "Ah-ah. *Over.*"

"But—"

"*O*-ver, Tilly. Done."

When the doors closed, Tilly turned back to the empty room.

"Damn," she said to herself. "I didn't even get to use 'pig-headed.'"

———

"You again." Culber sensed him more than heard or saw him, but when he turned, Ephraim sat against the yeel tree opposite him.

"I never left." He gazed up and slurped at some spores as they floated close by. *"But I am with you physically now as well."*

"I'm not haunted enough?" Culber spat. *"Why are you doing this to me? Am I a plaything? An experiment?"* He knew those questions were echoes of those he'd asked before as soon as the words left his throat.

"You are none of those things to me. Do you remember what has happened?"

"I . . . yes." But it was becoming a struggle to keep it all straight. His mind was muddled, his thoughts overwhelmed and chaotic. *"It was just yesterday? Or . . . no . . . it's been a week? A month?"*

"Yes." Ephraim skittered toward him.

His eyes closed to the burning wind, Culber snapped, *"That makes no sense!"*

"I know." The giant tardigrade settled in next to the human and put a clawed hand on his shoulder. *"Time works differently here. Do you remember?"*

"How can I remember when you won't let me forget?"

Rolling his upper body, Ephraim paused, confused. *"I don't know what that means."*

Picking up a piece of bark from the ground, Culber worked it with his fingers until it became a powder. He smeared the remnants on his forehead and his cheeks. *"Every time you're here, you give me hope,"* he grumbled. *"And every time you return, I remember there is none."*

"I think I understand," Ephraim said, and radiated a kindness that at that moment just enraged the man more.

"If you understood," Culber growled, oozing wrath and angst, *"you would put me out of my misery."* He lurched toward the tardigrade, bringing his nose just centimeters away from Ephraim's maw. *"Kill me."*

"That," he said sadly, *"is not within my power."*

Fury broiled in Culber's chest and became an explosive emotional charge that thrust through his body. *"I've seen the damage you've caused! I've seen what you've done to people in self-defense or anger or whatever it is that's inside you that can cause such harm!"* Fists in tight balls, he pounded on his own chest. *"Kill me with those claws!"* He struck the tardigrade's torso and even through his anger he marveled at the toughness of his skin. *"Kill me as you did Landry!"*

"So you remember. At least that much?"

Halted mid-rage by the question, Culber realized he did. *"Yes. Some. I think."*

"Do you remember Paul?"

Of course. But which Paul? *"I . . . Yes. But . . . I've met more than one."* He collapsed on his own haunches and rested his fists on his knees.

"*Yes.*" Ephraim put his closest claw on Culber's right hand. "*As you see it, you have.*"

"*The . . . one that wanted me more than my own Paul. The one I wanted to stay with.*" A heavy weave of guilt blanketed him. "*Can you take me back to him?*" He could feel hope intertwine with the thick remorse, and tried to cover his anxious sobs with words. "*Please. I can't live here. I can't live like this.*"

"*I cannot, my friend. That, also, is not within my ability.*"

"*Then what good are you?!*" He scrambled to his feet and thrust himself away from Ephraim and into the nearest tree. "*I'm not alive, am I? That's why you can't kill me! This is some kind of fever dream. The last thoughts of a man dying from lack of oxygen.*" He huffed out a series of short, frustrated, anguished breaths. Tears rolled down his face, mudding the yeel dust he'd rubbed into his skin. "*I died somewhere else, didn't I? I crashed in a shuttle, or was lost in a transporter accident.*" He hugged the tree, weeping. "*Or I've been stuck in an EV suit that's run out of air, or the ship has lost life support . . . or . . . or someone snapped my—*" He fell against the tree, sliding down until his knees reached the ground. He hugged the trunk, his cheek crushed against it.

"*I am . . . so, so sorry,*" Ephraim said.

Nose clogged, chest heaving, every thought Culber had felt like a steep climb. How long had he been here? How many eternities?

Suddenly, he lifted his head, sensing a presence. As always, just a hint—a whiff—a small mental scent. "*Is that him? Paul?*"

"*Yes.*"

Shifting his head again, he pulled himself to his feet. "*No, I sense him somewhere else now.*"

"*That, too,*" Ephraim told him, "*is Paul.*"

On the edge of hyperventilating, Culber shifted his weight from one foot to the other, looking left and then right. "*But— which is the right one? It that hi—*"

The tardigrade rolled his upper body, and closed the distance again between them. *"It is, and it isn't. It will—"*

"No, please don't," Culber begged as it dawned on him that it wasn't Ephraim who haunted him, but Paul. Not one Paul, not only *his* Paul, but a seemingly infinite number. Some wrong, some right, but all taunting him in his loneliness.

Rushing forward, Culber stumbled and fell into the bark dust. Hurrying to his side, Ephraim helped him up. *"You feel him entering the network. Seeking you."*

"He's waiting for me?" Culber asked. *"Where is he now?"*

Ephraim chittered sadly. *"I am sorry, Hugh. He is gone."*

"But he's searching for me." The man twisted toward the tardigrade, imploring him for some direction, some clear thought on how to escape exile. *"Will I keep missing him? Will he give up?"*

"Time here is infinite . . ." Ephraim's body heaved in and he drew two arms toward the sky. *"He and his forms are everywhere here. I can do nothing about this."*

His mind numb to the notion of limitless Pauls, Culber struggled to form a cogent, cohesive idea he could articulate. It was a battle, but in time he managed one: *"How often have I remembered myself, and then lost myself again?"*

"Time here," the tardigrade repeated sadly, *"is infinite."*

Wrapping himself around Ephraim, he collapsed into the tardigrade's many arms. The ghosts of all the clearings he'd been led to, all the loves he found and lost, taunted him from elusive mental shadows. The flood of too many lifetimes' memories nearly drowned him. *"Who am I? Who do I love? Anyone?"*

"I cannot answer that for you, my friend," Ephraim said, returning the embrace. *"But I can ask you if you can remember when you first knew you were in love."* He put his head against Culber's. *"I will try to give you the strength to do so."*

Whatever the tardigrade did acted as the mental bolster

Culber needed, and his mind cleared. *"Yes . . . it was our second? No! Third date—the one to the Metropolitan Museum of Art."* Culber pulled away, pacing in a semicircle in front of Ephraim.

"What happened?"

"The . . . uh . . . I don't know." He paused and tried to solidify the memory before it struck him like a snap of lightning. *"I was . . . I was so excited to share the de Kooning exhibit with him. So eager to show him . . . that part of me: my love for something. My love for him as much as, or more than, the art. He'd never even heard of de Kooning. But I was running around from piece to piece, and I just held my hand out for him, yelling for him to hurry up."* He laughed. *"It was a manic feeling. Safe and comfortable. You know, I didn't even look back to make sure he was following. I just knew that he was. And when he took my hand, I knew we were on a journey together and—"*

"And?" Ephraim prodded.

"I don't know." Culber looked at his hand and imagined Stamets's fingers holding his as if he had that day. *"Where is he?"*

"Out there," the tardigrade said. *"As we all are. Very few live in the network."*

"I do." Slowing his frantic pacing to a shuffle, he could feel his mind beginning to slip again, ever so subtly. *"Where do you go?"* he asked. *"And why do you come back?"*

"I am everywhere at once. I am here always."

"That means nothing."

"Time here is infinite," Ephraim tried to explain again. *"It is the bridge between and in between."*

"Riddles!" Culber barked angrily, his pace picking up again. *"Tell me in terms I understand!"*

"I travel. Because I am alone without you." The tardigrade gestured to the plane around them. *"I am here, but also outside here, because I need you to learn from me, and I need to learn from you."*

Halted in his path, he slowly turned toward Ephraim, unsure he understood the import of what he'd just heard. *"You don't mean me personally, do you?"*

"I do, and I don't," the tardigrade said, shifting to one side, then the other.

"Okay, okay, me, but also just life-forms like me."

"Yes. Linear beings, who conceive of the universe in moments. Who live in the clearings and not among the branches of these forests."

Culber laughed, because he thought he finally understood: The forest wasn't the thick covering of fungal trees, but the tunnels of connection through which he traveled. The network, which was infinite and eternal, is where Ephraim lived. And the areas of spacetime where beings such as Culber lived moment to moment . . . those were the clearings.

"There are others like you—I don't mean tardigrades, but beings who perceive the past, present, and future as one."

"They are one," Ephraim said.

Frustrated, Culber held his temples as if he could force his brain into staying lucid. *"I mean, beings who don't conceive it as I do, but as you do."*

"Yes," the tardigrade confirmed. *"But they isolate themselves. They can be curious and occasionally mingle, but they tend to find your conceptions of existence distasteful. Mostly, they keep to their continuums and passages . . . and avoid the clearings."*

"But you don't," Culber said, more accusatory than he intended.

"This is my forest," Ephraim said, looking into the sky, perhaps imagining—or actually seeing—the mycelial network, *"and all the clearings too."*

Culber thought he understood, at least for the time being. *"They stick to one universe, but you don't."*

Ephraim moved forward and put a clawed hand on Culber's shoulder. *"I do not shun the clearings, or beings like you."*

Struggling to use the musty air, Culber took a deep, focusing breath, then eyed the tardigrade suspiciously. *"D-did you let the* Glenn *capture you? In my universe?"* He pulled away from his touch. *"Or, did you at least know it would happen?"*

"Yes and perhaps."

"What does that mean?" His frustration faded into curiosity: Culber really wanted to know.

Lolling his head in a circle, the tardigrade seemed to be lost for a way to formulate his answer. *"I did not wish to harm anyone,"* he said after a long moment. *"And I knew my own actions would lead to certain consequences, but when I live in the clearings, I do not see all events. I get to experience time as you do. That is why I visit."*

"You didn't know they'd hurt you."

"I knew they might because they had before," Ephraim said. *"And hadn't. And will. And won't."*

"How many times are we talking here?" Culber asked. *"How often have you done this?"*

Chittering his tardigrade laugh, Ephraim said, *"There are no numbers for this."* He peered into the sky again. *"In many clearings, I will be hurt. And have been. In many, I am not. And won't be. In some, I am like you, in Starfleet. In some, I am just Ephraim. In some, I am never seen. All are happening. And will happen. And won't happen."*

Culber laughed as well, partly because he understood and partly because he knew this wasn't the first time, nor the last time, Ephraim would have explained this. *"You're the most unique being I've ever met."*

"An interesting concept, as you understand those terms. I suppose, if I must be categorized, I am . . . a singular being in a network of biology that connects an infinity of often similar universes, but also those that are just as different."

Culber circled his exceptional friend, trying to hold on just a bit longer to the mental stability he'd been given. *"And you give people—like Paul—the ability to travel here, to share what you experience, the way you share what they experience in their, I mean our, clearings. Did you help the Maligonq also?"*

"I have, and haven't, and will, and won't."

"There is no other way to say it for you, is there?"

"There is, and isn't—"

Waving his hands, the man cut Ephraim off. *"I'm sorry I asked."* He sighed, satisfied for now that he comprehended the tardigrade's nature, but still not getting why he did what he did, given the repercussions. *"Do you ever worry you're giving power to those who can't control it? That the abilities you share can lead to disaster?"*

"I do," Ephraim admitted.

"And, what? You just hope people won't be destructive?"

"Some see ways to destroy. Others see ways to build." The tardigrade roll-shrugged. *"I can't choose their vision and destiny. The network is a gift, the threads of which weave a life through existence. I must show this to others . . . and they will make what decisions they choose. And they won't. And they have. And also haven't."*

Losing his acuity, Culber laughed loudly until it turned into a sob, as the wind kicked up the yeel dust and the JahSepp jabbed at him more harshly. He cowered slightly and ran back to Ephraim, embracing him again. *"Nothing makes sense to me about this."*

"I am sorry," the tardigrade said, protecting him from the wind, *"for my part in your existence."*

Backing away, even though it meant the wind scraping pain into him again, Culber demanded, *"What does that mean? My existence."*

"I showed your Paul and he did not look to destroy," the tardigrade tried to explain, *"but he did create you here, and in doing so, I, too, am to blame."*

"*You—or he—created me . . . here?*" He pointed to the ground, less indicating that on which they walked and more the entire mycelial plane. "*Then, I did die?*"

"*A form of you did, as you understand death,*" Ephraim said. "*Paul created you here, but I gave him the . . . showed him the how.*"

"*I'm a doctor,*" Culber snapped, and could feel himself slipping further away from coherent thought. "*I understand death, better than you do!*"

"*You do, and you don't. And you will and you won't.*"

Panic seeped in where rational thought melted away. "*So, I can't go home, can I?*"

"*You can, and you will. But you also can't, and you won't.*"

Culber wanted to hit Ephraim again. He knew it wouldn't do any damage, and would only hurt his hands, but raw emotion was taking over now, and confusion, and it would feel good on some level to just lash out. "*I don't understand!*"

"*You are losing yourself again. Your mind cannot function well here. It was not designed for infinity. It is for clearings, not forests.*" He lowered his head. Regret? Sadness? "*Without my DNA, your Paul—any Paul—would not be able to travel these branches. Their minds could not handle it.*"

"*I'm . . . I am losing myself again,*" Culber said. He looked down at his hands. They were covered in yeel bark dust and small burns from the air. The very air burned. *Why does the air burn?*

"*You are.*"

"*I'm what?*" the man said. "*Oh, losing myself. Again.*" He gazed up at Ephraim. "*How do I keep . . . me?*"

"*In the clearings, my friend.*" The tardigrade took the human's hand. "*I have, and I will, lead you to them.*"

28

"Computer . . ." Stamets hesitated. Did he want to do this now? Should he dive in, open the channel, and see where fate took him?

Except he didn't believe in fate. He believed in mycelia. And in Culber. But the Culber he felt he really knew was gone.

Offering only a blip, the computer awaited his next command, if it ever came.

He sighed and considered turning in for the night, but the door chimed.

"Come."

When the doors opened, Captain Burnham stepped in.

"Great," Stamets said, burying his face in his hands.

"I beg your pardon?" Burnham asked, eyes narrowing. "That's not the reception I expected."

Blowing out an exasperated breath, he motioned to the chair opposite his. "It's less about you than about the lecture I sense is coming. Is this the one about the 'good of the ship' and the mission and how I need my A-game?"

The captain calmly lowered herself onto the sofa seat next to Stamets, rather than the chair he offered. "It's the one where you stop being an ass long enough to listen to your friends."

"Tilly sent you?"

"Tilly has voiced her concerns. With alacrity."

Pursing his lips but letting them slide into a smirk, Stamets said, "We wouldn't need spores if we could harness her zeal to power the ship."

The captain chuckled. "Well, that is true."

Allowing himself a brief laugh as well, Stamets quickly saddened.

Burnham leaned toward him. "Tell me what you're feeling."

He looked away, felt his lip quiver, and tried to keep himself composed. "I . . . I don't know," he lied. Sometimes saying that saved him from trying to articulate the depths of emotions he didn't want to admit he had. Bending forward until he was studying his boots, he repeated in a whisper, "I don't know."

"You know I'm not really Vulcan. I *will* understand."

"Unlikely, since I don't even understand."

She placed her hand on his, and the force of her will drew his gaze up to meet hers. "I see the wall you're building around yourself. I've been there. I've let people bang their heads against that same masonry."

He was silent, but didn't look away.

"Paul, the trouble with that wall is that, with time, you forget who built it. And that makes it damn near impossible to knock down."

"You tearing down yours anytime soon?" Stamets asked, hoping he hadn't pushed a bit too far.

Her lips curled up very slightly. "Captain's prerogative to keep a moat around her if necessary, mister."

He returned the expression, but his was a sweet, sad one— as much for his wall as for hers. "I'm sorry, Captain."

"You don't have to be sorry." She pushed herself up. "Just don't be a mason."

As she exited, he reflected that she was right: he always had somewhat of a barrier around himself and wasn't generally accepting of letting people in. Hugh Culber had climbed over that wall, so quickly. . . . It was hard to accept the possibility of beginning again—especially when the wound hadn't healed.

"Computer . . ."

"Working."

"Locate information on Hugh Culber, Starfleet Medical."

"Hugh Culber, Lieutenant Commander, Chief Medical Officer, U.S.S. Hood, *NCC-1703."*

Right where he should be, Stamets thought. He just wasn't the Hugh Culber he'd been pining for. "What time is it on the *Hood*?"

*"*U.S.S. Hood *ship time is twenty-two hundred hours, four minutes."*

"Not too late," Stamets said. And meant that in a number of ways. "Tell me if you would reach out to him, knowing he's not the same person you just fell for."

"Unable to comply."

He knew that would be the reply but sometimes enjoyed confusing the computer, just for his own amusement. "Open a channel to Doctor Hugh Culber on the *U.S.S. Hood*."

The computer beeped.

Angling himself toward the table as its holographic display sparkled to life, Stamets smoothed his hands over his shirt and made sure a cowlick wasn't sticking up in his hair. Which was stupid, because unless he'd just woken up, it never was.

"This is Culber." Written in three-dimensional photonic pixels, Hugh's visage appeared. The same face, the same close-cropped hair and tightly manicured beard, peered out at Stamets, expectantly.

"Hi." He wasn't sure what to say, as he hadn't planned to make the call at all until the captain came by. Now, sitting here, looking into the same eyes, Stamets was speechless.

"Hi," Culber repeated back, his face bright with curiosity. He was wearing dark maroon pajamas, or casual wear, and was perhaps ready for bed.

"Uh . . . hi." Stamets swallowed roughly, his mouth too dry.

"Can I help you, Lieutenant Stamets?" Culber asked.

His eyes bulged. "You remember me?"

Glancing down a moment, Culber said, *"It has your name on the screen."*

"Oh." Right, there'd be no reason for him to remember. Unless he kept a diary of insulting assholes he encountered on any given day.

"But," Culber said, a lighthearted lilt in his voice, *"I remember your lecture on space mushrooms."*

"Your saying 'space mushrooms' is an attempt to get a rise out of me."

"You're very astute. When did you join Starfleet?" His eyes flicked again to the information display on his screen. *"And do you know what time it is?"*

"Ten-ish? I think? Do you remember . . . uh, our rude encounter after the lecture?" he asked.

Culber thought a moment, or perhaps pretended to. *"I do now."*

"Sorry about that," Stamets said. "It was a difficult time and I know that's no excuse, but . . . I'm sorry."

"Has this been weighing on you a long time?" Culber asked. *"You've apologized twice now for something that happened years ago and I'd not given a second thought. What's this all about?"*

"I've been thinking . . . about life choices and I'm . . . trying to make changes . . ." His voice trailed off. He wasn't sure what he could say that wouldn't sound insane if he explained the events that led to his call.

"Are you looking for some medical advice? A program or medical regimen to follow? You must have a doctor there."

"No, it's not— Listen, I think this was a bad idea." Stamets looked away, but when he met Culber's eyes again, he saw a kindness he didn't expect. Perhaps he should have.

"I can't agree, until you tell me what's going on. Take a moment and try again. I can wait."

His mouth even more a desert than a minute before, Stamets stumbled. "Y-you said you'd not given me a second thought. Is that true?"

"I didn't say that," Culber said, seating himself to settle in for a longer chat. *"I said I didn't give your rudeness a second thought. It was your lecture that made the lasting impression."*

"I just hope I hadn't offended you."

"Annoyed, yes. Offended, no."

"Oh, well, I don't mind annoying people I know. But I didn't know you." Feeling more comfortable, more himself—and more like *this* Hugh was much the same as the one who disappeared back into the mycelial network—Stamets relaxed somewhat. "So would you . . . let me make it up to you?"

"All these years later?" Culber asked.

"Why not?"

Accepting that argument with ease, Culber said, *"Okay . . . where're you stationed?"*

"The *U.S.S. Discovery.*"

"Heard about that ship. Special, but no one really says how."

"Classified stuff." He winked. "I could tell you, but then I'd have to bore you to death."

"What if I'm interested?" Culber leaned forward and the holographic image shimmered with his smile. *"I mean, not bored."*

"Trust me," Stamets replied. "Give me half a chance, I'll bore you."

"We'll see. Do you still hate *opera?"*

Stamets looked down at his clasped hands, which he then

smoothed against his knees, wiping the clamminess from his palms. In retrospect, hating the artistic expressions someone else loved was one of the most foolish things he could imagine thinking, let alone saying. "No. I think I've learned that lesson."

With a contemplative look, Culber said, *"You don't seem like the same Paul from back then."*

"That's okay," Stamets told him in a soft murmur, his eyes welling with tears. "I'm sure you're not the same Hugh." Looking as deeply as possible into a hologram's face, he added, "I won't hold it against you, if you don't."

———

"Captain on the bridge."

Burnham headed for the center seat as her first officer lithely raised himself back to his station. "What've we got, Mister Saru?"

"Starfleet reports a series of anomalies they'd like us to investigate," he said, calling up the data on his console and sending it to the main viewer. "Long-range scans are inconclusive as to the nature of the phenomena, but they have determined they're not from any known stellar or planetary bodies."

Filled with the relevant data, the captain eyed the large screen as she lowered herself into the command chair. She gave herself a moment to review the information, and then clasped her hands, eager. "What do we think?" she asked her crew, opening the discussion wide.

Owo went first, reading information off her screen. "According to this, every subspace wavelength they've tried has bounced back nonsense telemetry. Gibberish."

Linus, at the alternate science station opposite Saru, chimed in as well. "Like Nah-pesh."

"Nah-pesh?" Burnham asked.

"If I'm not mistaken, that's akin to Earth's mythical Devil's Triangle," Saru translated, making the geometric shape in the air with his slender digits.

Still lost, other than understanding what a triangle was, the captain needed clarification. "I didn't grow up on Earth."

"Just an old sailor's story," Detmer explained. "An area in the western part of the North Atlantic, where people claimed ships more commonly disappeared under mysterious circumstances. Supposedly, electronic equipment or even magnetic navigational compasses would go haywire in that area."

"What was the reality?" Rhys asked. "*Were* there more vessels there than was common?"

"No," Detmer replied. "There were more losses because that area had more travel density."

"There was a brief coordinate fix on one of the signals," Saru said. "We've been ordered to investigate it."

"An honest-to-goodness mystery, Number One?" Burnham was ready for that, achingly so.

"So it would seem."

"Do you have the coordinates?" the captain asked.

"Already plotted," Detmer said, glancing back, excited. "At warp four, we could be there in twenty hours. Ready when you give the word."

Leaning forward, ready to push against the frontiers of space for as long as she could, Captain Michael Burnham was determined to learn what secrets these anomalies held . . . and more. "I don't want to wait twenty hours," she said, and swiveled to Saru. "You?"

He bowed his head toward her in agreement. "Most certainly not."

When Detmer looked back, the captain gave her a quick wink. "Keyla, how about warp factor five?"

"Warp five, aye."

Burnham waved her hand forward, toward the unknown. "Let's go."

Epilogue

"The air burns!" Culber howled. *"Make it stop! Please just make it stop!"* His demand turned into a sob and he scraped what protective dust he could off his shirt and pushed it into the open wounds on his face.

"You have strayed too far from the yeel," Ephraim said. *"You mustn't without good cause."*

"I . . . I had to come here. I think Paul is here." He peered upward, toward the bisected ship that was half-plunged into the mycelial plane. *"Is that Paul?"*

"Then you see it?" The tardigrade shuffled toward the vessel.

"The ship. Yes," the man said quickly, excitedly. *"Yes. Yes. Is it real?"*

"Yes. You must go, Hugh Culber," Ephraim told him. "This, *at long last, is* your *clearing."*

Guiding him, mentally pulling him forward, the tardigrade drew Culber toward the *Discovery*, and helped him on board.

Culber became a bit more cogent when he felt walls around him. He turned, frightened. The ship was familiar yet foreign. It smelled like the forest, but looked like the *Discovery*. The air still burned, but less than outside. For now. The JahSepp would take the ship away soon enough, and he'd be left alone again. That's how it always was. And wasn't. And would be. And wouldn't.

"If this is real, where is everyone?" he asked Ephraim, suspicious. But, physically at least, the tardigrade was gone.

Only his voice remained in Culber's mind: *"I fear your in-*

tellect is too shredded and feral to understand, or even to remember me," the creature said. *"But if you can, please listen. This is your clearing. These are your moments. This is your Paul."*

"Who are you?" Culber demanded to know. *"What do you mean 'clearing'? This is a ship! Is this . . . wait! I know this place!"* He heard a sound and twisted toward it. *"What was that? Who else is here?"*

There were voices: anxious in their tone, torturous in their familiarity. He feared them and he fled.

———

Turning toward the scuffling sound he heard, Stamets followed. The form ran and he chased after him. Was it possible? *Was that Hugh?*

Up the corridor and around the turn, the man ran away with fearful speed and it was hard to keep up. He lost him. But on the ground were patches of dirt and debris that slopped across the floor or floated eerily in the mycelial plane's air around them. It indicated the direction the man ran, and Stamets tracked him.

Until he lost even those when the smudges disappeared midcorridor. He spun about, searching, and the shift in his weight opened the door to crew quarters. There, on the deck, was more of the dust.

He entered to find Culber hiding, skittering behind the cover provided by a room divider. A stolen glimpse of the man showed his once-white uniform now in dirty tatters, his face and hands burned and scraped, and his hair and beard a scraggly, filthy mat.

Culber whimpered, covered his head with his hands, and sobbed, "You're not real!"

Stepping closer, hands pressed together, Stamets pleaded, "I am. W-when I was lost here, you found me."

He hid his face from Stamets.

"Do you remember?"

Unwilling or unable to answer, Culber seemed to be in agony. He clung to the half wall like a newborn infant to his mother.

"You found me in so many places," Stamets told him, thinking not just of the time he was in a coma, but their life long before that. "You . . . took me to the Metropolitan Museum of Art, when we were on leave. It was our third date. A-and you were walking so fast, because you were excited to show me the de Koonings."

Trembling, Culber huffed, panted, and still hid, but a connection *was* being made. Stamets could feel it.

"All of them in one room. I had to run to keep up. And . . . as you walked, you held out your hand behind you. Because you *knew* that I would grab it."

Shaking his head, Culber mouthed *no, no.*

"And I did." Stamets let out a nervous chuckle. "And I knew everything about you in that moment."

Culber looked up quickly, then pressed his cheek against the room divider again.

"And I'm here now," Stamets continued, reaching out as Culber shook his head again and again. "And here's my hand."

Pushing himself wearily, tentatively up, Culber's hand inched its way around the side of the wall, until he rushed forward, taking Stamets's hand only a moment before collapsing into his arms, sobbing.

The electricity of that moment, the solidity of it, steeled them both. *I'm taking you home, Hugh,* Stamets thought, holding on for dear life to the man he thought dead. *I'm here, and I'm taking you home. And I'm never losing you again.*

ABOUT THE AUTHOR

Dave Galanter has authored various *Star Trek* projects, including *Voyager: Battle Lines*, *The Next Generation* duology *Maximum Warp*, and *The Original Series* novels *Troublesome Minds* and *Crisis of Consciousness*, as well as numerous works of *Star Trek* short fiction. He lives in Maryland with his wife and family and can be found milling around smartly on Twitter @davegalanter.

ACKNOWLEDGMENTS

I always like to have a note such as this, because there are so many people to thank when a book is written and published. I assure you, what you see is not only my work but the effort of a team.

Perhaps most importantly I need to thank Kirsten Beyer. We collaborated on the ideas and themes of this book in a way that was both easy and fulfilling. I'm not sure I'd be able to tell someone where one person's ideas ended and another's began, and that's the best kind of collaboration. She's been a good friend for many years, and while I've always admired her skill and determination, it is her strength of character that reminds me to persevere in this craft, and for that as much as anything, I am forever grateful.

To the cast and crew of *Star Trek: Discovery*, I can only say this: you have helped to usher in a golden era of *Star Trek*, breathing new life into an iconic franchise. "Thank you" doesn't cover it. From acting and direction, to writing and casting, to design and effects, I honestly feel you are producing lightning in a bottle once more.

No less important for me, I always thank my family (especially my wife, Sam) and our friends, because through thick and thin, they help me to get the job done. I won't list *all* the names I could, but want to acknowledge Josh, Tamara, Deborah, Kate, and Shanna, especially. You are all appreciated.

This book also couldn't have happened without the support and professionalism of Ed Schlesinger and Scott Pearson. Thank you, gentlemen.

And Dayton Ward, you get your own singular line of thanks. It's difficult to express how much I appreciate your friendship, but it's more than I can say.

Perhaps the two people I owe most don't even know me, and other than through their portrayals I don't know them. Wilson Cruz and Anthony Rapp, who give life respectively to the roles of Hugh Culber and Paul Stamets, have been inspiring to watch. So to them I say this: In poring over "Disco's" thirty or so hours of television, I've tried to learn the patterns of delivery and mannerisms you have bestowed on your characters. I'd like to think that in watching so closely, I've also seen your hearts. And what big hearts they are. Thank you for showing the world a truly wonderful love story. I can only hope I've done it justice.

LLAP,
Dave Galanter